Aether and Ego

BY JOANNE MERRIAM

The publisher gratefully acknowledges the support of the Canada Council, Ontario Arts Council, and the Government of Canada, and Ontario Creates.

Canada Council for the Arts Conseil des arts du Canada

ONTARIO ARTS COUNCIL
CONSEIL DES ARTS DE L'ONTARIO
an Ontario government agency
un organisme du gouvernement de l'Ontario

Canada

ONTARIO CREATES

Library and Archives Canada Cataloguing in Publication

Title: Aether and ego / by Joanne Merriam.

Names: Merriam, Joanne, 1973- author. | Adaptation of (work): Austen, Jane, 1775-1817. Pride and prejudice.

Identifiers: Canadiana (print) 20260240486 | Canadiana (ebook) 20260240516 | ISBN 9781834210261 (softcover) | ISBN 9781834210278 (EPUB) | ISBN 9781834210490 (PDF)

Subjects: LCGFT: Steampunk fiction. | LCGFT: Novels.

Classification: LCC PS8576.E7398 A67 2026 | DDC C813/.6—dc23

INANNA
PUBLICATIONS & EDUCATION INC.
TORONTO, ONTARIO, CANADA
www.inanna.ca

Printed and bound in Canada

Inanna Publications and Education Inc.

210 Founders College, York University

4700 Keele Street, Toronto, Ontario, Canada M3J 1P3

Telephone: (416) 736-5356 Fax: (416) 736-5765

Email: inanna.publications@inanna.ca

Website: www.inanna.ca

PRAISE FOR AETHER AND EGO:

"*Aether and Ego* is enormous fun and a worthy tribute to Austen. It left me dreaming of a better world."

- KATE HEARTFIELD, AUTHOR OF *THE EMBROIDERED BOOK*

"A skillful reimagining of *Pride and Prejudice* with a speculative twist that casts familiar characters in a whole new light and breathes fresh life into a classic tale. *Aether and Ego* repeatedly subverts expectations and yet every twist feels utterly earned. Masterfully done!"

- A.C. WISE, AUTHOR OF *WENDY, DARLING*

"Elegant, smart, and transportive. *Aether and Ego* will delight *Pride and Prejudice* fans and alternative history readers alike."

- LAURA STANFILL, AUTHOR OF *SINGING LESSONS FOR THE STYLISH CANARY*

"If you love Jane Austen's *Pride and Prejudice*, you will enjoy *Aether and Ego*. Steampunk, the Regency in space - but interspersed with gardens and a lovely metaphor comparing life with a garden. Grab some Lady Grey, butter sandwiches and enjoy the book."

—JOYCE CHNG, AUTHOR OF *FIRE HEART*

"Like the original *Pride and Prejudice*, *Aether and Ego* features plenty of misunderstandings, lovelorn conversations, gleeful gossip, and barely averted scandals. But here, women are studying physics and playing daredevil stunts on the spaceship apparatus. Mothers are running businesses rather than scheming to marry off their daughters. The novel drew me in with its high-spirited characters and its moving depictions of solidarity among women."

—ROSALIE MORALES KEARNS, AUTHOR OF *KINGDOM OF WOMEN*

Aether and Ego

"The far and the near must be relative, and depend on many varying circumstances."

— JANE AUSTEN, *PRIDE AND PREJUDICE*

"Ships and sails proper for the heavenly air should be fashioned. Then, there will also be people, who do not shrink from the dreary vastness of space."

— JOHANNES KEPLER, CORRESPONDENCE TO GALILEO GALILEI, 1610

TABLE OF CONTENTS

CHAPTER ONE 1

CHAPTER TWO 18

CHAPTER THREE 35

CHAPTER FOUR 53

CHAPTER FIVE 72

CHAPTER SIX 90

CHAPTER SEVEN 106

CHAPTER EIGHT 120

CHAPTER NINE 138

CHAPTER TEN 155

CHAPTER ELEVEN 172

CHAPTER TWELVE 188

CHAPTER THIRTEEN 202

CHAPTER FOURTEEN 216

CHAPTER FIFTEEN 231

CHAPTER SIXTEEN 247

EPILOGUE 260

CHAPTER ONE

MISS ELIZABETH BENNET walked through the early morning aether in silence. Longbourn had been built opposite Lucas Lodge, and no dome had yet been built in the intervening space. She felt as though she had the whole world to herself. She breathed easily in her aether suit. The cold of the open spaces outside the main Meryton dome, to which Longbourn and Lucas Lodge were attached, sucked away her warmth, and she was glad the walk was so short. Going this way, instead of the safer route through Meryton, was not only shorter, but meant that nobody would see her to fuss at her about being unchaperoned. Her parents need not even know that she had snuck out. Humming, she skimmed her feet across the bare metal in the steps of the dances she had so recently been doing with the boys of Meryton.

She stopped at the opening to their 'lock to look out across the black expanse of the interior of the ship. The twinkling of the lights of the various domes spread out in an arc to her left and right, punctuated by the empty places where domes had yet to be built. The blackness of the spaces between domes looked almost velvet.

She went into the 'lock, sidestepping her mother's buckets and boxes of produce being kept frozen, and skimmed out of her suit, patting down the rumple of her dress. Nobody saw her come in amidst the general hubbub of the house, and she hung her suit on its hook without anybody noticing but Jane, who only smiled her usual Madonna smile. Jane already knew where she'd been; they shared a room, and every secret. Elizabeth smiled back. Lydia was yelling at Careful about something, the beagle barking back at her in a sharp assertion of his innocence, and Kitty was doing the dishes with more than her usual clattering. Mary was diligently plodding her way through some new piece of music on the pianoforte. Her parents were nowhere to be seen, but Elizabeth knew that at this time of day, papa would be in his library and mamma in her gardens.

She went to the foot of the stairs so it would appear that she was coming from her room, and then stuck her head in the library. "Tea?" she asked.

"No, I thank you," he said, and then, after looking her over, said, "You've torn your dress, my dear. You had better fix it before your mother comes in. She got that dress in Paris before the ship left Earth, you know."

"Yes," Elizabeth said. "I know." She twisted around until she located the problem. A good ten inches of hem was dragging on the floor behind her. She should have run upstairs and changed, she realized. "Oh dear."

"Did you and Charlotte have a good time?"

Elizabeth laughed and came into the library to sit by her father. He put down his book, holding his place with one finger. The dust jacket indicated that it was a book on mathematics, but the cover peeping above was the distinctive slate blue of their hardcover copy of *The Swiss Family Robinson*.

"You aren't angry that I snuck out?"

"I suppose I should be," he said, "but the two of you are far too sensible to get yourselves into any real trouble. At any rate, at your age your mother was pregnant with Jane, which makes it somewhat more difficult to maintain my firm belief in your childlike innocence."

"We went for a dance up at Purvis Lodge with the Harringtons," she confessed.

"And some young idiot trod on your hem."

"Walter Harrington, must have been."

He patted her hand. "Anything I should know about you and

Walter Harrington?"

Elizabeth laughed. "No, Papa."

"Very well. Now, Eliza, I have a serious question for you. I need to go to the London dome to work on some plans with a Charles Bingley, son of the famous Samuel Bingley. Would you like to come with me? I will be staying with the Gardiners. It's a very short trip, I warn you. I leave tonight and come back in three days."

Elizabeth sighed. "I would love to, but I've got signaling with Charlotte every night this week. I don't see how I could find a woman to replace me before tonight. We were just complaining last night that none of us has a day off all week."

"Next time, then."

"Take Lydia," Elizabeth suggested. "She is always saying she never gets to go anywhere."

"I should sooner shoot myself," her father said without any heat, turning back to his book. She laughed.

She went upstairs to change and find something to fix the hem, and decided to do a line of leaf embroidery along the whole hem and paste a narrow line of backing on the reverse of the torn part. It would look less like a patch job that way, and mamma might not even notice that the embroidery was not simply for fun.

§

When Mr. Bennet returned from London, Lydia met him at the door with, "What is he like?"

"I am glad you are home," Mrs. Bennet said, lifting Lydia out of the way to give her husband a kiss.

"Yes, yes, mamma, but papa, what is he like?"

"Who, my dear?" Mr. Bennet's eyes met Elizabeth's over Lydia's head, and he smiled a little when she grinned. "I am glad to see you too," he continued to his wife as his other daughters took their turns at hugging him in welcome.

"Charles Bingley, of course!"

"Lydia has spoken of nothing else," Mrs. Bennet said. "She is convinced that his moving to Meryton will mean eligible beaux for them all, and endless dances for her to wear out her slippers."

"My slippers, you mean." Kitty pouted. "She is forever borrowing them."

"That makes no matter," Lydia said, "because we will all get rich husbands and have new slippers every day."

"Slippers don't grow on trees," Mrs. Bennet said. "Get out of the doorway, Kitty."

"Did you have the chance to get any new books?" Mary said, and smiled as their father showed her a copy of something thick with a gray cover.

"It's the sermons you asked for. There's new sheet music in my suitcase, as well," he said, and Mary clasped her hands together in apparent joy before taking the book of sermons and going back to the drawing room. "And chicory from Hardwicke," he added to Mrs. Bennet, "so we can have a break from tea."

Mary's departure started a general exodus, and let him bring in his suitcases. Jane pulled Lydia by the arm into their drawing room and hugged her from behind until their father had stashed his things and come into the room to dole out his other gifts: a beautifully-carved new spindle for Jane, some hair ribbons for Kitty and Lydia, and a metronome for on top of the pianoforte.

"Lizzy, I couldn't find you any new novels."

"Never mind, papa," she said. "I'm just glad that you are safe home."

"Did anybody get into mischief while I was gone?"

"But what is he like?"

"Your daughters were models of good behaviour, but your beagle ate half a pound of pheasant."

"When it comes out his other end, it shall enrich your gardens," said Mr. Bennet.

Mrs. Bennet smiled.

"Disgusting," said Kitty.

"Papa," Jane said, "you have not answered Lydia's question yet, and I confess that I am curious about Mr. Bingley as well."

"He wore a blue brushed wool coat and rode a black horse and seemed very gentlemanlike. Unless you want to know about his architectural prowess, any further questions you will have to discover the answer for yourselves."

"He must be very rich, to have a horse," Mrs. Bennet said. "Well, it is very good that you were the first in Meryton to know him, since that will give our girls an advantage."

"At what, my dear?"

"Marriage, of course," Mrs. Bennet said.

"Is that why he is coming here?" Mr. Bennet asked. He picked up a book and turned it over in his hands, affecting disinterest, but Mrs. Bennet just laughed and ignored the question.

"It would be good to see them all settled with either a husband or a business to keep a roof over their heads."

"Is he tall?" Kitty asked.

"What colour is his hair?" Lydia asked.

"What colour are his eyes?" Kitty asked.

"I shall point him out to you at the next monthly assembly and you may make a list of all his attributes."

There was a brief silence, interrupted by Mary reading aloud, "Listen to this: 'The frailty of women has been frequently a topic of triumphant declamation. On this subject much unkind wit has been displayed'—"

"Oh, hang your frailty of women," Lydia said, trying to take the book of sermons and tearing the page halfway across in the ensuing struggle, which ended with Lydia letting go with one hand to punch Mary and Mary letting go with both hands to sit on the floor with a thump, covering her nose.

"Girls!" Mrs. Bennet held out a hand, and Lydia gave her the book, which she placed on one of the shelves nearby.

Mary took her hands away from her face and began to cry.

"I don't know where you get it from, Lydia, I really don't," Mrs. Bennet said.

Patting his wife's hand until she smiled, Mr. Bennet said, "How wonderful it is to be so quietly comforted at the tranquil center of one's family home."

§

Elizabeth stood at the new telegraph machine. *This ship is like a pressure cooker for human invention,* she thought. She touched one of the wires, half expecting to get a shock, but nothing happened.

"Do you know how to use it?" she asked Miss Charlotte Lucas.

"Oh, yes," Charlotte said. "Mr. Brown showed me."

Charlotte was a plain, rather horsey-looking English rose, her only pretension to beauty being her absolutely flawless skin. She had inherited her father's strong frame and a jolly, no-nonsense willingness to fix just about anything, mechanical or interpersonal.

They stood in the signal room, housed in a glass cupola on top of the Headfort dome. The ship was a giant wheel, whose spinning provided their gravity. Everybody lived on the inside surface of the wheel, except for those aethernauts on shift at the wheel's center. Twelve enormous glass domes sat at the ends of the wheel's spokes, and the insides of the hollow spokes were used to send shipments across the ship: metal and rock and ice and sundry other items sent to the central processing area at its hub, and then redirected down another spoke to its destination.

Each of the twelve superstructures sheltered a cluster of smaller domes, with the main dome providing some protection in case a smaller dome within it were to rupture. The main domes were each topped by a cupola, like the Headfort cupola Elizabeth and Charlotte were in now. Their location atop the domes put them closer to the hub of the ship, higher than even the tallest buildings, which gave them clear sightlines to signal the other superstructures. Theirs generally smelled of beeswax and smoke from the semaphore candles, but tonight it smelled more of clementines and rum from the cake that Charlotte had brought.

Charlotte cut two thick slices of the cake. It was a pound cake with rum-flavored icing and a generous garnish of clementine segments, which Lady Lucas had arranged in overlapping circles. The cake was already two-thirds gone, the Lucases having enjoyed it the day before; enough was left for another piece for each of them just before their shifts ended in about five hours, if they wished.

Elizabeth had learned the short and long flashes of the adapted semaphore that Mr. Ohm had invented for use across the ship. They used a candle and shield. The shield covered three-quarters of the candle, with the other quarter open to provide the candle with air and turned toward her body. She had always had to be careful to shield the light while keeping the candle far enough from the cloth of her aether suit not to scorch it.

It was seven-thirty in the evening, and the signal room on top of the Edgcumbe dome sent a brief series of candle flashes to confirm that all was well. Edgcumbe was slated to get the telegraph wires sometime in the next month. Soon nobody would need to signal with candles, she supposed.

The system of flashes had been developed in the first year of the ship's voyage, before she was born, when they had discovered that the aether that filled the spaces between each cupola didn't transmit any sound at all. Now they would use it as pulses through this new machine. The device had been put in the day before, and worked by breaking an electrical connection along the new cable that had been suspended between their signal room and the one on top of London's dome. Each break of the connection made a click. She glanced at the clock: not for another twenty-five minutes, unless there were some sort of emergency. They typically sent a message one way at the top of each hour, and the other way at the half hour, most of them simple confirmations that all was well. They also passed along messages for various businesses that didn't want to wait on the postal service, but this late in the day, those had all already been sent.

If she looked down, Elizabeth could see through the glass of the Headfort outer dome to the smaller domes within: Meryton,

Purvis Lodge, Longbourn and its greenhouses, Lucas Lodge and its aviary, the parsonage house of Haye Park, and all the others, surrounded and pierced through by a disordered tangle of pipes. But she was looking now across at the superstructure of London, a jewel sparkling with lights hanging at eye level across a broad expanse of darkness.

"Would you like a little honey on yours?" Charlotte asked, interrupting her reverie.

The honey, like the beeswax candles, came from Mr. Harrington's bees, and Elizabeth knew the Lucases exchanged honey for eggs, so it wouldn't cost them much of anything to give her a little. "Yes, lovely," she said.

Charlotte drizzled the cake from the small pitcher and handed Elizabeth her piece and a fork.

Elizabeth speared a clementine segment and a bite of cake and held out her fork toward her friend, saying, "Cheers," and Charlotte tapped her own fork against Elizabeth's as if it were a champagne flute and replied, "Tink." They both laughed.

"Happy birthday," Elizabeth said, though she had already given Charlotte her well wishes on her actual birthday the day before. They had few enough occasions on the ship to celebrate, so they dragged out each one as long as was sensible.

As they ate, she tried not to get crumbs down inside her aether suit. (The cloth of the suit, impregnated with gum elastic, was somewhat sticky.) They had removed their gloves and fishbowl helmets and attached them to their belts, in case of a catastrophic failure of the cupola—one always had to be careful—but there hadn't been an accident like that in decades, and it was always a temptation to take off the whole damn suit, except that the signal rooms were kept at just about five degrees above freezing. Her fingers chilled on the fork.

"I brought a few books for us to read," Charlotte said, and Elizabeth replied, "oh, me too!" and they spent a few minutes sifting through them. Charlotte had brought two novels, one of them in verse, and Sir John and Margaret Herschel's work of botanical illustrations of the ship flora using a camera lucida, and Elizabeth had brought a book on ornithology and another novel.

"These all look like great fun," Elizabeth said. "What gorgeous illustrations."

"I thought you would like that. Father promises he will finish with Faraday's new book tonight," Charlotte said.

The telegraph began rattling its slow series of letters and Charlotte grabbed her pencil. When she had finished, she read out the message, but Elizabeth had understood the Ohm code just fine: "5-A-R-R-I-V-A-L-S." They kept track of the number of people in each of the superstructures, as a rough proxy for determining weight, along with tracking shipments to each spoke. It was a short message, and Charlotte tapped back a confirmation.

In the little notebook chained to their station for this purpose, Charlotte wrote, "Friday, 5 September 1845: five arrivals."

They had nothing to do now until eight-thirty's communication from Edgcumbe dome.

"I suppose the five arrivals are the Bingley party," Charlotte said. "Your father has met Mr. Bingley, has he not?"

"Yes," Elizabeth said, "but he will not tell us a thing about him, no matter how much Lydia and Kitty beg."

"Father has promised to introduce us tomorrow. Mr. Bingley and some of his companions are meant to come for tea," Charlotte said.

Sir William Lucas had been the mayor of the town after which the Meryton dome had been named, and had spent his entire modest fortune to purchase himself, his wife, and his (then) only child, Charlotte, the promise of a dome adjacent to Meryton, a promise that had been fulfilled some years after the launch of the ship, by which time they had had several more children, including, to Lady Lucas's relief, the boy who would someday inherit the dome which had come to be known as Lucas Lodge. In the interim, they had lived in the Meryton dome with the other families also awaiting the construction of their personal domes, at that time including the Bennets, and the daughters of the two families had been much thrown together, resulting in Elizabeth and Charlotte's close friendship.

The London telegraph rattled again, and they both looked over at it for a moment of frozen dread—it was ten minutes past the hour, and any communication at such a time must be an emergency—but the Ohm code only spelled out, "W-H-A-T-S-Y-O-U-R-N-A-M-E."

So, word had gotten around that the Headfort signalers included a few girls this month. Elizabeth blew out her breath.

"G-E-O-R-G-E," Charlotte signaled back.

Elizabeth laughed.

There was no reply.

They went back to reading, Elizabeth keeping one eye on the clock. At eight-thirty, she exchanged signals with Edgcumbe that all was well, and at nine Charlotte showed her how to signal using the new device instead of a candle, then wrote a note for a runner to take to Sir William with the new population numbers and a suggestion that five workers be sent to Feilding, which would be building a counterbalancing dome to match Netherfield's, or to their neighbouring superstructure of Edgcumbe, which had the lowest population in the vicinity, if they could be spared from the Netherfield Park build.

Charlotte left in the elevator to take the note to one of the runners at the base of the spoke.

Elizabeth picked up her book on botany but found herself watching the London superstructure sparkling in the distance instead. Overhead was the same black it always was, interrupted by the slightly shinier black of the spoke leading up to central processing at the hub of the ship, but London was an irresistible sight.

Charlotte came back, and they read and spoke occasionally (Charlotte more than Elizabeth, since she kept pausing to read aloud some particularly amusing passages of her novel) and the time passed soon enough. A clockwork elevator used the outside of each spoke as its back, which made it trivial for the signal room operators to get to their jobs. When they finished their shift and their replacements had arrived, they headed back to the surface in the same elevator. Elizabeth smiled, as she always did, when the small counterweight dedicated to the signal room's elevator passed her. It was a heavy, pockmarked anchor with a curved, barbed bottom: to Elizabeth the barbs always looked like thick metal leaves.

On the other side of the elevator wall was the area where shipments came in and out of their dome, with a larger elevator system that reached all the way to the hub of the ship, which was open to the aether. The shipment and counterweights were similarly-sized cubes, each about as big as a carriage and standard through the ship, rather than the more fanciful historical objects used for the cupolas' elevators. Years ago, she and Charlotte and some of their friends had engaged in packet-dodging: they had dared each other to ride that larger counterweight on its way up to the hub, and then jump on to the incoming packet as it passed the weight on its way down. They had stopped when Charlotte broke her leg with a bad jump, but Elizabeth always thought about it when she was in an elevator, and bent her knees a little, imagining riding the weight up into the aether again.

§

"There is the topic of so much of your conversation these past few days." Mr. Bennet pointed out to his daughters a gentleman, handsome and well-dressed in the same blue coat as had been previously described to them, standing in the center of a party of five.

The September 1845 Meryton assembly was very much like any other month's: people stood about talking until the month's work assignments had been announced and any changes made, and then they danced. Punch was served by Lady Lucas, Charlotte's mother, who always treated the public assemblies as almost her own private affair. Elizabeth always felt brighter and more interested in her neighbours at the assemblies, when everybody was on their best behaviour, and fascinated by the immense size of the room compared to almost every other space she spent any time in. Only the unbuilt areas of the dome outside their back airlock could compete.

Mr. Bingley smiled upon the assembly, ready to be pleased with everybody, and shook hands with anybody who came near him. Mr. and Mrs. Hurst were more gracious than friendly, though finely dressed. Miss Bingley had a crystalline beauty: her radiance cold, like the bite of the aether between the domes against unguarded skin. She stood as if daring anyone to approach her, and then when she turned to the man on her right, her entire stance softened and she became a human again. The fifth member of their party, whom Elizabeth had by now heard whispered was named Mr. Fitzwilliam Darcy, was the handsomest of them all, with dark, glossy hair and dark, flashing eyes and dark, conventional clothes. His skin was luminously golden by contrast.

"The dark-haired man owns one of the oldest domes on the ship," Kitty whispered to Elizabeth. "Mamma says it was one of the first constructed after the launch of the ship."

Charlotte Lucas looked where Mr. Bennet was indicating, and leaned over to Elizabeth. "Why has Mr. Bingley been a topic of conversation in your household? Only because he is young and good-looking?"

"My sisters have heard that he also has a good fortune."

"Oh!" Charlotte looked upward, just stopping short of rolling her eyes. "And, of course, it is a truth universally acknowledged, that a single man in possession of a good fortune must be in want of a wife."

As Elizabeth grinned at her friend, Sir William Lucas signaled the musicians to pause the bagatelle they had been playing behind everybody's conversations. He called out, "Is everybody ready for their assignments? Yes? Excellent."

Bushy, barrel-shaped, and boisterous, Sir William had voluntarily taken on the task for Headfort of organizing the labour of those without structured positions within the ship, including all of the children over the age of twelve. Properly speaking, Thomas Taylour, 2nd Marquess of Headfort, after whom the superstructure was named, should have taken care of it, but he was famously reclusive and had been happy to pass the task along to Sir William.

"Following tradition, perhaps Mrs. Bennet may go first," Sir William said. A few of the younger attendees and newer transplants muttered amongst themselves, but everybody over the age of about twenty remembered the famine of '32 and what they owed the Bennets. In any case, in most places work assignments were given out alphabetically, so only the Andersons and Aylesworths were giving up their places. Miss Bingley and Mrs. Hurst, however, seemed to find it extraordinary, and whispered behind their hands. Mrs. Bennet pulled a pocket calendar and pencil from a concealed pocket in her skirt.

"Miss Bennet is to help in the communal kitchen on Tuesdays and Thursdays throughout the month," Sir William said.

Mrs. Bennet noted Jane's changed schedule in her calendar.

"Miss Elizabeth Bennet is to continue with signal-work with my daughter Charlotte, each Monday and Wednesday. Miss Mary Bennet is to change all the charcoal filters over, Tuesdays and Fridays. Mary, I have paired you up with Maria."

Mary and Maria Lucas joined hands and giggled.

"Miss Catherine Bennet is to work with Harriet and Penelope Harrington on Fridays and Saturdays in the bakery making bread. And Miss Lydia Bennet to work on finishing her courses on basic safety and first aid."

Mrs. Bennet busied herself writing down their new obligations after giving Sir William a nod on behalf of her daughters.

"And of course, we would like everybody's help with the Netherfield build," Sir William finished.

"Oh, yes," Mrs. Bennet said. "Thank you so much, Sir William. Will Elizabeth need to miss the build for her signal-work? I see on the calendar that Michaelmas is on a Monday."

"Thank you, no. I have arranged for some of the younger lads to take that evening."

"Much appreciated."

Elizabeth happened to be standing near Miss Bingley and Mrs. Hurst, and overheard one of them whisper to the other, "To speak for the family when her husband is right there in the room!"

"Thank you, Mrs. Bennet," Sir William said, with a deep bow. He went on to the next family. Some dates were not suited to some of the party, who called out their objections, with bystanders offering to swap times, and Sir William noting changes. This procedure took the better part of an hour.

"I am happy to be paired with you again," Elizabeth said to Charlotte. Sir William having drawn up the schedule, Charlotte generally received her first preference of partner, which meant she and Elizabeth often worked together. "Could you bring Faraday's new book?"

"Certainly," Charlotte said. "Father finished it, as promised. I must warn you, it is heavy going."

"They are all heavy going," Elizabeth said. "I really don't know if I even want to go to Babbage, except that it would get me out on my own."

"You could do that any number of ways," Charlotte said.

"Hmm," Elizabeth said. "But I must have a place to live, and since my aunt has told me she hasn't the room to house me for more than a few months at a time, my only other options are to go to school or find a husband."

"Heaven forbid," Charlotte said, her eyes dancing.

Mr. Bingley circulated amongst those who had already spoken for their families or were exempt due to their positions. Mr. Darcy stood looking on, silent and unreadable. Mrs. Hurst and Miss Bingley whispered between themselves and swallowed their yawns with ill-concealed annoyance. Mr. Hurst fell asleep in his chair. Finally, the music was able to start, and Mr. Bennet could disappear home to his books.

The string quartet, as Sir William styled them, or the fiddle players, as Mr. Bennet liked to call them, ironically but not inaccurately, struck up the first dance. Elizabeth danced out with her uncle,

Mr. Philips, who always danced the first two or three quadrilles with his nieces and then retired for the night. The ladies' dresses and the men's arms and legs made swirling shadows on the bright white floor.

After the first two dances, Elizabeth begged to be excused for the third, and laughed with Charlotte over a story her friend told involving her younger brother getting locked in the aviary. When she looked at him again, Mr. Darcy was speaking stiffly with Mr. Jones, the doctor in Meryton, not seeming to find much to say. After that gentleman bowed and went to dance, Mr. Chamberlayne attempted to engage Darcy in conversation, but he said little, looking out over the assembly as though he could see beyond them all to some far region. She had yet to see him smile, but when she looked again she realized Darcy was not so much older than herself. She wondered if he were diffident, self-effacing, or reserved, or simply too proud to speak with gentlemen he might consider his lessers. Impossible to say, with so little to go on.

Mr. Stone, with his tidy beard and short-cropped head, came over then with a friend to introduce to Charlotte, and asked Elizabeth to dance. She spent an hour or so pleasantly enough engaged. Finally she had to sit down, her face flushed from the exercise.

She looked about for Charlotte, but she was chatting in a corner with Miss Mary King, so Elizabeth merely watched the dance and drank some of the punch in the hopes that it would cool her in the hot room. She idly wished it wouldn't be considered unladylike to steal some of the ice still floating in the drink, which would have felt deliciously cool.

She watched Lydia lead Kitty out amongst the dancers; it was common for women to dance together when there was a shortage of men, but they were winding through the dancers as though playing tag, and liable to trip somebody up. She looked about for her mother, but she was deep in conversation with a group of men whom Elizabeth knew to be customers of her gardening business, and not attending to her children. Elizabeth motioned to her sisters, but could not catch their attention without making herself just as much of an exhibition as they were doing. Luckily, most of the dancers were smiling at their high spirits, and they grew tired of their game when Mr. Stone intercepted them to ask for a dance.

Mr. Darcy was standing several feet away, watching the dancers with what Elizabeth thought might be longing until Mr. Bingley joined him to say, "Come, Darcy, I must have you dance. I hate to see you standing about by yourself in this stupid manner," and Mr. Darcy replied in a low voice, "Absolutely not."

Laughing, Bingley said, "You never wish to dance."

"I hate being touched by strangers, as you well know. Your sisters are already dancing, and I know nobody else in the room. Go back to your charming partner," Mr. Darcy replied, pointing his chin at Jane, who was standing a little apart from them, waiting for their turn in the dance and giving Mr. Bingley privacy for his conversation.

All the Bennet girls had the same colouring: chestnut hair and green eyes; but Jane was far and away the handsomest, with her demure manners, gentle smiles, and adorable dimples, and yet something chic about the way her hair fell, the way her clothing fitted so neatly, the way she moved her hands or cocked her head ever so slightly at whichever gentleman held her attention. The colour was high in her cheeks from dancing. She was smiling gently as she watched the couples going down the line, though Elizabeth caught her glance straying once and could tell that it was only her modesty and innate sense of courtesy that kept her from watching Mr. Bingley as he talked.

"Is she not beautiful?" Mr. Bingley said. "But there is one of her sisters sitting down just behind you, who is very pretty, and I dare say very agreeable. Do let me ask my partner to introduce you."

"Which do you mean?" and turning round, he looked for a moment at Elizabeth, till, catching her eye, he withdrew his own, and coldly said, "She is tolerable: but not handsome enough to tempt *me*; and I am in no humour at present to give consequence to young ladies who are slighted by other men."

Jane walked a step or two closer then, and Darcy fell silent. It was Bingley's turn to lead his lady down the line. The couple floated off, and Elizabeth stood and began to thread her way through the crowd to Charlotte.

She supposed that he had thought he could not be heard in the crush of people, but imagine believing that merely dancing with him would increase her consequence! Perhaps his palms, resting lightly against hers, would magically cure her of having a merchant mother, like the magic cure of a faerie curse. The idea was momentarily attractive, but she shook her head, laughing at herself.

Charlotte met her halfway, and said, "You have gone all red, Eliza!"

Elizabeth told her the story, with a great deal of mocking detail, and Charlotte said, "Count your blessings you did not, after all, have to dance with the man."

"What do you mean?"

"Well, imagine the sort of person who could look at Miss Elizabeth Bennet and find her 'only tolerable'. He must have impossibly high standards, and your dancing is not quite as pretty as you are, you know. You would be bound to make a misstep and then he would be displeased and who knows what wild things he might say."

Elizabeth laughed. Turning toward the end of the room, she saw herself in the long, slightly fogged mirror that lined the side of the assembly hall, her reflection intermittently eclipsed by those of the other attendees, as they passed between her and the mirror, and the dancers behind her providing a kaleidoscopic backdrop. The scene seemed dreamy and unreal. Charlotte's reflection was looking at the other end of the room, and she followed Charlotte's gaze to see Darcy's mirror image now standing utterly alone. How could she have thought him anything but taciturn and proud? She considered him more closely: he seemed contemptuous of the crowd, and his proud expression took away all of the pleasure in contemplating his dark good looks.

CHAPTER TWO

AS THEY EXITED THE AIRLOCK OF ASSEMBLY HALL, Elizabeth and Mrs. Bennet put on their rebreathers. The others let theirs dangle from their hands, finding the thinner air of the Meryton dome equal to the lesser exertions of their slow stroll through town.

"And then for the two third I danced with Mr. Brown, even if he is so old, and then for the two fourth with Mr. Carter—" Lydia was saying, and Kitty was saying, "I *saw*, Lydia!" and giggling.

Jane hummed the music of the last dance she had had with Mr. Bingley, apparently unaware she was doing so, and Mrs. Bennet, noticing, gave Elizabeth a significant look.

They walked past the general goods store and the central spoke and the communal kitchen.

"Oh, there is Denny!" Lydia cried.

A little way ahead of them, a group of three maintenance engineers were walking. Lydia and Kitty ran to catch up with the trio, who stopped to talk with them. Mr. Denny introduced his companions to the two girls. The men were in cleaned and pressed clothes, nonetheless stained by the activities of their profession, for they must be of the group lately invited to Meryton to prefabricate portions of what would become the Netherfield dome, home, and greenhouse.

As they approached the group, Mrs. Bennet said, "See how your sisters put themselves forward, Mary? Now, I would not have you be as headstrong or thoughtless as they are, but you could learn from their example to be a bit more assertive."

"Yes, mamma."

Mr. Denny introduced his friends, a Mr. Haggerston and a Mr. Metcalfe, all over again when the other Bennet ladies reached them. Jane and Elizabeth stood a little apart from the group, Jane looking apparently blindly into the middle distance with a faint smile playing around her mouth, and Elizabeth leaning gently against her. The blue-white arc light overhead made the gloss paint on the building next to them look wet.

After a few rounds of everybody exclaiming over how much they had enjoyed the dance, Mrs. Bennet succeeded in extricating her youngest daughters from the conversation. They walked on, past the ladies' clothing shop and the little café that Mrs. Long's cousin ran, past the outskirts of Meryton, and they were soon at their own airlock.

They were met at the door by Careful, who whined for attention; Elizabeth knelt, crumpling her dress, and roughed up his ears and neck.

Mr. Bennet was sitting sideways on his overstuffed chair in the library, with his head propped up on one arm of the chair and his legs dangling off the other side of the opposite arm, reading a book.

"How was it?" Mr. Bennet asked, peering at them over the top of his book.

"Lovely," Mrs. Bennet said. "Mr. Bingley danced with Jane twice and Mr. Brown introduced me to one of the Edgcumbe suppliers for construction materials, who was in town on a personal errand, and we had quite a productive conversation about bamboo."

"A useful man to know, Mr. Brown," Mr. Bennet said.

"Lord, mamma, you have forgotten all the most important bits!" Lydia said, but before she could delight them all with a recitation, her face split in an uncontrollable yawn.

Mrs. Bennet dragged her three youngest daughters off to bed.

"And you, Elizabeth? Did any of his fine friends ask you to dance?" her father asked.

"No. The husband of his sister danced with nobody, and his friend would only dance with his sisters. In fact, when Mr. Bingley quizzed him on his reluctance to dance, he said that I was not handsome enough to tempt him." She made an exaggerated moue and then laughed when he crinkled his nose at her.

"His standards must be impossibly high."

"He was very arrogant and self-important," Elizabeth said, "but it signifies very little, since he will soon go back to London."

With that pronouncement, Elizabeth and Jane went up to their bedroom. Jane, as the eldest, could have insisted on having a room to herself, putting Elizabeth in with Mary, but thankfully had instead insisted upon the largest of the bedrooms after their parents', so that Jane and Elizabeth might continue to share a room.

"Two requests to dance," Elizabeth teased with a raised eyebrow once they had readied themselves for bed. "Practically a declaration of marriage."

Jane's cheeks dimpled when she smiled. "It was very unexpected."

"Only to you!" Elizabeth said.

Jane coloured, and paused, and then smiled again and said, "He was so lovely to talk to, and he danced so well!"

They had of course heard of the Bingleys before their arrival, though they had known nothing of their characters. Everybody knew the story of the astronomer Samuel Bingley, who had detected the asteroid heading for England and convinced a number of the nation's most prominent families and scientists (the inventor Charles Babbage, the physicist and chemist Michael Faraday, and a score of others) in joining with him to set out across the stars. Nobody knew what had happened back on Earth (there being no way to communicate and no telescope powerful enough on board the ship to watch the asteroid strike) but it was generally supposed that the asteroid must have wiped out England, and without England, the world would surely have fallen into chaos, and that it was only too bad that they hadn't been able to convince some members of the royal family to escape with them. Elizabeth strongly suspected that Samuel Bingley (who had never managed to do any other thing to bring himself renown, and who had been more interested in fame and status than knowledge or science once on board) had made some serious error or another in his calculation, but she kept that suspicion to herself.

Elizabeth grinned. "It is amazing, really, your gift for finding the good in everybody and overlooking our neighbours' follies, especially when you consider our father's earnest instruction. You liked his sisters as well, I suppose."

"Yes, of course!"

"Mrs. Hurst and Miss Bingley were certainly very well-dressed and handsome," Elizabeth said. "Everybody knows who their father was, though it seems to have made a stronger impression on them than one might like. To me they seemed quite haughty."

"You have only taken against them because of their friend's insult."

Elizabeth looked at her sister seriously. "They have no actual rank of their own, you know, and may be jealous of their family's success. They might take a dislike to you only because our father is merely an architect."

"I am sure they will not," Jane said.

"You are right. You are extremely lovable and so they must love you."

"Well," Jane said, and then couldn't come up with a demure response, and, laughing, blew out the candle.

§

When the two eldest Lucases visited a few days later, the Bennet ladies were already on their way to harvest. Longbourn consisted of the house and no less than three greenhouses, one each for fruits, vegetables, and bamboo, which required hours of daily work. Mrs. Bennet supplied the fruit and vegetables for the family from the greenhouses and sold her excess to Meryton. The bamboo all went for building supplies, in exchange for which her children were assigned fewer duty hours and could take time off to travel or study. Unlike the city children, though, they all helped out in the garden, so their hours were more variable, but not actually less than anybody else's. Charlotte and Maria often helped out, and in return Elizabeth helped with the aviary, and Lady Lucas had her pick of the choicest vegetables.

"Come, Maria," Mrs. Bennet said to the second-eldest Lucas when she saw her coming through the Longbourn airlock, "if you help me with the compost, I shall give you some fresh strawberries to bring home to your mother." Nudging Careful away from the door to the greenhouse, she continued, "Somebody needs to take this mutt out of here."

Elizabeth looked around, but Lydia and Kitty were ignoring their mother, and Mary and Jane had gone ahead into the building.

"I'll go," Elizabeth said.

"Thanks, Lizzy."

Charlotte had brought the promised book with her, and after putting the beagle into his kennel, Elizabeth ran up to her room to drop it on her bed. By the time she made it back to the greenhouse, Lydia and Kitty had started squabbling, and under the cover of their noise, she was able to speak with Charlotte without anybody, most especially Jane, overhearing.

The day before, Jane and Elizabeth had visited the Bingleys with their mother. Miss Bingley and Mrs. Hurst had rented a small house in the Meryton dome while they waited for Netherfield to be built; the usual guest quarters provided for workers had been, presumably, deemed insufficient. The house did not have its own dome, as it might have had in London, but there were no domed houses to be had in Meryton, and the ladies expressed a disinclination to be always travelling back and forth along the dismal corridor between the spines. The date for the building party had been set for Michaelmas.

"They found mamma intolerable," Elizabeth said quietly, "too independent, a distressing inclination for work instead of accomplishments, and dirt under her nails from the garden. Of course, they think my younger sisters are beneath them, but they claim a wish to be better acquainted with Jane and me."

"But do *you* wish to be better acquainted with *them?*" Charlotte asked.

"Not really. I do not like them," Elizabeth said frankly, "but Jane does, and I can pretend. You know she always believes people are exactly who they purport to be, without any suspicions."

"Do not leave without getting some seeds from me, Charlotte," Mrs. Bennet called from across the greenhouse, where she and Jane were doling out strawberries from a large bucket into smaller ones for future sale. "I have so many extra that your mother suggested I could trade them for one of her pheasants."

"By all means," Charlotte called back.

Their attention diverted, Lydia and Kitty stopped loudly whispering and poking one another and ignoring their work to turn to Charlotte.

"Do *you* have a secret beau?" Lydia asked.

Mary looked over with them, apparently curious enough to stop working.

Charlotte looked at Lydia for a long moment, as though she had forgotten the meaning of the word 'beau', and then said, "Life is not a novel, Lydia."

"I should *love* to have a secret beau," Lydia said. "Mr. Robinson said you have a nice figure at the assembly. Is *he* your secret beau?"

Charlotte made a face. "He's Father's age."

"He always comments on the young ladies' figures," Elizabeth said. "It *almost* makes me want to stop dancing."

Mary said, "Even Solomon included dancing amongst those purposes for which we should make time: 'a time to weep and a time to laugh, a time to mourn and a time to dance' and for my own part—" and Mrs. Bennet interrupted her to say, "Now is the time to plant and to uproot, Mary, so look lively with those berries!"

§

Elizabeth watched Mr. Darcy stride from one end of Lucas Lodge to the other in search of somebody acceptable to talk to.

This was the third dinner party at which Jane and Mr. Bingley had dined together, and the first to which Elizabeth had also been invited. Dinner over, Jane and Bingley were currently involved in a game of Vingt-un with Miss King and Mr. and Mrs. Hurst, with Mrs. Long dealing. Lady Lucas's sandy head was pressed close to Mrs. Bennet's chestnut one as they compared notes on healing tree trunk cankers. Most of the other attendees were standing around in small groups talking.

Finding nobody who met his standards, Darcy picked up a book and read a page, still standing, and set it down again. He stood looking inscrutably into the middle distance with his fingers just touching the book, as though he might pick it up again at any moment. Caroline Bingley came up to Darcy and took his arm. He turned to her and they spoke for a moment. She motioned toward the Vingt-un players and he said something to her that must have annoyed her, for she dropped his arm and flounced over to lean on her brother's shoulder, commenting on his cards and making Jane bite her lip.

"It is *just* as good as a play," Charlotte murmured to Elizabeth.

Elizabeth laughed.

Mr. Forster, an engineer in town to work on the Netherfield build, came up to them to ask Elizabeth about her signal-work. He said that he hadn't understood that they rotated through different positions, since they did things differently in the Castlereagh area of the ship, where he was from. Elizabeth obligingly described the code they used for each letter, demonstrating with a candle snatched from a table and a small plate for a shield.

"You engineers should all know this code," she told him. "You never know when you might need it."

"It shall be my constant study," Mr. Forster laughed, "so long as I have such a pleasant teacher."

She became aware of Mr. Darcy listening in on them. Elizabeth glanced at him, and caught a slight quirk of his lips, which she thought might turn into a sneer at any moment. All of his attention was on her. Meeting his eyes, she felt the weight of all that haughtiness and disapproval. Before this evening, Lucas Lodge had been its customary comfortable self. She had practically grown up here, since she and Charlotte had been the best of friends even before it was built. It was almost a home to her. Miss Bingley and Mrs. Hurst's fastidious glances at the Lucases' shipmade reading material and chipped china cups made it feel diminished. Mr. Darcy made it feel unsafe.

Elizabeth turned on him, chin raised and eyebrows arched. "Do you have a correction to make to my lesson?"

"You made an excellent demonstration." He bowed.

When he straightened, their eyes met. There was a short silence, in which Elizabeth distantly heard Mr. Bingley say to his partner, "Your deal," and then Charlotte broke the spell by saying, a little ironically, "She shall make another at the pianoforte. Eliza, you know I rely on you to entertain all of our guests."

"Oh, Charlotte, really," Elizabeth said. "You know I am only a mediocre player."

"A party needs music," Charlotte said with her usual cut-throat cheerfulness. "Mr. Darcy, you will help her with the sheet music."

Mr. Darcy went so far as to smile.

Elizabeth hesitated over the options for music, settling on a light, sprightly song: her listeners would enjoy her music more if it were cheerful and brief. She sat, and arranged the sheets, and Mr. Darcy was obedient to Charlotte's command and turned the pages for her, looming over her like the grave crane in Lady Lucas's aviary loomed over the koi pond. A prickling curtness shivered down the back of her neck.

She concentrated on her fingers and the music, determined to play well, but when she glanced away for a moment, she met his reflected eyes in the polished wood of the pianoforte's open keyboard cover. Was his faint smile a sneer? She almost fumbled her chords and dragged her attention back to her playing.

When she finished, she stood too quickly from the instrument, bumping one shoulder against his chest. He put out a hand to steady her and she stepped away from him.

"Thank you, Mr. Darcy," she said quietly.

He bowed.

Before she could collect the sheet music, her sister Mary had succeeded her. From an early age, Mary had applied herself eagerly to learning the pianoforte. She had a peculiar genius for selecting pieces that did not flatter her skills, but she was proud of her accomplished playing, acquired through consistent practice rather than any innate talent. She played, from memory, Beethoven's Sonata No. 17, striking every key with the same pressure as though her fingers were made of clockwork. Elizabeth kept her expression as smooth as an untroubled lake; the piece demanded more sensitivity, but she was hardly a good enough player to criticize.

As Mary played, Darcy moved closer to Elizabeth, but not so close as to invite conversation. She kept her eyes on her sister, though she could not help noticing his movements at the edges of her vision, and in the shadowed reflections on the side of the pianoforte. If he wished to talk to her, she wished he would do so, so that it might be over more quickly; if he did not, then why keep edging closer to her in such an importunate way?

The instant Mary was done, Lydia whispered in her ear, and she started playing a few Scotch jigs. Lydia and Kitty joined some of the younger Lucases and a few of the engineers in dancing. One of the younger Lucases was named Venus, which had seemed very exotic to Elizabeth at the time, but Lady Lucas had been a trendsetter, and now Meryton was dotted with infant Jupiters and Ganymedes.

Coming over to Mr. Darcy, Sir William commented on the charm of watching the group of dancers.

Mr. Darcy shrugged. "Every coxcomb can dance."

Oh, impossible man, Elizabeth thought.

"Do you not enjoy dancing?" Sir William asked.

"Only with a partner I know well," Darcy said. "And there are none such here."

She had known Sir William from birth, and knew he would not rest until he had inflicted Mr. Darcy on somebody, quite against everybody's wishes. To avoid it being her, she went straight to Charlotte. "Let us go to the aviary," she said, and Charlotte readily agreed.

On their way out of the room, Elizabeth saw Miss Bingley lay her hand on Darcy's arm and say something with a smile. She turned away so Charlotte could not again tease her.

Lady Lucas had reproduced the aviary from her childhood home inside her dome as faithfully as she could, nodding to practicality only by adding some types of birds for the family to eat and sell.

The aviary had its own aerator, a brass box suspended just above the metal mesh that contained the birds within their quarter of the dome. She had grown a mix of evergreen and deciduous trees studded with fruit-bearing bushes and enclosed them in a series of adjacent gazebos with metal mesh sides, then populated it with a mix of lovebirds, canaries, and finches from the great aviaries of the Saye and Sele superstructure for beauty, and partridges, pheasants, and Cornish hens for food.

From the doorway to Lucas Lodge, the aviary glowed with reflections from the candles and gas lamps shining out the windows of the house onto the gleaming metal mesh. Charlotte and Elizabeth climbed the steps that led up to the gazebos, which were on raised platforms to allow room for the trees' roots.

"Mr. Bingley has spent the whole evening so far with your sister," Charlotte said, opening the door to the aviary. From within, the birds warned each other about the human invasion: a trilling and cheeping and chirping canopy of music quieted only slightly by the thick greenery.

"It is quite plain that he admires her. Jane is at least on the way to falling in love, if not there already," Elizabeth confessed.

"Oh? She seems happy enough with him, but I did not notice any. . . particular regard."

"She is lucky to unite composure with unvarying cheerfulness.

If he drops her tomorrow, nobody can reproach her with improper behaviour."

"Listen to you, Miss Elizabeth Bennet, who never saw a fence she would not climb nor a packet she would not dodge, talking about improper behaviour. It makes me almost fear to confide in you all of my own wicked secrets." She knocked her shoulder against Elizabeth's.

"That you go to dances at the Harringtons?" Elizabeth laughed. "You have no secrets from *me*, Charlotte Lucas." She bumped her shoulder in return and smiled at her friend. "Anyway, Jane has always been very mindful of her reputation. It comes of being the eldest, I think." She looked up at the glass canopy reinforced with copper that she remembered had once been brassy, but had turned a deep green. "She is not *wrong*. I am careful too, in my own way. I would stay out overnight to dance with a large group, but I would never risk being alone with a man in a way that would suggest I had—"

"The horror." Charlotte shuddered comically.

Elizabeth laughed.

They were companionably silent, walking a little further in, past the koi pond, and finding a bench near the still central fountain, its clockwork exposed on one side where it had evidently been opened for repairs. A pair of goldfinches splashed their wings in the water left in the basin. After brushing some sort of beetle off the seat, Elizabeth curled against the metal armrest, though Charlotte remained standing.

"I tried to read your book last night," Elizabeth said after a while. "You were not lying when you said it was heavy going."

"Mary King finished her engineering courses. If she can do it, Eliza, you can." Charlotte said.

"Oh, yes, I noticed she had come home. I *am* glad she returns victorious. We will have to be sure to tell Walter Harrington so he can stop saying women have no brains for physics."

"That oaf. Do you know, he is the only man who ever proposed to me?"

"No! Charlotte, you never told me!"

"Obviously I said no. That was a decade ago, and I thought I would have better offers."

Elizabeth turned the conversation by asking, "Does that make Miss King the first woman to graduate from Babbage Academy?"

Charlotte reached up a finger. "I believe so."

"That is amazing," Elizabeth said.

"*She* is amazing," Charlotte said, looking up at the little green birds with their scarlet heads. "I like her *so* much, Eliza."

"Yes, I have noticed you are becoming intimate friends."

Charlotte laughed as though Elizabeth had made a joke. "Yes," she said after a moment. "Very intimate."

A lovebird fluttered over to perch on her finger. It looked at her with its bright eyes and then took flight again when she didn't immediately offer it any birdseed. Another perched on a branch above them, eyeing them speculatively, and began grooming itself. Charlotte let her hand fall, then reached out to pick off some moss that was growing up the side of the fountain and throw it into a bucket with skimmings of algae from the koi pond, which would undoubtedly end up as fertilizer for their garden.

"I am happy for you to have found a new friend," Elizabeth said, "even if she is very daunting."

"No, you're wrong. She is quite unassuming, once you get to know her. She is only a little prickly after the way the male students—and even the professors—have treated her. You know her uncle had to make quite a sizable donation to Babbage to entice them to actually award to her the degree she had earned?"

"Shocking," Elizabeth said. She wasn't shocked, but she felt as though she ought to be.

"Anyway, Eliza. About Mary King—"

The doorway to Lucas Lodge opened for a moment, spilling out light and laughing voices calling for somebody, and then the door slammed shut again. Charlotte spooked at the noise, exactly as a horse might have, and seemed to forget whatever she had been about to say as she watched Lady Lucas stand out on her doorstep, look up at the stars, and walk slowly around to the other side of the house.

"Perhaps it is too soon to say anything," Charlotte said to herself, and when Elizabeth raised her eyebrows, said quickly in a higher voice, "Oh! I mean about Jane and Bingley, of course."

But they had been speaking of Mary King, not Bingley. Elizabeth supposed that her friend had been about to task her with more about Babbage, and was glad for the turn of the conversation. "It's far too soon for him to declare himself," she said. "It doesn't mean he won't. They now know which games the other prefers, and which type of punch and flavour of cake. They are nearly well enough acquainted to be married."

Charlotte laughed. "But Eliza, she would do better to be less careful and more affectionate. She might lose him if she does not give him the confidence to know that his attentions are welcome. When I—that is—they only see each other at parties and dinners, where they can scarcely talk. She can fall in love after he has proposed."

"An excellent idea, if all she wanted were to get married. But she has only known him, what, three weeks? She does not know yet what sort of man he is."

"Just as well if she does not know all his flaws when they walk down the aisle. It will delay the inevitable."

Elizabeth laughed. "But you would not do that."

"No, I would not," Charlotte allowed with an unsmiling sidelong look. "I did not, that is, and I am now unlikely ever to get married. Especially—" She shook her head and did not complete the thought.

Elizabeth raised her eyebrows at this, but didn't argue. Her friend was accounted a spinster at the age of twenty-seven, which was foolish and a waste, but Elizabeth could not make some gentleman ask for her friend's hand.

§

"Father," Elizabeth said, coming into the drawing room.

Mr. Bennet had his head in a book and did not hear.

"Our aunt told me that if we should go to the communal kitchen more often, we might run into Mr. Forster and Mr. Carter," Lydia said to Kitty. "She sees them going there very often from her window."

"Father," Elizabeth repeated.

"Yes, dear," Mr. Bennet said without looking up. He turned a page.

"Could you come to your library with me, and explain to me these equations?" Elizabeth said, holding up Faraday's new book.

"I saw Mr. Metcalfe when I was going to work yesterday," Kitty said. "He had on his blue coat! So handsome!"

Mrs. Bennet came in just then, still wearing her dirt-covered gloves and an apron. "Lizzy, I need you."

"Not just at present, my pet," Mr. Bennet said to Elizabeth.

Mary came into the room behind Mrs. Bennet. "Excuse me, mamma," she murmured, and walked around her to the family's shabby pianoforte.

"I think he has a weak chin," Lydia said. "Denny is much more to my liking."

"But I cannot follow them, Father," Elizabeth said.

Mary cleared her throat, and Elizabeth looked over to see that she was gathering her sheet music into a pile and shuffling through it to find a song.

"Oh, no," Kitty said. "Metcalfe has much nicer hair."

"Lizzy," Mrs. Bennet said.

"It is just as well that you have such bad taste, Kitty! Less competition for the good men!"

Mary began to play a sonata.

"I am speaking with papa, mamma." Elizabeth said.

The sonata sounded as though it were a military march.

"I have not!" Kitty pouted.

"I am sure you can work them out on your own, Lizzy," Mr. Bennet said mildly, still reading.

"My taste is every bit as good as yours," Kitty went on.

Her father still did not look at her. "And in any case, you will have no need of that sort of knowledge when you are married."

Elizabeth put down her physics book with a thump.

"Now, Lizzy."

"I will help you, Mother," Jane said, rising from the window seat where she had been looking out at the lights of their greenhouses and apparently daydreaming.

"Why do we even have a window?" Elizabeth said, motioning at her. "What is the point? There is nothing to look at."

"Thank you, Jane," Mrs. Bennet said, looking pointedly at Elizabeth.

"Oh!" Elizabeth threw up her hands. "I am going for a walk."

"I want to come!" Kitty said, and Lydia said, "Yes, let us go into Meryton with you!"

No wonder Mary King had been the first woman to graduate. She was an only child.

"Lizzy," Lydia said, "did I tell you that Mr. Denny said I look two entire years older than my actual age!"

Elizabeth put her hands over her ears and walked out of the room, but Lydia and Kitty followed.

"We shall go to the Philipses'," Lydia said, and Kitty agreed.

Mrs. Bennet's sister was married to a Mr. Philips, a clerk to a lawyer in Meryton. Her sisters enjoyed visiting their aunt to collect interesting gossip, which they called news. They grabbed their rebreathers and slipped on their boots and skipped a little ahead of her.

Elizabeth concentrated on the rhythm of her breathing, in the hopes that a calm exterior would lead to a calm interior, and trailed after her sisters.

As they walked through Meryton, Elizabeth looked up at the thick sheets of glass that formed Meryton's dome, and then the larger Headfort dome that encompassed it, and the metalwork junctions that held them in place. A crew was clambering across a temporary walkway far overhead, oiling or repairing something she couldn't see. Even farther above, somebody stood in her old place in the signal tower, telling London and Edgcumbe that everything was fine here, and that some few people, probably in the single digits, were lucky enough to travel from one place to another.

When they reached the most populated area of the Meryton dome, Lydia saw Mr. Denny and waved her hand as she called his name. Elizabeth briefly closed her eyes. Mr. Denny, smiling, crossed the street with a friend following him. The friend was handsome, tall, well-built, with a ready smile and gentlemanlike appearance, and evidently clever enough for engineering, for Mr. Denny immediately said, "Allow me to make known to you Mr. George Wickham, who has come to help us with the Netherfield build."

"So, you are an engineer?" Kitty said.

Mr. Wickham smiled and said, "I am well on my way to becoming one."

Mr. Denny then shared a little news of a Mr. Morris, an acquaintance of Lydia and Kitty's, who had moved to Edgcumbe a few months before and had lately been married. Mr. Wickham shared some thoughts on the attractiveness of marital bliss. Lydia contributed a few statements about a most interesting sermon their clergyman had given the previous weekend on the subject of marriage, which as far as Elizabeth could recall were entirely fabricated for the sake of the conversation. Kitty complimented Mr. Denny on his excellent new hat. Finally, Mr. Wickham commented on the prettiness of all of the ladies' dresses.

"Especially yours, Miss Elizabeth," he said.

"Oh! I am glad you like it," Elizabeth said, swishing her skirts a bit.

"It does not look shipmade," Denny said.

Indeed, the shipmade fabrics, so often made of wool, had a distinctive roughness, but Jane had repurposed some old bedding that had torn to make Elizabeth's dress. "Jane made it. She is very skilled at sewing. I did all of the embroidery, though."

As she was speaking, she heard a strange sound that almost sounded like a child's cry. Only after she turned and saw the horses did she identify it as a whinny. She had only ever seen Sir William's elderly nag, but these glossy creatures were in their prime, she was sure from their shiny coats.

Elizabeth realized then that she had been hearing the hollow clip-clop of hooves against metal coming toward them for some minutes, but had been too distracted by Mr. Wickham's compliments to notice.

Darcy and Bingley were just dismounting.

"What luck our running into you!" Mr. Bingley said, coming up to Elizabeth and smiling at her sisters. "We are just on our way to Longbourn to inquire after your sister."

"I am certain she will be very pleased to see you," Elizabeth said with a smile. "Do not be discouraged if you get no answer to your knock. Papa hears nothing when he is deep in a book. Jane will most likely be in one of the greenhouses with mamma."

Eyes crinkling, Bingley bowed and took the reins for his horse back from Mr. Darcy.

"Allow me to introduce you to Mr. Denny," she indicated him, "and Mr. Wickham," she went on, and as Denny stepped forward to clasp Bingley's hand, Elizabeth's eyes went to Mr. Darcy, whose head jerked a little, just as if she had slapped him. He was staring at the newcomer, face white. She looked back: Wickham had turned quite pink. They must have known each other, yet nobody spoke.

Darcy's eyes went far away, as though he were willing himself somewhere else. Wickham looked hard at him, and bowed. Mr. Darcy made only the slightest bow in return.

"Most pleased," Mr. Bingley was meanwhile saying in the most natural way, shaking hands all around, and laughing at something Mr. Denny said with his untroubled, honeyed laugh. He remounted with easy grace and they took their leave. Darcy bowed once more, more deeply, to Elizabeth, his face strangely grave, and she watched them ride away.

CHAPTER THREE

THE NEXT MORNING, MR. BENNET HELD A LETTER up as he sat for his eggs and toast. "I hope, my dear," he said to his wife, "that you can accommodate a visitor in a few weeks."

"Why, who is it?"

"A total stranger."

Mrs. Bennet said, "A stranger?"

Lydia said, "Oh, let it be an engineer or if not, then at least an architect!"

Her father, the architect, bowed ironically in her direction.

Jane said, "Father, do tell us!"

He ate some eggs and drank some of his chicory coffee, enjoying the suspense, then finally flapped the letter between his thumb and forefinger and said, "This letter is from my cousin, Mr. William Collins. The younger one, who will inherit this dome and any buildings therein immediately upon my death."

"*Any* buildings?" Mrs. Bennet's voice, pitched high in horror, rose above the general hubbub of the girls' responses. "No, it won't do, Mr. Bennet. When Mr. Collins is here you absolutely *must* be sure to emphasize to him that the entail only covers the house and dome, and that the greenhouses, as only *semi*-permanent structures, are not included, by a strict reading of—" Mrs. Bennet paused, her usual composure shattered, and then she wailed, "Oh *why* could we not have had a boy?"

Kitty said, "Mother, we could not *help* being girls," and Mary said, hopefully, "But he is the cousin who is a pastor?" and Lydia said, "Will he bring us any presents, do you think?" and Mrs. Bennet continued, saying, "And when you die, Mr. Bennet, are we to lose not only our house but the very business that keeps us alive?"

Mr. Bennet dropped bites of toast under his chair for Careful.

"I am in good health," he said only. This set off another flurry of commentary. Finally, his daughters ran down, and he said, "Shall I tell you what he says? His terrible father has died, and he has received ordination and been given a living in Hunsford, Meryton's counterpart in the Castlereagh dome, by a Lady Catherine de Bourgh, who he sounds half in love with. He wishes to, well, I will let him speak for himself: let me see, here it is—'As the pastor of Hunsford, I must make an example to my flock and am, accordingly, haunted by the unmended breach between the two branches of our family. I sincerely pray that you will not reject the offered olive branch. I am distressed that my father should have—' well, anyway, we need not revisit those events. He writes, hum-te-hum, here is the strangest part—'In mending your argument with my late father, I appeal to you as a Christian, but in this second respect, I appeal to you as a father. I am sorry to be the instrument by which your daughters should be harmed, and hope that we may discuss a possible remedy.'—etcetera etcetera. And then he invites himself here. I must write him back soon and let him know whether or not we accept his self-invitation."

"What an odd, pompous letter," Elizabeth said after a short silence.

Mary pursed her lips. "The idea of the olive branch perhaps is not wholly new, yet I think it is well expressed."

"What could he mean to offer us as amends?" Jane took the letter from her father to peruse the words he hadn't felt worthy of being read aloud, but it seemed to shed no light on the matter, since she handed it back to him with a shrug.

Mr. Bennet looked at his wife, who stood to clear the dishes. "He does not seem quite so odious as his father," she said. "If he wishes to visit, I will not discourage him."

After breakfast, Elizabeth and Jane were in charge of cleaning up. "What do you think of papa's letter?" Jane asked, but Elizabeth merely waved her hand to indicate how inconsequential she considered the whole affair.

"I want to tell you about something that happened yesterday," Elizabeth said, and she described the strange meeting between Darcy and Wickham. "After I introduced Mr. Wickham, there was the most awkward silence, and both men looked thunderstruck. Yet nobody said a word about it, and Mr. Bingley did not look as though he recognized Mr. Wickham at all."

Jane's brow furrowed slightly, and she put the kettle on so they might have a hot tea when they were done. "How strange," she said. "Did Mr. Wickham say anything after Darcy had left?"

"Not at all." Elizabeth frowned as she scraped the dishes clear of food. "I might almost have imagined it, but then, if they *have* had some sort of falling out, he could hardly discuss it with somebody he had only just met."

Jane accepted one of the plates for scrubbing. "They must have had their reasons for such a display. Perhaps we will find them out someday."

They fell silent, and began to wash the dishes, moving around each other in the small kitchen with the ease of long years of practice: scrubbing and drying and putting the dishes away, and afterwards having a long hot drink.

§

A day later, Mrs. Philips invited the Bennets to dinner along with her friends in town and a number of the visiting engineers.

The Philipses liked to entertain, so they maintained a simple, though beautiful, dining room and a sumptuous drawing room. Elizabeth had been through her aunt and uncle's whole house, and the rest was meanly furnished just so they could afford the display of these two rooms.

Mrs. Bennet had kept her daughters busy all day in the greenhouses, and they arrived just in time to go in to dinner with the group.

"Perhaps Eliza might catch the eye of one of the engineers," she told her sister when they all arrived, making no effort to keep the statement confidential.

Elizabeth wrinkled her nose at her aunt and mother, who were congratulating each other on their cleverness. As she passed her jacket and rebreather to one of her young cousins, she saw that they had arrived too late to choose where they might sit, and Mr. Wickham was already leading in a Miss Grantley, who was annoyingly pretty and fashionably dressed. They ate (what, Elizabeth hardly noticed, though she dutifully exclaimed over the spread) and she spent the meal fending off the advances of a friend of her uncle's, wheezing sherry fumes down her cleavage. It was a relief when the meal ended and the ladies could withdraw while the men smoked over port wine and madeira.

The drawing room had a fireplace with fluted columns and carved garland, which had pride of place opposite the door, and in between were scattered an assortment of sofa sets, side tables, armchairs, end tables, and so on, with one corner of the room devoted to velveted card tables and damask chairs. The walls were painted a dark honey colour, nearly the exact shade of Mrs. Philips's hair.

Next to the pianoforte, white inset shelving matched the crown molding and displayed real Chinese porcelain behind glass. This, Mrs. Philips removed for use, as she offered tea, chicory coffee, and muffins. The ladies spoke lightly of the magnificence of the meal, the charm of the room, and those little details about the visiting engineers that might entertain the group. Nobody had anything to share of Wickham, except for one comment from Miss Grantley on his pleasing manners.

When at last the gentlemen joined them, Wickham immediately sat with Elizabeth and Lydia.

"An excellent meal," he said, and Elizabeth agreed.

Lydia struck up a sprightly conversation with him, and, in no mood to compete, Elizabeth looked around the room. Soon enough, Lydia grew too entranced with the whist games not to have her own share of the excitement and wandered off to comment on Mr. Denny's bets.

"How long has Mr. Darcy been in Headfort?" Wickham asked after a pause.

"Not more than three weeks."

"Do you know him well?"

"Not at all, nor do I wish to." Elizabeth leaned forward and lowered her voice. "He is said to be wealthy, and he is a great friend of Mr. Bingley's, and otherwise I know very little about him, except that he is quite disagreeable." *And he finds me not handsome enough to dance with,* she thought.

"His estate in Darlington was one of the first on the ship. Pemberley is quite beautiful, and very large; I dare say it is a similar size to all of Meryton, just for the one family and their retainers. I lived there as a child."

Elizabeth sat back in astonishment.

"Indeed, the coldness of our encounter the other day might have suggested otherwise." His smile was sad. "Your opinion of him as disagreeable would surprise most people."

"Not in Headfort. He offended almost everybody at our last assembly."

"Did he?" Wickham's smile broadened a little. "I *am* surprised. Those with a fortune can usually get away with a lot more than those without. Perhaps the people here are more discerning than usual."

"Ha!" Mrs. Philips could be heard across the room over her husband's bass laughter. "Trump ace. Oh, well done!"

"Do you know if he plans to stay here long?" Wickham asked.

"I have not heard anything one way or the other. I hope you will not change your plans to stay here on his account."

"No. If he wants to avoid me, he can do so. It distresses me to see him, it is true, on his father's account, but *I* have no reason to regret *my* behaviour."

"But he has reason to regret his?"

Wickham paused. "The late Mr. Darcy was a great man, a pioneer in aetherflight and a great inventor, as well as a kind and generous friend, to me and to my father, who devoted his life to Pemberley. The current Mr. Darcy is. . . less so."

Elizabeth hardly knew what to say, and at that moment Mr. Denny won his bet and a tumultuous cheer came from that corner of the room. Wickham gazed across at the commotion and then seemed to come back to himself with a start, and turned to her with an easy smile, some of his intensity seeming to evaporate. "Do you enjoy living near Meryton? Your family has their own dome, do they not?"

"Yes, we are only a short walk away." *Oh, please only be making conversation,* she thought. Strangers occasionally thought that their dome was evidence of wealth they did not have, rather than a reward for all of the work her father had expended helping to design the ship and its domes. She wanted this young man to like her for herself, and not some imagined fortune.

"I have enjoyed the society here," Wickham said.

"People here are in general very friendly," Elizabeth agreed. "For myself, I would like to travel and meet with different sorts of people. Except for my uncle's house in City dome, in London, I have hardly been anywhere."

"But you seem so—I was going to say sophisticated, but that is not quite the right word. Perceptive, I think. I am surprised to hear you are not much traveled. But perhaps you have had an extensive education."

Elizabeth laughed, unconsciously putting both hands to her cheeks to stem a blush. "Father does not believe we girls need it. However, I have learned to do a lot of different things due to Sir William Lucas's views on cross-training."

"I like him. Everybody in Meryton has impressed me with how friendly and organized they are. It seems a good choice for a second chance."

"What was your first chance?" Elizabeth asked, almost sure the question might lead the conversation back to the mystery of his strained relations with Darcy.

"The church. I should have had an excellent little dome near Pemberley," he said with a trace of bitterness. "The late Mr. Darcy bequeathed it to me, but when the previous incumbent died, Darcy gave the living to somebody else."

"But how could he?"

His expression was almost blank, but for a slight twist of his lips. "The wording of the will was vague. Mr. Darcy—the late Mr. Darcy, that is—spoke of it in front of us both, but the current Mr. Darcy pretended not to understand his father's intentions." He looked down at his hands in his lap, and took a deep and steadying breath. "He accused me of whatever came into his head in the moment, based on nothing, to justify denying me the bequest, only because he was jealous of his father's love for me."

"How shocking! I have never liked him, but I would not have thought him capable of such maliciousness! He deserves to be publicly shamed."

"I beg you," Wickham said, "please keep this secret."

"Of course," Elizabeth said. "You alone must judge when, or if, to reveal his actions to the world."

"I loved his father too well to say a word." Wickham ducked his head a little and looked up at her from his new, lower vantage point, smiling shyly and shrugging his shoulders. It was a pose that smacked of artifice, and yet with him seemed entirely natural. "I have only told you, because our behaviour was so strange the other day, that I felt I owed you an explanation, and I thought that you would have the wisdom to understand. I cannot trumpet these circumstances around the world, but it is a great relief to have an understanding listener like yourself."

"Thank you. I hope—I mean, I am happy to—any time," Elizabeth said, feeling her colour mount. "But, oh, it is so confounding! You would think his very pride would prevent his acting in such a dishonourable manner, for surely he lives to be thought highly of."

"Yes, I believe he does. How insightful of you. He is generous with the poor, and helps his tenants, and so forth, and he has a great deal of pride in his sister, who is a very handsome, accomplished girl of sixteen, just the same age as your Lydia. Miss Darcy reflects well on the family, you see, and the family's reputation is what matters to her brother."

Wickham could not have hit upon an explanation that would endear Mr. Darcy to Elizabeth less. "Oh, I hate all of this concern with family reputation," she said. "I am sure we would do better to treat each person according to his own behaviour, without reference to his wealth or his parents' status."

"Alas, we live in a fallen cosmos," Wickham said with a mischievous tone.

"Says the man who should have been a parson," Elizabeth teased.

He smiled in return.

"You must have known Miss Darcy. Is she more like her father or her brother?"

He frowned. "I wish I could give you a good report of her. Unfortunately, she is just as proud as her brother. They are both apt to be agreeable to the rich and unpleasant to everybody else. Your friend Mr. Bingley no doubt only sees him at his best. He is supposed to be very rich, is he not?"

Since Lydia chose that moment to return to gloat over having won five hours off duty at whist, Elizabeth was spared the necessity of replying. Lydia said that she intended to take the rest she had won the very next day, and could not be persuaded that it was too short notice for a replacement to be found, as Denny, from whom she had won them, was unavailable. Kitty promised to go in her place, prompting Mrs. Bennet to complain of thereby being shorthanded in the greenhouse, which meant that she would require Lydia's help. This argument continued all the way home.

Once they had turned in for the night, Elizabeth whispered the entire sordid story to Jane. Wickham had asked her to keep it secret, but it was too shocking not to share, and she knew Jane would never breathe a word of it to anybody. Telling Jane was always just the same as keeping a secret, and she never felt that she had betrayed a confidence in sharing it with her.

"I cannot believe it of Mr. Darcy," Jane declared when she was finished. "And yet I am sure Mr. Wickham would not lie. They must have both been deceived in some way."

"That is indeed the only way in which they might both escape blame." Elizabeth reached over to lightly tickle her sister. "Just think, though; if they were deceived, then you shall have to think ill of whatever villain lied to them both. Twist it however you can, you cannot excuse *everybody*."

"No," Jane said, "but I cannot believe that Mr. Bingley could be deceived in his friend, or that Mr. Darcy should have acted so disgracefully."

"And I cannot believe that Wickham should have invented the whole complicated history."

They were both silent a moment.

"If this scandal becomes public, Mr. Bingley may have to suffer a lot of unmerited blame, if he *has* been deceived."

"Wickham swore me to secrecy, so you may rest easy on that point."

"I wonder if his sisters know anything."

"You are uniquely positioned to find out," Elizabeth said, "but do not ask on my account. I am only curious."

§

Michaelmas. The day of the build.

The day before, William Goulding, the clergyman in Meryton, had based his sermon on an old Earth story that when St. Michael banished Lucifer from Heaven, he fell from the firmament to land in a blackberry bush. The prickles of the blackberry were compared at length to the prickles of conscience when one knew one had done something wrong, and Mrs. Bennet had muttered the whole way home about the blackberries she had just started, and how now nobody would want to eat them, until Mr. Bennet had said to never mind about that because she could just take them out of the dome to dry them in cheesecloth and aether, and put them in his muffins year round.

Elizabeth had a foggy notion that on Earth, Michaelmas had been part of the turning of the year, the beginning of the shortening of days. Or maybe it was when days began to get longer? Days had been shorter in winter, had they not? She would have to ask her parents. Every day was the same on the ship, and years were a matter of convention. In hundreds of years, when they reached Alpha Centauri, they might have to adjust to a different year, but for now it was simpler to stick to a calendar that no longer touched them.

The Bennets arrived early at the Netherfield site, currently bare metal except for the enormous mounds of supplies, tidily stacked and labeled, and the scaffolding and lighting that had already been erected. Mr. Bennet immediately went to speak with the foreman, and Elizabeth expected that they wouldn't see him again until the end of the day.

Elizabeth looked for Mr. Wickham amongst the engineers, but he was nowhere to be seen. *I bet Darcy ensured he was kept away,* she thought, but it wasn't the sort of thing one could ask about. Of course, that didn't stop Lydia.

"Mr. Denny," her sister called, and when he came over to the family group, she said, "Where is Wickham?"

"London," Mr. Denny said. "He had business there." Lydia turned away, apparently satisfied, and Denny leaned toward Elizabeth to add, "though it might have waited if he had not wanted to give a certain person a wide berth."

Elizabeth nodded her understanding. Perhaps it was just as well, she thought: for this work, she had worn her oldest and most patched dress with an even older apron over top. Her hair was pulled out of her face and covered with a piece of linen splotched with old paint. She looked just fine for the likes of Denny, but as much as she had looked forward to seeing him, maybe Mr. Wickham could wait for a day when she looked at least a little more fashionable and tidy.

"Put me to work," she said.

Mr. Denny motioned her to the bottom of the scaffolding. For the next several hours, she helped to shift pre-fabricated pieces into place to form the inside of what would be Netherfield Park. The floor plan had been chalked directly on the metal, over which they laid an insulating layer, followed by sections of unpainted underflooring. Then load-bearing beams sketched the skeleton of the house, slotting into place with a distinctive *thunk*. The outer walls, glowing with panels of oak and glass, were wrestled into place behind her while Elizabeth and Jane lifted the much lighter panels of bamboo that formed the base for the inner walls. They interlocked according to Mr. Bennet's pattern with quiet clicks.

By mid-morning, skilled workmen were plastering over the bamboo and Elizabeth's group was moving up the stairs to lay out the ceiling and underflooring on the scaffolding that had seemed to sprout overhead while she had been busy with the first floor. Harsh shadows from the arc lamps far overhead splayed across the unfinished floors, and one of the workers called for lights to be brought in the house.

By mid-afternoon, the roofing was being put on by one set of workers while bamboo flooring, stained a deep brown, was installed behind the plasterers as they finished each section of wall. In the heart of this orchestration, Jane brought Elizabeth some water as they took their hourly break, sitting without ceremony on a patch of unfinished floor. Sweaty and considerably wilted, Elizabeth felt conspicuous amongst the many workmen, but when she looked around, nobody was paying either of them the least attention. She pushed the strands of her hair that had come loose back into their ribbon and took two bread and butter sandwiches handed to her by one of the workers.

"We should eat these outside," Jane suggested. "The air in here is so close."

Once outside, Mr. Bingley came up to thank them both, and Jane walked a little distance off with him to converse privately. Elizabeth smiled as he took one of Jane's hands, then looked away to give them what little privacy was possible amidst the hubbub.

She couldn't help but notice that neither Miss Bingley nor Mrs. Hurst had come to help out. How extraordinary to expect so many people to do so much work on one's behalf without once lifting a finger to contribute.

Elizabeth looked up at the house as she ate. From the ground, it looked stately and serene, even as the workers finished nailing on the roofing. A worker who was crouching in the glare of the arc lamps on the scaffolding overhead moved to his next section, and Elizabeth saw that it was Mr. Darcy swinging the hammer. Without his coat, his hair disordered and his fine linen shirt sticking to his torso, he looked like an entirely different man. He was smiling slightly as he concentrated exclusively on his work; he seemed more in his element here than he had ever seemed in a drawing room. She started to smile, and then remembered his ill-treatment of Mr. Wickham.

He looked in her direction then, or perhaps in the direction of Bingley and Jane (he was at such a distance that she couldn't be sure) and his smile dropped away, and then he stepped away from the edge and was lost to sight. Elizabeth turned away. Seeing Charlotte Lucas, she walked over to check that she had also eaten and had some water, and then her break was over. She went with Charlotte to the closest engineer, a Mr. Pratt.

"Do you have anything for us to do?" she asked.

He directed them to the outer dome. Workers clambered over scaffolding to rivet together the metal ribs of the structure; all that she and Charlotte were called upon to do was to pass up the next piece to the line of men. Charlotte climbed up the scaffolding a few feet.

Elizabeth turned to grab a piece, and Mr. Darcy was standing there with it in his hands. She instinctively jerked back from him.

"I do apologize. I did not mean to startle you," he said.

"I am fine. Thank you," she said, taking the metal joist from him and passing it up to Charlotte, who was now perched just above her on the first horizontal brace, to pass further up the line.

She turned back, and he had picked up the next piece. She pursed her lips. He wasn't needed here, and furthermore wasn't welcome, but she would not be the first to be uncivil. Silently he handed her piece after piece, and silently she accepted them, until, suddenly fancying that it would be the greater punishment to her partner to oblige him to talk, she said, "It will be a great advantage to the neighbourhood to add another dome."

He agreed.

After he had passed a few more pieces to her silently, she said, "And now it is *your* turn to say something. Perhaps you can comment on the number of people who turned out to help, or the rapidity of the build."

His mouth quirked at one corner. "I will say whatever you like."

"Excellent. Maybe in a little while, I might share my ideas on how Netherfield ought to be furnished, but for now we may be quiet."

Above her, Charlotte, who was making no attempt to hide that she was spying on their conversation, barked a laugh.

"Do you always talk when you are working?" Darcy said.

"Of course. Usually, I am working with people I have known my whole life, and we have little to learn about each other, but it helps to pass the time more pleasantly."

"And with people you know only slightly?"

"It would look strange not to talk at least a little, and rumours may start that we are enemies."

"And you do not find it distracting?"

"It does not require my full attention to pass these bits of metal up the line."

He nodded. "I find it easier to converse when I am otherwise at leisure, so I can give proper thought to my statements."

Elizabeth was silent for a minute as she continued to pass the metal pieces up to Charlotte, but then the workman above her friend engaged her in conversation, and she noticed that they would soon come to the end of their pile. If she didn't say something now, she might never again have the opportunity.

"When you met us last week, we were just making a new friend."

His face coloured; his mouth tightened; his eyes cut away from hers. After a moment, he said, "Mr. Wickham makes an excellent first impression. Whether he may *keep* your friendship remains to be seen."

"He lost yours," Elizabeth said, "in a way that haunts him."

Darcy only bowed and handed her the last of the metal pieces.

When she turned from handing them on to Charlotte, Sir William Lucas was approaching. "Your roofing skills were unexpected," he said. He turned a genial smile in Mr. Darcy's direction.

Darcy smiled politely. "I am accustomed to helping whenever maintenance must be done at Pemberley," he said.

Sir William shook his hand. "Excellent, most excellent," he said. "I hope we may take advantage of your skills in the future when you visit your friend," he added, with a nod to Bingley, who had moved to sit on a pile of supplies with Jane, their heads close together.

Darcy glanced in the direction of Sir William's nod.

"But do not let me interrupt. I was just coming to fetch my daughter," Sir William went on, and Charlotte stopped chatting with the worker above her to hop down from her perch.

Turning back to Elizabeth, Darcy said, "I have forgotten what we were talking about."

"Then it cannot have been very important." Elizabeth dusted off her hands on her apron and looked about for something else to do, but she didn't have the strength to hoist the enormous panes of glass into their proper locations on the outside of the dome, a job currently being handled by teams of men with complicated pulley systems.

"Come, have some supper," Darcy commanded.

Elizabeth pursed her lips. "It is early for supper, but I admit I am famished."

They headed for the house, into which all this time people had been carrying furniture, food, and other items. The plaster would need a few days to dry, but the family had decided to move immediately and simply pile most of their things in boxes in the middles of rooms, rather than continue to live in the cramped house they had been renting in Meryton. Darcy and Elizabeth found a few trays of food that had been prepared, presumably, by Miss Bingley and Mrs. Hurst, who had both finally deigned to show up.

Darcy grabbed a muffin and continued into the house while Elizabeth made herself a plate. Miss Bingley pulled her to one side and said, "Jane has been asking me about George Wickham, I gather at your behest, and I hear that he forgot to tell you that his father was the steward when he was complaining of his so-called ill treatment. As your friend—" here Elizabeth raised her eyebrows, but Miss Bingley went on "—I have to caution you not to believe his lies, for Mr. Darcy has been nothing but kindness to the man."

"You have this on whose authority?"

"Mr. Darcy himself, of course. I am not privy to all the details, but rest assured what I have told you can be relied upon."

"I have heard you say nothing worse of Wickham than that his father was the late Mr. Darcy's steward, which I already knew!"

"I was only trying to be helpful." Miss Bingley walked away.

Elizabeth picked up her plate and angrily ate a wedge of cheese. She then sought out Jane, who had finally parted from Mr. Bingley and was watching the glass of the Netherfield dome being raised and put into place, causing the light from the arc lamps above them to split into rainbows. Her sister turned to her with outstretched hands. "What a wonderful day this has been," she said.

"Am I to wish you joy?" Elizabeth teased.

"It is far too early for that," Jane said, "but Lizzy, I am so happy."

"If you have been too busy, I forgive you," Elizabeth said, "but have you discovered anything about Mr. Wickham?"

"No," Jane said. "I asked, but the Bingleys only know what Mr. Darcy has told them. Mr. Bingley speaks so highly of Mr. Darcy that I am afraid Mr. Wickham must be quite disreputable, unless he is mistaken in his friend's character."

"What did he say about the late Mr. Darcy's bequest?"

"He believes the living was only left conditionally, though he could not remember the details."

"I am sure that Mr. Bingley believes Mr. Darcy, but that does not mean that *I* must. But let us speak of something else. What did you talk of for so long?"

"Nothing of consequence." Jane dimpled. "We just talked, about anything and everything. I do believe he may actually be growing fond of me."

"I am sure of it, for who could resist you?" She hugged her sister.

It was now time for supper, and all that was left to do afterwards was to form the smaller dome in which the greenhouse would eventually be installed. Many of the workers had gone home with packages of cold chicken and bread from the Bingleys to take with them, and she was able to sit with Mary, Kitty, and Lydia before her three younger sisters headed home with their mother.

"You and Jane will make sure to drag your father home when you are done?" Mrs. Bennet said. "I dare say he would stay until dawn if they were not done before then."

They promised sincerely and ate their dinners, and then it was time to put up the greenhouse.

The Netherfield greenhouse was not on the scale of the Bennets', which were used not only to feed the family but to provide extra produce for sale. It was a small structure for the Bingleys to grow roses and peonies to decorate their house, and for guests to take a small turn in after dinner. Miss Bingley had declared her intention to use pots and containers to hold all of their efforts, and so the greenhouse didn't need to be raised to allow room for a soil bed. Accordingly, they required many fewer people to put it together. The pots would arrive later.

Elizabeth had expected to be swaying on her feet by this time, but the rest and food had revived her, and when Mr. Bingley asked for volunteers she stepped forward along with Jane, Darcy, and perhaps twenty others. Mr. Bingley selected the youngest and fittest eight or nine of them to marshal the joints and glass, and despite having volunteered, Elizabeth was surprised to find herself and Jane chosen. Usually men liked to keep these tasks to themselves, but either Mr. Bingley was unusually egalitarian, or, more likely, he simply wanted to keep Jane by his side.

Miss Edevane, a sturdy nurse of middle-age who had a genius for organization and often stepped in when a group in Meryton lacked a leader, instructed the others in how to lay out all of the parts, and they quickly had the metal frame in place, with some of the neighbourhood boys of Lydia's age tasked with climbing the entire thing to make sure all of the screws were tightened. They pressed the straight panes of glass into place around the outside of the greenhouse and secured them. At Miss Edevane's direction a few of the boys climbed ladders to put into place the two curved panes that formed each half of the ceiling.

The first was lifted by Mr. Denny and Mr. Dawson on one end and Mr. Darcy and Elizabeth on the other. Unlike the panes that had been used for the larger Netherfield dome, these were only a little taller than Mr. Darcy and about as wide, but with an even curvature. They weighed enough that Elizabeth was not quite sure she could manage, but she listened with her body to every movement of Darcy's projecting itself to her through the glass. Through her gloves, the smoothed edge of the pane pressed hard against her fingers, and she was sure she'd have marks there later. Some of the workers above them used a winch to begin lifting the glass with a rope threaded through the curved area, with Denny, Dawson, Darcy, and Elizabeth keeping the pane steady so it wouldn't slip off the rope, until the boys clambering all over the frame could grab it from above. Soon it was in place, and she looked up at it from below. A wobble in the glass distorted Mr. Darcy's reflected expression as he looked in her direction. She turned her gaze to him, but he was already looking away.

Jane and Bingley held one end of the second pane of glass as Chamberlayne and Haggerston held the other, replicating the procedure for the second pane. The boys above began operating the winch, and the glass was at face-height when disaster struck: Jane missed her footing and swayed. She let go of the glass to stretch out her hands for balance, but her rolled ankle wouldn't take her weight. She was falling. Bingley reached out to steady her and lost his grip on the pane of glass, which slid toward Haggerston and Chamberlayne. Chamberlayne protected his face, rather than letting his nose get smashed, and the pane of glass slid off the rope and fell, smashing into the floor more or less simultaneously with Jane, and breaking next to her.

Shards of glass ricocheted into Jane's body from boot to hip, and she cried out in pain.

CHAPTER FOUR

MOST OF THE GLASS CUT JANE IN TRANSIT and kept going, skidding on the metal floor, but a few pieces embedded themselves into her side, sparkling under the arc lamps.

"Jane!" Elizabeth ran forward and crouched to help her sister sit up.

"I will fetch the doctor." Chamberlayne left at a run.

"I am fine," Jane said, but it was clear she wasn't. Blood was oozing down her left side, and a few jagged pieces of glass stuck out of her leg. Miss Edevane began staunching the bleeding with strips of cloth from her petticoat, working around the glass rather than removing it.

"Do not try to stand up." Mr. Bingley's brow was etched with worry. He had a small shard of glass embedded in his cheek and several cuts on his arm, but appeared to be otherwise unscathed. He seemed entirely unaware of his own injuries in his worry for Jane.

"I am so sorry," Jane said. "I must have lost my balance."

"Shh," Mr. Bingley said. "Please do not trouble yourself about that now."

"We must stop all this blood," Elizabeth said, seeing that Miss Edevane's efforts seemed insufficient, but then Mr. Jones came back with Mr. Chamberlayne.

The doctor had been on a house call in the neighbourhood and he had happened to see him just outside the dome, about to head home, Mr. Chamberlayne explained as Mr. Jones called for bandages and ice. Once the glass was removed and Jane's leg was securely wrapped, all the men but the doctor turning their backs to give her privacy, he said, "Under no circumstances should she be sent home. Is there a bedroom ready?"

"There are six," Mr. Bingley said, "and at least one of them should be ready by now, though the plaster—"

"Hang the plaster," the doctor said brusquely.

"Of course, of course," Mr. Bingley said.

"The bed may be pulled out from the wall," Mr. Darcy said. "It would allow Mr. Jones better access to his patient in any case."

Mr. Jones had a few of the boys carry Jane into the house. Elizabeth followed part of the way, and then at the door to the house, worried that she would only be in the way, she paused in indecision. As her sister was carried out of sight, Elizabeth turned to Mr. Darcy to say something; afterwards she could never remember what, because he was eyeing her left elbow, which she was surprised to see was soaked a bright red.

"Oh," she said.

He said, "Let me have a look," and led her into the receiving room, stopping one of the workers en route to tell them to get Mr. Jones when he was done attending to Jane. The furniture hadn't been brought in to this room yet, though the center of it was taken up with boxes.

He pulled one of the boxes out of the pile for her sit on. "Does it hurt?"

Of course it hurt, but in a distant way. Elizabeth supposed she was in shock; even the calm way she thought that seemed a confirmation. She bent her elbow and wiggled her fingers. The red stain might have spread a little; she couldn't be sure. "Everything works. I am sure mamma can attend to it."

"Your mother has gone home," Mr. Darcy said, giving her a concerned look. "I think we had better wrap it up now. May I?" and he pulled a utility knife out of the pocket of his trousers.

"Men always have such useful things."

"I am going to cut off the sleeve." He paused, looking at her eyes for permission, then at her slight nod, slipped the knife into the cloth above the blood and half-tore, half-cut, keeping the blunt edge against her skin.

Peeling the cloth off the wound was worse than bending the elbow had been, and seeing the long, deep cut in her forearm was worse still. It glittered in a long line, which, it took her a few seconds to realize, was a shard of glass. She set her teeth, determined not to embarrass herself by swooning or crying. He sucked air through his teeth, and then pinched the thin shard embedded in her arm between his thumb and forefinger, pulled it out, and dropped it into a handkerchief which he placed next to her on the box, presumably to dispose of later. Then he was wrapping her arm, and although she was sure she hadn't swooned, Mr. Jones was suddenly there too, bending and squeezing her arm in a most unhelpful manner.

"I am fine," Elizabeth said to the doctor at the same time as Mr. Darcy said over her, "It needs a few stitches."

The men ignored her to unwrap her arm again, the scrap of what Elizabeth realized belatedly was a piece of Mr. Darcy's shirt discarded on the floor. Then Miss Edevane was there holding a shot of whiskey to Elizabeth's lips, and one of the workmen, called over by Miss Edevane, was bringing a pitcher of water and fresh linens to wash the blood away. Elizabeth lost track of time when the doctor was putting in the stitches. Then he was finished, and while they rinsed her arm again, she looked around for Darcy and saw him at the edge of the little crowd of people, shouldered aside by the workmen. Darcy was looking at her helplessly, and it was the same look he had given the dancers at the Meryton assembly, and Elizabeth thought, *my God, he is shy*, as he stepped back, something shuttering in his face. He picked up the handkerchief and the torn piece of red shirt and strode from the room.

Mr. Bingley was all apologies by the time Elizabeth made it into the house. "I cannot believe how quickly everything went wrong. One moment, all was perfect and the next, disaster! I will never forgive myself." His face had a small plaster where the glass had been, and his arm was bandaged in such a way as to indicate either a more serious injury than Elizabeth had suspected, or excessive care from the doctor. "If only I had not been so foolish as to let go of one side of the glass," he continued with an unconvincing attempt at his usual easy smile. "Perfectly daft. I am so sorry."

Elizabeth started to reassure him but was interrupted by Mrs. Hurst.

"Jane was the one who swooned. It is not your fault, and anyway she will be just fine in a matter of hours."

"May I be taken to her?" Elizabeth smiled to soften her tone, but she was wondering if Mr. Bingley was so charming because he so earnestly wanted to please everybody he encountered, or if it was just easier to be charming when one had an easy life. The work that day had been the first work she had seen him do the entire month. But he always displayed a ready charm, even when exhausted or, as she was finding out, injured, whereas she could only be charming for a few hours at a time and then needed a good book and a nap.

He was motioning her toward the stairs when Mr. Bennet walked through the front door, saying, "Mr. Jones just told me on his way out," and all of the apologies had to be gone through again before they were finally escorted to where Jane lay on a settee placed against a jumble of boxes, looking wan, her injured leg propped up on an embroidered ottoman.

"I am fine," she said despite her pallor, "really. I have lost a little blood, but Mr. Jones said that so long as I had a good long rest, I would have a complete recovery." She indicated Elizabeth's arm. "Perhaps you also need a rest."

"More from our long day than this minor injury," Elizabeth said.

"It looks serious enough," her father said, touching the bandage with concern. "I will get you home as quickly as possible." He kissed the top of Jane's head and said more softly to her, "I am glad you are not more seriously injured."

Once they had ensured that Jane would be well taken care of, Mr. Bennet and Elizabeth headed home.

"It has been an extremely long day," Mr. Bennet said. "Well, Lizzy? Have you fallen in love with any of the fine young men we saw clambering all over that building today?"

Elizabeth laughed. "You are thinking of your other daughters," she said.

The Meryton dome was very quiet at this late hour. Dust motes drifted in the gas lamps. They walked past the central cluster of homes, sturdily built of brick and steel, towards their own airlock.

As she moved about the kitchen, setting dishes that had been left to dry on the rack back in their places and avoiding too much movement of her arm, Elizabeth overheard Mr. Bennet tell his wife about Jane's accident, and Elizabeth's lesser injury, followed by her shriek of dismay.

Kitty came into the room. "What did you do to your arm?" she asked as she took a cookie from the jar.

As Elizabeth was explaining, Mrs. Bennet joined them. "I am sending for Mr. Jones," she said.

"He has already seen her," Mr. Bennet called from the hallway.

"I am going to bed," Elizabeth said. She was allowed to do so only after her mother had embraced her several times, threatened her again with the doctor, and exclaimed over her narrow escape.

The next morning, after insufficient sleep, Elizabeth stopped at Lucas Lodge to let Sir William know about her and Jane's injuries so he could adjust the work duties. As it happened, they were both scheduled solely for her mother's greenhouses for the week, since they had worked the Netherfield build, so she only needed to make private arrangements within her family. Charlotte, passing his office, poked her head in the doorway to volunteer to take any tasks Elizabeth couldn't manage, and pressed a cup of tea on Elizabeth when she refused breakfast.

When she accepted, Elizabeth was surprised to find Mary King already sitting at the Lucases' long table. She held a mug of chicory coffee in one hand and a newspaper in the other. Looking up as they came in, she smiled only with her eyes. Charlotte introduced them, and Elizabeth said, "Miss King, this may sound silly or presumptuous, but I want to thank you for making going to Babbage seem more possible—"

"Oh, no, not you too," Mary King laughed. "If it hadn't been me, it would have been any number of others. There are at least five girls ready to graduate this spring, if Babbage allows it."

There was a little silence, and feeling as though she were intruding on the pair, Elizabeth said, "I must be going. I want to see how Jane is doing."

To her surprise, Miss King said, "Are you heading into town? I will walk you over."

They left together, Miss King immediately saying, as though embarrassed, "You must be wondering how I came to be at the Lucases so very early in the day—"

"No!" Elizabeth said, surprised.

"I was actually there to see Sir William," said Miss King. Her stride was long, so that Elizabeth did not have to shorten her own to keep pace with her, and Elizabeth could see the exercise bringing up Miss King's colour. "I needed to notify him of my uncle's convalescence, and Charlotte was kind enough to ask me to breakfast with the family. Lady Lucas had just gone upstairs to rouse Maria when you arrived."

"Is Mr. King very ill?"

"Yes. My cousin William expects him to die any day now, but I think he will outlive us all. He has had these spells before, you see. His heart," she said breezily. "He always recovers after a little rest."

"I hope he will be better soon," Elizabeth said, a little amused over the bald way that Miss King talked. She was a very forthright sort of person. Elizabeth found herself warming to the woman. "Is William his son?"

"No, he is his other brother's child. My uncle was the oldest, and took me in when my parents died. His wife died a few years ago, so it is only us now, but William often comes from Oakham Mount—" this was the dome closest to Meryton on the Edgcumbe side— "to visit and lend a hand on various projects. You were working with him yesterday, I heard."

"Was I?"

"When you and Charlotte were helping with the joists. She mentioned it to me."

Elizabeth wondered if William King expected to inherit anything from his uncle. It might be good for Charlotte if he did; so many young men chose to wait until they could support a wife, rather than tolerate a long engagement, and he had certainly seemed interested. *But no, I am as bad as Lydia. Surely Charlotte may speak with a person without being suspected of having a secret beau.* So, she said only, "You and Charlotte have become good friends."

"Jealous, Miss Elizabeth?" Miss King asked with a smile.

"I am devastated." Elizabeth laughed.

She turned in at Netherfield's 'lock and waved goodbye to Miss King. Miss Bingley greeted Elizabeth with every expression of pleasure and immediately took her to see Jane, who had been moved to a bigger bed in the same room, and the boxes moved to a more tidy stack a few feet from the still-sticky plaster walls. Jane was sleeping, her forehead slightly feverish against the back of Elizabeth's wrist. Elizabeth judged it best to let her rest and went back down the stairs to the nascent drawing room.

Mr. Hurst, napping on a chaise longue with a newspaper spread open over his belly, said with a yawn, "Ah, Miss Elizabeth Bennet. Pleasant journey?"

"Lovely, thank you." She pulled up a box to sit on, all the furniture being already occupied, and Mr. Bingley sprang to his feet to offer her his seat, insisting that they switch places. This put her next to his elder sister, who was holding a book but not attending to it.

"And how is your sister?" asked Mrs. Hurst.

"She seemed slightly feverish to me," Elizabeth said, "but I could not be sure."

"Mr. Jones should be by in an hour or two," Mr. Bingley said.

The hour ticked by slowly, though Mrs. Hurst and Mr. Bingley gamely attempted to make conversation with Elizabeth. Bingley's conversational sallies, in particular, often trailed off with no end. His frequent glances toward the stairs betrayed the cause of his distraction. Miss Bingley and Mr. Darcy had gone for a walk with Miss Bingley's lady's maid, she learned, and the men were expected at Haye Park to help Mr. Goulding to repair something in the rectory when Darcy returned.

In her turn, Elizabeth shared that her parents sent their best regards, and that she had seen Sir William and she and Jane were both excused from work duties.

These topics exhausted, Mrs. Hurst said, "you are both so *brave* to take on these little tasks" and then pretended to return to her book, and Mr. Bingley pressed a bewildering variety of refreshments on Elizabeth until Mr. Jones finally came and went with nothing but reassurances that Jane was mending fine, though she wasn't to be moved.

Mr. Bingley took her up, and, seeing that Jane was awake, gave her a warm smile before he bowed and departed.

"Lizzy, thank goodness," Jane said with a faint smile. Her dimples stayed hidden. "I am so glad you have come."

"How do you feel?"

"Sore." She laughed a little. "As you might guess. It feels as though I have been stabbed all down my leg. Which is easily explained!"

Elizabeth put the back of her wrist to Jane's forehead again. "I cannot tell if you are feverish or not," she said.

"I do not feel particularly warm. Is our mother here?"

"No, the doctor said you were in no real danger, so she is working, though she asked after you most anxiously. I am to send a letter if I am not back before dinner with particulars of your recovery. She said she could not disappoint Mr. Harrington."

"Of course." Jane smiled. She was their mother's chief admirer.

"She sends her love and concern and told me to tell you to stay in bed and let me wait on you. Father said it would be good for my character." This did make Jane's dimples appear, and Elizabeth grinned back. "Do you need anything?"

Jane shook her head, and Elizabeth perched on the edge of her bed to take her hand. "How is Mr. Bingley?" Jane almost whispered, no doubt to keep her voice from carrying down the stairs.

"Tolerably well. Worried about you."

"I wish he could come sit with me."

Elizabeth went to the door and saw that Mr. Bingley was lingering in the downstairs hallway. She motioned him to come up, and sat on the other side of the bed with her book while he and Jane conversed in low voices.

After another hour, the slam of a door and calling voices announced that Mr. Darcy and Miss Bingley had returned from their walk, which meant Mr. Bingley was needed at the rectory. The men all set out, and, not too much later, thumps on the steps heralded the arrival of the sisters to Jane's room. They were accompanied by a maid who carried in three light bamboo chairs, one at a time, and went back out.

When she came back in with a table suitable for cards, Miss Bingley gestured to the area near Jane and said, "Clara, set it over there."

The table was fashioned in thick wood, marking it as a piece from before launch. The girl couldn't have been older than twelve. Her arms shook with the effort of lifting it. Elizabeth jumped up and helped to carry the table over to the bedside.

"Your arm," Miss Bingley said. "Eliza, you must sit and let Clara do her work." Yet she made no move to take Elizabeth's place.

"I am just fine," Elizabeth said through her teeth.

The ladies kept themselves entertained around Jane's bed for some hours while the gentlemen were out.

By mid-afternoon, Elizabeth said, "I think I had better head home."

Miss Bingley offered their carriage.

"Could she stay?" Jane asked, her voice almost weak enough to be a whisper.

Mrs. Hurst and Miss Bingley exchanged a glance. Normally Elizabeth would have read their expressions and said firmly that she would come back in the morning, but the incident with the maid and the sheer extravagant amount of space their house took up made Elizabeth feel that a little inconvenience would be beneficial to their souls. She gave them Jane's Madonna smile, pure and innocent, and waited.

"Of course she must stay," Miss Bingley said after a pause that was almost, but not quite, long enough to be awkward. "We have plenty of room. Please do stay, Eliza."

"I would be delighted," Elizabeth said insincerely.

Clara was sent to Longbourn for her clothes, and Elizabeth gave her a note for her mother which read, "The doctor says Jane is well. Please give this poor child a slice of the pie Mary made last night, if Lydia has not finished it off already, while she waits for you to pack a small valise, and make the valise as light as possible, please. All I really need are fresh underthings and a nightdress, and I suppose something suitable for dining. My old blue dress will do. Lord knows I am not trying to impress these people."

§

During the day, the Bingley servants had been bustling about making everything comfortable, so that by the time Elizabeth returned to her room to dress, it was reasonably well-appointed and comfortable (even if everything *was* pulled away from the walls). Dinner seemed to drag on, and Elizabeth left as quickly as she could, with the excuse of needing to take Jane a tray. She left for the kitchen, and once the tray had been prepared, walked alongside the dining room to the stairs, and overheard Miss Bingley criticizing the Bennet sisters' "nonsensical attempt to work the whole day like a man, and see what became of it!" which made her remind herself with a grin that eavesdroppers never heard good of themselves.

Jane was sleeping, so she only put the tray on her nightstand and crept away again. She found on coming back down the steps that the Bennet sisters were still the subject of conversation. She would never have dreamed of eavesdropping on her family or friends, but these people? It seemed to her justifiable. She stopped just out of sight of the door to hear Mrs. Hurst saying, "Did you see her sleeves rolled up as though she were about to go into surgery?"

Miss Bingley said, "Just imagine, being such an *excellent worker.*"

Elizabeth smiled.

"And what else do we need on this ship, Caroline?" Mr. Bingley said.

I like you, Elizabeth thought.

"You would not want your dear sister to work so hard, I am sure, Mr. Darcy," Miss Bingley said.

"No."

Clara (who, Elizabeth couldn't help thinking, must have 'worked the whole day like a man') came around the corner just then, so Elizabeth had to continue into the dining room as though she had never stopped.

She remembered her epiphany the day before that Darcy's disdain was a mask for shyness, but the epiphany itself now seemed a symptom of shock. His declaration that he would not like his sister to work seemed evidence that she had been right about him all along. He was disdainful because he was proud, but if she meant to be fair (because she still had an inner Jane that told her to be fair to everybody, even Darcy) she should look for signs that her shock-addled epiphany had been true after all.

She was sure that the evidence of her having overheard them was written all over her face, but nobody seemed willing to meet her eye, perhaps in mortification in case she *had* heard anything. She prepared a chicory coffee for herself at the side board and quitted the room. Halfway back up the stairs, she heard a flurry of whispers, among them Miss Bingley whispering, "Do you think she heard us?" and Mr. Hurst, who had appeared to Elizabeth to be nearly asleep, saying quite clearly, "Who cares if she did?"

Elizabeth leaned against the banister to sip her coffee, stifling a laugh. Jane had better be sure she loved Mr. Bingley very much to put up with his family.

Their embarrassment was short-lived, and she was rewarded for her nosiness with hearing Miss Bingley speak slightingly of her family to Mr. Bingley's protests that they were all that was charming, and if Mrs. Bennet *did* have her own business, that only spoke well of her intelligence and wasn't inappropriate at all, not nowadays. Miss Bingley went on to criticize her uncle in London and her aunt in Meryton as being "rather low connections" and Mr. Bingley stoutly declared that he didn't care. Mr. Darcy, Elizabeth couldn't help noticing, was silent throughout. She wasn't sure what to make of that. She continued her walk upstairs.

Jane was just waking as she came in, and she brought her the cooling tray of food and spoke of very little. Mr. Bingley visited for a while, along with his sisters. All were perfectly appropriate in wishing her well soon, the brother rather more sincerely than the sisters.

Late in the evening, after Jane had gone to sleep, Elizabeth went to her own room, but the coffee had made her jittery, so she decided to go downstairs, where the light was better. She brought the book on physics which Charlotte had loaned her, earning an incredulous look from Mr. Hurst. Mr. Bingley and the Hursts were playing a card game, Mr. Darcy was seated at a beautifully polished desk doing something mysterious with a magnifying glass and an orderly pile of gears, and Miss Bingley was splitting her attention between both activities. Elizabeth opened her book and began to review the section she and Charlotte had gone over together earlier in the week.

"Your craftsmanship is impeccable," Miss Bingley said, looking over Mr. Darcy's shoulder. "I dare say Miss Darcy has the cleverest little pets in the whole ship."

He continued to work without looking up.

"Please let her know that we miss her very much."

"After your previous request," Mr. Darcy said without looking up,

"I have already done so. I sent the letter during our walk earlier, you will remember."

Elizabeth kept her eyes bent to the page, hiding a smile.

Darcy picked up a tiny gear with a pair of tweezers and fitted it into something in his hand. Miss Bingley leaned over him to see better, and he said, low, "Miss Bingley, you are in my light." She went around to his other side.

Mr. Bingley called out from the card table. "Darcy, did you see that play? Quite a move!"

Mr. Darcy, glancing over at the game, said, "Well played, Bingley."

They played in silence for several rounds of the game, and Miss Bingley contented herself with passing Darcy tools he might like to use next and walking around the card game to see everybody's cards. Elizabeth was soon deep in puzzlement. She flipped to an earlier page to see where she had lost her way.

"How lucky Miss Georgiana is to have such an attentive brother," Miss Bingley said. "I have often commented on the cleverness of your little animals."

He nodded.

Elizabeth had looked over at them when Miss Bingley spoke, and Darcy saw her looking, and opened his hand. A small brass bird flexed its wings in his palm and shook its tail. Miss Bingley and Elizabeth both exclaimed. He put it on the table, and it waddled over to the remaining gears, which he swept out of its way.

"What is it?" Elizabeth asked.

"A baby duck," he said. He put it on the ground, and it began to waddle in a series of concentric circles centered on the spot where he'd put it down, fluffing up and smoothing down fine brass plates along its back end as if shaking water off feathers. "They have them in Arkwright, along with a host of other waterfowl."

"I have read about them in books," Miss Bingley said. "Oh, how charming!" Turning to Elizabeth, she said, "Mr. Darcy makes them for Georgiana's birthday. She has a chickadee, a rabbit, a little dog... and several others. It is so impressive. I could not do it!"

"How lucky for you that you do not have to," Mr. Darcy said, sorting the remaining gears into separate compartments in a steel case with handsome brass detailing.

"Are you an engineer, then?" Elizabeth said. She hadn't noticed him working on anything in the Netherfield build that would have required any specialized knowledge, but then, Sir William had made the assignments and might not have known his background.

"It is more of a hobby than a profession," he said. "I have not had much time to devote to it since my father died."

"But you went to Babbage?"

"You know it?"

"Indeed," Elizabeth said. "I have thought about applying to get in."

Darcy put down his tools and looked at her with focused intensity. She met his gaze, lifting her chin a little in defiance, and he began to smile, very slowly, as though he could not help himself. She felt her lips soften into their own smile.

She had entirely forgotten Miss Bingley until she drawled, "How extraordinary," and broke the spell.

Darcy's smile fell away.

"I heard they just had their first female graduate," Mr. Bingley said, looking up from his cards. "A Miss King, I believe."

"Yes," Elizabeth said. "She lives here in Meryton."

"How capital! Young ladies are all so accomplished nowadays."

"A *lady* should be accomplished in modern languages and pianoforte and drawing," Miss Bingley said to her brother. "Not physics and construction."

Mrs. Hurst, absorbed in twisting her wedding ring around and around her finger as she stared at her husband, murmured agreement.

Mr. Darcy said, "Pursuing a career in engineering must make any young lady's marriage prospects much slimmer."

"Is that the first consideration a woman must have? Whether or not her *current* actions will please men whom she might meet at some point in the *future*?" Elizabeth asked.

"Miss Eliza Bennet," said Miss Bingley, "despises marriage. She is a tireless student and has no pleasure in anything else."

Elizabeth looked closely at Miss Bingley, who smiled back as innocently as a head of cabbage. In an attempt to soften the tone of the conversation, she replied, "If I am honest, I have little pleasure in my studies at the moment, as I find the mathematical element quite beyond my education."

Mr. Darcy sat with a gear suspended between two fingers, his work forgotten. "Where did you receive your education?"

"Since my father always refused to teach his daughters any mathematics, and my mother was never taught any herself, neither of them taught me much beyond simple sums."

"How are you understanding this?" Mr. Darcy gestured toward her book. "It is fairly advanced."

"I perfectly understand the theories themselves, I think, but I cannot follow the mathematical proofs. I am sure I could with a little help."

"There is a remedial class at Babbage for the chaps who need to get up to scratch on subjects they have missed, is there not?" Mr. Bingley asked.

"Yes." Mr. Darcy looked thoughtfully at Elizabeth for a moment.

The duck hit the leg of Elizabeth's settee and stopped, sitting still for several seconds before beginning a new series of circles. Elizabeth picked it up and it stopped again, this time in her palm. She could feel, more than hear, the faint ticking of its clockwork.

"How does it know to stop?" she asked.

Darcy said, apparently expecting her to know the word, "gyroscope." She determined to look it up later.

"How clever," Miss Bingley said, taking the device from Elizabeth. "You have put your learning to such good use. Miss Georgiana will be ecstatic." She put it down on a side table, and after sitting a moment it began to waddle again and almost immediately fell off the edge of the table. It spread its wings and made a graceful landing at Miss Bingley's elegantly slippered feet.

§

The next morning, Mr. Jones said that Jane's wounds were scabbing over nicely and that she ought to stay in bed another day, but since he didn't outright ban her from getting up, she asked Elizabeth to send a few lines to their father asking for the carriage.

"I am ready enough to go, but I would have thought you would want to extend your stay with Mr. Bingley as long as you could."

"I feel so grubby," Jane said. "It is impossible to get properly washed with all these bandages. I know I am being vain, but I hate for Charles to see me so disheveled."

"Oh, you call him *Charles* now, do you?" Elizabeth laughed. "I will take extra care over combing out and styling your hair before we go down to breakfast."

At breakfast, the Bingley sisters exclaimed over how well Jane looked and how dreadful her injuries had been and how much they would have hated to be trapped upstairs all day. They heard that she was leaving later that day with smiles and made only the most perfunctory protestations at their leaving so soon.

Mr. Bingley offered her blankets and bacon and anything else that came into his head, eventually sitting by her side when he ran out of comforts to offer her. Their heads close together, they spoke quietly, until Miss Bingley said, "Pray, what are you speaking about so intently?" and Mr. Bingley replied, "Advancements in pneumatic mechanisms in the ship's delivery systems," with a laugh that implied that they hadn't been discussing anything of the kind. Miss Bingley tossed her head as she left the room.

After awhile, the Hursts finished their breakfast and left, and then Jane and Mr. Bingley went out to examine some books he had mentioned, Mr. Bingley supporting her on his arm as she walked a little gingerly, clearly still in some pain.

Mr. Darcy entered the room as they left and eyed Elizabeth sipping tea. He helped himself to some toast piled on a plate at the side board. He folded himself into a chair across from her. She sipped her tea, and he sipped his, and had a bite of toast, and she sipped again, waiting for him to introduce a topic of conversation. After a few moments it became clear that he would not talk, and Elizabeth compressed her lips.

"Did you sleep well?" she said.

"Tolerably."

She smiled a little into her cup. Any accusation of unsociability was now sufficiently diverted, and she declined to make any further effort until he had put forth some himself. She had a final bite of eggs, and then slowly finished her tea, drawing out the drink from curiosity, but he didn't say another word, or betray any discomfort at the silence. She found herself more amused than annoyed, and when she left the room her eyes were fairly dancing, though the gentleman did not notice, with his eyes steadfastly trained on his toast.

After breakfast, Mr. Darcy went on an errand he didn't bother to explain, and Miss Bingley and Mrs. Hurst went along with him for the exercise. Mr. Hurst had a nap with a newspaper for a blanket. This left only Mr. Bingley to entertain Jane and Elizabeth, and Jane asked to see the greenhouse. Mr. Bingley found a wheeled chair for her, and took them both out to the empty greenhouse. The glass had been swept away by the silent hands which did so much of the labour of the household, and the panes put into place, barring the one that had shattered, a replacement for which was on the way. Mr. Bingley sketched with his hands where he wished to place the pots for the dwarf citrus trees he intended to grow, and where Miss Bingley's baskets of marigolds and container gardens of roses and peonies would be located.

At mid-afternoon, their father's carriage arrived for them with Mary in the driver's seat. The sisters all hugged their greetings, and then, as Mr. Bingley said his goodbyes to Jane, Elizabeth bounded up the stairs for their luggage. It had already been gathered up by a pair of servants, who ducked their heads at her and took it down the stairs. Elizabeth stood in the empty room that had been so briefly her own, and lightly brushed the plastered walls with her fingertips to find them still tacky to the touch. "We had better get out of here before the walls harden around us," she said to herself.

One of the servants helped Mary with the hand-crank to rewind the mainspring of the clockwork for their return trip, and they were soon off. In the carriage, Elizabeth leaned back against the cushions and laughed. "Lord! I do not think that I have ever left a place where the inhabitants were more relieved to see my back."

"What do you mean?" Jane asked.

"Mr. Bingley, of course, heard with real regret that we were leaving. I exempt him absolutely from my judgement."

They passed the central spoke, where the shift must have been changing: a small crowd of people in aether suits was going in as others came out, peeling off their suits as they passed through the door. Wickham was one of them, laughing with another man whom she recognized as Mr. Metcalfe, which made Elizabeth realize that, since her sister had been injured, she had hardly thought about Wickham. He was merely a person she would have liked to know better. She had marked him out for special attention at her aunt's, and then abandoned him. She felt a little thrill of guilt for her lack of constancy. Then they were past the knot of people. She glanced back at Jane, and saw that her sister was shaking her head.

"But you must have seen how insincere Miss Bingley and Mrs. Hurst were when they said that we were welcome to stay as long as we pleased," Elizabeth went on.

"On the contrary, I thought they seemed most affectionate."

The communal kitchen rolled past the window, Mrs. Clark just opening the door, and then Harrington's, with its beautiful picture window full of shipmade dresses and hats and its discreet sign promising imperceptible patching and tailoring of the more valuable old Earth items, and then the cafe. As they passed, Elizabeth said, "Mr. Darcy is more of a puzzle. He was interested enough in our conversation last night, but do you know, we were alone together at breakfast for fully twenty minutes and he did not say one word to me? No, I am wrong, he said exactly one word to me. He is so strange; sometimes he seems to almost admire me, but then at other times he seems to positively detest me."

"But he is often silent even with his closest friends. You cannot judge by that."

"That is true enough."

"And Mr. Hurst?"

"Oh, Mr. Hurst. I forgot about Mr. Hurst, which I am sure will not surprise you in the least. I suppose he does not care who is there as long as they are willing to play at cards or let him nap."

"You *are* severe, Lizzy." Jane smiled, her dimples springing to life. "Come now. We had a perfectly pleasant convalescence at Netherfield, and we have leave to rest for another few days. And two days hence I shall dine with Mr. Bingley again!"

They reached their dome at that point, and fell into the waiting arms of their parents and younger sisters.

CHAPTER FIVE

BY THE TIME MR. BENNET'S COUSIN MR. COLLINS arrived the following week, Jane and Elizabeth were both recovered from their injuries and Meryton's October assembly had passed by without incident or insult, though Wickham, to Elizabeth's disappointment, had missed it.

Mr. Bennet cycled his cousin through the 'lock. "Mr. Collins, welcome to Longbourn."

Mr. Collins was a tall and thick young man whom Elizabeth would have guessed was a construction worker rather than a rector, except for his serious and courtly manner. "You keep a lovely house," he said to Mrs. Bennet almost as soon as he was in the door, "So clean and neat."

Mrs. Bennet interjected, "That is the girls' doing, not mine."

But he was still talking: "The furniture is so stately, for who does not love a dark wood and cream theme in the comfort of their home? I have long intended to paint the interior of my own little cottage and that is just one of the combinations of colours that I have considered. So soothing to the eye."

Nobody quite knew what to say to this, so Mr. Bennet suggested that they show him his room.

"I am indebted to you, sir," Mr. Collins said, "for this luggage is quite heavy."

Mr. Bennet took another of his bags.

"I must remember to express my appreciation for the honour of my reception here at Longbourn," Mr. Collins said. He had a middle-aged voice, hard and slightly adenoidal, much older than he was. "What a fine family you have. I had heard before of your daughters' famous beauty and bounteous good health and am so relieved to see these reports were accurate, perhaps even understated."

"How kind," Mr. Bennet said. A certain way he held his mouth signaled to Elizabeth that he was at his most ironical, but his face was perfectly serene as he continued, "I trust you will find my daughters' characters also worthy of your commendation."

"I am sure. I hope you may see them all well married."

Elizabeth and Jane exchanged a glance.

"They will marry as it suits them," Mrs. Bennet said. "On Earth, I suppose I would have worried terribly about their prospects, though it is hard to remember the way we thought about things back then. It *does* seem a shame that our staying here is dependent on Mr. Bennet's health. A most outmoded way of distributing property, I have always thought."

"You allude, perhaps, to the entail of this dome."

"It is such a relief to me to know that my business, at least, will not suffer, since the greenhouses are not covered by the entail."

Mr. Bennet turned with the luggage to raise his eyebrows at his wife, as if to say, 'you don't need to attack the man the instant he arrives.' She widened her eyes at him in return, as if to say, 'I must do it if you won't.' Mr. Collins, looking about the house with no self-consciousness of being its unearned inheritor, entirely missed the byplay, but more importantly did not challenge her assertion, only saying, "As to that, I have come—but perhaps it is enough to say that I will not see my cousins destitute."

"Very kind," Mrs. Bennet said, "and I am sure we are all grateful, though nobody really need worry about becoming destitute on the ship when anybody who works hard is provided for, and my girls have proven to be quite adept at a number of tasks." Enumerating the many different duties that Sir William assigned and the way folks in Meryton cycled through them according to his clever schedules, she led Mr. Collins off.

Elizabeth went upstairs to change into older clothing and grab her gloves, and then went out to greenhouse two. She had no assigned work to do, but thought that getting her hands in some dirt would be a nice change, especially as her mother was busy with Mr. Collins and would not, therefore, be there to interpret her unsolicited help as an offer to join the business. She could rely on Lydia to take credit for the work, if the question even arose. She began turning their mulch through the empty beds, using her fingers as a rake, and then just walked around the greenhouse, touching the plants and examining seed trays, before consulting her mother's crop plan schedule and putting in succession plantings of beets and cucumber. She hummed while she planted, and although she worked steadily, she felt entirely at her leisure.

"Oh, thank you, Lizzy," her mother said behind her as she was midway through the cucumber.

"I thought you were entertaining Mr. Collins," Elizabeth said.

"I passed him off to Jane. I really just could not take any more gratitude. Strange thing to be annoyed by, but there it is."

Mrs. Bennet began to help her. For a while they just worked together silently, passing each other tools as needed. Then her mother said, "I do so enjoy this, dear. I know you have said no in the past, but I wish you would consider apprenticing with me instead of all this engineering."

"I do not want to be a salesperson, mamma," Elizabeth said. "I enjoy this part of your business, but the actual *business* part is at best tedious and at worst aggravating. I have no diplomatic instincts with customers."

"But none of your sisters are the least interested."

Elizabeth sighed.

Luckily, Kitty came in then to say, "Mamma, nobody can find the key to the refrigerator on the edge of the dome, and Lydia is trying to pick the lock, and Father said to let you know."

"That girl will be the death of me, I swear," Mrs. Bennet said, rising.

§

Dinner was served at seven.

"You are fortunate to have so comfortable a home." Buoyed by the cordial reception and a late afternoon nap, Mr. Collins made a circuit of the table, nodding at the fashionable china and the many flickering bayberry wax candles. "And what an elegant dining room. Every detail is a testament to your good taste."

He followed his compliments with a long and florid grace.

"Thank you," Mrs. Bennet said when he was done.

Mr. Collins served the ladies to either side of him, then helped himself to the array of dishes, which included a clear broth, a variety of stewed and roasted vegetables from greenhouse two, pheasant in port wine sauce, and small pies. He paused to admire his plate, then savoured a bite of carrot. "An exquisite balance of earthiness and sweetness and fairly bursting with natural flavour. To which of my cousins should I direct my thanks for this delicious meal?"

"Catherine and Mary, today," Mrs. Bennet said.

"My compliments to you both." He applied himself to the serious business of eating, and silence ruled the table for a few minutes, broken only by the clink of silverware and Careful's distant complaint at being contained in his kennel.

"You seem very happy with your neighbour, Lady Catherine de Bourgh," Mr. Bennet said as he finished his soup.

"Indeed, as I mentioned in my letter, she has given the most remarkable consideration to my progress as the rector of her parish. She has asked me to dine at Rosings, her dome in the Castlereagh superstructure, you understand, several times since I moved to Hunsford. She sets an extremely generous table, including every kind of meat. Our last meal had not only two different kinds of fowl, but ham and sturgeon, and calf's head soup."

He took a bite of one of the pies, filled with vegetables in gravy from the pheasant drippings, and continued, "Her pies even contained a liver paté."

Mrs. Bennet looked at the laden table with an unreadable expression. Elizabeth bit her lip. They didn't have meat at every meal, since it was so dear. She knew that her mother had made a trade with Lady Lucas expressly to have this pheasant on hand for Mr. Collins's welcome.

"Of course, she can hardly expect to compete with your vast array of fresh vegetables," Mr. Collins said hastily. "She grows some fruits and vegetables on her property but nothing like your very impressive operation here."

Mrs. Bennet smiled thinly.

Mr. Bennet said, "She sounds like an invaluable acquaintance."

"Indeed. Just last Saturday, she asked me to join her in a game of quadrille, and she says that I am a good enough player to become a regular attendee. Within the week of me starting, she even visited my parsonage, where she was so kind as to make some suggestions on how best to use the space, and gave her blessing to all of my alterations."

"Does she live near you?" Mr. Bennet cut up some of the pheasant, swirling it through its sauce and spearing a bit of carrot as accompaniment.

"The dome in which the town of Hunsford is located abuts Rosings, from which the parsonage is separated only by a short walk and a 'lock."

"You have not mentioned a Lord de Bourgh."

"No, sadly. She is a Lady through her father; her husband was Sir Lewis de Bourgh. He tragically passed away in 1821, leaving her with an infant in arms and Rosings."

"1821!" Jane said. "Did his death have anything to do with the ship leaving Earth?"

"As to that, I do not know. Her Ladyship does not speak of him. I am sure her grief is still too great."

"Is that her only family?" Elizabeth asked.

"She has two nephews, but Miss de Bourgh is her only immediate family."

"What is she like?" Lydia said. "Miss de Bourgh, I mean. Is she pretty?"

"She is an attractive little creature, but is often ill, which has sadly interrupted her progress in a number of areas. I understand she was once thought a prodigy at pianoforte but was obliged to give it up." He paused to carefully cut a green bean into a few inch-long segments, which he stacked on his fork.

"Our Mary is quite a prodigy as well," Mrs. Bennet said with more motherly pride than accuracy.

Mr. Bennet's mouth quirked once. He glanced at Elizabeth, who had to compress her lips to hide her smile.

"Miss de Bourgh has been most affable when I have conversed with her at Rosings. She is engaged to her cousin Mr. Fitzwilliam Darcy—"

He was interrupted by a few gasps. Lydia whispered something to Kitty, and Jane looked with wide eyes at Elizabeth and mouthed, "Poor Miss Bingley."

"Is this Mr. Darcy of Pemberley, the same man who has been engaged in a major build in our neighbourhood?" Mr. Bennet asked.

"The very same, though I did not know that he was lending his undoubtedly considerable talents here."

"And he is to marry Miss de Bourgh?" Elizabeth asked.

"That is my understanding," Mr. Collins said.

Poor Miss Bingley indeed, Elizabeth thought.

"I have not yet met him, but Lady Catherine de Bourgh and Lady Anne Darcy were sisters. Consequently she is aunt to the present Mr. Darcy."

"Jane and Elizabeth spent a few days last week in the company of Mr. Darcy," Lydia said, and at his surprised exclamation, explained Jane's injury in the most dramatic terms.

Elizabeth glanced at Jane, who shrugged slightly, her face blooming with pink. "I am fully recovered," she said without raising her eyes from her plate.

"Shall we bring in the second course?" Mrs. Bennet said, raising her eyebrows at her two youngest daughters.

"Yes, mamma," they chorused as they rose to clear away the hot dishes and bring in cold ones: mince pies, a bread pudding, strawberries, and nut cookies.

"A well-prepared dinner is a balm to the soul," Mr. Collins said. "This is a very excellent meal, very excellent. Lady Catherine de Bourgh herself could not be happier with your first course, and I declare her cook is quite a marvel, with a calf's head soup that is entirely the best I have ever eaten, and her pheasant! But your pheasant was equally good, which really you could not ask for better."

Mrs. Bennet only smiled at this, and the gentleman continued: "I do hope you will forgive the question, arising as it does only from curiosity: when you hold a dinner party, do you find it inconvenient to do without servants?" He helped himself to a cookie and only then offered them to the ladies on either side of him.

"We do not often hold large parties of the type you mention," Mrs. Bennet said. "Mr. Bennet and I are so busy with our work, you see."

"I will admit," Mr. Bennet said, raising his glass in an ironic toast, "that when we first came onto the ship, our lack of servants may have seemed us making a virtue of necessity, since we could not have afforded to pay them in any case." He took a sip and smiled slightly. "We have found that we get on very well on our own, with occasional help for parties as you describe. Mrs. Bennet must sometimes hire some young men to help with harvesting, but that is a business expense, and, I hope you agree, an entirely different species of help than a servant who is dependent on your goodwill for their food and lodging."

"Indeed, indeed," Mr. Collins said.

"Your late father and I often disagreed on the necessity of having servants. It was one of the reasons for our falling out. I hold that the practice leads to people believing that they are superior to others based only on accidents of birth, which I hope you will agree is unchristian."

"Treating one's servants well is, of course, a moral imperative that demonstrates our conscience. We must always endeavor to support human dignity and prioritize the well-being of all, not only those at the top, as it were; or the bottom for that matter. Lady Catherine de Bourgh mentioned something along these lines to me just last week; that providing sufficient opportunity to one's inferiors to improve their health and broaden their minds is the sacred duty of those fortunate enough to have been born with rank."

"Hmm," Mr. Bennet replied.

"Let us retire to the drawing room," Mrs. Bennet said, and then continued in a lower voice with a gesture to the table. "Lydia, Catherine, please."

They did so, Lydia and Kitty lagging behind as they took away the remaining dishes. Elizabeth took up Charlotte's book and soon put it down again; she thought perhaps physics was just not her forte. Her mother kept a few books on a little shelf: a few novels, a book on the operation of the ship, and several books on gardening. Elizabeth selected the thickest of these, which she had been reading in sections for the past few years, and resumed three-quarters of the way through the book with the section on composting. She always seemed to come back to the books on gardening: the subject itself was so interesting, but she didn't want to take over her mother's business, which seemed to involve just as much haggling and deliveries and *other people* as it did gardening, so she tried not to show too much enthusiasm.

Mr. Bennet and Mr. Collins went to his office and came in an hour later smelling of tobacco.

"You must tell us of any other interesting people you know in your parsonage," Lydia said to Mr. Collins as soon as he was seated. "I am just dying to know what life is like in another dome. Do you have any intrigues? Castlereagh is such a romantic name, much better than stodgy old Headfort. We sound like a cheese."

"I am sure we do not have anything that could be called an intrigue," Mr. Collins said. He then suggested that he might read aloud to the ladies to edify their minds. Mr. Bennet having no objection, Mr. Collins opened Mary's copy of *Fordyce's Sermons* where Lydia had torn it all those months before and spread it open on the table. He began to read in an adenoidal singsong, steepling his fingers. "Hardly can one go into a company of men, where licentiousness of tongue passes for freedom of conversation, without hearing the poor women abused for their worthlessness, or weakness, or both."

In his corner behind Mr. Collins, Mr. Bennet quietly opened his own book and began to read. He was the only family member so blessed; the rest sat in front of Mr. Collins. Elizabeth endeavored to look lively and interested. Jane was looking in Mr. Collins's direction, but her eyes were unfocused, and Elizabeth was sure she was thinking only of Bingley; Mary was focused, eyes shining; Kitty and Lydia were slumped in their seats.

"But supposing them particularly frail, is it noble to exult over them—"

Elizabeth caught their eyes and made a stern face; Kitty sat up a little straighter, but Lydia only crossed her eyes back at Elizabeth.

"—on that account, and in their absence too, when they have not an opportunity of defending themselves?"

Lydia whispered to Kitty, "Oh! I nearly forgot—"

"Should not the strong rather pity and support the weak? Yet after all—"

"—Mrs. Forster has promised us to have a little dance some evening."

"—how does it appear that any singular strength of resolution belongs to our sex—"

"Lydia! Kitty!" Elizabeth whispered. "Shh!"

Mr. Collins cleared his throat. "—or that yours stand chargeable with peculiar infirmity?"

Kitty whispered, "Oh! When?"

Mr. Collins went on: "The loss of virtue is, no doubt, often followed with extreme depravity in women."

Lydia whispered, "Maybe next week!"

Mrs. Bennet said, "Lydia, please; Mr. Collins is reading."

Mr. Collins put down his book, and drew a breath.

Before he could say a word, Mary said, "How *can* you two be so silly? Mr. Collins seeks to improve your mind and behaviour and this is the thanks he gets."

Mr. Collins bowed to Mary, but did not reopen his book. He offered himself, somewhat stiffly, to Mr. Bennet for a game of backgammon, and by-and-by the household was at peace.

§

The aerator turned itself off with a sigh. Mr. Faraday's ingenious invention normally made relentless, muted ticktocking noises as it let out its slow leak of newly-made air. Elizabeth no longer heard the ticking consciously; when it stopped, the silence woke her up as thoroughly as if she had woken from a nightmare. Dense shadows hunched against the walls. They could do without the aerator for some time, and had others in the house, but none of the domes were quite air-tight enough to go without them indefinitely. She sighed and rolled out of bed. She groped for the breadbox-sized device in the dark, and once she had found it, fussed with it for a few minutes by feel before she found the problem: something soft (it felt like a scarf) had become ensnarled in the clockwork. She pulled the cloth out and set it to one side to darn later, and the clockwork started back up again on its own, to her relief.

Now wide awake, she pulled on her housecoat and padded downstairs as quietly as she could. Mrs. Bennet was likely to be up already tending to her vegetables, but the rest of the household would be still asleep, and she'd never hear the end of it if she woke Lydia or Kitty at the ungodly hour of five in the morning. In the crate of his kennel in her father's library, Careful whined, and she went into the room to pet him and check his water dish.

Next to his crate was a small avalanche of papers and pamphlets and open books. Mr. Bennet would stack them untidily, and every now and again a mound of reading slid onto the floor in this manner. She began to tidy and stack them, closing the books that were open with bookmarks, so he wouldn't lose his place, and attempting to keep everything in the same order he had originally tossed it on the heap, except for the books which she put in their own separate pile. This accomplished, she patted Careful one last time and moved on to the kitchen. The beagle put his head back down, content to nap a little longer.

In the kitchen, she went to start the fire and put her father's leftover chicory coffee grounds in a bucket for mulch. The wood stove was rarely cold: her father stayed up late reading over coffee and her mother woke up early for tea before she left to turn on the arc lamps for the greenhouse. She opened the little door with a rag around her hand; the embers had been stirred, so her mother must be awake. She stuck a length of bamboo on top and closed the door again. She put the kettle on and perched on the edge of a chair, watching her copper reflection look bored. The fire hissed and muttered. The water always took forever to boil, and she had left her mother's gardening book upstairs. She blew out her breath, and then headed for the bookshelf in the breakfast room for something light to pass the time. The room was already occupied.

"I doubt it," her mother was saying as she began to pull the door open. "Lizzy would have told me."

Elizabeth froze at her name.

"If Jane is likely to be soon engaged," Mr. Collins said, "then I feel that my duty is to choose one of the younger daughters."

Oh no, Elizabeth thought. It all became obvious in a flash: his hints about 'making every possible amends' and being 'prepared to admire' them. He was here looking for a wife. She should have realized. Somebody like him *would* think they should be flattered by the attention. And Elizabeth, next to Jane in birth, would be his next natural target.

"As you like, if they will accept you." Her mother sounded non-committal. "If you were to become my son-in-law, it would be a comfort to know that the entail won't take the property out of the family, as you say."

"Indeed," Mr. Collins said, "and while I agree your greenhouses would not be included, and I thank you for your very convincing explanation on that score, in case I did not say it earlier, most edifying, indeed yes. Still, it would be a shame for anybody to be made homeless—"

"I will not marry off my daughters to secure my own comfort," Mrs. Bennet said, "but you have my blessing, sir, in the attempt to woo them. And the parsonage-house does sound nice."

I have to stop this, if mamma won't, she thought. Elizabeth swung open the door as Mr. Collins said, "Indeed, a tranquil residence."

Mrs. Bennet was carrying a bucket with a mess of roots sticking out of the top in one hand, the tendons of that hand standing in bas relief. In the other, she had a mug of tea, which she was just setting down to support the bucket with her second hand. "Ah, Lizzy," she said and went out without another word, leaving Elizabeth alone with Mr. Collins.

"Good mor—oh, cousin," Mr. Collins said. "I do not think we—that is, your clothes—"

Elizabeth looked down at herself and realized the problem. Although she was wearing many more layers than usual, they were bedclothes, and improper for her to wear in his company, especially without a chaperone. Properly speaking, her mother should not have left them alone, but then her mother only remembered those sorts of rules in fits and starts.

"Right," she said. "I will just—excuse me." She left, taking her mother's mug, which she dumped in the kitchen sink. It was just as well; she had been completely unprepared, and needed to concoct a plan to divert Mr. Collins's attention. She needed to think.

The kettle was singing now and she lifted it off the stove. She went to the window, still absentmindedly holding it, and watched her mother walking away. The steam on the glass made her a ghost even before she had vanished into her work.

§

"The best you can do with that scarf is tear it apart and refashion it into ribbons," Jane said, coming into the room. Careful squeezed in at her heels and ran around the room, auditing all of the changes that had occurred to every item since his last incursion. "What happened to shred it so?"

Elizabeth explained the incident with the aerator. "It is probably not salvageable, except maybe to trim a hat. I am really just hiding from Mr. Collins."

"Well, Papa is asking for you," Jane said. She patted her bed, and Careful scrambled up, where she stroked his ears for a moment. "I must get ready; I am visiting with Miss Bingley. The gentlemen, except Mr. Hurst, have gone to London, but the sisters were insistent that I visit to save them from boredom and each other. Do you think the blue or the purple dress?"

"Ruff," Careful said.

"Yes, you *are* a good boy. You wore the blue to the Lucases' dinner." Elizabeth dropped the mangled scarf over Careful, who nosed it into a nest along with Jane's blankets, and went to see her father. She heard the muted thump behind her that signified the dog following to see where she was going and if there was food involved.

When she put her head in the door of her father's library, the beagle passed her and leapt up into one of the chairs in front of her father's desk.

Mr. Bennet said, "Please take Mr. Collins out somewhere."

She came all the way into the room and sat in the one chair unoccupied by person, beagle, or piles of books. Careful daintily stepped down again from his chair and sniffed at her feet, and she petted his silky head until he grew bored and began sniffing around the room (her father's feet, the difference engine built along the back wall, a broken aeolipile he was always saying he would fix one day, a stack of chipboard, an old painting of a man on horseback that had not been hung up and collected dust leaning against a stack of leather-bound books, the desk) before finally lying down in his open kennel with a huff. Her father's request could not have been more unwelcome, and she told him so.

"I am sorry, Lizzy," he said, "but he has been talking at me continuously ever since breakfast of Lady Catherine and his Parsonage, and the former's cook's amazing calf's head soup, about which he is in ecstasies, and the latter's shelving arrangements, over which he is very worried for some reason (and since the man does not read much at all I cannot imagine why) and I have gotten nothing done all morning, and the plans for the Blenheim dome in Hardwicke must be completed by tomorrow latest or we shall have to set back the build date, which will have downstream effects on the computations for balancing—well, never mind, please just take him for a walk."

So, over a cold luncheon of mince pies and leftover pheasant, and trying not to look too mulish, Elizabeth said, "I must go into Meryton to meet with Charlotte and Maria Lucas for my turn of duty at the communal kitchen. Mr. Collins? Girls? Would any of you care to accompany me for the walk?"

"Oh, yes, please!" Lydia cried, and Kitty nodded.

Mr. Collins said, "The healthfulness of the exercise must be to our benefit. I would be most pleased and gratified to accompany you."

As a party of four, they would naturally split into the younger and the older, and she would have Mr. Collins's sole attention for the length of the walk. Elizabeth turned to Mary, and widened her eyes at her, as good as begging her to come.

Mary was not a famed walker, and usually declined these family outings in favour of practicing the pianoforte, but she rose now, saying, "I am persuaded by Mr. Collins's commendable thought on healthfulness. One must exert oneself regularly or risk ill health."

"Indeed," Mr. Collins said, taking her arm.

"Thank you," Elizabeth mouthed to Mary, who smiled back at her serenely.

Elizabeth walked with her youngest sisters, slightly outpacing

Mary and Mr. Collins, though she could hear the rise and fall of their conversation. Mr. Collins did most of the talking, and, amazingly, Mary let him.

Drowning out whatever he might have been saying, Lydia said, "Lizzy, you will never guess what happened last night. Kitty and me and Ganymede and Bill and Tom snuck out to go for a walk and Ganymede dared Tom to ride the counterweight all the way to the shipping hub—"

"You should not be sneaking out behind everybody's backs, especially with boys, and especially going packet-dodging," Elizabeth said.

"Like you never did it," Lydia said.

Elizabeth found herself without an answer. Anyway, she had known William Lucas and Thomas Purvis since they had been in diapers, which made it difficult to see them as threats to her sisters' virtue.

"Anyway," Kitty said, "that isn't even the most shocking thing! On our way back, we happened to pass that little house where the old Cats live—"

"Oh, Kitty, don't call them that," Elizabeth said. The nickname referred to two mature spinsters, Catherine Blythe and Kathryn Edevane, the latter of whom had been so helpful when Jane had been cut by the falling glass at Netherfield. They had lived together as long as anybody could remember, and were sometimes rumoured to be a romantic pair, which was supposed to be terribly shocking, though Elizabeth couldn't see the harm in it.

"You could be called a Cat yourself," Lydia said to Kitty, laughing.

Kitty made a face at her. "But not an old one. But who do you think was visiting them, but Mary King! What do you suppose *she* might have had to say to them? Denny says—"

"Never mind what Denny says," Elizabeth said. She made her voice quite firm. "You mustn't repeat gossip, Kitty. You don't know what harm you might do. In any case, Mr. King is quite ill, and Miss King probably needed Miss Edevane's nursing advice."

"Oh," said Kitty, sounding disappointed.

"Speaking of Denny," Lydia said, and enthused about the potential of seeing Mr. Denny and Mr. Wickham in town.

At Elizabeth's turn, she reminded Lydia and Kitty to behave and waved to Mr. Collins and Mary before going into the communal kitchen. She counted herself lucky to have made it nearly the whole day without exchanging more than a few words with the man.

§

The dining area was a large metal box full of battered metal chairs and rough wooden tables. Somebody had painted one wall in a landscape not unlike the ones she had seen in books; it had faded in the years since, and in a few places the metal wall had been scrubbed bare. When she walked into the kitchen, she was immediately engulfed in the competing smells of lemon cleaner and baking bread. She was put to work peeling potatoes, and when she reached her station, was surprised to see Mr. Wickham.

"I did not realize you were on the duty roster," Elizabeth greeted him. "I assumed your engineering duties would have exempted you."

"You forget," he replied with a smile. "I have not yet sat my exams. I could still fail them, and then I should be grateful for such employment as this."

Elizabeth laughed. He handed her a peeler from a bin full of them, and she started peeling.

"Your sister Lydia played a very creative trick last week," Mr. Wickham said. "Did she tell you about it?"

"No, I do not believe so."

He put down the potato he had just finished peeling, and leaned back a little. "Mrs. Forster had a little party, and invited the Harrington sisters to attend, and afterwards a group of the attendees went packet-dodging."

Elizabeth looked up, surprised, and at her expression Wickham quickly said, "Oh, not me. I only heard about this later."

"Oh, I see," Elizabeth said, her objections dying on her tongue.

"Well," he said, slouching against the back of his chair, "somehow she and the Harrington sisters inflated an empty aether suit and put some bags of wheat or something in it to make it a plausible weight for a person, and got it up to the top of the outgoing counterweight with them, and when they jumped, they let it fall down on its own. Of course everybody waiting in the packet area thought somebody had been killed."

As he spoke, Wickham gestured with his hands, ending his sentence by spreading out his arms with a broad 'can you believe it?' gesture.

"No!" Elizabeth said, peeling industrially.

"Mrs. Forster told me they only realized when Lydia could not stop laughing."

"Oh, Lydia!"

They were silent a moment, and he shifted on his chair, then continued, "She mentioned that you and your elder sister had both been injured. I should have asked as soon as I saw you. Are you both quite well?"

"Yes," Elizabeth said. "I only had this cut on my arm—" she showed him the angry red line that was still visible on her arm "—and Jane, though more grievously injured, seems now to be completely recovered, although I do wonder if she hides her aches and pains. She is very reserved."

"I am relieved to hear you are both recovering." He put down his peeler and stretched out both arms as if working out a sore muscle. He hesitated, and then asked, "And do you still share my opinion of Mr. Darcy after staying in the same house with him for so long?"

Elizabeth remembered Darcy's awkwardness when he thought he wasn't welcome, and the silent breakfast they had shared. She said, "I cannot say we spoke much," and Mr. Wickham's shoulders relaxed slightly. "But why were you not at the build?"

"I decided that I had better not meet Mr. Darcy, after all. Scenes might arise unpleasant to more than myself."

"Very wise," she said, and handed him a potato.

Charlotte and Maria Lucas came into the kitchen then, and the four of them made a merry party for potato peeling, succeeding in getting through the entire shipment before their shift ended. He walked the three of them to Longbourn, and once they had arrived, Elizabeth was pleased to introduce him to her father, and refresh her mother's memory of him. Mr. Bennet only nodded at him over the top of his book and then went back to reading, but Mrs. Bennet invited him to join them for tea ("just, please, no potatoes!" Maria said to general laughter) and then Wickham escorted the Lucases home and Elizabeth lay on the couch spinning daydreams until Mr. Collins and her three younger sisters all came happily in the door, Mary listening with unlikely but apparently sincere interest to Mr. Collins's extensive thoughts on the advisability of purchasing a steam-powered percolator.

CHAPTER SIX

THE NEXT DAY AT BREAKFAST, A LETTER ARRIVED from Netherfield Park addressed to Miss Bennet, in an envelope of much finer parchment than Elizabeth had ever had the opportunity to use. She gave it to Jane, who opened it immediately and read through it, her face slowly turning more and more somber until she stood still as stone. After a moment, she put the letter away and rejoined in the conversation with a counterfeit cheerfulness.

Mr. Collins entered the room soon afterwards. He said to Mrs. Bennet, "May I ask for the favour of a private word with your daughter Mary?"

All was astonishment: Mary looked more smug than usual; Jane and Elizabeth exchanged surprised looks; Kitty gave Lydia a sly smirk; Lydia actually laughed out loud.

Mrs. Bennet, notably unsurprised, said, "Of course, Mr. Collins. Come, girls," and stood to go. Kitty scooped up Careful as they went.

Mary moved to the window, and waited for them to leave, a small smile playing across her lips.

Jane took advantage of the excitement to pull Elizabeth upstairs and take out her letter. It was as thin and delicate as a butterfly's wing, and covered in graceful writing that Elizabeth recognized as Caroline Bingley's.

"It is from Miss Bingley," Jane confirmed. "They have left Headfort for London, this morning; they would have handed the letter off to be delivered on their way out of the 'lock. Caroline and Louisa did not give me any hint of their travels yesterday, but she says they are headed for London, and will not be coming back. Such a removal would have required planning; they must have known already when I saw them. I do not know what to think."

"I do," Elizabeth said. "But go on."

Jane read out the beginning of the letter. They were gone to Mr. Hurst's personal dome, Grosvenor, in New Mayfair, and hoped Jane would write them often, to make up for the loss of her visits. They would not return this year, or perhaps ever, but when Jane was next in London (it was unthinkable to these ladies of fashion that anybody might not go to the London dome regularly) she could come to visit them.

"Mr. Bingley will have further duties to get Netherfield up and running," Elizabeth said. "His sisters may relax in London—I understand the family puts all the work on the gentlemen—but he is not completely at leisure to come and go as he pleases. Father will confirm that he must mean to return."

"But listen," Jane said. "She writes, 'My brother has discovered that his business will take many months, rather than the days he had expected; something about repairs to the superstructure's charcoal air scrubbers that has gone quite above my head. We wish you could have come with us, but naturally you have your family and work duties to absorb you; please do not entirely forget us.' As if I could! But it seems clear enough that I will not see Charles until next year at the earliest."

"It is clear enough that Miss Bingley means to keep him away."

"No, Lizzy. He could easily come to see me if he wished: Caroline is not his master, and you know he has his weekends; even in emergencies engineers get days off."

"And why should he be particularly needed to help with air scrubbers when his specialty is building domes, and London is chockablock with other engineers?" Elizabeth sensed the hand of a person of influence behind the scenes, possibly even Mr. Darcy, but without proof it wasn't worth mentioning to Jane. "It is very strange. But at the worst, you might see him in January; that is only three months from now."

"But you do not know everything. Let me read you the end of her letter. 'Mr. Darcy talks of nothing but his sister, who we expect in London any day. Georgiana Darcy is one of those women whom both men and other women cannot help loving. We hope she shall be hereafter our sister.' And she goes on to say how much Charles admires Georgiana, and how she hopes I might have many beaux at Christmastime to distract me."

"Oh! That. . . oh, Jane, there is no polite way to say what I am thinking."

"If she has seen how I feel about him, she is very thoughtful to warn me of his attachment elsewhere."

"Or he has no attachment elsewhere, only Miss Bingley wishes he did! You must have seen how she dotes on Mr. Darcy, and how resistant he is to her charms. *We* know that he is engaged to Miss de Bourgh, but Miss Bingley does *not* know, or she acts as if she does not, and she must think that if *her* brother marries *his* sister, that will throw them together and give her the opportunity to wear him down."

"How horribly cynical of you, Lizzy," Jane said. "Although you do make a horrid sort of sense, I know that Caroline is incapable of dishonesty."

"Anybody who has seen you with Mr. Bingley would know he loves you," Elizabeth said. "She will not be able to sway him. Even if he is held over in London for a few months, you will see him soon enough. I dare say he will not be able to keep away."

Jane smiled at this, her dimples flashing into and out of existence. As she was putting away her letter, Lydia came knocking at their door, demanding to know what they were doing closeted away when there were celebrations to be had, for Mary and Mr. Collins were engaged.

§

Mr. Collins had planned to leave on Saturday, and would not alter his plans due to his engagement. Accordingly, they took their leave over breakfast, and Mrs. Bennet invited him to stay at Longbourn again whenever his work might allow him to visit. Mr. Collins thanked her at length and they fixed the final Monday in October, a few weeks away, as the start of his next visit, pending Lady Catherine's permission.

"I am deeply grateful for your welcome here," Mr. Collins said, "For I have never seen such a welcoming and comfortable home, and, I am certain, I will endeavor to model my own home after the pattern of Longbourn in all things, helped, I am sure, by my most perceptive and wise future wife."

"I look forward to it," Mr. Bennet said, and the ladies made all the proper civilities until they could at last close the 'lock behind him.

"Papa," Lydia said after a whispered exchange with Kitty, "may we go to Meryton? Only Mrs. Philips should be told—"

"Yes, my dears," he replied. "You have my blessing to spread the gossip throughout Meryton."

They settled on the whole party of girls walking into Meryton, with Mary for once the celebrated leader of the group. Jane held a letter for Caroline Bingley which she was to mail, and Kitty and Lydia hoped to buy some new ribbon to trim their hats.

"But however did this happen so quickly?" Elizabeth asked Mary on the way home. "I can hardly believe you have fallen in love over the space of one walk to Meryton and a few family meals."

"I expect that love will come later," Mary said calmly. "We are already of a similar mind about many subjects."

"I am happy to find you so practical," Elizabeth said, hiding her smile. She really thought that Mr. Collins would make Mary happy. She was perhaps the only girl in Meryton for whom that was at all likely, and by taking him on, she saved the happiness of some other girl, and so, marrying him was almost a charitable act. She saved this thought for Mr. Bennet's future amusement.

Mrs. Bennet was as pleased as Mary. "One of my daughters married and provided for," she said to her daughters as they prepared that night's meal, "and my business secured. How lucky we are in Mr. Collins."

A letter from his future son-in-law arrived on Tuesday on handmade stationery, which was full of thanks and apologies; Mr. Bennet declined to read it to them, saying that it was for his own entertainment only, but handed the third page over to Mary so she could see the confirmation that her fiancé would come for another visit in a fortnight, having secured permission from his patroness.

No letter came from Miss Bingley, and Meryton whispered that the family had quitted the dome and would spend the rest of the year in London while work continued on the grounds. After suffering for a week, Jane finally permitted Elizabeth to ask their father when Mr. Bingley would come back to Netherfield.

"As the architect," he answered her, "my job is finished. I know no more than the neighbourhood gossips."

"Could you write to ask him?" Elizabeth asked.

"Certainly I *could*, my dear," he said with a stern look, "and he will know immediately *why* I write. We are not friends, you know. Bingley, as amiable as he is, should not be confused with a fool. It will be quite transparent that I am writing on Jane's behalf. You know she would not like that."

"No," Elizabeth agreed. "But it is so stupid that his sisters should come between them."

"Do you think him indifferent?"

"I think he could be convinced that his duty lay elsewhere, or that Jane herself did not care a pin for him. He is awfully diffident and London is so diverting."

"Well," Mr. Bennet said. "He is a grown man, and will do what he likes." He turned back to his book, and Elizabeth understood herself to be dismissed.

§

At last a letter arrived on creamy stationery, written closely by Miss Bingley. It was organized as if from an etiquette guide to invoking heartbreak: it assured Jane of their happiness in London, described their plan to stay there at least through Christmas, and conveyed Mr. Bingley's regret at failing to say goodbye by wording that managed to suggest that Miss Bingley had fabricated her brother's regrets only to comfort Miss Bennet, and that in fact he never thought of her at all. Her closing paragraph described their many outings with Miss Darcy, who she again predicted would soon be her sister. Nowhere in the letter did she ask one question of Jane to provide a start for return correspondence.

"Oh, Jane," Elizabeth said when Jane had shown her the letter. "I do not believe that he *is* partial to Miss Darcy any more than he was a few weeks ago, but I admit, that as angry as this makes me at Caroline, I am more furious with Mr. Bingley, for allowing his easy temper to make him his sister's pawn."

"We made each other no promises, and I merely misunderstood," Jane said. Her eyes grew a little glassy with unshed tears. "I took his amiability as interest, that is all. In time, I will quite forget him."

"Anybody could see how much he liked you. But—no, do not cry—" Elizabeth hugged her sister close and kissed the top of her head. "You are too good."

"I beg you, Lizzy, do not think he is to blame."

"What are you girls doing in here?" Mrs. Bennet asked as she opened their door, and Jane busied herself putting away the letter to keep their mother from seeing her face.

"Coming, mother!" Lizzy sang out in a light tone, and went downstairs to help prepare some partridge from Lady Lucas.

For Mr. Collins's welcome dinner, to balance their numbers, they had invited Mr. Wickham and Mr. Denny as well as two of Mr. Bennet's friends. The latter were a Mr. Haggerston and a Mr. Dawson, respectively pugnaciously stout and fashionably narrow, in town to deal with something to do with the ship's mechanisms, which Mr. Bennet had characterized as nothing that need worry them, and declined to explain any further.

One end of the table (Mr. and Mrs. Bennet, and Mary and Mr. Collins) spoke of nothing but wedding plans, while the other end of the table were less focused and much louder. The only moment that marred their merriment was when Lydia complained of never having had the opportunity to see Netherfield Park completed: Jane hardly knew where to look, and Elizabeth, catching Wickham's eye, saw his skin flush, no doubt at the thought of Darcy.

"We completed the essentials," Haggerston said obliviously, "and if Bingley does not want the place, I am sure he will sell it soon enough and you will have a chance to see it completed."

After the meal, the men went to Mr. Bennet's study to drink and smoke, while Mrs. Bennet updated the ladies on all of their duties for the wedding, which had been set for a fortnight Saturday, on the eighth of November. Mary favoured them all by playing some music on the pianoforte, and was in such high spirits that she played as well as Elizabeth had ever heard her.

After everyone had gone, Jane and Elizabeth turned in early so that they might talk in private. As they lay in bed, Jane whispered, "Do you really think they influence him to stay away?" Who she was speaking of did not need to be specified. Elizabeth indicated that her views had not changed, and Jane sighed. "It makes no sense to me. I cannot stop thinking about it. They have assured me of their regard and love for me, and if he loves me, no other woman could make him happy."

Elizabeth leaned so close she could smell Jane's soap. "His happiness may not signify. They may put more importance on his wealth and reputation, or on his bride's connections."

"If they do want him to marry Miss Darcy over me," Jane said, "their feelings may naturally arise from their love for her."

"I have a sister's partiality," Elizabeth said. "I cannot imagine anybody loving anybody more than they love you."

§

Two days before the wedding, Elizabeth, Lydia, and Kitty put on their aether suits to make ice cream. Their back airlock had been put in place to allow them to connect to the next dome to be built in the future. It was little used, although the sisters had been known to go that way to sneak over to the Lucases without walking through town. It was also Mrs. Bennet's secret weapon: she had become accustomed to using it as a freezer, sending one of her daughters out every morning with a pot of water covered by a close-fitting lid to freeze in the aether outside, and placing that in the center of the chest she kept in the kitchen for cold foods. She also allowed some of her wares to freeze so they would keep for longer periods, and these boxes filled half of the space of the 'lock.

On this occasion, the ladies took out several closely-lidded pots filled with boiled mixtures for apricot, rosewater, and vanilla ice creams, tied tightly shut. They stood shaking them until their arms ached, so the air at the top of the container would combine with the liquid mixture at the bottom as it froze and make a smooth and slightly fluffy dessert instead of one big block of ice. Once they were done, they set the pots just outside the airlock to stay frozen, until they would be retrieved the day of the wedding. The Lucases could certainly be trusted not to steal them, and nobody else had any reason to come by their airlock.

That afternoon, Mrs. Bennet's younger brother and his wife arrived from London. Mr. Gardiner had the same green eyes and chestnut hair as his sister and nieces, though his face was somewhat more florid. He shared with his sister a genius for business, and shared with his wife the fashionable elegance so common to Londoners. His wife had a long, narrow face, long nose, pert lips, and long, shining black hair always dressed in the most recent style. Having married their uncle when she was eighteen and Jane was eleven, she had become good friends with her two eldest nieces as they had grown into young women.

Mr. Gardiner and Mr. Bennet took themselves off to smoke cigars and Mrs. Bennet immediately put her sister-in-law to work shelling peas. Mrs. Gardiner shared a few juicy bits of London gossip about people Mr. and Mrs. Bennet had been acquainted with in their youth, and Mrs. Bennet shared some unsavoury details about one of the vendors she did business with, who had lately left his wife for a much younger woman. When Lydia had finished washing their linens, she came into the kitchen for a cold drink and collapsed in a chair to tell Mrs. Gardiner everything she knew of Mr. Bingley's desertion of Jane.

"Really, Lydia," Elizabeth said.

Jane said, "Lydia exaggerates, aunt. It was no desertion, for we made no promises to one another."

Seeing her daughter distressed, Mrs. Bennet forbade further discussion of the subject. "We should be concentrating on Mary in any case," she went on. "Tomorrow is her big day."

Later that night, Mrs. Gardiner found Elizabeth alone, and said, "What a shame that Jane should have been disappointed in her young man. I am sorry for her. It is a sad but common story: men easily fall for a pretty girl, and then just as easily forget about her."

"It is much less common that friends should deliberately draw him away," Elizabeth said. "He was really in love, I believe. His sister I once watched spend five whole minutes speaking to him on some matter or other, and at the end he turned to her and said, 'I'm so sorry, Caroline, what were you saying?' for he was too busy watching Jane from across the room to attend to anything else."

"Poor Jane!"

"Do you think she could come stay with you for a few weeks? I feel certain she would enjoy a break, and we could certainly arrange with Sir William for her to have a little vacation. I can take on any extra shifts, if needed." *And perhaps when he hears that she is in town, Mr. Darcy will not be able to keep him away,* Elizabeth thought.

"Of course. Perhaps we can bring her back to Longbourn when we come for Christmas. That will give her about a month of respite."

The next day, Jane was told of her aunt's suggestion, and readily agreed, but then, growing pale, said, "Oh—perhaps I—had better not. He—my—my mother may need me—with Mary leaving."

"You need not fear meeting the Bingleys," Mrs. Gardiner said, guessing the real reason for Jane's hesitancy. "New Mayfair and City domes are quite opposite sides of the superstructure. I am sure we have no connections in common, and we need not go out much. You will not meet, if he does not come on purpose to see you."

"I should love to see him, when I am quite prepared," Jane said quietly, "and it would be a pleasure to see Caroline and Louisa, but I admit that coming upon them all unaware would be a little difficult."

Elizabeth thought that Caroline Bingley and Louisa Hurst would most likely drop their acquaintance with Jane immediately rather than pollute themselves by visiting the City dome, but said instead, "Caroline is staying with her sister, and Mr. Bingley with Mr. Darcy, so you might visit one without risking seeing the other."

So it was decided: Jane would spend the rest of November and most of December in London.

That night, to make room for the Gardiners, Mary and Elizabeth shared a room, with Jane on a cot in Lydia and Kitty's room. Mary spoke at length on how satisfied she was with the wedding preparations and with everything that Mr. Collins had told her about Hunsford, and then turned to Elizabeth suddenly. She said a little wildly, "It is so strange, Eliza. Tomorrow I will be Mary Collins. I can hardly believe it. I am excited—I am—but also—"

"You will soon get used to it," Elizabeth said, "but if you do not want to marry him, after all, it is not too late."

"No, no. No, I am only nervous. But I hope that after a few months, you or Jane might come to see me. Mr. Collins's plans for renovations will delay me from any visits home."

"Of course I would be happy to visit," Elizabeth lied.

"I thought I would die in this house," Mary said dreamily, "or in some dingy rental house if Father died before me. I thought I would spend my life in the kitchen and the drawing room. I was not sad about it, you understand. I knew the four of you were prettier and I would be left here to fetch and wash up after our parents, and live quietly, and it sounded tolerable. Then I took mamma's advice and asserted myself a little and it turned out that I was just as attractive to a good man as any of you. I cannot believe I am the first of us to marry. I keep pinching myself. I hardly know who I am anymore, Lizzy." Then she seemed to come back to herself, and added primly, with the same smile she had given Elizabeth when she had, in Elizabeth's place, led Mr. Collins off to walk to town, "I shall help my husband with his flock and be a model for my sisters to aspire to."

Elizabeth doused the light and whispered, "Good night, Mary. Do not worry. Everything will be well."

§

Mary's wedding day arrived. She wore her best dress, the leaf-green trimmed with pink satin, with her mother's best pink nasturtiums in her hair, and pink satin shoes. Mr. Collins looked as well as he ever would, in a navy cut-away coat with tails and a white cravat, and his hair stiff with pomade. The whole Bennet family attended, along with Maria Lucas, and a friend of Mr. Collins whose name Elizabeth never caught. Elizabeth contemplated the couple, thankful that neither her present happiness nor her future depended upon their brevity or wit. Mr. Goulding performed the prescribed service; Mr. Collins stuttered over his vows; the rings were exchanged; finally, the marriage lines were entered in the parish register book and Mary given her copy. The new couple, able at last to style themselves Mr. and Mrs. Collins, were celebrated at a breakfast back at Longbourn, along with the Philipses, the rest of the Lucases, a good fifth of the population of Meryton, and a towering wedding cake. In his high, old-person's voice, Mr. Collins thanked everybody assembled at such length, the hot buns grew cold.

By Elizabeth's design, she was seated next to Wickham, who loaded up her plate with pastries, tongue, and eggs. Mrs. Gardiner was seated on his other side, where she watched them both narrowly. As Mr. Wickham piled Mrs. Gardiner's plate high with food, he asked her, "Do I detect a Darlington accent?"

She replied, "You do! Well spotted."

"I grew up there. Where are you from?"

"I spent most of my life before my marriage in Lambton."

"Oh! I am very familiar with the area," he said. "I grew up at Pemberley. My father was steward to the late Mr. Darcy."

"What a coincidence!"

"I have not visited since my father died four years ago," Wickham said, "but I remember fondly all of my old friends there."

"I am the same. We write, of course, now and then," she said, "but it has been so long since I have seen them."

"Do you remember old Mr. Pilchard, the clergyman?"

"Yes! What a funny old gentleman. But he must have long since passed. He was nearing eighty when I left to be married twelve years ago."

"Yes, I am afraid he passed a couple of years ago, though he continued working almost until the end."

"I have often wondered whatever happened to Miss Pope. She must have married, I suppose."

They spoke of several other acquaintances, and Elizabeth turned to the gentleman on her other side, Mr. Brown, as a break from hearing about people she supposed she would never meet. Mr. Brown had very little to say for himself, and their conversation limped along for only a few minutes. When Mrs. Gardiner turned the conversation to Pemberley, Elizabeth turned back with an interest she could not entirely hide.

"The late Mr. Darcy was such a lovely man," Mrs. Gardiner said. "I remember his generosity during the famine of '32 very well, but I was married soon after and moved to London with Mr. Gardiner."

"He was a very great man," Mr. Wickham said, and then hesitantly added, "His son unfortunately has not held to that tradition."

Mrs. Gardiner expressed surprise.

"Elizabeth can attest to his pride," Mr. Wickham said, "but I would not mind him being proud, even arrogant, if he treated his inferiors with kindness."

Mrs. Gardiner leaned past Wickham, and Elizabeth laughingly related the story of his snub at the dance. "But do not pity me, aunt," she finished, "for to have the attentions of a man like that would surely be a punishment."

"His conduct as a boy was always—" Mr. Wickham paused, searching for the right words, and settled on: "—technically blameless, you could say, but certainly did not encourage affection."

"Did you know him well?" Mrs. Gardiner asked.

"We were thrown together often, since we were the only children in the Pemberley dome of a similar age, but even as a boy, to be his friend required a very obliging nature."

"I can only imagine," Elizabeth said dryly, thinking of Bingley.

"I have been trying to remember if I had ever heard anything about him when I lived there," Mrs. Gardiner said. "We hardly moved in the same circles. Was he ever cruel to you?"

"Not as a boy," Wickham said. "He would never have done anything to invite his father's disapproval. But as an adult—his father intended me for Mr. Pilchard's replacement, but Mr. Darcy chose to give the living to another man after he passed away."

"How extraordinary," Mrs. Gardiner said.

Wickham made an embarrassed hand gesture, and they moved on to other topics.

The moment of the new couple's departure arrived. Mr. Collins simpered and bowed repeatedly. Mary cried a little, and was angry at anybody who commented on it. The sisters all embraced. The parents assured their daughter and each other that she would be well. Mr. Collins thanked everybody for their welcomes. Finally they cranked up the carriage and went.

In the ensuing melee of guests all departing, Elizabeth found Charlotte Lucas, to whom she had been unable to speak earlier. "Would you like to take any of the ice cream home?" she asked after they had exchanged hugs and greetings, Charlotte's face strangely grave for the occasion. "You can keep it frozen in your back 'lock. I know rosewater is Maria's favourite, and we have quite a quantity left."

"Yes, but may I come by in the morning to get it? I'm going directly to see Mary King."

"I was sorry not to see her and her uncle here today," Elizabeth said. "Is he recovering at all?" She had heard at her last work session that his heart problems had worsened.

"She sent me a note this morning to let me know that the worst has happened, and Mr. King passed away in the small hours of the morning. She is not quite alone in the world; she has her cousins in Oakham Mount. She has not decided if she will quit Meryton to go to them, or—oh, Eliza, everything is so unsettled."

So, this accounted for Charlotte's gravity, Elizabeth thought. She might be losing a dear friend. They would no doubt keep a lively correspondence, but when would Charlotte ever have occasion to go to Oakham Mount? "Please give her our condolences," she said. "And take anything you think might tempt her to eat. Do you want me to go with you?"

"No, you have far too much to do here."

"I assure you, my mother will not miss me. Let Kitty and Lydia have their share of the work for once."

Charlotte smiled for the first time. "I appreciate it, Eliza, but I think Mary would be happier if she didn't have to talk to too many people."

"She cannot stay entirely alone," Elizabeth said. "If she needs you to stay with her for a few days, please just send me a note and I will cover your shifts. Jane leaves on Monday, and now that the wedding is done, I will be quite at my leisure."

"You don't know what that means to me," Charlotte said. "Eliza, I have wanted to tell you—"

Yelping rose behind them, and Elizabeth turned to find Careful almost upon her. "Careful!" she yelled, and the beagle reversed course, his ears flapping behind him as he ran between legs and under dresses. Kitty dove for him and missed, but Wickham caught him by his collar and put him squirming into Elizabeth's arms before leaving with a lop-sided smile. In the confusion, Charlotte had slipped away, whatever she had wanted to say forgotten, and before too long only the family was left.

"I could not be any more entertained," Mr. Bennet said to Elizabeth. "You would never tolerate such a man, but I have high hopes for Kitty and Lydia's husbands giving Mr. Collins a run for his money."

Elizabeth thought of Wickham. *Papa would be hard-pressed to find* him *entertaining*, she thought with a smile.

That evening, Mrs. Gardiner followed Elizabeth up the stairs and pulled her into the room she usually shared with Jane, but which had been given over to the Gardiners during their visit, where she warned her very seriously away from Mr. Wickham.

"But you seemed to like him so much," Elizabeth said.

"Yes, he was perfectly pleasant, my dear. But he has no way to provide for you. If Darcy had given him the living he spoke of, or if he had settled into a career that would provide comfortably for you both, it would be different, but he did not, and so, you must hold yourself back. He could have been trained and been working for several years already, as an aethernaut or fabricator, or the law or even medicine. He has come late to engineering, and may tire of it. You cannot afford to marry a man with so little, who has reached his mature age without having actually embarked upon a career."

Add Wickham to the stack of wrongs Darcy has done me, Elizabeth thought.

"I do like him very much. I do not love him, at present," Elizabeth said. "But he is very agreeable. I would be sad to disappoint you. But every day young people get engaged who have no fortune. And we are changing, aunt: mother has her business, and I might have my own. What was wise for your generation might not be for mine. Perhaps I will work, and he will raise the children."

Her aunt's mouth quirked a little at the idea. "Does he support you in your plans? Would he welcome a wife who went to university? Who made her own money?"

Elizabeth had never even considered these questions. "I do not know. I do not even know if I truly want to go to university, aunt."

"Speak with him about it, in a general way, and see what he thinks of modern women like Mary King. You may be surprised."

"I will do so, and I will let you know in my very next letter," Elizabeth said.

Mrs. Gardiner expressed herself contented with this promise, and they parted for the night.

CHAPTER SEVEN

MARY'S LETTERS ARRIVED PUNCTUALLY EVERY Tuesday, and were uniformly positive: she wrote at length on the moral uprightness of her neighbours, Lady Catherine's excellent judgement and excessive kindness to them both, and the comforts of her new home. Elizabeth did not believe that it could be quite so wonderful as she painted it, but supposed she would find out for herself soon enough.

A much better correspondent, Jane wrote Elizabeth daily, first to let her know they had arrived, and then to update her on all of her activities, which were mostly the sorts of things she would have done in Meryton, but spiced with new people, different fashions, and varying sights. After several days, having heard nothing in return from Miss Bingley, she supposed that the letter she had sent on her first morning had been lost. Mrs. Gardiner was going to New Mayfair the following day, and Jane had resolved to go with her and call at the Hursts' dome.

She wrote again the next day: "Caroline was most gracious. It seems that my letter went astray. Mr. Bingley, she says, is well, but they see very little of him. Mr. Darcy has kept him busy with some engineering issue or another. They expected to see him this evening, however, along with both Mr. Darcy and his sister. I long to see Miss Darcy and confirm for myself the beauty and accomplishments that Caroline claims for her. I have little to write to you about my visit; it was so short, as they were on their way out the door for another engagement. However, I look forward to seeing them here at the Gardiners.'"

But they did not visit, and neither did their brother.

In her reply, Elizabeth wrote Jane of progress in the greenhouses, and her struggles with her varied studies. She ended her letter by saying, "Everybody in Meryton now knows what you and I have known for months: somehow word of Darcy's cruelty to Wickham has become public (he told our aunt at Mary's wedding, and I know she would never betray a confidence, yet somebody may have overheard us speaking). I continue to believe he and Miss Bingley keep word of your visit from Mr. Bingley."

Jane wrote that she had seen a play, and read several books, and gone to all the best dress shops; every letter ended with a postscript that she had heard nothing from Miss Bingley.

On the first of December, Miss Bingley and Mrs. Hurst finally visited: "Caroline returned my visit this morning," Jane wrote, "and was so brusque in her apologies for not having already visited that I was quite surprised. She was distracted, such that we hardly spoke. I must conclude that I was mistaken regarding her affection for me."

At least one good thing has come from her stay with our aunt and uncle, then, Elizabeth thought.

Jane looked for ways to excuse Caroline's conduct: it must have arisen from love of her brother and anxiety on his behalf. These explanations went on for half a page, as Jane worked to convince herself that she had hardly been wronged at all. Elizabeth shook her head lovingly. "Miss Bingley writes that she made sure to mention my being in London to Mr. Bingley, and that he asked her to be sure to give me his regards (what a cold word it seems, *regards!*)."

Oh, Jane, Elizabeth thought. *All hope of Mr. Bingley's regard seems gone, and Jane will not even accept the relief of a cleansing anger. I hope Bingley is punished in his marriage to Mr. Darcy's sister, since, at least based on Wickham's portrait of her, she would make him quite miserable.*

With this latest letter came another from her aunt, asking if Elizabeth was adhering scrupulously to her promises: "I hope that you are keeping your guard up around the young man we spoke of."

Elizabeth wrote back with bracing sympathy for Jane, and in a separate letter, news that would give her aunt relief: Wickham had transferred his attentions and admiration to another young lady. "I was not able to carry out my promise to you of asking him how he felt about women going to university, but we have our answer with his choice: you may remember that Miss Mary King, before her uncle died and left her all that money, was already notorious as the first woman to graduate Babbage."

Charlotte had spent a week helping Miss King to recover from her uncle's death, and Elizabeth had been as good as her word in covering her shifts for her. After a week, Lady Lucas, chafing at the extra work she had to do around Lucas Lodge, persuaded Charlotte to return home. Mrs. Clark, whom Elizabeth knew from her shifts at Meryton's communal kitchen, had been hired as a temporary lady's companion, there being no Mr. Clark, until Miss King could receive her inheritance and decide her next steps. The famous Mary King had, if not prettiness, a self-possession and playfulness that was very pleasing, and Elizabeth had found that she liked Charlotte's friend very much. Consequently, Elizabeth had been able to watch the transfer of Wickham's affections with no pain or embarrassment, and only a little wonder at Mary King's composure in the face of all his flattery. He seemed like the sort of man who would require a lot of management, and Elizabeth privately thought Miss King's detachment boded well for managing the high-spirited Wickham in marriage.

Charlotte spent every spare moment with Miss King, and though Charlotte included Elizabeth in several of her visits, they never seemed to have time alone together any more, and Elizabeth was more jealous of this than of Wickham's desertion, though she would never have admitted it to a soul.

She finished her letter to her aunt, "Since I have no ill feelings toward him or Miss King, I find that I could never have been much in love with him to begin with."

§

In December, the monthly Meryton assembly fell on St. Nicholas Day. Mary King being exempted from her work duties for the moment, Charlotte and Elizabeth were once again paired up, and Elizabeth was delighted to find that they were assigned to the signal room.

Wickham was assigned to the communal kitchen but came to visit the Bennets often, frequently with Charlotte and Mary King in tow, lightening Mrs. Bennet's mood when she dwelled on Mary's absence too much and inspiring Lydia and Kitty to pay more attention to their textbooks so they could impress him with their learning. Elizabeth could not see that Wickham was making any great headway with his courting of Miss King, and Charlotte explained this one afternoon by saying, in a rare moment when it was only the two of them alone, "Eliza, I have a matter of great seriousness to speak with you about."

They had been sprawled on her bed, to gain privacy from Elizabeth's sisters, Charlotte reading and Elizabeth adding embroidery to a plain top Jane had pieced together for her from bits of an old blanket, until Charlotte had the moment before sat up abruptly and let her book fall onto the bed.

"I am in love with Miss King," Charlotte said.

Elizabeth opened her mouth to respond and found she had no words.

"I understand you are probably shocked—" Charlotte began.

"More surprised than shocked," Elizabeth said. "I thought you and William King might be—"

"Will King!" Charlotte laughed.

"But you and Miss King. . ." Elizabeth trailed off, not sure what to say.

"We love each other," Charlotte said.

Elizabeth noticed her friend's shoulders were held tight and high, as though bracing herself for a physical blow.

"Oh, Charlotte," she said, reaching out to touch her hand. "However did it come about?"

Charlotte's shoulders came down to their usual level as she breathed out a sigh. "It was the most natural thing in the world. But I thought that it was just me—that of course she esteemed me as a friend, but that was all—but yesterday, she kissed me!"

Elizabeth smiled at her friend's pink cheeks. "But what will you do? How will you live? Two women alone—but then I suppose she has her wealth—"

"That is exactly what I wished to discuss," Charlotte said.

Elizabeth said, "Our generation is learning to do so many things differently from our parents. I suppose, if a woman can be an engineer, what is to stop her from being something like a husband?"

"The trouble is, my father will disown me. You know he has always been cold towards the Cats."

"Oh," Elizabeth said. "Yes, I see. Perhaps you can ask their advice."

Charlotte fell back against the pillows, and then wailed, "What am I to *do?*"

But Elizabeth could only pat her friend's hand and say, "We shall come up with something."

The Gardiners brought Jane home for their annual Christmas visit on the following Thursday, making her time in London exactly one month. Their children, who had been left in a neighbour's care during their previous visit for Mary's wedding, descended on the household in force, and the afternoon passed quickly until they could be consigned to the nursery the next day when the hired governess was to arrive. Jane was, by all appearances, perfectly composed and happy; but her aunt sat next to Elizabeth at their family dinner that evening, and told her in a low tone, masked by the surrounding merriment, that Jane still struggled to stay cheerful. She was confident that in time her niece would fully recover from her attachment to Mr. Bingley, perhaps eventually being able to approach the whole affair as calmly as Elizabeth was treating Wickham's desertion.

"What do you think of Miss King?" Mrs. Gardiner asked, toying with her soup. "I should be sorry to think our friend mercenary."

"Last month you were warning me away from him, because he might like me despite my relative poverty, but now that he likes another with some money, you disapprove."

Mrs. Gardiner had to spend a few moments then correcting the behaviour of her sons, who were more focused on getting under the table with the dog than on eating. While she was thus engaged, Elizabeth helped herself to a ragout of celery and some herb pudding. Women were supposed to wait to be served by the men at the table, but those old rules, like so many, seemed to be slipping away. Finally, the disturbance having been solved by lifting the boys into their parents' laps, Mrs. Gardiner said to Elizabeth, "If I knew about Miss King, I would know if it were plausible that he could really love her."

Elizabeth laughed a little. "She is extraordinarily intelligent, and has a good sense of humour in company." She had to pause then, because Careful had put his chin on her knees. She rubbed his silky fur and the insides of his ears, and then turned back to her aunt, shoving the dog's head back under the table. "She is a great friend of Charlotte Lucas's, which means that I must defend her, and though I do not know her very well, I know her well enough to be sure that she would not be fooled by a mere mercenary." *And* that she was unlikely to actually marry Wickham, but that was Charlotte's secret to tell.

Mrs. Gardiner sighed and finished her soup, feeding half of it to her son, who was indignant at not being allowed to feed himself. "But he showed no interest in her until she received her inheritance? Ben, stop that, for goodness' sake."

"Not in the least, but if he should not have pursued me, because of our mutual lack of fortune, why should he have pursued anybody else equally poor?"

"Just hold still for mummy. If he did not have any use for her before, it simply seems questionable at best, Lizzy."

Elizabeth slipped Careful a sliver of carrot, which he nosed sadly two or three times before consenting to eat. He settled between her feet and leaned his head against one leg, and she put a hand down to scratch his head. "Have it as you choose. *He* shall be mercenary, and *she* shall be foolish."

§

With the sprigs of pine and holly and the wreaths of bamboo and flowers that Lydia and Kitty put up everywhere, and the paper garlands that Jane had the little Gardiners make, the house looked like a perpetual party. The weeks fell quickly away, full of signal-work and gardening, cleaning the house from top to bottom, weaving garlands and decorating the house, baking, and visiting their neighbours. Before long the house was permeated with the scents of sugared almonds and brandied cakes and the honey smell of the beeswax candles Mr. Harrington had sold them.

Christmas came, full of music and baking and eating. Wickham, Haggerston, and Denny joined the family party for part of the day. Mrs. Gardiner taught her nieces all the latest ways of dressing their hair and helped them to modernize a few of their dresses in the London fashion. Lydia and Kitty disappeared the next day for hours and came back excited to report that they had gone packet-dodging, and that Lizzy and Jane weren't to tell their parents, on any account, and an argument about the dangerous practice spanned three entire days. Charlotte and Mary King and Elizabeth snuck out to the Harringtons for an illicit dance on New Years' Eve, where Miss King only danced in groups of other girls, telling Walter Harrington that it was because Mr. Wickham had not been invited. Upon their return, this time, Elizabeth was not caught by her father, and she returned the favour by asking no questions about her parents' and the Gardiners' obvious headaches from excessive wine.

And then suddenly it was January. Before they left, her aunt and uncle asked Elizabeth if she would like to join them on a pleasure tour later in the year.

"We have not decided exactly where we shall go," said Mr. Gardiner. "Perhaps to the Arkwright superstructure, or that of Saye and Sele."

"I should love to see the vast water reservoirs of the one, or the aviaries of the other," Elizabeth said. "In fact, I would be delighted no matter where we went."

The next two months were spent in work and study, and study and work, varying little beyond the monthly Meryton assembly, at which Elizabeth did not even have much pleasure in dancing, most of the engineers having melted away to other projects, and Wickham absorbed in his courtship of Miss King.

They found themselves working together again in the communal kitchen on the first of March, this time washing dishes. There was a strong smell of tea, with the omnipresent undertone of some astringent cleanser. Elizabeth had arrived first, and when she saw him heading for her station, she smiled.

"I am here to interrupt your solitary work," Wickham said, taking his place beside her at the sink.

"Whatever shall I do," she said with an arch look and mock distress.

Mrs. Clark, one of the older ladies who always seemed to be there when Elizabeth was, brought them both cups of tea without asking, and Elizabeth took a polite and scalding sip and then set hers to one side to cool. She plunged her hands back into the lukewarm water to bring up a pot that had been set to soak, and began to scrub at it.

"Thank goodness for that," he said. "Now that I am courting Miss King, I feared our friendship would suffer."

"Never," Elizabeth said with a smile.

"As though a rose could ever shut, and be a bud again," he said, misquoting Keats. He sipped his tea, leaning against the counter, angled toward her in a confidential pose.

She could feel the warmth of his body just inches from her own.

Remembering Mrs. Gardiner's warnings, Elizabeth shifted her weight to lean a little further away from him, and said, "It is a wonderful thing to find a companion who aligns with one's needs."

He looked a little uncertain at this, but only replied, "You and I shall always be good friends, I am sure."

She nodded, smiled, and scrubbed a second pot.

"I ran into Miss Lydia Bennet last week, and she mentioned that you were going to visit your sister in Lambton."

"Complained that she was not going as well, no doubt," Elizabeth said.

He laughed and sipped more tea.

She finished with the pot, and moved on to a third. "She would complain just as much if she were to go. The half-day in London there and back, at our uncle's, would be the highlight of the trip for her. We shall spend most of our time in the Parsonage, I would imagine, which is not exactly Lydia's idea of fun."

"Will you visit Rosings while you are there?"

"If Mr. Collins has anything to say about it." She laughed.

He was finishing his tea, and as soon as he set down the cup she handed him the washcloth and picked up her own cup. He rubbed the rag over a casserole dish crusted with cheese and said, "I will be curious to hear if Lady Catherine de Bourgh improves upon further acquaintance."

He was having trouble with the lumps of cheese baked onto the dish, and she put down her tea and said, "Let me," taking the dish from him and sliding her thumbnail under the crust to get it off. "Yes, I will report back if she does. Mr. Collins is so overawed by her, I half expect an actual dragon."

He laughed again, and swished a little soap into their teacups to clean them. Elizabeth threw the sodden casserole crusts into the garbage and turned the conversation to his work, and spent a happy hour listening to his anecdotes about Denny and Haggerston's antics as the men prepared the pieces for the next build. When they had finished the dishes—or when she had, for Wickham was both slow and inept at the job (*to be fair,* she thought, *it* is *beneath him both as an engineer and as a gentleman*)—she carefully cleaned her nails before heading home, humming to herself, convinced that he was the most amiable man of her acquaintance.

§

Two days before the March assembly found Elizabeth on her way to Hunsford with Maria Lucas (who was Mary's particular friend) and Maria's maid, who was introduced to Elizabeth only as Sara, no surname. She was sad to leave Jane, who promised to write faithfully, and her father, who did not, but the prospect of going anywhere at all was very welcome, even if she ended up having to spend most of her time listening to Mary read extracts from pious books.

The trip took them out of the airlock from the Meryton dome to the long dark corridor between Headfort and London, where they were to stop for a lunch with Mrs. Gardiner, and then along the corridor from London to Castlereagh. Elizabeth had never liked the trip to London: the corridor was only wide enough for perhaps three coaches to ride abreast, and was not heated; they had to wear their heaviest coats and carry rebreathers in case anything should happen while they were en route, since the corridors had only one layer of dome to protect their air in case of a rupture, and they were not rich enough for the specially-reinforced carriages. She had heard talk of the ship's engineers building steam-powered trains to travel from one superstructure to the next, so that the journey she was about to take would be completed in hours rather than days, but it hadn't happened yet, and her father always argued that it was absurd to spend so many resources on luxury travel when what really required improvements was the system for moving raw materials from one superstructure to another.

They passed through the bruised shadows of the corridor. Their breath rose in little white puffs, and Elizabeth sank her hands gratefully into the fur muffler that her mother had loaned her. The carriage began to slow, and the driver had to get down and crank it back up again, shivering.

The corridor side of the airlock was neat as a pin, but they passed through it into London's comparative chaos: the calls of women selling fried foods in paper cups stacked in baskets hung over their arms, the brawl spilling into the street from a nearby pub, the jingle-jangle of various conveyances passing over the broad metal street. Garbage was scattered in the road, and somebody had painted a luridly coloured advertisement for a new type of men's razor on the gray blank side of a warehouse, over which somebody else had roughly painted several short words, of which Elizabeth was sure she didn't want to know the meaning.

Lunch was neat little vegetable pies and biscuits at a small restaurant Mrs. Gardiner knew of near the corridor's 'lock, and then they were on their way through London to reach the corridor to Castlereagh. To one side of the restaurant, chickens scratched the hay scattered on the floor of a small coop. Women in patchwork clothes carried tubs of laundry. The glass-blowing and metal-work buildings radiated enough light to see carts and carriages and crisscrossing lines sagging under the weight of gray washing. Pedestrians stepped into the roadway without looking. They turned a corner onto a long straight throughway lined with black wrought-iron fencing, and then they were passing through the Castlereagh-side airlock.

In the corridor to Castlereagh, the lamps' fulsome yellow light glittered on a fog of dust motes. Elizabeth was officially farther from home than she had ever been. She assumed the jittery feeling in her stomach was excitement, but after a few hours of monotony it resolved to nausea. Castlereagh crept closer. She nodded off, and when she awoke they were still in the corridor, Maria Lucas swaying against her, fast asleep, and her maid in the opposite seat looking steadfastly out the window at the darkness of the aether, separated from them only by the corridor's glass exterior and the carriage itself. Sara could have been thinking anything, but her manner did not invite questions or intimacy, and Elizabeth turned to look out herself. Another half-hour passed, and the driver bellowed down to them, and then they were through the 'lock to the Castlereagh superstructure.

Castlereagh looked largely similar to Headfort, to Elizabeth's irrational disappointment: tidy and clean and, after London, seemingly barren. They passed through the small market-town of Oneoak, which consisted of one attractive street surrounded by ten ugly ones, a handful of shops, and the titular oak tree drooping in a huge container in the center of an open-air market. Oneoak existed primarily to service travelers like themselves. Finally they reached the slightly larger Hunsford, and then traveled its length to get to the Hunsford Parsonage. As they got close, another dome could be seen through the glass of Hunsford's, which must be Rosings.

Finally, they reached the laurel hedge in a planter crafted from an old horse trough and painted a gunmetal gray, cornered by orange trees in rust-coloured terracotta pots, as described in Mary's letters.

"This must be it," Elizabeth said.

They were met at the gate by Mr. and Mrs. Collins. Elizabeth climbed stiffly down from the carriage and wished it were ladylike to stretch. Mary hugged Elizabeth hard and Maria harder, all smiles. Maria and Mary went ahead, chattering, and Elizabeth was left to walk up the gravel drive with Mr. Collins, who inquired minutely after her parents and sisters even though her mother had written Mary every week since the marriage. The driver and maid followed with their luggage despite Elizabeth's protests that she could carry her own valise.

They had some tea in the parlour, and related the details of their journey, and admired the handsome furniture in the room. The house was neat and tidy, and though they did not have a servant, Mary mentioned a Mrs. Hill, who lived in Hunsford and was paid by the church to help her with meals and cleaning the kitchen, three days per week. Mary was very satisfied with the arrangement, which met the requirements of her upbringing while appeasing the pretensions of her husband.

They had scarcely each drunk a sip of their cups of tea, when Mr. Collins insisted they join him in the garden, his particular project. It consisted of a series of containers arranged in wide spirals to give a geometric effect, inside the bounds of the long horse troughs he had arranged to mark the edges of the property, since the Parsonage had no dome but merely existed within the larger Hunsford dome. He spoke of his arrangements with the gardener at Rosings, who allowed him to bring those items with blossoms to their little dome for the use of their bees, although the hive already had the many flower varieties of Rosings to choose from and did not need what he termed his poor offerings, transparently fishing for a compliment, which Elizabeth immediately provided. Mary smiled her thanks behind his back. The garden led to an airlock through which they could see the dome of Rosings. Mr. Collins mentioned that Elizabeth would have the pleasure of seeing Lady Catherine in church that Sunday. "Her Ladyship will include our guests in any invitation to us. She has been nothing but kind condescension to my dear Mary and I fully expect that she will extend that courtesy to you both. She often invites us to dine or play cards, and insists upon providing a carriage to bring us back to the Parsonage."

Finally, Maria Lucas confessed herself fatigued by the trip, and they all returned to the house.

Around noon the next day, as Elizabeth prepared to go for a walk to see Hunsford, she heard voices calling below and glanced out her room's window to see two ladies, one old and one young, sitting in a low phaeton at the garden gate talking to Mr. Collins and Mary. She met Maria on the landing, who said, "Eliza, come downstairs and see! No, I will not tell you who they are! Come down."

"But it is only Lady Catherine de Bourgh and her daughter," Elizabeth said, following her down the stairs.

"Oh, no," Maria said, "that is Miss de Bourgh, but the elder lady is Mrs. Jenkinson, her companion."

They reached the dining room, whose windows looked out over the container garden in front of the house. The elder of the pair was speaking through the window of the phaeton, while the younger looked on mutely with every evidence of boredom.

Miss de Bourgh was dressed in bright colours that emphasized rather than distracted from her sickly complexion, with white flowers set against her mouse-brown hair, and her mouth had a satirical turn that made Elizabeth think she felt ready to consider herself superior to anybody who might cross her path.

"She is almost birdlike," Maria said. "So tiny."

Mr. Darcy's future was revealed in a flash to Elizabeth: he would marry Miss de Bourgh, and they would live at Pemberley, and she would bear him two sickly children, the heir and the spare. Miss Georgiana would join them from time to time to demonstrate her accomplishments and play with the clockwork pets that he would no longer make her, being so busy with his wife, until she could be married off herself. Mrs. Darcy would have two cats, thin and white, whom she would dote on, in stark contrast to her parenting, which would be outsourced to a succession of nannies. Mr. and Mrs. Darcy would retreat into their wealthy and entitled life, and Elizabeth would never see him again, which was just as it should be.

Finally, Mrs. Jenkinson ran out of things to say to Mary and her husband, and drove on.

"Congratulations," Mr. Collins said to Elizabeth and Maria as he swept into the house. "You are most fortunate. Yes, I really have no hesitation in saying that you are very fortunate girls indeed."

Elizabeth raised her eyebrows, and Maria exclaimed, but instead of specifying what had happened, Mr. Collins walked away into his office.

"We have been invited to Rosings tomorrow," Mary explained.

CHAPTER EIGHT

THE AIRLOCK TO ROSINGS WAS A SHORT WALK further along the lane that had brought them to the Parsonage the day before, and they cycled through a good fifteen minutes before the invitation had specified, Mr. Collins having been quite anxious that they not be late. (Lady Catherine objected to being kept waiting, especially by anybody who ranked lower than she, which Elizabeth supposed comprised everybody on the ship.) He had warned them at breakfast and again several times before they dressed, until Maria Lucas was quite agitated, that the consequences of the lady's displeasure were sure to be dire, without actually appearing to know what those consequences entailed, since he would not himself have ever dreamed of inviting them.

"Hurry, hurry," Mr. Collins said as they grew close to the Rosings airlock.

A servant who had been waiting at the 'lock led them up the lane. In front of them was the grand stone house, with the tops of beech trees peeking over the roof. To their right were a series of containers filled with low citrus trees and herbs, no doubt for the de Bourghs' enjoyment.

To their left, to Elizabeth's delight, was a large park, most likely taking up half the dome; the expense must have been enormous, but the first families had had earth and trees transferred from their estates to the ship before launch, Elizabeth had read. How extraordinary to see it now for herself: only a low stone wall to hold in the dirt perpendicular to the lane; no pots under the trees and no glass to hold in the air, aside from the dome itself. The entire place smelled like a greenhouse, with their distinctive, slightly fizzy, green scent. As she walked, she also occasionally caught a smell like cloves, which she was sure was attributable to one of the flower beds they passed.

At intervals along the lane to Rosings were glass spheres on waist-high pedestals filled with greenery and a variety of flowers in various shades of purple. Clockwork swallows in gleaming copper swooped on a track around the spheres. Mr. Collins called Elizabeth back when she approached one, warning her again of the necessity of being on time.

"You must not worry yourself over how grand everything is at Rosings," Mr. Collins finished at last. "Lady Catherine will not hold your inferiority against you."

Even Mary, who had visited several times before, looked a little awed at this long speech.

The servant, looking down their nose, passed them off to two more in the entrance hall, who led them to the grand room where her Ladyship sat with two men, one old and the other ancient. The trio sat on one sofa facing another on which sat Miss de Bourgh and Mrs. Jenkinson.

Lady Catherine and the old man rose to receive them. Behind her Ladyship, a large gaunt dog with grey fur and white around his muzzle slowly rose up to look at them. He was a breed Elizabeth did not know, and Mary whispered that it was called a wolfhound. He was shaggy and moved stiffly with age, but had a certain improbable canine dignity.

Mary had arranged with her husband in advance that she would introduce her sister and friend, and did so. It transpired in turn that the men were both named Davies, one being the father of the other.

"I apologize for failing to rise," said the older of the men. "I can't stand very much nowadays."

He had been an Admiral, his son had been a Brigadier, and they were both long retired. The Brigadier was fashionably, if sedately, dressed in civilian clothes, while the father wore threadbare uniform pants and a form-fitting waistcoat and jacket that must have gone out of fashion in his youth.

Lady Catherine and Miss De Bourgh could hardly have been any less alike: where the mother was tall and sturdy, with a striking face which must have once been beautiful, and an authoritative self-importance, the daughter was sallow and ailing, with unremarkable features and no conversation, except that whispered to Mrs. Jenkinson, whose only concern was to cater to her needs. Querulous and impatient, her Ladyship dominated the conversation and its participants, and it became clear that for her entire life, every little thing that she had desired had appeared the instant she expressed a wish for it; the only difficulties that had not been made smooth for her by her rank and fortune were the death of her husband and the ill health of her daughter.

When her Ladyship was seated again, the dog left her to come up to them and sniff at their boots. They all sat in turn: Maria on the edge of her seat as though she might flee at any time, Mary and Mr. Collins with slightly more self-possession, and Elizabeth completely distracted by the dog, who leaned heavily against her leg. She petted it, and after a moment it yawned and laid down across her feet.

She looked around with lively interest at the rich furnishings and artwork. The room contained an elegant, navy-and-gold chinoiserie rug which covered much of the floor, over which had been placed a rosewood sofa, a Chippendale sofa, a grouping of four mahogany elbow chairs and a low kidney table with candles at either end, a circular table with a white urn, presumably Sir Lewis's, and a navy satin-backed settee that appeared to be more for the display of its bright, detailed embroidery than for regular use. Against one wall ran a marble slab side board and a separate breakfast table, bookended by two Pembroke tables with their leaves dropped and decorated with flower-filled chinoiserie vases, and behind them all a long mirror, spotted with age. Space had been left, somehow, for card tables at one end of the room, and at the other end a pianoforte and a harp were arranged as if in conversation with one another. No normal family had been permitted to bring so many heavy items with them: almost all of the furniture at the Bennet's house had been manufactured on board the ship. The contrast made for a room that probably felt, she thought, a bit like being on Earth must have felt. The house had so much to admire that Elizabeth was able to ignore quite a bit of Mr. Collins's fawning conversation until they were finally led in to dinner, all but the wolfhound who was taken in a different direction by a servant.

What a shame, Elizabeth thought, watching him go. *Since the wolfhound is male, he could have helped to balance the numbers at table.*

Lady Catherine sat at the head of the table, with Brigadier Davies and Mary on either side. Elizabeth was seated between the Brigadier and Miss de Bourgh, and Mrs. Jenkinson sat at the foot. Maria Lucas was seated with the Admiral and Mr. Collins on either side. The arrangement put Mr. Collins as far as possible from her Ladyship while still having a gentleman available to serve each woman her meal, which made Elizabeth wonder if Lady Catherine did not enjoy his fawning servility as much as she seemed. Later she decided that her Ladyship merely liked having the Brigadier at her side.

The first course was the inevitable calf's head soup, as well as consommé, a whole sturgeon, a leg of mutton boiled with capers, calf's heart, jugged hare, rabbit pâté, and roasted partridge with orange sauce made, Mr. Collins informed them, from the oranges that grew on the property. Such an extravagant array of meats amazed Elizabeth. She glanced at Mary and Maria, whose mouths had dropped open, and remembered to close her own. The Brigadier carved.

"Now, Brigadier," Lady Catherine said as he served the foods closest to them on the table to her Ladyship on his one side and Elizabeth on his other. "I must know if my advice on the proper functioning of your steam cooker has solved the issue."

"Have a little of this soup, my dear," Mrs. Jenkinson whispered to Miss de Bourgh, who consumed two spoonsfuls of consommé.

"Yes, thank you," the Brigadier said. "Would you like some hare, Miss Bennet? I know it is a little rich for some ladies' tastes."

"Thank you very much, Brigadier," Elizabeth said. He added it to her already laden plate.

"Yes, you were exactly right about what the issue was, your Ladyship," the Brigadier said, "and my cook was very grateful."

"Very delightful to sit next to such a handsome young lady," the Admiral could be heard to say into his bowl of calf's head soup, whether to Mary or Maria, who were seated on either side of him, was not clear.

"Have you enough to eat?" Mrs. Jenkinson asked Miss de Bourgh, who nodded.

"Your cook should have known how to fix it herself," her Ladyship said. "Nobody should use a tool they do not fully understand."

"Too right," said the Brigadier.

"Oh, I am so worried that you are indisposed, my dear," Mrs. Jenkinson said to Miss de Bourgh, who shook her head.

"Now, Mary," her Ladyship said. Mary sat a little straighter. "Do you have a steam cooker?"

"I cannot help but worry when you eat so little, you see." Mrs. Jenkinson said to Miss de Bourgh, who placed a sliver of partridge between her lips.

"No, your Ladyship. We cook over the stove."

"Would more orange sauce tempt you?" Mrs. Jenkinson said.

Miss de Bourgh said nothing.

Elizabeth tried to exchange an amused glance with Maria, but she kept her eyes studiously on her plate for the entire meal.

The second course was a couple of roasted ducks, vol-au-vents, green peas, asparagus, stewed cucumber, braised cabbage, plum pudding, and blancmange. For dessert, apples in pastry and various fruit ices.

After dinner, the gentlemen went off for cigars and the ladies went to the drawing room.

Lady Catherine spoke widely and decisively on Mary's domestic arrangements, the organization of her kitchen, the necessity of canning her husband's garden's largesse, and the need for her to begin sewing clothes for her anticipated offspring now; and then quizzed Maria on her accomplishments, the number of her brothers and sisters, the circumstances of her father's knighthood, the quality of her governess, and Lady Lucas's maiden name.

Maria quavered through sufficient answers for Lady Catherine to then turn her attention to Elizabeth. "Mrs. Collins has told me only one of her sisters plays, which I suppose refers to you?"

"Yes, your Ladyship."

"None of you draw either? Mrs. Collins has told me so, and I find it very strange. But she has told me several shocking facts about your upbringing: I hear that all five of you are out at once? Very odd! Although I suppose it has benefited Mr. Collins that your younger sisters did not have to wait for *you* to be married. And no governess, she tells me; is that possible?"

"Yes."

"She was quite unable to account for your mother's decision not to engage one. A governess might have provided a more rigorous education than I gather the five of you have received."

"We learned gardening from our mother, and useful aspects of running a business and a household, which are very similar," Elizabeth said.

Her Ladyship sniffed.

"And our father taught us rudimentary mathematics, and made his large library available to us. The aspects of our education that were neglected were not such that a governess could have corrected."

"To what could you possibly be referring?"

"Mathematics and physics," Elizabeth said. "Engineering. Um, biology."

"Pshaw," Lady Catherine said. "Women do not need to learn such things."

"I think we do, Lady Catherine, at least now that we are aboard ship. Perhaps it was different on Earth, but here we need every person to give their utmost, female as well as male, to figure out the planning and keep everything running. If I cannot carry heavy timber and do heavy labor, at least I can free up a man for that labor by doing the heavy intellectual lifting. Women have as good a right to the pleasures of the mind as men. To be kept back only out of tradition would not be very likely to promote the survival of our species."

Lady Catherine stiffened at Elizabeth's answer. Mary compressed her mouth as she stifled a smile that still made it to her eyes. Elizabeth wondered how often anybody failed to give a direct answer to her Ladyship's questions.

Since Mr. Collins came in then with the two older gentlemen, what Lady Catherine might have said in reply is lost to history. Servants came in to silently place card tables, and Elizabeth, in thanking them, earned a glare from her Ladyship. Lady Catherine chose quadrille, and ordered Brigadier Davies and the Collinses to sit down with her, leaving Elizabeth to play Vingt-un with Admiral Davies, Maria Lucas, Miss de Bourgh and Mrs. Jenkinson. At her table, Lady Catherine narrated the errors of the others in an overpowering voice.

Elizabeth had the merrier table: Miss de Bourgh limited herself to statements directly related to her cards, as if every syllable shortened her life span, but Admiral Davies so aggressively complimented every lady on her cards and manner of playing that he was impossible to resist, and soon they all, excepting Miss de Bourgh, began to laugh and tease each other in the most harmless way possible. Eventually even Miss de Bourgh condescended to smile.

§

The next day being Sunday, Elizabeth had the honour of hearing her cousin's ponderous sermon and then the pleasure of sitting with her sister in the dining parlour, which looked out onto the lane and Mr. Collins's container garden. For the next fortnight, sitting in the dining parlour was their chief activity: twice per week, they dined at Rosings, and on the remaining nights, Mary and Maria whispered between themselves while Elizabeth continued to study the book

Charlotte had leant her, which she was almost halfway through, thoroughly sick of reading, and determined to finish.

Mr. Collins periodically came in from his garden or his office to share a thought with Mary, or to point out carriages passing the Parsonage. Although they could easily see for themselves, Mary never failed to thank her husband or, when Miss de Bourgh stopped, to speak with their patroness's daughter. Elizabeth observed as well that Mr. Collins seemed particularly anxious that Mary approve of his sermons, bringing her several drafts throughout each week and sitting with her to go over all of his changes.

On their first weekday, Elizabeth proposed a shopping trip in Hunsford, which Maria eagerly agreed to, but which Mary vetoed, saying that she would infinitely prefer a book. Elizabeth did not make that suggestion again, though Maria did prevail upon Mary for one shopping trip a few days later, just, she said, to see something of the town, since she had slept through their travel. Once the outing had been reframed as educational, Mary made no further objections.

Mr. and Mrs. Collins often walked to Rosings, Mr. Collins to provide spiritual guidance and Mrs. Collins to practice the pianoforte. When they did so, Elizabeth went as far as the airlock with them so she could walk through the extraordinary park that made up half of the Rosings dome. She thought the clockwork terrariums on the main path charming and pretty, but fussy, and once she had had her fill of looking at them once, she forever after concentrated on the grounds.

A small stand of beech trees grew at the highest part of the manmade hill close to the back of the house, with the rest of the garden consisting of tulips and azaleas, set in lawns dotted with hawthorn, cherry and mulberry trees and surrounded by ornamental gravel walkways lined with white rocks. The hawthorn trees were covered closely with pink and white flowers and yellow butterflies keenly interested in the blossoms. She followed a different path every day: sometimes winding through the trees, sometimes to the central flowerbed of azaleas with their strong clove scent, and sometimes leading to the back of the house, where the beeches towered overhead and grew brown where their tips almost touched the freezing top of the dome. It was strange to look at the trees and see the house behind them, when she had been so accustomed to trees which knew their proper place, in the cramped corners and spacious middles of greenhouses and aviaries, or as bonsaied miniatures in container gardens. She tried not to spend too long staring: once, Brigadier Davies had walked by an upstairs window inside, and she had had to hide before he saw her. Seeing him in the family area of the house had of course made Elizabeth wonder about the likelihood that Lady Catherine was having an affair with him (or if it were Mrs. Jenkinson!) and she made great sport over the topic in her next letter to Jane.

On their third visit to Rosings, Lady Catherine said, "My nephew is coming to visit, and I dare say that even if we were not related, I would still contend that he is one of the finest gentlemen one could hope to meet."

"Do you mean Mr. Darcy?" Elizabeth said, looking up from petting her Ladyship's wolfhound, who was by now her great friend, despite nobody having formally introduced them.

"Yes," her Ladyship said. "I suppose you met him when Mrs. Collins did, at Meryton?"

"Yes," Elizabeth agreed. *When I see his affection for Miss de Bourgh, I may even feel sorry for Miss Bingley,* she thought.

The day of his arrival, Mr. Collins spent the whole day gardening, no doubt to get a glimpse of the great man. Elizabeth was in the dining parlour, looking out the window instead of at the book in her lap, when Mr. Darcy's carriage went by; she did not see him, but Mr. Collins bowed and hurried inside to confirm the sighting. "I will call on them in the morning," Mr. Collins said, and the next day he made good on his promise. When he returned, Mr. Darcy and another gentleman followed him.

Once inside, Mr. Darcy greeted the ladies and then gestured to the gentleman next to him. "Colonel Fitzwilliam, my cousin," he said.

Colonel Fitzwilliam was perhaps thirty, and, while not handsome, had the easy affability of a gentleman. He and Mr. Collins carried the conversation for some time, until Mr. Darcy, turning to Elizabeth, said, "And how is your family?"

"They are all very well." She smiled gently, keeping her expression innocent as she continued: "My sister Jane was in London until just before Christmas. Did you see her there?" She knew that he had not, but hoped his reaction might give her a hint as to why Mr. Bingley had never called on Jane.

He might have coloured a little (so very little, that she could not be sure) as he said, "I did not," but showed no other symptom of discomfort.

She asked no other questions, though the gentlemen stayed for another half hour of gentle conversation about very little.

§

Mr. and Mrs. Collins stood in the hallway between the dining parlour and Mr. Collins's office, speaking in low voices which nonetheless carried into the room adjacent, where Elizabeth and Maria were waiting in their church clothes for the rest of the household to be ready to go.

"It has been almost a fortnight," Mr. Collins said.

"You are worrying yourself over nothing. Lady Catherine is simply busy with her guests."

For the past twelve days, the usual visits to and from Lady Catherine had been suspended. Mr. Darcy had greeted them at church the previous Sunday, but had not visited them either. Their only visitor had been Colonel Fitzwilliam, who had called on them every second or third day, and seemed happy both for the company of three pleasant young ladies and for the respite from his aunt.

"And why should she not be," he said, "when they are such august gentlemen? And yet, I cannot help but be concerned that we have done something to displease her Ladyship."

Over Mary's answer, Elizabeth called from her seat, "I am certain her Ladyship would let you know if any of us had displeased her, cousin."

"Do you think so?" Mr. Collins said.

Elizabeth smiled at Maria, and Maria smiled shyly back.

"I agree," Mary said, "but she *will* be most displeased if we make her wait for your sermon to start this morning, so we had better get moving."

They departed for church immediately thereafter, and were asked after the service if they were free to visit Rosings that evening. Mr. Collins very nearly stopped fretting.

Once they were ensconced in Lady Catherine's drawing room, her Ladyship was too interested in her conversation with Darcy to pay them the sort of attention she did when her family was not present. The wolfhound seemed to be of a like mind with his owner, and laid alertly across Darcy's feet, his head raised sphinxlike to receive Darcy's attentions. Darcy scratched around his ears and ruff, somehow making the activity look dignified, and called the dog Neptune, which solved one small puzzle for Elizabeth. After a few minutes, Lady Catherine jealously signaled a servant to take the animal away.

Miss de Bourgh sat limply at the other end of her mother's chaise, occasionally nodding at something her Ladyship said and otherwise apparently not listening at all. She looked into the distance with the kind of placidity usually ascribed to lakes. Elizabeth hoped that she had a rich inner life to sustain her, but she supposed that she would never have an opportunity of asking.

Colonel Fitzwilliam seemed delighted at the addition to their usual party; even conversation with Mr. Collins was diverting for him. He finally settled by Elizabeth and entertained her with stories about his adventures as an aethernaut. "My most recent voyage, like most of my voyages, was to a nearby asteroid. It's hard to see from inside the domes, but we are quite close to the asteroid belt. I go with a crew to capture the smaller rocks so we can tow them back to the central hub of the ship, where they are broken apart and any useful metals and water claimed for our use."

"It all sounds terribly dangerous," Elizabeth said.

"Most days are routine," he said. "I have had a few close calls, though."

"Like what?"

"Well." He shifted a little closer to her, his voice dropping confidentially. "A few months ago, I had to go out to rescue another ship that was just hanging in the aether by one of the asteroids, slowly tumbling. The people on board were not replying to our signals—"

"Oh!" Elizabeth interrupted. "Do you use the signal language?"

"Yes," he said. "We blink the electrical lamps on the fronts of our ships. Do you know it?"

"I have learned it for signal work," Elizabeth said. "It is very useful. But what had happened to them?"

"They had maneuvered into the path of the asteroid and been hit by it, and it had damaged parts of the ship. The pilot and crew had been knocked unconscious. After we towed them back, everyone recovered, but if they had been out there for much longer, they might have frozen to death."

"How gruesome," Elizabeth said. "Do you use the difference engine to calculate your trajectories? I know my father depends upon it for his architectural work."

"No, not often," Fitzwilliam said, smiling. "It takes far too long. We do often use it to calculate our plans before leaving, but once I am in the pilot seat, everything happens far too quickly to depend upon such a cumbersome device."

Despite Colonel Fitzwilliam's anecdotes being by far the most interesting she had heard in months, Elizabeth found her attention straying inexorably to Mr. Darcy.

Perhaps it was simply that she had decided ahead of time to keep watch over him to see if he showed any love for Miss de Bourgh whatsoever, so she would know whether or not she could luxuriate in feeling sorry for Miss Bingley, as a sort of revenge for that lady's interference in her sister's life. At no point had she seen him converse with his cousin beyond the barest civilities. Miss de Bourgh seemed equally indifferent. Elizabeth had seen no sign of any particular regard, let alone love.

Perhaps it was the soft smile he gave Neptune, making his bottom lip look soft and vulnerable.

Perhaps it was that every time she looked at him, he seemed to have just looked away from her. She had counted four times that evening when she had nearly caught him staring at her, and she wondered that nobody else seemed to have noticed, and she also wondered if it was only her nerves, stimulating her imagination and making it so difficult to think properly.

She rubbed her arms and forced herself to attend to Colonel Fitzwilliam's story of being knocked off his ship and saved only by a well-placed tether.

When they had finished their tea, Lady Catherine raised her head from where she still spoke with Darcy, and said, "We must hear Miss Bennet play."

Elizabeth allowed herself to be persuaded, seeing that her Ladyship was, as usual, adamant (her Ladyship seemed to have no other mode). Colonel Fitzwilliam pulled up a chair to turn the pages. Lady Catherine spoke to Darcy throughout the first song, until he abruptly stood and paced across the room to stand by the harp, whereupon she condescended to speak with Mr. Collins instead. Elizabeth wished her father could have been there to enjoy the sight of him bowing repeatedly in his chair.

Mr. Darcy put a hand on the harp as if he might lean on it, thought better of it, and paced with his hands behind his back to stand against the wall at one end of the pianoforte. He could see her hands on the keys; perhaps he wished to watch her play. He was too far away for conversation. After a moment he unbent enough to lean against the wall. Elizabeth made an effort to ignore him.

At the end of the song, she thanked Colonel Fitzwilliam for turning the pages. Over his shoulder, Mr. Darcy's reflection showed in the mirror behind the chinoiserie vase, his face rendered unreadable by small constellations of brown dots where the silver had worn away from the mirror.

She played two songs, and then yielded the instrument to her younger sister, who was eager to play.

"An instrumental," Lady Catherine said firmly, by which Elizabeth knew that she had heard Mary sing.

Mary attempted a Mozart piece for which Lady Catherine had the sheet music, and made a creditable effort. Elizabeth looked over at Darcy, despite herself, but he had retreated to that lack of expression that seemed to mean he was at pains not to let anybody guess his true emotions, or else that he was absorbed in his own thoughts. Mary continued playing until it was, thankfully, time for them to return to the Parsonage.

§

The Collinses' home smelled of oranges. Mr. Collins had not grown up with much in the way of fresh produce, and went to some trouble to show his wife, who had, that he could provide for her in this department, by placing an enormous bowl of oranges on the dining parlour's side table, and another in the kitchen, and a third in his office. These came from his container garden, along with many of the herbs Mary used to cook with, and blended with the almond scent of the laurel hedge coming through the front window.

Elizabeth was trying not to drip juice on Charlotte's book while eating one of the oranges (and, indeed, struggling to keep her attention on the book itself) when the doorbell sounded. She rose as Mr. Darcy let himself into the room.

"Oh!" He looked around the room, seeming astonished to find her alone. "I apologize for my intrusion. I had understood Mrs. Collins and Miss Lucas to be within."

"They went for a walk. Mr. Collins is at Rosings."

"Yes, I saw him before I left."

Elizabeth wiped her hands surreptitiously on her skirt and motioned him to sit. When he folded himself into a chair, she sat across from him, and inquired after the health of his aunt and cousins. He assured her they were all well.

"Tea?" she asked.

"I thank you," he said. "I am not thirsty."

They fell silent. The pause lengthened; she had a brief visual of the floor opening up to swallow them both and put them out of their misery. She cast about for something to say, and her eyes fell on a half-finished letter to Jane that she was currently using as a bookmark. "Did you come here from London, when you arrived a fortnight ago?"

"Yes, indeed."

"Was Mr. Bingley still staying with you at that time?"

"He had left a week or so earlier."

"He is well?"

"Yes."

"And Miss Bingley and Mrs. Hurst?"

"Both are well."

After another short pause, she said, "Will he return to Netherfield?"

"I do not know."

She nodded, and thought that she had better not say anything further on the topic.

After a moment, he said, "The Parsonage seems much improved since Mr. Collins came. I believe my aunt provided some advice to him."

"He often comments on her kindness."

He smiled briefly. "He appears very happy with your sister."

"Yes," Elizabeth said. "And she with him."

"It must be a relief to have her settled so close."

"I would not say she is close."

"Anything beyond your own superstructure, I suppose, would appear far." He smiled a little, superiorly or teasingly Elizabeth could not discern.

She felt her face heat. "We do not have your family's fortune. The expense of travelling does not allow of frequent journeys."

He made a sound of vague agreement or acknowledgement; they fell silent again. This silence felt more dire than the previous ones. Elizabeth blurted out, to fill the silence, "I have been thinking about parks."

"Oh?" he smiled a little.

She had been turning over the idea in her mind for days: "Your aunt has this large expanse of land that she does not use, except for show—"

"You think she should open it to the public?" His face still displayed the little smile, as though he had forgotten to sneer.

"It would be a wonderful gesture," she said, "but I was really thinking, why should the public have to wait on the generosity of the rich? We could have public parks. We have space enough. On Earth—"

"But on Earth, parks were basically free," Mr. Darcy cut her off. "Pemberley has its own park area, and it is a considerable expense. To take that kind of expense from the public purse would cut into the budget for items we need for survival."

"Oh," Elizabeth said. She could not argue with that. "I see."

Mr. Darcy leaned towards her. "*You* cannot mean to throw yourself away. *You* cannot really wish to go to Babbage."

Elizabeth opened her mouth to reply and found that she had no idea what to say. At her silence, he lost his sudden intensity. He sat back in his chair, and ran one hand through his hair, and, picking up one of Mr. Collins's books, glanced through it before putting it down again. Finally he said, in a calmer tone, "And you are enjoying your travels?"

They spoke briefly on the subject of her visit, before Mary and Maria came home. Mr. Darcy rose, and greetings were exchanged. and Darcy said, "I thought you and Miss Lucas were at home, Mrs. Collins."

Mary smiled at him. "Well, we are home now." With a quick glance of reproach at Elizabeth, she added, "Would you like any refreshments? We have some excellent orange juice from my husband's garden, and Hill has made some very nice cake."

"I thank you, but I am not hungry."

"How is everyone at Rosings?"

"Very well."

He stood another moment, and then said, "I am very glad to have seen you all. Please give my regards to your husband, Mrs. Collins," and showed himself out.

Mary raised her eyebrows as soon as Mr. Darcy was gone. "You should have called for Sara to join you, Eliza. A woman must guard her virtue—"

"But is he in love with you?" Maria Lucas said over her, with a very Charlotte-like air of getting straight to the point. "Why else would he have stayed?"

Moralizing from Mary she could take, but being teased by Maria Lucas over Mr. Darcy, of all people, was not to be borne. Elizabeth said, "He was silent nearly the whole time he was here. If he was trying to woo me, he did it very ill, and you know that Lady Catherine has stated it as a rule that Mr. Darcy does not do anything badly."

Easter came and went. Mr. Darcy began to visit every day, sometimes with his cousin and sometimes alone, and once with her Ladyship. He was often silent and occasionally taciturn, while Colonel Fitzwilliam was uniformly friendly and funny. Once, he teased Darcy for his silence, by which Elizabeth understood he was acting differently than he normally did, but nobody knew why. Mary thought Darcy was in love with Elizabeth, and searched her books for extracts with which to advise her sister. Maria Lucas thought it would be terribly romantic if it were true, but couldn't agree with Mary, given how often he just sat there. A man in love should show more energy, she said. Elizabeth only laughed at the idea.

Worse, she often ran into him when she walked through the Rosings park. He always felt it necessary to walk with her. They didn't talk much (he was silent apparently by nature, and she refused to take the trouble of carrying along a one-sided conversation) but on their third walk together, he stirred himself to ask her how she fared, and how her family fared. They had the usual conversation these questions elicited.

Finally he said, "It must be agreeable to you to be so long with your sister," and when she absently replied in the affirmative, he continued, "Next time, when you are at Rosings, is there any particular place you would wish to visit?"

Elizabeth held her breath a moment. He seemed to think she would be staying at Rosings when she returned. Could he believe that Colonel Fitzwilliam was going to propose, or perhaps even had already done so? Perhaps he had only misspoken, or she had misheard.

"This is my turn," she said instead of answering, and they were silent the rest of the way to the 'lock. His reflection in the glass of Rosings dome looked at her with shadowed eyes.

CHAPTER NINE

THE WEDNESDAY BEFORE MR. DARCY and his cousin were due to leave Rosings, Lady Catherine informed them that they were to help her with her monthly charitable outing the next day. "I started the tradition shortly after the ship left Earth," she said. "We will bring the men dinner."

She did not see fit to explain who the men were, but Mr. and Mrs. Collins seemed to know. He said, "Oh yes, I suppose it *is* the fourth Thursday tomorrow. How I look forward to this day every month. You are so good, your Ladyship, to be so generous to the townsfolk."

The next morning, they met Lady Catherine, Mrs. Jenkinson, Mr. Darcy, Colonel Fitzwilliam and a handful of servants by the endlessly looping metal sparrows in the Rosings drive. Miss de Bourgh was, Mary whispered to Elizabeth and Maria, far too ill to come on these outings. The servants handed out baskets to everybody but Lady Catherine, which proved to contain lunches done up in packages.

"Are we not taking a carriage?" Maria asked Mary in surprise when they began to walk.

Lady Catherine, overhearing, said, "No, I always walk."

"It only goes to show your excellent condescension." Mr. Collins said, "In meeting the men on, as it were, the same level, you are making the physical reflect the metaphorical."

Maria looked confused. "I thought we were giving them sandwiches," she whispered to Mary. "What does he mean?"

They passed through the airlock into the lane. Colonel Fitzwilliam came up to Elizabeth, and she ignored the whispered conversation to ask him, "Do you still leave on Saturday?"

"Yes. I must get back to work. Asteroids do not tow themselves."

Elizabeth smiled. "I suppose I assumed that you could take whatever time off you wanted, being the son of an earl."

"Second son," he said. "Younger sons must work for a living."

"Ah," she said. "Then it was very good of you to take the time off to see your aunt."

"She does not think so," he said. "She is annoyed with me for leaving so soon, but I must save some of my time to see my cousin."

Elizabeth thought he meant Mr. Darcy for a moment, and then realized. "Miss Georgiana?"

"Yes. She is living in London these days. I am one of her guardians, and make two annual visits to see how she gets on."

"I have heard more about her from Miss Caroline Bingley than from Mr. Darcy. Perhaps you know her?"

They had sorted themselves into groups of two walking abreast: Mr. Darcy alongside Lady Catherine in the front, followed by Mr. Collins and Mrs. Jenkinson, and then Mary with Maria. Colonel Fitzwilliam and Elizabeth took up the rear, and he allowed the others to outpace them a little now.

He said, "Oh, yes," with a slight air of disapproval, from which Elizabeth guessed he did not like Miss Bingley very much either. "And her sister and brother. They are often with Darcy."

"I am not surprised. Mr. Darcy is practically a guardian to Mr. Bingley."

"How funny you should put it that way, because I think he really *does* take care of him in some respects. On our trip here from Pemberley, Darcy made a few comments that led me to believe he had saved Bingley from an imprudent marriage."

The gas lamps overhead hissed.

"Imprudent in what way?"

"Oh, he had some objections to the family, I gather. Darcy is not always very forthcoming, you may have noticed."

His objections must have been her having a mother and uncle who were in business, and another uncle who was a clerk. And that nobody could be good enough for Mr. Bingley compared to his sister, whom he hoped to unite with his friend.

She looked ahead at the pairs of walkers, and wished she could just sling the basket of sandwiches and snacks into the road, and march ahead to Mr. Darcy, and perhaps sling *him* into the road as well. She had imagined Mr. Darcy as a supporting character in Miss Bingley's machinations. Mr. Bingley's sister would merely have had to hide Jane's presence in town and prey on his insecurities as only a sibling could do. But now she knew that Mr. Darcy had been a more active participant in Jane's heartbreak than she had suspected.

For the sake of Mary's prospects here, with Darcy's aunt such an integral part of her husband's success as a parson, she would have to swallow what she knew. She could not make the scene she so dearly wished to. She would have to smile and be polite to the man for the next two days. Somehow.

"We are falling behind the others," Elizabeth said, walking ahead.

Soon they reached the workplace where Lady Catherine intended to dispense her beneficence. Colonel Fitzwilliam had told Elizabeth a few more anecdotes of his adventures in the aether, which had helped to divert her. Her turbulence of spirit no longer showed by so much as a tremble of her hand.

The men whom her Ladyship was feeding this month were fixing something very high overhead outside the Hunsford dome. They met halfway: her Ladyship's group put on their aether suits and rode the elevator to the Castlereagh cupola at the top of the larger Castlereagh dome within which Hunsford and Rosings and Oneoak were all nestled, and the men met them there after crawling across the scaffolding allowing them to make their repairs to the underside of the Castlereagh ceiling to come in through a side 'lock.

(Elizabeth was surprised to see the cupola's extra airlock; she was quite sure that Headfort did not have one like it.) The men cycled through the 'lock two or three at a time.

It was a tight fit with the eight of them and their baskets plus perhaps twenty workers. The workers ducked their heads to Elizabeth as she passed out the contents of her basket: sandwiches, bundles of matchstick-cut carrots and cucumbers, and cool drinks in glass bottles sealed with wax. They looked at her with smiles of faint resentment, like she was a Darcy or de Bourgh, and she found it strangely embarrassing.

"Are you putting new sheets of metal over a hole?" she asked one of them. "That's what it looks like from here, but it's an awkward angle."

"Yes," he said. He was a stout, bearded fellow of middle age and middle height. "We got hit by something small, so we're just patching it up."

"Did it go through anything else?" she said. "Was anybody hurt?"

"Not that I know of," he said, answering her second question first. "It only went through the outer dome, so we'll just have the aerators going overtime once we've finished the patching, that's all."

She looked out at the area where they were working and saw in their faint reflections that Darcy was watching her, or at least that his eyes were turned in her direction. She turned to look at him challenging, raising her chin, and instead of looking away, he paced over to them.

"Mr. Darcy," the worker said, subdued again, as though the gentleman's glance had been a reprimand.

It irritated Elizabeth, but she still remembered that she should not make a scene, for Mary's sake, so she merely turned her back on Darcy.

"Do you like the work?" she asked the worker. "I always found soldering rather nerve-wracking."

"You really know how to solder?" he said, and when she smiled her assent, he turned to the man next to him and said, "Liam, this one knows how to solder."

"Get out of here, McCormick."

"It is true," Elizabeth said. "I have only gone out once, but Headfort requires everybody to learn every skill."

"Smart," another man said. They chatted a moment longer, and then the men were done their sandwiches and everybody began to pack up. Elizabeth turned away from Mr. Darcy and fussed with repacking her basket with the leftover paper from the sandwich packets the men had left, so that she need not meet his gaze.

"You handled them very well," he said after a pause.

She gave him a look. "They did not require *handling*."

"They were very familiar with you."

Elizabeth looked around for help or a distraction. Mr. Collins was just leading Colonel Fitzwilliam on to the elevator to leave, deep in conversation. Lady Catherine and Mary had already left, and Maria and Mrs. Jenkinson were too far away to be any help.

"I suppose you think I acted inappropriately by speaking with them?" she said.

"Not at all," he said. "I was surprised by how well you handled—how well you treated them. You might have been her Ladyship's nearest relative, instead of. . . that is. . . you seem born for the role."

She frowned, even as she knew that he thought he was paying her a compliment. "Thank you, I think."

"It has given me an image of you playing that role at Pemberly."

She stared at him, astonished, and then as the intense quiet all around them sank into her consciousness, she became aware that Maria and Mrs. Jenkinson had left. The signal room had been cleared for her Ladyship's party, and the signalers might come back at any moment, but in the meantime, they were alone.

"What do you mean?" she said.

He folded into a chair, and then unfolded again to pace the room. She watched him. He walked across to a table and then back toward the elevator and then, turning, came toward her in a rush.

"In vain have I struggled. It will not do. My feelings will not be repressed. You must allow me to tell you how ardently I admire and love you."

Elizabeth startled. She leaned away from Darcy abruptly. She felt her cheeks heat, and thought, *I cannot have heard him correctly,* but then he took her hands, and she was so astonished that she did not withdraw them as she should have.

"I have been in an agony these past eight months. . . When you were injured at Netherfield, I. . . you have to have seen how I admired you. You must become my wife."

Elizabeth took a breath to say something, but she knew not what. His eyes now held a fraction of that same helpless appeal they had had when the doctor had taken over bandaging her arm and he had no longer been needed, and she thought, *I could love him for that hesitancy.* Then she remembered Jane and Wickham. Still, she was trying to think how to reject him in a way most calculated to spare his feelings, but then he did not stop there.

"Despite the inferiority of your connections," he said, "despite the familial obstacles which will face us. . . my aunt will never receive you as Mrs. Darcy. . . I will lose friends over this. I may become the laughing-stock of all of London for all that I care. In spite of everything that should keep us apart, I love you."

Elizabeth became aware of their positions, seeing them as a third person would: the man with his dark hair and eyes, his impeccable clothes, the woman pale, her chestnut hair still mussed from sleep, her skirt stained with juice, her hands limp in his, the man drawing closer, his lips and cheeks reddening, his eyes never leaving her face, their breathing intertwining.

"Mr. Darcy," she said.

He said, "Your wild ideas about engineering, no doubt put into your head by your mother, you will have to let go."

Diverted, she said, "You disapprove of women going to university?"

"Not at all," he said. "But Pemberley needs a mistress, and you are already well-suited to that task. Pemberley will be your chief concern. It is a life-absorbing task to care for it. You will soon forget those dreams in favour of better ones."

"Mr. Darcy," she started again.

"I am convinced that we can be happy together, indeed, that I cannot be happy with any other woman. I have found that I cannot conquer my attachment to you, and I hope you will reward me by accepting my hand in marriage."

Elizabeth stepped back from the small sphere of their exhaled breaths and slipped her hands from his. His voice had ended on a note of triumph: he really believed she would be grateful to improve her station, as the older generation put it, by marrying him; indeed, he had no real doubt as to her answer. She could feel her face burning and frown lines forming.

"Do you remember," she said slowly, "I asked you some time ago if you had been aware that my sister was in London? But I know that you *were* aware and that you kept them apart."

His exultant smile began the process of disappearing.

"I know that you lied to me. I know that you separated my sister and Mr. Bingley, to her great grief, and she has hardly been happy since." Her chest hurt, and she took a deep breath before going on. "How could I accept such a man?"

His expression closed into a blank courtesy colder than anger. He just looked at her.

"And if that were not enough, how could I accept a man who would be the means of ruining a young man's dreams only because you were jealous that your father loved him better?"

At this, his nostrils flared. "I treated Mr. Wickham better than he deserved."

"Because he was the steward's son? As I am only an architect's daughter? As my family is inferior?"

His mouth opened, but her words were swept along by her anger, and she overrode anything he might have had to say for himself.

"You are very sure of your place in society, but I do not think much of *gentlemen* who have to put everybody else down to raise themselves up!"

He reared back as though slapped. They regarded one another in some astonishment, both of them panting a little with rage and some other emotion.

The elevator doors opened, and the Castlereagh cupola's signalers stepped out looking uncertain as to why Elizabeth and Darcy were still there, keeping them from their duties.

After a moment Darcy spoke. "The others will be wondering where we have gone," he said in a tone somehow both calm and violent. "I am sorry to have wasted so much of your time."

At least, Elizabeth thought darkly, *if any rumours arise about the two of us having been alone together for so long, nobody will suspect my virtue, with witnesses to those bitter parting words.*

They stood in the elevator together silently for the agonizing minutes it took to sink to the dome's base. The counterweight, when it passed them, was a stainless steel rendition of a castle's tower, complete with turrets.

At the base, Elizabeth only shook her head when Mary asked what had taken them so long. Lady Catherine had already gone ahead with Colonel Fitzwilliam and Mrs. Jenkinson, and the others made a quiet group on their way home, with only Mr. Collins apparently oblivious to the general mood. He rhapsodized happily all the way to the Parsonage about her Ladyship's generosity and the affectionate gratitude of the working man. At the gate by the laurel hedge, Mr. Darcy merely bowed to the company, eyed Elizabeth with a devastating gentleness, and turned away.

Although it was only mid-afternoon, Elizabeth pled a headache (not entirely a fabrication) and went up to her room for a nap, stopping in the bathroom first to brush away the sour taste in her mouth.

Her room was exactly the same: the clock ticked the same rhythm, the scent of oranges continued to permeate the air, the warm untroubled light suffused the room with the same soft glow. It was as if it had never happened. The longer she thought about it, the more astonishing the proposal seemed. She remembered his many silences in the past, and thought now that he had been trying, then, to conquer what he saw as a shameful affection. She remembered his light touch when she had been injured, and the moments when their eyes had met and the way her awareness of everything around her had seemed to fall away. She had so often thought he was sneering at her when all of that time he had loved her. Astonishing.

Her headache was a lance between her temples. She made herself lie down in the narrow bed. How she slept was recorded only by her wrinkled and twisted covers.

§

Elizabeth flew through the park, angling her wings to just barely rustle their tips against the leaves, and the leaves she touched almost seemed to wave at her; as she flew deeper into the park, they turned gild-edged, bright with fresh brass and polished copper surfaces, and when her wings brushed against them, more and more it hurt: one of her feathers got caught in a gear turning on the surface of a leaf, and then another, and she was bleeding bright with the copper gears turning on their surfaces, her wings cut and feathers falling; the trees closed in on her path, until she was unable to fly any further, her wings, gore-encrusted, were squeezed shut against her sides; she kicked and rolled until she became aware of the blankets tangled around her body, and blinked herself awake.

The events of the previous day came back to her in pieces: Colonel Fitzwilliam's confirmation of Darcy's guilt; the proposal; Mary's scathing, but thankfully private, comments as they prepared dinner about the propriety of being alone with a man to whom she was not wed, even one so unimpeachable as Mr. Fitzwilliam Darcy of Pemberley.

She kept seeing Darcy's eyes as he turned away at the gate.

It is Friday morning, she thought. *They leave tomorrow. I need only get through one more day.*

Downstairs, she could hear Mr. and Mrs. Collins departing, Maria's voice floating up the stairs to wish her well, and the others shushing her ("shh, she is asleep, let her sleep") and they were gone.

After a brief breakfast of toast and oranges and tea, she went for a walk. Instead of walking in the beautiful wood at Rosings, which would have been so much more soothing to her agitation, she went down the lane to Hunsford expressly to avoid him. Mindful of the previous night's admonishments, she asked Sara to come with her. The girl trailed along behind her like a shadow and would not talk. After two attempts at conversation went nowhere, Elizabeth left Sara to her thoughts and walked ahead, trying to outpace her own.

A few minutes later, a movement in the corner of her eye caught her attention. Waveringly, through the glass of first Hunsford's and then Rosings' domes, Elizabeth could see a figure standing in the park. He was waving something at her, and when he saw that he had her attention, he held out his hands as though to entreat her to stay where she was, and rapidly walked away in the direction of the airlock. It was Mr. Darcy, she was sure, though the glass distorted his face.

She walked the same few feet of ground back and forth several times, in an agony of indecision as to whether she should obey his gesture and stay where she was, and get whatever conversation he wished to have over with, or if she should run to Hunsford and hide, perhaps in a ladies' dress shop or somewhere else he couldn't follow, or meet him on the road on the way back, so that at least if he insisted on walking with her, the way would be shortened.

Sara sighed and idled by a lamppost, unwilling to catch up to Elizabeth and be forced into more conversation. Elizabeth laughed a little at how she must appear to this girl, and stopped pacing, facing in the direction he must come. Soon enough she saw him hurrying towards her.

He smiled perfunctorily, his eyes unreadable. He was holding a letter. He said, "I have been hoping to meet you on your usual walk. Please read this," and tried to hand it to her.

She crossed her arms. "Whatever you have to say to me, just say it."

He looked at her for a long moment, clearly at a loss for words. He had expected her to take the letter and allow him to abuse her family further (for what else could the letter be but a defence of his position?) with no protest. "Very well," he said at last, "but our conversation cannot happen on a public street." He led the way back to Rosings, and she allowed it. Privacy would be better for all concerned.

As they passed Sara on their way back, Elizabeth murmured, "You may go back to the Parsonage, if you like, since we are only going to Rosings," and the girl shrugged and turned in at the little gate.

When they passed through the Rosings 'lock, Mr. Darcy turned back to her and said quietly, in a somewhat stilted, formal manner, "Do not worry that I will repeat yesterday's sentiments."

"Thank you," Elizabeth said. "What have you to say that cannot be said on a public street?"

"You accused me of interfering in your sister's marital schemes, and of ruining the blameless Mr. Wickham."

She frowned at the word "schemes." But at least he had been listening.

"You have been misinformed," he said, still in that stilted tone, "on the second matter, and I should prefer your rejection to be based on an honest assessment of my character."

They were walking up the drive instead of into the park as she had expected, possibly to avoid the gardener she could see kneeling at one of the flower beds. Before they reached the first of the clockwork decorations, she steered them to their right, to pass the container gardens with their herbs and dwarf trees laden with oranges and lemons. (It occurred to her that Mr. Collins had probably been gifted his trees from this garden.) She stopped to touch one of the oranges, which were almost perfectly ripe. Somebody should be harvesting them. It would be a shocking waste of food to let them rot on the tree.

"I can only refute your accusation by explaining Wickham's history with my family," he was saying, and she returned her attention to him.

"Go on."

"I trust you will not share any of this with anybody," he said, "although if you must have a confidante, make it your worthy sister."

She smiled a little bitterly. He could not possibly mean Kitty or Lydia. "Do you mean Jane, or Mary?"

"Jane," he said, with no sign that he understood his implication that Mary was unworthy.

Elizabeth sighed.

"Wickham's father," Darcy said, "managed my father's estate very well, and my father wished to help the family. Wickham charmed him and consequently my father held him in high esteem. He supported Wickham's education and intended that when it became available, Wickham might be given the living in Lambton, near to Pemberley."

"This much I know," Elizabeth said.

"We were close in age," Darcy said. "I—I am afraid this will upset you—"

"Please just say what you have come to say."

"He gambled, he drank to excess, and he. . . behaved toward women in a way that cannot be admired. . ."

Elizabeth frowned. This was not her Wickham. "You are being very vague," she said. "Do you have any specific ills to complain of?"

"I am sure, as irresponsible as your parents are, they have not allowed you to be exposed to. . ." Darcy trailed off.

"I see," Elizabeth said. She knew *why* she was never supposed to be alone with a man. Her mother had made sure to tell her so that she could protect herself. That she was alone with a man right now—and one who would probably judge any other lady who was alone with any other man—was not lost on her.

"Well," Darcy said, evidently relieved not to have to spell out Wickham's alleged crimes to her. "My father died five years ago. He left Wickham one thousand pounds and had me promise to support him in whatever profession he chose. He chose the law, and since the fees were less than for the church, requested the difference in what I should have to pay for his education, a sum of three thousand pounds."

"That is a considerable sum," she said. "Wickham did not mention a settlement, I remember very particularly." He had said that the wording of the will was vague, and that Darcy had chosen to disregard his father's wishes because he was jealous of his father's love. They walked a few paces along the metal paths around the citrus trees. "If you helped him to study law, why is he not a lawyer?"

"He did not study law. He ran through his funds while living without prudence or morals instead. Three years later, the Lambton parson died, and he wrote to me to ask for the living."

"But you refused."

"Naturally. Last year, he came again into my orbit." He turned to her at last, the stiltedness which had accompanied all of his words and gestures of the morning seeming to slide away. "I am sharing with you a potentially volatile secret," he said, "but I know you can be trusted."

"Thank you," Elizabeth said, touched, despite herself.

"But I wish you would read the letter I wrote," he said, pressing it into her hand. "I fear I shall make a hash of this." She took it, taking pity on him, and shoved it into the pocket of her skirt.

"Please go on," she said quietly.

One of the kitchen maids came into the area where they had been pacing back and forth amongst the trees, and they fell silent. She put a bucket on the ground and began picking the oranges. Darcy steered Elizabeth silently past the clockwork swallows to the park on the other side, his hand lightly touching her elbow, the warmth of his hand seeming to burn through the cloth of her dress. They walked until they were out of earshot. When he took his hand away, the impression of his warmth stayed a moment longer, and she found herself rubbing her arm.

Darcy said, "My sister Georgiana is a decade my junior, just the age of your sister Lydia."

Elizabeth raised her eyebrows. How did his sister figure in this story?

"Wickham met her in London, with the assistance of her new governess, a Mrs. Younge. It turns out that she was previously known to him, and she seems to have applied for the post at his direction. He courted my sister, and persuaded her to elope with him."

"An elopement!"

"Fortunately, I happened to be in London upon business, and Georgiana confessed their plans to me the day she was to leave with him. You know me too well to have any doubt of my reaction."

"There must be some mistake," Elizabeth said.

He frowned at her. "I understand your disbelief," he said, "but I promise you I would not involve my sister in a falsehood of this nature."

"I—I—" Elizabeth pinched the bridge of her nose. *Darcy has to be lying. Yet nobody would tell such a monstrous lie about a beloved sister!*

She could easily remember what Wickham had said of the circumstances of Darcy's refusal to give him the living. One or the other was lying. She found it impossible to imagine that Wickham was guilty, but equally impossible that Darcy should involve his sister's reputation in a lie. He trusted her not to gossip about it, but if she chose to do so, his sister could be ruined, at least in the sphere to which she was accustomed. She couldn't help but hesitate. If Darcy's account were true, then Wickham was a scoundrel and Darcy blameless; and vice versa.

She thought back to every interaction with Mr. Wickham. Nobody in Meryton had known him for more than the span of weeks, or could testify to his good character. She tried to remember him behaving not merely charmingly, but generously or selflessly, but could not. She, and everybody, had assumed him to be a good person by virtue of his social graces and charm.

"I see," she said at last, shakily.

"Of course, I could not expose him without involving my sister in his disgrace. He was after her fortune, of course," Darcy said.

Elizabeth remembered her aunt asking her about Wickham's sudden courting of Mary King. "I have to admit I am, um, very shocked," Elizabeth said. "The man whom I met did not seem like he could have been capable of—but—" She fell silent.

"Colonel Fitzwilliam and I are her guardians. You may ask him for confirmation."

She said nothing. They walked for some minutes, going around the back of the house by the beech trees. She could hear him breathing, his emotions having been riled up by his sister's story despite the clinical way he had described it. She glanced at him sidelong through her lashes, and saw that his colour was high.

She remembered Wickham telling her about Darcy. It hadn't even been a week after they had met. For the first time, she was struck with the impropriety of such communications to a stranger. He had told her that he had no fear of Darcy, but then had avoided the Netherfield build, the very thing for which he was supposed to have come to town. Only she and apparently Mr. Denny had known his story, and then, she remembered, the story had been everywhere only after Darcy had returned to London and could not know what was said behind his back.

And his attentions to Mary King! How mercenary those seemed now, and how right had been her aunt's warning. His marked attentions to her, before Miss King had come into his sphere, could only have arisen from vanity, unless he had assumed that any family with a dome must have money to inherit.

As for Darcy, now that she was among people who had known him all his life, she saw that he was respected and loved. Despite all of the time they had spent together over the past month, she had never seen him act wrongly, and though he had certainly said many things that had irritated her, none of them had been dishonourable. She had observed his courtesy toward his cousins and his patience with his aunt. If Darcy were the man that Wickham had painted, he could never have hoped to conceal that from the world.

And then there was the mute testimony of Neptune, the wolfhound, who preferred Darcy over everybody, including his own mistress. And even over Elizabeth, despite her regular bribes of forbidden foods. Neptune could not be influenced by Darcy's high connections or fortune, which was why dogs were such superior judges of human nature.

"How wrong I have been," she said.

"No, no, I beg you, do not blame yourself," Darcy said. "Wickham is to blame. I am sure he told you any number of lies."

"Yes, well," she said. "So it would seem."

They stopped under the beech trees. He looked down at her, his face partially shadowed by the leaves. She looked away for a time, watching an ant circumnavigate a leaf without attending to it, and then turned back to him. "I am sorry," she said, "but you mentioned earlier having two charges to defend against, and you have only talked about one. You have still ruined my sister's happiness, and I am sure there is no defence there."

His face closed off once more. "I observed their behaviour closely. Your sister was very pleasant to him, but no more than she is pleasant to anybody. I noticed no signs of love and believed that her heart was not involved. However, you must know her better than I do. I admit, I may have made an error."

Elizabeth laughed once, shortly. "I should think so," she said. He seemed to feel no regrets over his mistake. "And *did* you hide her presence in London from him, or was that all Miss Bingley?"

"Miss Bingley was not difficult to engage in the project," Darcy said, "but it was I who convinced him. He still does not know she was in London. If they had met there, his efforts to extinguish his feelings for her might have been defeated, and I felt at the time that it was best for them not to meet." He paused, and then said, "Perhaps this concealment was beneath me."

"Of course it was!" Elizabeth said. "Playing games with Jane's heart, and treating Bingley as a child who could not make up his own mind? Yes, it was beneath you!"

"I—"

But she was relentless and would not let him speak. "And why? Because my mother's father was in trade back on Earth? Because my father is only a gentleman with a small property and not all this—" she gestured around her "—excess, that requires a small army of people to maintain? What about all your money makes you believe it makes you a better person than me and my sister?"

"My motives may appear unsatisfactory—" he began.

"*Appear* unsatisfactory!" Elizabeth said.

"Yes. My family name is a responsibility! A responsibility you should be grateful you have never had to suffer."

"The Bennets are every bit as well-respected in our dome as the Darcys in theirs."

"Impossible! Your sisters' impropriety—"

"Jane is not—"

"No, no," he cut her off. "You and Jane—even Mary—have always been very proper, I am sure. I am speaking of Kitty and Lydia, who so frequently flirt and—"

"Oh!" Elizabeth turned away from him, and then turned back and flared, "Your own sister was going to elope with Wickham!"

"Do not criticize my sister!"

"I am not! You must see that any fifteen-year-old, no matter how carefully brought up, might be prone to—"

"I hardly think it is the same thing!" Darcy said, his nostrils flaring. "Not to mention your mother's business—"

"No!" Elizabeth overrode him. "Do not criticize her business. I know you people insist on living by the old rules and think yourself so much better than the rest of us, but my mother is twice the woman any of the ladies in your circle could ever be!"

With that, Elizabeth walked almost blindly away from him, her hands shaking, and he did not follow her.

CHAPTER TEN

SHE EMERGED FROM ROSINGS PARK onto the long drive down to the 'lock. She could not face her sister or Mr. Collins, and so she turned toward town, her feet eating the ground in her haste to outrun her conversation with Darcy. She gave one thought to stopping for a chaperone and decided that Mary could be angry, if she liked, if she ever even heard anything about it.

Something crinkled in her pocket, and she pulled out his letter. She almost threw it down onto the street, but remembered that it must have an explanation of Georgiana Darcy's indiscretion, and could be found by anybody. She put it back in her pocket, determined to burn it unread. Mr. Darcy deserved no more of her attention.

"Odious man," she said to herself. But she could not help rehearsing her grievances against him in her mind (going over and over their conversation, and thinking of all the things she should have said to him) and without thinking about it she found herself opening his letter. It consisted of a sheet of thick, creamy paper, written closely on both sides in a spiky, masculine hand. It turned out to repeat the same points he had already said to her at more length.

She reached the heart of Hunsford. She looked around herself with a shiver as she realized she had been crossing roads while reading with no attention to the other pedestrians or carriages that might be upon them. Fortunately, at mid-morning, traffic was very slight. She waited for a steam-powered conveyance to make its ostentatious way down the road, and then turned to go back to her sister's house.

She walked almost blindly through the town, dwelling on certain turns of phrase in his letter with indignance. She only noted other people and vehicles to avoid them. Later she would account herself lucky that nobody knew her there, for her behaviour could not have brought credit to herself or her family; she did not remember absolutely snubbing anybody, but could not imagine that she had failed to do so.

Elizabeth returned to the Parsonage, folding Darcy's letter back into her pocket. With Mary and Maria's laughter ringing from the windows and candles shimmering along the windowsills, the house was as cheerful as she had yet seen it, and yet she dreaded going in. She had no desire to share intelligence of Darcy's proposal (or indeed the shifting stories of Bingley and Jane or Wickham and Darcy) to her pious sister, let alone to Mr. Collins or Maria Lucas.

She folded the letter inelegantly and shoved it in its envelope, then had to take it out to refold it more carefully when it wouldn't fit. She tucked it into the deep pockets of her skirt, took a deep breath, and squared her shoulders to go inside.

As she walked through the door, Mr. Collins said, "You have missed Mr. Darcy and Colonel Fitzwilliam, who called perhaps an hour ago, to take their leave of us."

"The Colonel almost decided to go looking for you, but he had not the time," Mary said.

Elizabeth performed the appropriate disappointment at missing them, and attempted to follow the topics when they moved on. She picked phrases out of the flow of conversation (—the garden will—the oranges in particular—Lady Catherine—dine at Rosings this week—) but she was a broken signal-tower; the sense of things went all undecoded.

She and Charlotte had long ago settled it between them that a refused proposal was an event you could not get past quickly enough. It had finality and pathos and the definite feeling that the universe was splitting in two: forever after was the version of you who said no, and, ghostlike and theoretical, the version who had said yes. You might record the event in a letter to a very close friend, but you never dwelled on it: what if the man turned out well, and you regretted your loss, or worse yet, what if he turned out so badly you were embarrassed he had ever seen you as a possibility? Better amnesia. Better to look back and entertain doubts that anything had happened at all. But Darcy's communication made this impossible so long as it demanded her attention. She soon went upstairs to study her letter and remember all of his more extemporaneous comments on their walk that morning.

His belief that her mother lowered herself by running a business she dismissed outright; of course somebody like him would believe something like that. The great and high-ranked people of the ship were rarely in the Sir William mold, but then Sir William had not been born to his rank, but earned it through some attentions given the King on Earth, when he had been Mayor of the original Meryton, she thought, or some story like that. Since he had not been born to it, he had been able to move past it to join the real world, where rank was something one noticed, to be sure, but the overriding concern was that everybody be clothed and fed, that the systems continue to operate so that they had air and soil and water, that everybody work together, or they would assuredly die together. She remembered the pinch of hunger during the famine, and the way that strangers had come up to her mother for years afterwards, tears in their eyes, to thank her. People like the Darcys had never run out of food, she was sure; nothing had changed for them, and so they were still part of that old world, where the worst thing a woman could do was be useful.

But his opinions about her sisters' behaviour, their silliness in company which Darcy styled in his letter as a "total want of propriety"—he was wrong, based on what he had seen. They were sometimes a little more flirtatious than was strictly proper, to be sure. But he was not actually wrong. He had not seen the worst of it—she remembered Lydia punching Mary in the face just to get hold of her book. Darcy's observation plowed a little fertilizer into the disregarded areas of the garden of her mind. The nourishment fed weeds she had never meant to encourage. Weeds and buried crossbreeds. Lydia loved to be the center of attention, which sometimes led her to act out in company, and Kitty would follow wherever Lydia led, even though she was the older of the two. Elizabeth supposed that Miss Georgiana would never play tag on a dance floor or start a jig at a family party, let alone go packet-dodging or punch her brother in the nose.

Her eye sockets felt somehow both hollow and swollen, and the inside of her skull felt unpleasantly dry. She held the letter for a moment to her breast with an open hand, feeling herself breathe. She could see the entire structure of his argument all at once, and understood it, and rejected it, and yet she knew that many on the ship would share his ideas and judge her family as he had. She could only hope they were in the minority.

§

The next morning, Mr. Collins came upstairs to wake everybody, announcing loudly outside their doors that they were invited to dine at Rosings that night.

"From the Parsonage gate," he said, "I saw the gentlemen leave Rosings and head toward the airlock to Darlington. Naturally, I headed to Rosings immediately. Her Ladyship was so good as to invite us all to dine with them this evening."

As she dressed, Elizabeth could not help but imagine the scene that would have transpired on this visit had she accepted Darcy's proposal. Lady Catherine shouting; Darcy at his most cold and sneering; Mr. Collins at his most servile; Neptune barking at the rising babble of angry voices; Elizabeth shaking off the hand of the butler as he threw her from the house.

On the threshold, she stopped, patted the doorframe slowly with one palm, and turned back. The letter was still peeking out from under her pillow, where she had stashed it the night before, and she put it in the deep pocket of her skirt, safe from discovery. It made a faint, satisfying rustle there.

At Rosings, the wolfhound snuffled at her skirt pocket and whined at the scent of his favourite on the hidden letter. Elizabeth petted the dog distractedly, neither of them happy.

Her Ladyship opened by lamenting the loss of better company. "Such wonderful young men, my nephews. They will miss Rosings so much. Darcy seemed to feel it most acutely. His attachment to Rosings certainly increases." She smiled over at her daughter, who raised her eyebrows slightly, and then slowly looked away.

"Keen observers of character," Mr. Collins said, "are often laid low by having to part with such excellent examples of fine breeding and discernment."

Her Ladyship smiled.

After dinner, Lady Catherine looked at Elizabeth and said, "I notice that you speak less than is usual, Miss Bennet. I suppose Mr. Collins has begun to teach you a more feminine reticence. Your own parson has been shockingly lax. I am sure that when I was your age I never spoke more than two words in company."

Elizabeth opened her mouth to reply, and then thought better of it.

"Or are you merely unhappy at having to go home again? You must stay until June, which would allow me to take you and Miss Lucas as far as London in my barouche-box."

Mary looked at Elizabeth, her face quite blank, and Elizabeth thought that Mary would be disappointed for her guests to stay any longer. She had been happy to have them, but their departure was still a relief when it meant getting back to her books and the husband she unaccountably doted on.

"We cannot change our plans," Elizabeth said.

The following Saturday was the night of the monthly Meryton assembly, and, having missed March and April's, Elizabeth did not mean to miss May's and create a scandalous deficit of completed shifts, for her family and friends to have to make up, and especially when she had been promised a trip in not so many months with her aunt and uncle. As it was, she expected to have extra shifts every week for the next few months. But people like her Ladyship did not engage in communal responsibilities like work shifts, and she expected that any attempt to explain them would only end in confusion and clueless remarks. Fortunately her Ladyship was easily distracted by an exhausting number of suggestions for their method of packing, their best way home, and their stops along the way.

For the remainder of the week, she was able to take a daily solitary walk, determined to enjoy Rosings park as long as it was available to her. She knew the letter, now crumpled and dog-eared, nearly by heart. When she considered how she had spoken to him of Wickham, she was filled with shame, but when she thought about his bold interference in Jane's affairs, her shame was forgotten in the swell of her indignation. She went over every line again and again, and remembered what he had said both in his proposal, and in his defence the following day, and compared both to his wording in the letter as though she were preparing to write a thesis on the slight differences in tone, the shades of meaning that could be ascribed to this adjective versus that, to the way his eyes had glowed while declaring his love and the way they had gone empty when she had rejected him.

It was no surprise that Elizabeth felt despondent, but she play-acted a light-hearted, untroubled person well enough that none of her sister's household noticed the deception.

§

From the back of Rosings park, Elizabeth could see the lights of Darlington. The empty space between the end of the dome and the end of the superstructure shaded from the bare metal almost bright from Rosings' lights, to a band of gray outside Castlereagh, and then the absolute black of the unlit interstitial spaces, and upwards to the anonymous lights of the closest dome in that direction of the giant wheel their ship formed. It might have been Lambton or even Pemberley, though she thought that Darcy would have probably mentioned if Pemberley was visible from Rosings. Bolsover maybe, or Dovedale; she wasn't sure of the arrangement of the domes in that superstructure, and didn't know which was closest. Quite possibly it was some more anonymous and practical space, for growing food or bamboo.

The wall of the dome was cold, the thin air outside unable to hold much heat. That was how her mother often kept vegetables from spoiling, but Elizabeth was still always a little surprised. People whose domes were in the center of town never experienced cold like this. She reached out, splayed her fingers on the slightly frosted glass, and then snatched them back, unable to stand the cold so intense it felt like a kind of heat. The ghost of her hand was left behind, waving at her briefly and then fading away. Her real hand throbbed, and she stuck it under her opposite arm to warm it back up more quickly. *Foolish thing to do,* she thought.

She backed up a few steps to the wide, hard metal bench. The lack of comfort, in stark contrast to the luxurious furniture inside Rosings, made her assume it was for the servants. That would be like her Ladyship. She sat.

She had been coming here almost daily since she had arrived in Hunsford, at all times of day, and had never seen Lady Catherine or her daughter out walking. Miss de Bourgh might have benefited from a walk now and again, and Mrs. Jenkinson might have considered it a break from her duties, but she was sure they never ventured out, unless they came out when they ought to be sleeping. Miss de Bourgh did not strike her as the sort to sneak out at night, but then Elizabeth took care not to strike others as the type, either. Not that she did it often. She was really very well-behaved, she thought, but the rules for gently-raised women were so stupidly strict, it was almost impossible not to break them. Even coming here to walk was breaking a rule—she ought to have a chaperone—but

Sara was usually busy and Mr. Collins had no servants of his own, and she would not ask her sister or Maria when half the point of the walks was to get away from the Parsonage and all of the people in it. Everybody winked at the rules about chaperones; they were from Earth, and assumed a much larger excess population than existed on the ship. People might be rather shocked if she walked around town alone, but to go to a private garden during the day for a ramble was only a little eccentric.

She had seen a few of their servants: the gardeners, of course, and one of the kitchen maids often came out after breakfast for a walk (she had shied away the one time Elizabeth had tried to talk to her) and one of the male servants brought the wolfhound out at mid-morning every day for exercise, which, when Elizabeth's walk overlapped with the dog's, turned into as much of a romp as Neptune's dignity would allow. She began carrying cookies in her pocket to sneak to the wolfhound when she next saw him. Once, the footman who set up their card tables, and a different maid, had been kissing in the shadows of the beeches, and Elizabeth had pretended she didn't see. But except for Lady Catherine giving Mr. Collins permission for Elizabeth to walk here, none of the ladies of the house even seemed aware of the park.

What does it do to a person to have all of this at their own personal disposal? What kind of person could have this and not delight in it?

She stood, the bench having become more uncomfortable than standing. Still facing the empty space between Castlereagh and Darlington, she paced a little and began worriedly rereading Darcy's letter. She heard a twig snap behind her, and, on turning, found to her surprise that it was her sister. She folded her letter back into her pocket.

"Mary!" she said.

"I thought you might be here," Mary said. "The carriage is ready earlier than we had thought. But I am glad of the opportunity to speak with you alone before you leave."

"I can hardly believe it is already time for us to go home," Elizabeth said.

They began to walk back toward the 'lock. They passed under a cherry tree, and she lifted a low branch over her sister's head.

"Thank you for coming, and for bringing Maria," Mary said. "I know we have little here to keep you occupied, though my husband's sermons perhaps have been improving."

The branches of two trees had been carefully braided together by some long-ago gardener to form an arch over a fork in the path. Mary turned there to the easier path down the long lane with the globes decorated with swooping clockwork swallows.

"Not to mention your sermons to him, which I think have improved your husband," Elizabeth said, more politely than accurately.

Mary snorted. "You joke, but I find that we are remarkably attuned to one another. I do think my habits of scholarship have helped him to become more studious himself."

"I am so happy for you, Mary. I will be sure to let mamma know how you delight in your life here."

"Please give our love to mamma and papa, and all of our sisters, and our aunt and uncle," Mary said.

By this time they had reached the Parsonage, where they found the carriage was indeed all ready to go. Elizabeth ran up to her room to check that she had not missed packing anything, and then came back down and hugged her sister goodbye. Mr. Collins helped Elizabeth and Maria into the chaise. Turning back to take a parcel from his wife, he left Sara to get into the chaise without assistance. Maria gave Sara a hand up and Mr. Collins a dark look, but he did not notice. "Oh!" he said as he handed the parcel in. "I am sure you did not mean to forget to express your gratitude to her Ladyship." He suggested how they might most appropriately convey their respects and gratitude, and Maria agreed. The parcel proved to be a box of oranges, pastries, and meat pies for the road. Elizabeth called their thanks for the food to Mary. Finally, the door was shut, and the driver let go of the hand crank so the clockwork could begin to turn the wheels with its steady ticking.

By mid-afternoon, they were at the Gardiners', where they were spending the night. That evening, after the usual topics had been exhausted and all of the interesting news of their visit that Elizabeth judged *could* be told, *had* been told, Mrs. Gardiner drew Elizabeth to one side and said, "There was not a private moment on your way to the Parsonage to ask: is there any further news of your friend Mr. Wickham?"

Elizabeth hardly knew whether to laugh or cry. "I can tell you honestly, that I am in no danger in that department, dear aunt. He is still courting the famous Miss King."

Although she thought Miss King was not in too much danger from Mr. Wickham, either.

The next day, the driver took the three of them through the corridor to Headfort and home, first to Lucas Lodge and then to Longbourn. The whole family met Elizabeth at the front door, and she forgot her troubles for a moment in embraces and laughter. Careful got underfoot and whipped everybody's legs with his tail.

Mrs. Bennet had made a heavy spread of pea soup, sourdough bread, Cornish hens roasted with stewed gooseberries, and every kind of stewed and roasted vegetable from her greenhouse.

"You must tell us all of your news," Lydia said, passing a plate of carrots. "Did you meet anybody new? Did anybody ask to correspond with you? I do not suppose you had any dancing? I suppose Mary kept you from having any fun."

"Oh, Lydia," Elizabeth said.

"I have the most delicious news," Lydia said, not waiting for Elizabeth to answer any of her previous questions. "It's about your favourite—indeed, everybody's favourite."

Elizabeth closed her eyes.

"You will never believe it. Miss Mary King, of all people, has turned down dear Wickham. She is not nearly handsome enough to be turning down eligible men. But Wickham is safe!"

"And you are safe home," Mrs. Bennet said, "and if Lydia will eat her pie and cease speaking for a moment, we might hear how Mary fares."

"She is very well, and exceedingly pleased to be a regular visitor at Rosings, and shares her husband's awe of a certain Lady who lives there. She sent you a letter I have packed away in my box."

Once the family was done eating, Mr. Bennet came with the ladies to the drawing room to hear all about Elizabeth's trip, and she entertained them with whatever amusing tales she could recall, mostly centered on Neptune or the absurdities uttered by Mr. Collins and Lady Catherine, so that she wouldn't have to tell them anything that really mattered.

She longed to tell Jane about everything that had passed between Darcy and herself—nothing could hold her back once they could have a private conversation, except her worries of how any mention of Bingley, even to reveal that he had not known she was in London and therefore had not snubbed her, would grieve Jane when she seemed to be mostly recovered from her heartbreak. Still undecided at bedtime, she allowed her exhaustion to overcome her.

§

They went together to that month's assembly, where Elizabeth was gratified to be paired with Charlotte for the next month's shifts, and relieved not to see Mr. Wickham, and even more relieved to hear, via Mr. Denny, that Wickham was completing the training he had undertaken in town that week, and would leave the following week for Brighton, where he would be apprenticing with Mr. Forster. She need never see him again.

The following morning before church, Elizabeth finally had the time, privacy, and clear head to tell Jane some of what she had redacted in her recital to the whole family the night before. She had decided that she would not pain her sister by mentioning Bingley, including the first portion of Darcy's letter which showed how Bingley had cherished her sister, but otherwise share everything. In the moment of relating her story, she found herself also softening Mr. Darcy's harshest statements towards their family. She wanted Jane to feel positively toward him, or as positively as possible under the circumstances, though she could not say why, even to herself.

Jane was surprised at his proposal, but not as astonished as Elizabeth had been. "It is perfectly natural that he should admire you," she said. "I have once or twice surprised such an expression on his face that made me think he might."

She was grieved for Mr. Darcy, and pointed out how his unhappiness must have been increased by his certainty of success.

"Yes," Elizabeth said, "but he can console himself by reflecting that he has not been driven by love into a disadvantageous marriage."

Jane waved a hand to express her opinion of his judgement.

"It would have been a great advantage to *our* family," Elizabeth said, "but I must admit, that never crossed my mind. And then he spent the next morning delineating his whole history with George Wickham, and oh! Jane, it is shocking."

She relayed the entire contents of her conversation with Darcy as they related to Wickham. Jane was shocked and grieved. Even the discovery of Darcy's innocence could not console her. She spent twenty minutes altogether trying to think of ways they might both be blameless, since the Wickham she knew could not be capable of such wickedness, while surely Darcy could never lie about anything so dreadful concerning his own sister.

"You must be contented with one good man between them," Elizabeth said. "I believe it is Mr. Darcy, despite appearances."

"Poor Mr. Darcy! And poor Wickham!"

"Wickham's misfortunes are all of his own making."

"And what do you mean, 'despite appearances'? I always thought Mr. Darcy was rather handsome," Jane said. "His dark eyes did give the impression that he might be a little wicked, to be sure."

Elizabeth shivered, and looked around for her shawl, though

it was not cold in their room. "I cannot argue with you there," she said. "I made so much fun of him only because he did not want to dance with me, and did not like my looks. I drowned my hurt pride in laughter. Jane, I am ashamed."

"Oh, Lizzy." Jane patted her hand. "And then to have upbraided Mr. Darcy for his treatment of Mr. Wickham when it was really the other way around."

"You can hardly censure me more than I have already censured myself." They sat silently for a moment while Elizabeth dragged on her shawl. After a moment, she said, "Do you think I need to expose Wickham publicly with what I know—or rather, with that portion of it that can be shared?"

Jane thought about it, and then said, "Without revealing the shocking elopement he had planned to make to steal Miss Georgiana's fortune, which of course you must not make generally known, nobody will believe the rest was not fabricated by Mr. Darcy. And Mr. Wickham may be sorry for his actions, and want to redeem himself. I do not see that you could do any good."

"And in any case, once Wickham leaves, it will not matter."

"Then we are agreed."

§

After church, Lydia came into the drawing room with two aether suits. "Should I take the green one or the white one?" she asked. "Or should I take both? I should not like the engineers at Brighton dome to think our family poor."

"Well, we *are* poor," Kitty said brutally, though this was an exaggeration: they had no fortune, but they were considerably better off than most.

"Brighton!" Elizabeth said. "Why are you going to Brighton? When was this decided?"

"And anyway you know I sometimes use the green one when I am wearing my green dress," Kitty continued.

"While you were away," Lydia said. "Mrs. Forster invited me, because we are *such* good friends."

Elizabeth had heard something at the assembly about Mr. Forster going there for his next build, and of course his wife would go too, as well as many of the engineers, who followed him like iron filings following a magnet.

"Mrs. Forster is only a year or two older than Lydia," Jane said. "I know you have hardly met her, Lizzy, but the two have become fast friends."

"On very short acquaintance," Kitty said, pouting. "They only just met. It is horribly unfair! Everybody gets to travel but me."

"I am going to take both," Lydia said, and left the room. Kitty flounced after her.

At dinner there was a renewal of the topic, when Lydia said, "It is so difficult to decide what to bring when I have only the one suitcase. Mamma, might I borrow yours?"

"No," Mrs. Bennet said. "You only need your large valise, Lydia. You will be spending most of your time alone with Mrs. Forster helping her to set up her new household."

"I shall be courted by every eligible engineer on the ship," Lydia said. "You would not want me to miss my chance because I only have room for two or three frocks!"

"You may borrow my suitcase," Jane said.

"Oh, no, please let me have it, Jane. I will be with the Gardiners before Lydia returns, and the suitcase I used for Hunsford was so small," Elizabeth said at the same time as Lydia was eagerly saying yes.

"I will leave you to it, my dears." Mr. Bennet left for his study.

Mrs. Bennet sighed. "It must be nice to be a man," she said. "Settle it amongst yourselves, girls, but you do not need a great deal of frivolous luggage, Lydia, for Heaven's sake."

"It is not frivolous!"

"And you have another two weeks to pack," Mrs. Bennet said. "I don't want to hear another word about it until at least next Sunday." She began to cut up her chicken.

"If I ever want to be married, I must meet eligible men, and engineers are so clever!"

"You are fortunate that I was able to move into Mary's room," Kitty said to Lydia. "If I had to share a room with you, I am sure I might smother you in your sleep."

Without looking up from her chicken, Mrs. Bennet said, "No murders while I am eating," and Elizabeth choked on her food and had to get up from the table.

Lydia did not say another word about packing around Mrs. Bennet, but continued to rhapsodize about her chances of meeting eligible beaux in Brighton for the next several days.

Careful's excavation of Elizabeth's covers woke her on the Thursday after she had returned from Hunsford. She turned her head; the door was open, though Jane was still sleeping in her bed on the other side of the room. The beagle must have gotten out of his crate, as sometimes happened, and nosed at all the doors until he found one with the catch not quite latched. She lifted the covers, and the beagle rushed under to flop against her side. She rolled over to hug him against her, and he squirmed against her until he had gotten his head out from under the covers. He thumped his tail against her belly a few times and then, yawning, closed his eyes.

She lay on her side, enjoying the dog's warmth, and tried to let her mind empty, but she could not stop worrying about Lydia's forthcoming trip. When she heard her father moving around downstairs, she got up, dressed quickly, and took Careful down with her, despite his protests.

"Thank you," said Mr. Bennet when she handed him the beagle. "I was wondering where he had gotten to."

"He is my alibi," Elizabeth said, closing the door. "I must speak with you about something very important, and I would really rather you did not let the others know about it. Lydia would never forgive me."

"Very well," Mr. Bennet said. "When the Inquisition comes, you were only ever here to reunite me with my beloved pet." He put

Careful down on the floor; the dog promptly began his usual audit to make sure nothing in the room had been moved and no new interesting smells had escaped him.

"I am very concerned about her trip to Brighton," she said. "Lydia has not learned to act properly in company, and she exposes herself to ridicule and even condemnation with her wild ways. You know it is true; you have laughed at her often enough."

"Go on," he said, his tone almost aggressively neutral. He moved some papers around his desk.

"Mrs. Forster will not be an improving influence, nor will she rein her in. The probability is that both of them shall be more imprudent and rash in Brighton dome, with no countervailing forces to sway them towards being even slightly more responsible, and where the opportunities for wickedness cannot help but be greater than in a small dome like Meryton."

"So you would have me make her stay here," he said, looking up from his papers.

"Yes."

"Lydia will never be easy till she has exposed herself in some public place or other, and we can never expect her to do it with so little expense or inconvenience to her family as under the present circumstances."

"When she exposes herself," Elizabeth said, "she exposes all of us as well."

Mr. Bennet took her hand. "You need not worry, my dear. Nobody could make you ridiculous. Or Jane, I dare say. You are, both of you, loved and respected wherever you go."

"But Father—"

"Lydia has her own path to forge," Mr. Bennet said. "She cannot come to much harm: Mr. Forster will keep Lydia and his wife out of trouble."

Elizabeth went next to her mother, where she was sorting seed packets that had gotten jumbled together, and made, in substance, the same speech as she had to her father.

"Your father has already said that she may go," Mrs. Bennet said, "and I do not think it will do her the harm you think, my dear. I was just as silly at her age, and I learned to grow up. Lydia will learn some things in Brighton that she cannot learn here, comfortable in the center of her family home, and that will expand her horizons." She vented a short laugh. "Well, there are no horizons inside this ship, but you know what I mean. We cannot teach her to be wise, but hard work will save her as it has saved you and Jane."

"What work will she—"

Mrs. Bennet held up a hand. "She will have to keep up with her shifts there, or so I have told Mrs. Forster—" this was news to Elizabeth and she suspected would be to Lydia as well "—no, do not raise your eyebrows at me; we will cover for you when you are away, for you truly need the break. Now, come help me to plant these."

If Lydia had known about Elizabeth's interference, her indignation would have outstripped her triumph at both parents taking her side. It was clear, from her voluble transports of fancy whenever the conversation turned to Brighton, that she dreamed of becoming a celebrity amongst the engineers, many of them new to her, for the build was much bigger than the one at Netherfield, and would span several weeks. She imagined herself seated on a chaise with a colourful drink, beating off one admirer after another until the man of her dreams should come along and fall in love with her at once.

CHAPTER ELEVEN

WHEN ELIZABETH DROPPED IN AT LUCAS LODGE the next day, she found Charlotte seated with Mary King. She remembered Charlotte's prediction that she would never marry, and smiled. Charlotte had told her only the week before that they were destined to be star-crossed lovers, for she couldn't bring herself to choose between Miss King and her family—"What if she tires of me? I will be on my own with no wealth of my own," she had sighed, and Elizabeth had said that nobody could tire of her, and Charlotte had said her one consolation would be in discovering an instance of Eliza Bennet being proved wrong.

A little embarrassed, she handed Charlotte back the book on physics which must appear remedial and elementary to Miss King. "I thank you, and apologize for taking so long with it," she said. "Miss King, I can only admire your accomplishments more; I found it interesting, but I fear I could not hold the mathematics in my head."

"What should you like to do instead?"

"Truly, I do not know," Elizabeth said. "I like everything well enough that I have studied, but nothing strikes me as really exceptional."

"Must you be exceptional?" Charlotte asked. "Some women only want to make a home, and raise children, and we have need of them as well."

Elizabeth laughed. "How wise you are," she said. "Miss King, what will you do next?"

As she was explaining that she would be going to London soon to help maintain the City dome, Lady Lucas and Maria came in with cucumber sandwiches and strawberries that Elizabeth thought she recognized from her mother's greenhouse. They asked after her mother and sisters, and the ladies spent a pleasant half hour chatting. Gradually, Elizabeth became aware of how quiet Charlotte and Miss King were being, and noticed that, seated together on the chaise, they were tapping each other on the side of the leg, in patterns of long and short finger taps.

"-A-N N-O-T S-T-O-P T-H-I-N-K-I-N-G A-B-O-U-T Y-O-U-R K-I-S-S-E-S," Miss King was tapping.

"I L-O-N-G T-O T-O-U-C-H Y-O-U A-G-A-I-N," Charlotte tapped back.

Elizabeth wrenched her eyes away. Charlotte noticed her attention to their conversation then, and, with a slight blush, shrugged slightly at her.

"Has Charlotte told you her news?" Lady Lucas said. She was a tan-coloured woman, with sandy hair and wheat-coloured skin with tawny freckles, and a penchant for beige in her plain, though excellent and unmended, clothes. At a distance her hair and skin blended together, and her eyebrows could hardly be discerned. She raised them now as she widened her eyes, evidently about to share something fabulous.

When Elizabeth did not answer, Charlotte said, "No, mother. I had not gotten to it. Eliza, Miss King has asked me to come stay with her in London, as her companion."

"Has she," Elizabeth said. Charlotte to go to London? She would have only Jane to talk to, then. She heard how flatly she had asked, and cleared her throat and took a hasty sip of tea. "Excuse me," she continued, more brightly. "Will you go to London as well then?"

"Indeed."

"It is a very good position for Charlotte," Lady Lucas said with obvious satisfaction.

"Yes," Elizabeth said. "How wonderful."

It was, in fact, a little beneath Charlotte, to be a lady's companion, but Lady Lucas was obviously relieved to be spared the maintenance of an unmarried daughter, and was imagining some relationship like Mrs. Jenkinson's to Miss de Bourgh.

When everybody else had left, Charlotte walked her home. They were silent most of the way, Charlotte apparently deep in thought and Elizabeth barely looking where she was going. The flat metal surface luckily offered no occasion for tripping.

Finally, Charlotte said, "When you have had time to think it all over, I hope you will be satisfied. I am convinced that my chance of happiness with her is as fair as most people can boast on entering the marriage state, and this way, if we should separate, our reputations will remain intact. But our friends shall know the truth."

They had reached the 'lock for Longbourn, and Elizabeth turned to seize Charlotte's hands. "I *am* happy for you," she said. "but I will miss you so! Miss King is very lucky indeed. Please visit before you go."

Charlotte said, "And you must visit us in London, where—oh, Lizzy!—I am sure we shall be so happy."

The two embraced, and Elizabeth watched her friend walk away from the 'lock, her feet making little dance steps every few meters.

§

For Lydia's last day in Meryton, she invited all of the remaining travelling engineers to dine at Longbourn. Mr. Bennet was very glad to have them all, so they put the extra leaves in the dining table to make room and hired a few people for the day. Despite her best efforts, Elizabeth found herself seated next to Mr. Wickham.

"How was your trip to Hunsford?" he asked her immediately.

"It was an excellent break, and of course I was very happy to see my sister so well settled." She smiled, showing her teeth. "Mr. Darcy and his cousin, Colonel Fitzwilliam, both visited Rosings during the same time. Do you know the Colonel?"

Frowning into his soup, he said, "I formerly saw him very often.

He is an upstanding gentleman, I always thought. How did you like him?"

"Oh, very much," Elizabeth said. "I saw him very nearly every day, and I do not think I ever saw him annoyed or out of sorts."

"And how long were he and his cousin there?"

"Nearly a month."

"He is a gentleman in spirit, as well as lineage, unlike his cousin."

Elizabeth had to work hard to keep her countenance smooth. After a moment of consideration, she said, "Colonel Fitzwilliam exerted himself more to be pleasant and to keep the conversation going, but he is a second son, and they must generally work harder, since they have no guarantees in life. Mr. Darcy felt no embarrassment at a silence, and was indifferent to the opinion of half of the people in the room, I am sure, but he was not rude, nor did he treat anybody badly."

"We spoke before of his conceited indifference to opinion, I believe," Wickham said, smiling.

"It may sting to be the person to whom he is indifferent, but I admire his attitude now that I understand his disposition better," Elizabeth said.

Wickham's spoon shook a little as he ate. For a minute or two they were both silent, Elizabeth with satisfaction and Wickham with apparent annoyance. Eventually he said, "I imagine he is better behaved on visits to his aunt."

Elizabeth had no desire to hear Wickham's grievances again, so she only nodded and turned her face a little away from him. Soon afterward, he turned to speak with Kitty, who was sitting on his other side and answered him only in stammers, making her the perfect audience for his self-aggrandizement. Elizabeth listened to his portion of their conversation while appearing absorbed in eating, and he said nothing to Kitty about Darcy, or which otherwise might impose on her sympathies, and so Elizabeth was satisfied. At cards after the meal, Elizabeth allowed her time to be dominated by Mr. Chamberlayne, but she needn't have worried: Mr. Wickham spent the rest of the evening speaking only with the other engineers.

At the end of the evening, their parting was notably cool.

The Forsters were the last to leave. He and Mr. Bennet stayed involved in a long technical discussion even as their other guests were making their goodbyes. Lydia was going with them to their house for the night, to avoid having to double back to Longbourn for their journey in the morning.

"Work hard," Mrs. Bennet said as she hugged her daughter goodbye.

Lydia drew back with a laugh and replied, "Work! But Mrs. Forster and I will be so merry, we shall have no time to work, mamma—" and talking over her, without raising her voice, Mrs. Bennet said grimly, "you may be merry while you help keep the ship going. I have arranged everything, and Mr. Forster shall hold you to your shifts."

Elizabeth was glad that everybody but the Forsters had left so that they did not hear Lydia's wails, but wished that her mother had prepared Lydia better—though after they had gone, her father said to Mrs. Bennet, "Well done, darling, we got off very lightly indeed," and kissed her forehead before he went laughing back to his library.

Elizabeth had observed Lady Lucas and Mrs. Gardiner both to intervene quite firmly when their children acted improperly or inconsiderately, and the contrast with her own parents was always a puzzle. Yet her parents both gave their children no doubt of their affectionate good will, and perhaps allowing them to learn through experience made the lessons more effective. Elizabeth could only hope that her father's confidence in Mr. Forster, and her mother's in the benefits of hard work, were not disappointed.

Lydia had promised to write long and detailed letters to Kitty and her mother, but failed utterly. Her letters to her mother, when they came at all, were brief and full of the vaguest outlines of her life, and the slightly longer missives to her sister were full of gossip and rumours without much information about Lydia herself.

Elizabeth threw herself into working, to make up for her earlier absence to Hunsford and to cache some credit before going to Arkwright with the Gardiners, as well as to give herself something to do in the absence of the engineers. Mr. Harrington made no overnight trips, so the motherless Harrington twins and their brother threw no dances. Elizabeth's birthday came and went with only a cake and small family dinner to mark it. She was paired with Jane for most of June, and the two sisters found consolation in each other; though Jane was not as cheerful as she had once been. Elizabeth became certain that the worst was behind her, and Jane would soon be her old self, though perhaps a little less serene. They washed hundreds of dishes and peeled thousands of potatoes.

If she could have had Jane come with her on her trip, everything would have been as she wished it, but her aunt and uncle, while comfortable in their smart London house, nonetheless had limited means. Asking them to add another person was not to be considered.

They were only two weeks away from their trip across the ship when Mrs. Gardiner wrote to say the trip was both delayed and shortened. "My husband is needed at work until Friday, 3 July, and then will have to be back within the month. Since we shall, accordingly, have only three weeks for our rambles, we do not believe there will be time for the more extensive travel to Arkwright—everybody says that you need at least a month to tour the area properly, and it would take us days just to get there and back. Your uncle and I propose a new plan, wherein we travel to Darlington and visit the famous beauties of some of our oldest domes, like Haddon Hall and Pemberley, etc. I am most eager to see the town of Lambton, where I spent my first years on the ship. You heard me talk about it with your friend, Mr. Wickham, and I confess that the pleasure of seeing my friends again after so long away almost makes up for disappointing you with this news."

The mention of Pemberley and Wickham inevitably brought Mr. Darcy to mind. Of all the moments in her life that haunted her when she felt awkward and alone—the faux pas she had committed at social events, the arguments she had made that had turned out to be based on misunderstandings, the times she had laughed at an unkind joke rather than defending an acquaintance or failed to shrug off a slight—her intemperate and misinformed defence of George Wickham on refusing Mr. Darcy's proposal caused her the most embarrassment. To then follow that up by intruding herself onto his notice, by actually going to his home, would be insupportable. But surely she could convince her aunt and uncle to give Pemberley a miss, and to see something of the dome in which he had been raised might give her a better understanding—but what could she be thinking? She most likely would never see the man again. She did not need to know him better.

Finally, it was July. The Gardiners arrived with their four children and an improbable amount of luggage. The two oldest, girls of eight and six years old, were fashionably named Jupiter and Luna, while the younger boys had been christened the more traditional Theodore and Oliver. Jane and Kitty were to take turns taking care of them while the Gardiners were gone, and were sharing a room so they could turn over Mary's room to the boys and Lydia's to the girls. Elizabeth had made sure to buy Kitty a very handsome hat ribbon of braided blue, white, and green threads in gratitude for what promised to be an aggravating month; to Jane she promised faithful correspondence.

While Mrs. Bennet showed her brother the improvements in her greenhouses, Mrs. Gardiner sat with Elizabeth, who was engaged in packing some last-minute items in her travelling chest. Elizabeth decided that she had better take advantage of the moment without her uncle, who would be present most of the time during their trip, to have a private word with her aunt.

"I wanted to thank you for your valuable advice," Elizabeth said, "regarding Mr. Wickham."

"Oh?" said Mrs. Gardiner. "I am glad to have been helpful, my dear. Has he married, then?"

"No," Elizabeth said. "As it turns out, Miss King's heart is engaged elsewhere. But I do not want him anymore, and I find that I really never did."

"You said before that you found you were not jealous of Miss King."

"No," Elizabeth said, "I think I merely liked being admired, for once. I was mistaken—"

Kitty and Careful came in then. "Mamma sent me up to help with packing," she said, dumping the beagle on the bed. He began sniffing the pillows.

Elizabeth had been about to say that she had been mistaken in Wickham's character, but to explain about his lies regarding his inheritance in front of Kitty seemed beyond her patience, and Mrs. Gardiner did not really need to know. So, the topic was dropped.

On the first week of their trip, they saw the reconstruction of Haddon Hall, the market dome of Bolsover, and, for Elizabeth the highlight, Calke Abbey, which was much smaller than the house which had been left behind on Earth, but which boasted a very fine rose garden, arranged in individual variety beds to emphasize the special attractions of each cultivar, with a domed orangery bursting with ripened fruits. Elizabeth spoke with the gardeners at length on every aspect of the garden, and as a reward for her interest, they permitted her to pick one of the roses to dress her hat. She dried it very carefully, wrapped it in tissue, and put it away in her hatbox where it would not get crushed, with plans of making it a gift to Jane.

In Bolsover, Elizabeth liked the steaks that were marbled with fat in every establishment and the berries which grew on container bushes the town had placed on every corner, a variety of blackberry that was fatter and sweeter (and the bush itself thornier), than any she had previously eaten. Mr. Gardiner lauded the good beer and spent more than he had budgeted on their very fine neckties, and Mrs. Gardiner commented over and over on the friendliness of every person they encountered.

At the beginning of their second week, they headed to Lambton, where Mrs. Gardiner had lived before her marriage. "I have been corresponding with some of my old friends," she told Elizabeth en route, "and they have mentioned several acquaintances with whom I had lost touch, so we will have no shortage of people to visit."

"Excellent," Mr. Gardiner said.

"I would be curious to see Pemberley again as well," Mrs. Gardiner said, and Elizabeth involuntarily said, "Oh, no."

"Oh no?" her uncle echoed. "Why, oh no?"

"You have heard so much about it already," her aunt said. "You must not let your dislike of its owner turn you away."

I have no business at Pemberley, Elizabeth thought, but she could not explain why to her aunt without a great deal of explanation, and she was certain that any explanation would be met with very tiresome comments from her uncle, who had always found the very idea of his nieces' love lives to be hilarious.

"I should not like to meet him there," she said. She looked out the window of their coach: her reflection in the window was superimposed over an inquisitive tortoiseshell cat which was running along the edge of the coach's shadow looking up at the driver. Her reflection looked worried. "That is true. But really, I am merely growing tired of all this architecture. That is papa's passion, not mine. Perhaps we might examine historical models of Mr. Babbage's inventions. I have heard there is an excellent museum at Lambton."

"That is for children," her aunt said. "Pemberley has some very famous grounds, almost unique in the ship for not being containered."

"And my sister will be very curious to hear how they handle the particulars of their gardening," Mr. Gardiner said.

Elizabeth had only seen the Rosings version of a forest, which she supposed the little stand of beech trees behind the house might be called. She had to admit to herself a curiosity to see another. But what if Mr. Darcy were to be there? It would be awful. He would think—she could not imagine. She decided she would tell them about his proposal, and therefore the awkwardness of them visiting, *only* if the family were at home. With any luck, they might be away.

That night, before she readied herself to sleep, she asked the chambermaid, "Are the Pemberley grounds as fine as we have heard?"

"Don't know what you've heard," she replied, "but they're very pretty."

"Is the family there, do you know? We thought about going tomorrow, but did not wish to intrude."

"Oh," the chambermaid said, "people go anyway. But they're away in London now. They're mostly away in London, they've a house there." She sniffed disapprovingly, but Elizabeth smiled. "Anything else, miss?"

"No," Elizabeth said, "thank you very much."

Accordingly, the next morning, when Mr. Gardiner said, "How about it, Lizzy? Shall we visit Pemberley?", Elizabeth was able to reply with complete nonchalance, "I have no objection."

§

The whole of Pemberly dome was raised some ten or twelve feet off the ground, and they had to ride up a steep slope to approach the airlock. It put Elizabeth in mind of a glass terrarium, so closely did the grounds crowd the edges of the dome. They asked at the airlock if they might see the place; and were let in by a smiling young man who sat by it in a comfortable-looking chair and who passed the word along to a young girl in pigtails and breeches. She tore off toward the house, Elizabeth assumed to give them some warning of visitors. The air smelled green.

"We were told in Lambton that Mr. Darcy was away from the house. Is that right?" Mr. Gardiner asked the man.

"Yes, but both Darcys are coming home tomorrow."

Elizabeth felt that she could breathe more easily. What luck that they had chosen today to visit!

They rode to the house along a straight lane lined with large porous gray rocks bordering the famous Pemberley Woods. The oaks and Spanish chestnuts grew in essentially straight lines, and must have been re-planted on a grid; the effect was that the forest seemed a series of grassy lanes. At the end of the lane loomed the stone façade of Pemberley House. They parked their rented and somewhat battered carriage next to the stables as instructed, admiring the fine velvet-lined carriage waiting there for the household to need it, which a stable hand was busily winding up.

The housekeeper, an older woman named Reynolds who was more friendly than Elizabeth had expected after the snobbery from the servants at Rosings, led them into the family's dining room. After glancing at the handsomely outfitted room, Elizabeth wandered to the window. From this vantage point, she could see that the forest behind the house led to a lake with a fountain, which was lit with blue and green lights. The lake's edges were all overgrown with vegetation, in a charmingly haphazard pattern.

They moved from room to room, and she couldn't help but imagine if she had accepted his proposal. The place was beautiful, but she found herself largely uninterested in the house, as well-proportioned as were all of its rooms, and as elegant, well-made, and surprisingly practical as were its furnishings. To visit, it was gratifyingly immense, like stepping out of the small confines of the usual dome-dweller's compact house, but to be its mistress? She would have to have spent all of her time managing the staff. And she would not have been permitted to invite her aunt and uncle, as the lowly connections they were. Her mouth compressed a little at the thought. But to be in charge of that forest and that lake! They were glorious.

Turning, Elizabeth ducked before she had consciously registered that something had swooped at her head. Mrs. Reynolds snatched it out of the air with an apology and handed it to her. It was a clockwork chickadee, its body moss green; the top of its head and chin had a blue patina, with the crown rubbed to a brassy brightness. It ticked against her palm. Elizabeth rubbed its crown and it turned its head to face her.

"Our master made this for Miss Darcy. I believe it was aiming for its nest."

Mrs. Reynolds indicated a little basket on the crowded table next to Elizabeth, which also contained a small locked rosewood box, probably for jewelry, with an inlaid star in blocks of various woods, a palm-sized painting of an older man whom Elizabeth recognized, from the house's other paintings, as the late Mr. Darcy, a fan, a pair of silver ostrich candlesticks, a pair of porcelain monkeys, a cut stone obelisk used as a paperweight on a small stack of folded letters, a walnut clock, and a small stack of books, with *Glenarvon* on top and *Experimental Researches in Electricity* just underneath, which made Elizabeth smile. Miss Darcy must be a reader. Everything that could be polished was shining, and there was no dust to be seen.

"Does it have a name?" Elizabeth asked of the chickadee, charmed. She turned it around and around to consider every brass feather.

"I don't think so," Mrs. Reynolds said. "You can open it from the middle, if you'd like to see the clockwork, but be careful. Sometimes the mechanism to make the head move falls out."

"I had better not."

The chickadee was trying to hop against Elizabeth's palm, so she placed it in the nest, where it huddled into a spherical shape and buried its head into one wing.

"It seems very lifelike," Elizabeth said. Lady Lucas had some chickadees in her aviary, and she thought Darcy might have had one as a model.

"Mr. Darcy is very talented," the housekeeper replied.

They passed through a room that Mrs. Reynolds said had used to be the late Mr. Darcy's, and was kept furnished to his taste. Mrs. Gardiner pointed out a set of miniatures to Elizabeth: one of Mr. Wickham and the other of Mr. Darcy. Her aunt, she could tell, meant to tease her a little, still being ignorant of Wickham's actual character, but Elizabeth could not play along. She walked a little ahead and followed the housekeeper into a room lined with sculptures.

Imagine having an entire room set aside only for artwork, Elizabeth thought.

Several paintings hung on the walls, grouped in clusters, of forests, and epic battles, and luminous cityscapes, all set on Earth, where they must have been painted. They had that patina that Elizabeth associated with old paintings. Between the groups of paintings were sculptures set on the floor and on pedestals. One was a bust of Mr. Darcy, and Elizabeth paused to look at it. He still had a little baby fat around his chin, and she guessed that he had been perhaps eighteen or twenty when the sculpture had been carved. His eyes were straight-forwardly, even challengingly, staring at the viewer, but the hint of a smile played around his mouth and his eyes crinkled very slightly in their corners. His face was more open than she had ever seen it. She thought that it must have been done before his father died. Mrs. Reynolds was speaking to her uncle and aunt about one of the paintings, all of them with their backs to her, and Elizabeth paused to look at him much longer than she would have had she been observed. She clasped her hands behind her back to resist any temptation to touch the marble.

When they turned, she drifted toward the paintings on the wall, and considered a gorgeous landscape, at least five feet tall, with a very pale sky overhanging some vegetation, a large oak at one end dominating the scene, with some tiny houses sketched in very far away in distant fields, their windows lit with pinpricks of gold. It was a little like looking across the ship's expanse of darkness to see the tiny lights of distant stars. What could it have been like to have the entire outdoors outside your house, like an enormous greenhouse? What could it have been like to see the stars every night, with no wobbly old layers of dome glass in the way, like it was nothing special?

Mr. Gardiner asked Mrs. Reynolds if Mr. and Miss Darcy were often at Pemberley and what they were like to work for.

"He is very correct, and everything must be done just so, but he is never cross or mean when we make mistakes, but always says he must not have explained himself properly, and takes all the blame on himself. She is much less particular, and very dreamy. A big reader, but also a very accomplished girl."

"Do the staff wish that he would marry?" Mrs. Gardiner asked.

"It would be good for the family," Mrs. Reynolds said, "but I sure don't know who would be his equal. He is very kind to the poor, just as his mother that was, and an excellent administrator of the estate, like his father."

The Gardiners smiled, and Elizabeth stared.

Elizabeth's one fixed idea of Mr. Darcy, from almost the first moment of their acquaintance, had been that he was a difficult personality. She thought of his behaviour at Rosings. He had not been what most people called amiable: he had no ready smile or easy conversation, but in the company of those he knew well, or later in the evening when he had had time to relax into the conversation, he became friendly and almost talkative. She thought of Wickham, and realized that she had conflated an easy manner with goodness, along with most of Meryton.

Next, they were ushered into a room decorated in creams and pale yellows, with a few pale pink accents, which the housekeeper said were Miss Darcy's favourite colours. The room was simply furnished with airy lace curtains over wide windows, a few overstuffed sofas and chairs, several narrow side tables, and one whole wall devoted to shelving for books. The whole room was overseen by a white porcelain candelabra decorated with tiny pastel yellow and pink roses and crazed with age, which implied that Miss Darcy's taste in colours was hereditary. Looking closer, Elizabeth could see that the room also housed a variety of unobtrusive clockwork animals, all in attitudes of repose at the moment: a sleek rabbit with long ears folded onto its back, a turtle with its head pulled into its shell, and an owl perched on a bar holding the curtains.

An attentive brother, thought Elizabeth.

A remarkably lifelike clockwork cat painted a porcelain white regarded them from the other end of the room with bright green eyes, until the housekeeper hissed and ran over to it, whereupon it disappeared around a door there, which Mrs. Reynolds promptly closed. Elizabeth exclaimed.

"Miss Darcy's cat," Mrs. Reynolds explained. "He's forever getting out of her apartments into the rest of the house. I would leave him be, but he is fascinated by the clockwork animals and will either break them or injure himself trying to make friends."

When they had seen all they were permitted to see, they were handed by the housekeeper over to the gardener at the hall door, which suddenly opened.

Mr. Darcy walked in.

He stopped in the doorway when he saw her, one hand going out to brace himself against the frame, all his sophistication leaving him for the moment in his astonishment. His mouth hung a little open, as though he were panting, and his eyes darted around the room. A moment, and then his elegant mask fell back over his features. He came forward and greeted her.

She blushed.

His voice gentle, he asked after herself and her family; they soon established that everybody she knew was well, that she had been in the Darlington dome for a little over a week, and that she was staying at the Lambton Inn.

"I—we were told the family was away," she said by way of explanation for her presence, hardly able to raise her eyes. "I *never* would have—"

He did not interrupt her, but she didn't know how to finish her sentence. He finally nodded in his usual blank, composed manner. Some instinct made her begin to reach out to put her hand on his arm, but she aborted the gesture, and then feared he had seen it. She asked after his sister and aunt. He asked again after her family, and at her repetitive answers, fell silent. He stood looking at her for a minute, and then abruptly went inside.

"He is very handsome, is he not?" Mrs. Gardiner said after he had gone, joining her. "His portrait barely does him justice."

"A fine figure of a man," Mr. Gardiner agreed.

She would have left at once, but still felt the necessity of appearing unaffected to her aunt and uncle, who were entering the woods along a beautiful trail that circled the lake. The land there had been built up a little to mimic a hill, so that the lake could be commensurately deep, and she could see a few shadows swimming, though they fled when people came near.

What was he thinking right now? He must have been surprised

to see her, but had he been pleased? He had seemed pleased, after his initial amazement. Could he still care for her, despite everything?

When they had looked at one of the chestnuts close up, Mr. Gardiner said to the gardener, "Might we go around the lake?"

Elizabeth closed her eyes briefly, and felt her temples throb. "I think we had better leave, now that the family is here," she ventured.

CHAPTER TWELVE

"YES, WE HAD BETTER HEAD BACK if we wish to do any shopping before dinner," Mrs. Gardiner said, and as they stood debating the matter, Mr. Darcy stepped out of the back of the house and approached them.

I will be calm and open and friendly, she resolved, but once they had exchanged greetings again, she said, "What a delightful—a charming—" and then remembered how any praise of his property might be interpreted. She blushed and fell silent.

"Would you do me the honour of introducing me to your friends?" Mr. Darcy said, ignoring or not noticing her confusion. His dark eyes were guileless.

She led him a little closer to them. She was glad that she had helped her aunt to braid her hair in such a complicated fashion that morning, and had agreed with her uncle on the necessity of wearing one of his new, more flamboyant neckties. *He will be amazed,* she thought, *that these genteel people are my uncle and aunt whom he believed such lowly connections.* "Mr. Darcy, this is my aunt and uncle, Mr. and Mrs. Gardiner," Elizabeth said. She looked sidelong at him, and saw his surprise, but after the slightest hesitation, so slight nobody who wasn't looking for it would have noticed it, he shook their hands warmly and expressed his pleasure at meeting them very sincerely.

"I am very pleased to meet you," Mr. Gardiner replied.

After they had been talking some minutes, Mr. Darcy asked, "Do you fish?"

"I have done, once or twice, on trips to domes with large, stocked pools. London has none," Mr. Gardiner said.

"You must fish here while you are in town. We stock it with a variety of fish; it is a complete ecological system, and the work of several biologists who come here regularly to study and monitor the health of the lake."

While Mr. Gardiner replied, Mrs. Gardiner and Elizabeth exchanged glances. "That is generous of him," her aunt murmured to her, and she replied, "Yes, and how wonderful that they keep the lake in such good condition."

But she was thinking that the compliment to her uncle must really be to her. What else could it mean? He had only just met Mr. Gardiner. And yet, it seemed impossible that he could have retained any affection for her after her rejection.

Darcy led them deeper into the woods. Mrs. Gardiner moved up to lean against her husband, whether from real fatigue or as a ploy to make Elizabeth walk with Mr. Darcy, Elizabeth could not have said. Mr. Darcy took his place by her side readily enough.

"Your arrival was very unexpected," Elizabeth said as soon as she could bring herself to speak.

"Yes, I was supposed to come tomorrow, but had some business with my steward." They walked in silence for a moment, and then Mr. Darcy said, "My party joins me tomorrow. You know some of them: the Bingleys."

Her eyes, which had been raised to his, fell back to the ground. "And how are they?"

"Very well," he said. "They expect to visit here through the end of the month."

They walked for several paces without speaking. Elizabeth looked around at the trees, but could not attend to any details.

"My sister is also coming tomorrow," Mr. Darcy said abruptly. "I would like to introduce you, if you are free."

"I—yes," Elizabeth said. "Certainly."

"Perhaps I might bring her to visit you in the morning, when she arrives?"

Elizabeth indicated her agreement, and reminded him again of the name of the inn where they were staying.

After a moment, Mr. Darcy said, "She has lately mentioned some idea of becoming an engineer," as though explaining why he wished them to meet.

"How interesting," Elizabeth said slowly. "I thought you disapproved."

"Did I?" he said.

"That, as a profession, it did not help a woman's marriage prospects."

"Factual," he said, "though possibly not politic to mention."

The lake, visible to one side, had some sort of wheeled contraption moving around its edges, glinting with brass clockwork above and below the water line. She asked him about it, and he explained that it was his own invention. The wheel created ripples in the water in a way that mimicked Earth weather, which helped the health of the stocked fish. It had a tendency to push itself to the shoreline, which he was trying to solve. One of his staff wound it back up each day and rowed it back to the middle of the lake. They walked in silence for a while, then he said, "We all have our roles to fulfill. I love Pemberley, but its management is a full-time job; my role is to handle that before I may indulge my own desires."

"And owning Pemberley is such a hardship."

He smiled down at her. "Quiet, peasant."

Elizabeth was surprised into laughter.

"My sister is in the peculiar position of having wealth and no competing responsibilities that would prevent her from doing as she pleases."

"That seems to me to be the position of nearly every wealthy woman."

"The women of the ship must maintain the population, but my

sister would have help that would allow her to also do other work."

Elizabeth frowned. "Being a woman need not mean merely raising the children. Look at my mother."

"She has the help of her daughters in running her household. And I would not say 'merely'. I raised Georgiana, and it was not an easy job to do."

"This proves my point—men can do some of this work, and women can take on some of the men's responsibilities." Elizabeth looked out over the lake. "Do you remember the famine of '32?"

"Somewhat. I was eleven. I remember my parents had all the staff's children over for dinner every day for a few months, to make sure everybody had a proper meal at least once per day." He smiled in reminiscence.

"That was good of them," Elizabeth said. After a pause, she continued—"My family nearly starved. I was six; Lydia was just a baby. Mother did not have any more children after Lydia, even though they were trying for a boy, and I always wondered—well, anyway, she had just the one greenhouse then, and she had only planted flowers, to be ladylike, you know. When supplies started getting scarce, and Father could only bring home so much food—we did not have the money to pay the inflated prices—Mother was smart enough to plant radish and lettuce and carrots, which all grow quickly, and to harvest the flowers that were edible. We were lucky that the fashion then was to put nasturtiums on salads, to look pretty, or we would have only had the roses. That, and the occasional supplement from one of my uncles, got us through the bad first months, until she could harvest some real food. And her greenhouses were never hit by the blight, for whatever reason, so we helped to feed our neighbours as well. Her business started because of that—we did not charge our neighbours for food then, but once things stabilized—and what could be more motherly than feeding her children? If she had stuck to her role, I think some of us would have died, Mr. Darcy; I really do."

He bumped his arm against hers, comfortingly. They had just reached the end of the trail, and while waiting for Mr. and

Mrs. Gardiner, they ventured closer to the lake, the fish darting off, and stepped onto a short bridge there, which covered some of the machinery moving the water around. They leaned against the railing, and looked down at the water and each other's reflections. Somehow it was easy to meet his reflection's gaze. They were quiet for a stretched moment, his silence now seeming to arise from an inner calm, rather than the arrogant wish not to be troubled by his social inferiors that she had always presumed. She smiled at his reflection, and his reflection smiled ripplingly, and a little sadly, back. At last, he said, "I do not think I realized it had gotten so bad."

"Well, no. Of course, your parents would have sheltered you from it. They sound like they were very worthy people."

"Thank you," he said mechanically, as though his mind was elsewhere.

Her aunt and uncle were soon close enough to make further private conversation impossible. He offered them something to drink, which they declined, and finally they drove away in silence. Elizabeth felt as though bubbles of light were rising from her stomach to her lungs, and could scarcely tell if she were happy or nauseated.

Once through the airlock and safe from the ears of any Pemberley servant, Mr. Gardiner said, "He is not what I expected."

"He was friendlier, and more interesting, than I would have expected from your reports, Elizabeth. I thought you had said he was disagreeable."

"I thought him so, in Meryton," Elizabeth said, "but I liked him much better in Castlereagh, and he was even more pleasant today."

"It hardly seems possible that this was the same man who disinherited poor Mr. Wickham."

"I think Mr. Wickham embroidered the facts there," Elizabeth said slowly, "I have it from—from an authority who may be relied upon—that Darcy gave Wickham the value of the living he was promised when Wickham turned it down, quite a generous sum."

"So, Mr. Wickham was stretching the truth for sympathy from a pretty girl," Mr. Gardiner said, and Elizabeth, unable to refute such a forgiving interpretation without betraying Mr. Darcy's confidence, could only shrug and look out at the town.

After some meat pies from the inn, they spent the rest of the day visiting Mrs. Gardiner's former acquaintance. Mrs. Gardiner was entirely caught up in seeing her friends, but Mr. Gardiner, to whom they were mostly strangers, turned the conversation to Darcy and Wickham a few times, winking at Elizabeth across the room when nobody was looking. Darcy was reputed to be generous to those less fortunate, but a little proud, a criticism that could be made of every great family on the ship. Wickham was almost unknown, but a few people remembered him leaving behind large debts which Mr. Darcy afterwards discharged.

§

The next morning, she let them know that she was expecting Mr. Darcy and his sister, and consequently could not join them for further visiting. "You must stop giving me such knowing smiles," Elizabeth whispered to Mrs. Gardiner soon afterward, "for I am already all nerves, and you are not helping at all."

"But he shall be so willing to be pleased that it will not matter if you are nervous," Mrs. Gardiner replied unrepentantly. "It may even add to your charm, my dear."

Elizabeth paced by the window of her room at the inn until Mr. and Miss Darcy appeared. They stepped out of the lovely carriage she had seen by the stables the day before. Miss Darcy wore a bonnet, which meant that Elizabeth couldn't see her face from her second-story vantage point, but it wouldn't have mattered: she had caught her breath at the sight of Mr. Darcy's dark head, a cowlick she hadn't noticed before curling a single lock of hair against the grain of the rest of his head, his shoulders moving under the cloth of his waistcoat as he helped his sister across a puddle.

Mr. Darcy looked up, and before he saw her, she stepped away from the window. She hadn't breathed since he had stepped out of the carriage, and when she started again, her chest felt strangely light. The noise of the inn and the vehicles outside and the sound of her own heartbeat crashed into her. She skipped down the stairs, smiling broadly, and met his sister with fewer nerves than she had expected. Miss Darcy was tall and womanly, but her manner was that of a bird perched on a branch, watching for any little movement before flitting away. She was reputed to be very proud, but Elizabeth saw very quickly that she was merely shy, which, by some curious alchemy, caused the remainder of Elizabeth's nervousness to fade away.

After ten or so minutes of conversation, Darcy mentioned that Bingley would be joining them soon, and only a few more minutes passed before they heard his quick step on the stairs. He greeted her warmly, and asked after her family, and was pleased to be introduced to her aunt and uncle. He might have been a little more subdued than he had been previously, but otherwise was just the same. It was quite clear that neither he nor Miss Darcy entertained any particular tenderness for the other.

"Has it been many months since you have seen each other?" Miss Georgiana said.

"More than nine months," Bingley replied, "I have not seen Miss Elizabeth Bennet since the beginning of October, at Netherfield."

"I am pleased to find your memory so exact," Elizabeth said.

Bingley bowed a little, the tips of his ears turning pink. "And are *all* of your sisters at Longbourn?"

"All but one," Elizabeth said.

He looked up alertly, his face telegraphing his anxiety that she might follow up this statement by saying that Jane had lately been married, or some such. "Oh?"

"My sister Mary has moved with her new husband to the Hunsford Parsonage."

Bingley's face broke out into a broad smile. He made the appropriate congratulations, and found no other way to ask about Jane. Elizabeth considered asking him if he had seen her in London, as she had previously asked Darcy at Rosings, just to give him a hint that his sister and friend had kept it from him, as Darcy had confessed, but her courage failed her. Miss Darcy began to speak of the beauties of the little garden at the Lambton Parsonage, and Mr. Bingley shared a recollection that the Parsonage near to him growing up had been very plain indeed, a very Puritan expanse of bare metal, and Mrs. Gardiner shared an anecdote about the late parson who had inhabited it when she was first on board the ship. Her aunt must have realized who the young man was to Jane, but gave not a hint of it, and Elizabeth followed her lead and allowed the conversation to move on.

While she spoke with the others, Mr. Darcy was speaking with her uncle. The sight, in itself, was not very exceptional: they both looked very sophisticated and fashionable in their flowing neckties, tightly-fitted breeches, and the high glass-faceplate-topped hats that men of means had recently started wearing, which could so easily be converted into the helmet of an aether suit. Except for the difference in age, and Darcy's darker eyes and leaner build, they looked really rather similar, and yet the difference in how Darcy acted now to how he had acted when she had first met him at the Meryton assembly was so stark that she could not help but be astonished.

They stayed another twenty minutes, and before leaving, Miss Darcy, after several significant looks from her brother, invited them all to dine at Pemberley. Elizabeth dropped her eyes in confusion, and Mrs. Gardiner had to answer for them. They set the date for the dinner for the day after next, with the ladies to more informally visit Miss Darcy and Miss Bingley the following morning, and Mr. Gardiner to accompany them for fishing with the gentlemen.

§

Georgiana does not belong on a vessel blasting through the aether, Elizabeth thought the next day. The whole effect of the room's high ceilings and light-coloured furnishings, which could have put them in Grecian or Roman times, and of all of the party's fine clothes and beautifully-dressed hair, put Elizabeth in mind of an elven court from the fairytales she and Jane had used to make up. The clockwork animals that had adorned the room previously had been put away, so that the only modern touch was the aerator quietly ticktocking in one corner.

In the second-floor sitting room that they had admired so much only two days before, Elizabeth and Mrs. Gardiner had been received by Miss Darcy and the Bingley sisters, and been introduced to a Mrs. Annesley, the lady with whom Georgiana lived in London, a young widow with an angular, cut-glass beauty. Miss Bingley and her sister barely spoke, and Miss Darcy merely nodded slightly at every point with which she agreed. Mrs. Annesley and Mrs. Gardiner carried on most of the conversation.

"I understand from my brother that you excel at the pianoforte," Miss Darcy said to Elizabeth after a while.

Miss Bingley scoffed under her breath.

"Your brother exaggerates my skill," Elizabeth said with a smile.

Miss Darcy nodded. Half a head taller than anybody else in the room, and wrapped in an airy white dress, Miss Darcy could have played the elf queen in a family theatrical, but Elizabeth thought her overly-mannered regal nods arose from shyness rather than pride.

"He has said that *you* are very adept," Elizabeth went on.

Before Miss Darcy could do more than brighten at the praise, Miss Bingley said, "Mr. Darcy cannot say enough good things about Miss Darcy. He is a most attentive brother."

"Yes," Miss Darcy said, looking back and forth between Miss Bingley and Elizabeth.

"And how is your brother, Miss Bingley?" Mrs. Annesley asked.

"You shall see him later, and may judge for yourself."

After twenty or thirty minutes, servants entered with cold, thin slices of beef layered to look like rosettes, beautifully-decorated cakes, and pyramids of grapes, nectarines, and peaches. Miss Darcy led the way to the table, and they all followed and took the tiny bone china plates offered, and placed on them their selections.

Mr. Darcy entered the room then, and all of the ladies watched him. He bowed generally to the room, sweeping off his hat, and helped himself to a peach.

"How are the gentlemen enjoying their expedition?" Miss Bingley smiled at him from across the room.

"Very much," Mr. Darcy said, "although your brother has had to come back to change his clothes."

"Whatever has happened?"

"He fell in the lake."

Miss Bingley was surprised into laughter, and Elizabeth realized she had never heard Miss Bingley's natural laugh; all of her past laughter in Elizabeth's presence had been calculated or contemptuous. "How like him."

Mr. Darcy settled on the arm of the chair where his sister sat, and placed his hat on the table, where its glass top glinted from the lights in the candelabra. "I have left Mr. Gardiner in good hands with Mr. Pope and our gardener," he said to Mrs. Gardiner, and after she thanked him, added, "Perhaps I misspoke by saying 'good hands'; Mr. Pope managed to take a fish to the face while reeling one in."

There was general laughter, and Miss Darcy began to speak much more easily. Elizabeth exclaimed over the cake, and Miss Bingley said it was enough to tempt her to eat sweets, in the same tone one might say one was tempted to eat arsenic, and then went on, "Pray, Miss Eliza, are the engineers that came to build our house all gone now? They must be a great loss to *your* family."

Darcy looked at Miss Bingley, and then at Elizabeth. His sister looked back and forth between them, puzzled by the undertone of scorn in Miss Bingley's tone, but Darcy must never have mentioned to her Wickham's new profession, for she showed no confusion or distress. Elizabeth could tell from her tone that Miss Bingley had hoped to embarrass Elizabeth somehow, perhaps by making her betray the feelings Miss Bingley must think she had for Wickham or by reminding Mr. Darcy of the flirtatiousness of her younger sisters.

Her shot was misaimed, however. Elizabeth only smiled and said, "Yes, I believe my father feels their absence."

Miss Bingley tried again: "And how is your *mother's business* faring, Miss Eliza?"

"Very well," Elizabeth said composedly, and raising her chin, turned to Miss Darcy and said, "In fact, I would be obliged if we could send these peach pits to her, and see if she can do anything with them. These peaches are exceptional, and perhaps if they will germinate, we might make you a gift of one of the trees."

Miss Darcy was only too glad to agree, and the conversation turned to gardening, which Mrs. Annesley dearly loved. Elizabeth, able to show her own interest in her mother's absence, spoke more than previously, despite Darcy's gaze settling on her whenever she opened her mouth.

They left after another half hour, when Mr. Gardiner returned from fishing, and Elizabeth and Mrs. Gardiner spent the ride back to the hotel speaking of the beautiful house, the exceptional food, the excellent company, and the gracious hostess—everything except Darcy, on Elizabeth's side from fear of saying too much, and on Mrs. Gardiner's side from observing her niece's embarrassment.

They stopped at the Lambton post office, where Elizabeth sent to her mother the package of peach pits she had been given by a servant on her way out of the Pemberley dome. The rest of the day passed in letter-writing and visits to Mrs. Gardiner's friends, and, for Elizabeth, anticipation of the dinner the following evening.

§

They spent the morning of the dinner shopping; Elizabeth wanted a new dress, and when that turned out to be outside her budget, she purchased some new cerulean ribbons to brighten up her best pelisse, which she thought she had time to sew on before they went to Pemberley. However, when they returned to the inn, the barman gave her a letter from Jane, dated the day before. Her aunt and uncle left her to read her sister's letter in peace, setting off for a walk to give her privacy.

Jane started with an account of a goodbye party for Charlotte Lucas and Mary King, which Elizabeth was sorry she had missed, but then she wrote, in a far messier hand,

> "I have come back to add the most alarming news. Mr. Forster has sent an express to let us know that Lydia has eloped. She must have left Sunday night. She left a note for Mrs. Forster making it clear that the gentleman involved (if indeed such a word can be used to describe him) is Wickham! Mr. Denny, however, was overheard saying that he believed that W. had no honourable intentions. Mr. F. wrote from Herschel to say he has traced them there, and they were last seen on the Hardwicke road, which could mean they intend to stop there, or to go on to Darlington, where he has a large acquaintance from his youth, or even Kent or London, where they might be less noticeable in the crowds. Mr. F. is making further inquiries. I hope you will come home directly. Mamma is sick with worry. And if you are here, our uncle might join our father. Papa has already left for London to find her. I fear that even if he succeeds in discovering them, his anger and distress will result in some form of violence. Our uncle's presence may save everything. Please do what you can. Affectionately yours, Jane"

Elizabeth turned the page over frantically for more news, but there was no postscript. *It was not like Jane to waste paper*, she thought irrelevantly. She put down the letter, unconsciously squeezing it into a wrinkled mess. Lydia could be anywhere between Brighton and London—which comprised half of the ship! She might be almost anywhere. How was she to be found? And once found, what could they do to save her?

Elizabeth jumped up to run out of the inn to look for her uncle.

She opened the door to find Mr. Darcy with a servant who was in the act of reaching for the doorknob. Darcy looked at her, startled, and began to say something, but she spoke over him, saying in confusion, "I am so sorry, Mr. Darcy, but I must find my uncle immediately."

"May I fetch him? Or the servant?" he said, putting a hand on her arm. "You look distressed. Please, you must have a seat."

Elizabeth turned to the servant, a lanky boy of perhaps twelve, and said, "John, isn't it? Could you fetch Mr. and Mrs. Gardiner? They have gone walking, toward the church."

As he left, she sank down into a chair. A few tears fell onto her cheeks.

Darcy said, "How may I help you, Miss Bennet? You must know, I will do whatever I can. Only let me know what you need."

"I am not unwell," she said. "I have just—Jane has written—" She passed him the last page of the letter so he might see for himself. He read it, and his eyes raised to hers in horror.

"Wickham," he said.

"I know," she said. "I knew what he was. Had I but explained some part of what I had learnt, even only to my own family!"

He, too, turned the letter over in hopes of some scrawled lines on the back, and then, seeing none, passed it back to her. She folded it with the page about Charlotte's party, and shoved it into her pocket with some violence, as though it could not hurt them if it were out of sight.

"You have seen why I have asked for my uncle," she said, "but I do not see what he can do. Wickham cannot afford to marry a girl with nothing to her name but a partial share in a gardening business, and we cannot afford to bribe him to do so, nor can we hope to cover this affair up. Lydia's reputation will be in tatters."

But Darcy was no longer listening. He paced back and forth, frowning into a distance beyond the walls of the room they were in. She understood all at once that if he had been entertaining any further affection for her before, he must be conquering it now. Lydia was about to become the lowest of lowly connections. Elizabeth pinched the corners of her eyes to keep herself from crying any further, and occupied herself with sniffling and waiting for her uncle to come.

After a long pause, she heard Darcy say, "I am afraid you have been long desiring my absence."

He has such beautiful manners, she thought distantly. She looked over at him, and saw how implacably his face had stilled to an expression that might have been pain or might have been distaste. The light seemed to have gone out of his eyes.

Elizabeth said, with an attempt at mirroring his dignity, "Please give Miss Darcy our apologies and regrets for tonight's dinner, and conceal the reason for our abrupt departure as long as possible."

They were both retreating behind their good breeding, and each perfectly cordial word was another brick in the wall between them.

"Of course," he said, heading for the door. "You can be assured of my silence. I am sorry. I will leave you now. I hope this affair ends more happily than we could hope."

Mr. Gardiner opened the door just as Darcy reached it. They exchanged greetings, and her uncle went with him out into the hall. Mrs. Gardiner made to take Elizabeth's hands, but she held up a hand to ward her off, and followed the men out of the room. Consequently, she heard when Darcy said to Mr. Gardiner, "I have an idea of where he may have gone, sir."

"Where?" Elizabeth asked.

The two men turned to her. "Let me deal with this," her uncle said.

"Take me there," Elizabeth said.

"Your uncle can—"

"My uncle can accompany us," Elizabeth said. "Then there can be no question of impropriety on our part. But I am the only one who can convince Lydia to come home before she is ruined forever."

"It is too late for that," Mr. Gardiner said, gently.

"She is only just sixteen," Elizabeth said, despairingly, "and she has not been protected as she should have been."

The men were looking at her owlishly, and she could see their judgement of Lydia hardening on their faces.

CHAPTER THIRTEEN

ELIZABETH EXPECTED THAT NEARLY THE WHOLE SHIP would share in the men's judgement. Her heart sank.

Yet Miss Darcy had escaped that judgement.

She turned to Mr. Darcy. "She is the same age that—" and then, remembering that the Gardiners were right there, and that Georgiana's reputation could still be ruined if the story got out, she changed her sentence midstream "—that the other lady you knew, was," she said, and she saw Darcy understand her. "Would you have sentenced her to marry him?"

"I—" His eyes went far away as he considered that averted future, and then returned to her. "I do not see an alternative. They have been three days on the road."

"But you know where they are," Elizabeth said. She remembered Lydia's blithe mentions of packet-dodging, and an idea came to her, almost wholly-formed. It only depended on timing. "Where is that?"

He was plainly puzzled. "Hardwicke. It is the next superstructure after Herschel en route to London, and it is where Mrs. Younge, a friend of his, now runs a lodging-house."

Elizabeth recognized the name from his letter. "I see," she said, thinking furiously. "If we could find them quickly, if we could remove her back to Brighton, or, if we could bring her to Longbourn, I am sure if we said she had to come home for, for, say, an illness of our mother's. Jane said mother was very ill with worry. I am sure the

Forsters would support us in such a lie."

"The timing does not work," her uncle said. "It would take far too long."

"But if she arrived in Longbourn tomorrow," Elizabeth said.

Brighton was in the superstructure of Feilding. Between there and Longbourn was Herschel, Hardwicke, Darlington, Castlereagh, and London. Each was about half a day's distance from the next by carriage. A fast horse could do it in less than a quarter of the time, with a higher top speed and no need for stops to rewind the mainspring, which was how Jane's express had gotten to her so quickly.

It took three days to travel from Feilding to Headfort by carriage. Lydia had first been missed on the thirteenth of July. For the lie that she was travelling to see her mother to be plausible, she would have to arrive at Longbourn three days later on the sixteenth, or four days later if her aunt and uncle were in the carriage, which their neighbours would understand meant that she had stayed overnight in London.

It was the sixteenth now.

Elizabeth continued, "If she was seen arriving with me and my aunt and uncle from London... I think that would work."

"But Lizzy—" her aunt said behind her, as she turned to Darcy to ask, "Do you know the dome and the street address?"

"Fifty-six Edward—in St. Clement's dome—but—"

For her uncle to travel from Darlington where they were now, to Lydia and Wickham in Hardwicke, would take a full day, assuming they were staying where Mr. Darcy believed they were. Then to bring Lydia back to Longbourn would take another two days, assuming he could get her to leave Wickham, putting her at Longbourn on the nineteenth at the earliest; gossips like the Miss Harringtons would be certain to ask questions.

The other difficulty to be overcome was Wickham's silence. He would not want to let Lydia go until he had been paid off, and Elizabeth couldn't see how that was to be done. In the immediate term, perhaps a promise of payment would suffice. She felt all of the pressure of time slipping through their fingers, and trusted in her own ingenuity to think of something while she put the first part of her plan into place.

Darcy and her uncle were still discussing their own plans, and she could see from their expressions that they would never agree to her plan, and never let her help. They would say it was too risky.

"You are right, of course," she said to her uncle. "It will take too long. You must go to Hardwicke and convince Mr. Wickham to marry her. My aunt and I will return to London to intercept my father. We must set out at once."

Mr. Darcy said, "Please allow me to send a manservant to accompany the ladies back to London."

Elizabeth and her aunt went to write quick notes to the friends they had planned to meet later in the week, while Mr. Darcy went to fetch a manservant from Pemberley and make their apologies to Miss Darcy. Her letters finished quickly (and possibly illegibly), Elizabeth threw her things into her suitcase any which way and went to her aunt.

As she packed her and her husband's clothes, Mrs. Gardiner said, "Jane may be right. How could he plan to take advantage of a girl who is protected by his own employer? We may all be panicking for nothing. They may even already be married. Lydia would think that was a great joke."

"So she would," Elizabeth said, "but Wickham will never marry a poor woman. Lydia has no brothers, and papa is so sardonic in his criticisms, that I could easily imagine Wickham thinking he will not do much to defend her honour. And anyway, had they truly intended to marry, why must it be a secret? Lydia certainly intended marriage—her note to Mrs. Forster shows that, at least—but she is only just sixteen, and easily talked around by such a man. If we find them already married, then your question is answered." She sighed. "The worst of it is, I knew that he was bad. But that he might look at Lydia simply never occurred to me."

Mr. Gardiner stuck his head in the door, and said, "Is everything ready? I have settled up with the innkeeper."

They took the luggage downstairs, and found Mr. Darcy with his manservant waiting at the entrance to the inn. They loaded up the carriage with luggage while the manservant cranked up the carriage's mechanism, and Mr. Gardiner removed a small valise for his own use over the next few days.

Mr. and Mrs. Gardiner took their leave with affectionate murmurs and clasped hands, leaning their heads together, and Mr. Darcy said to Elizabeth, "I hope you have safe travels."

She shook his hand and said, haltingly, "Thank you again—for your welcome, and—and for, for your assistance."

He nodded and handed her up into the carriage next to her aunt, then put his hands deep within his pockets and leaned back against the wall of the inn, the brim of his hat hiding his expression.

The ladies looked back at the gentlemen as they rode away, Mrs. Gardiner watching her husband pick up his valise from the dusty metal floor of the dome, and Elizabeth taking a last look at Darcy, whom she was sure she would never see again.

When the men were out of sight, Elizabeth acquainted her aunt with her plan.

"I do not like it," Mrs. Gardiner said, when she had finished talking. "You take too many risks, and there are too many uncertainties."

"Only do what I ask," Elizabeth said. "Wait by the London spoke for us with your family's carriage, and be prepared to leave London as soon as we arrive. Bring my bag. And write your husband, and my father, to let them know what we are about, so they may join us at Longbourn when your letters reach them. Oh, and write Mr. Forster to call off his search, if he is still trying to trace them."

"It is too dangerous, Lizzy. I ought to forbid you from doing it."

"I have to try."

Mrs. Gardiner shook her head and then nodded, and just in time, because they were approaching the turn for the Darlington spoke in the center of the dome. As they slowed to wait for a break in traffic, Elizabeth flung open the carriage door and rolled from the carriage to the edge of the thoroughfare. She looked back to see her aunt pulling the door shut, and the manservant apparently oblivious as he drove on.

She put on her aether suit and clipped the straps of the bag she had been carrying it in through a loop on the hip of her suit. The men could shove the bags down one pant leg, but the women had added these loops years back after a female aethernaut had died from a mishap caused by it tangling up her feet in the bottom of her suit's skirts. She cycled through the airlock. Some workers were shouting at each other by the receiving area, and nobody saw her come in. She went quickly around the other side of the counterweight, both so she wouldn't be seen and to block out the glare of the lights fixed to illuminate the area for loading and unloading supplies. Unlike the counterweights that operated the elevators to the cupolas, these were brute, hollow cubes with space inside for more weights to be added to counter especially heavy shipments. The area for the counterweight was not lit; people were not supposed to go into the unlit areas. She climbed up the boxy counterweight, able to gain purchase on its straight sides only because they were pockmarked with the wear and tear of operating at varying gravities in the open aether. Unlike most items in the ship, these moved regularly between the weightlessness at the center of the ship to its heaviest simulated gravity.

She flattened herself on its top so the workers wouldn't see her, and grabbed the first man-sized link in the chain which rose out of its top. Shipments came and went all day in Headfort, and she could only assume it would be the same here. When the shipping container leaving central processing began its descent, the counterweight started to rise with a jerk. After a moment, she pulled herself to a standing position, the counterweight under her swaying a little. She flexed her legs, taking care not to lock her knees.

The words of Jane's letter repeated in her head: "She left a note for Mrs. Forster making it clear that the gentleman involved (if indeed such a word can be used to describe him) is Wickham! Mr. Denny, however, was overheard saying that he believed that W. had no honourable intentions."

She had to save Lydia. *Idiot headstrong child.*

Years before, when Elizabeth had gone packet-dodging with Charlotte Lucas and the Harrington sisters, they had ridden up the counterweight and jumped onto the container coming down, then jumped to the ground and rolled, before it hit; she had stopped when Charlotte had landed badly and broken a leg four or five years before. Now, she would be riding the counterweight all the way to the top, which she had never done before, and jumping to the central shaft that ran through the middle of the ship, and hopefully not missing and killing herself.

For several minutes, she had nothing to do but to cling on to the chain link and look around. The sight was amazing, and although she had always claimed to be packet-dodging to prove that she was no coward, in response to the dares of the others, she thought the real reason they wanted to climb the packets was to see the stars all around them.

From inside the domes, the stars were merely a smeared impression of dots of lights. Each superstructure had an outer dome which was made of thick glass with a metal mesh laid over it, and then each town had its own dome within that, and the glass of the smaller town domes had wobbles and air bubbles and other imperfections running all through them, so that seeing the stars clearly was impossible. To climb out of their habitats was a revelation every time: the blackness of aether, with the spinning stars, and the loneliness of the giant wheel of the ship. Within the domes, it was easy to be caught up in the day-to-day tasks and emergencies that kept them all busy, but out here, she was confronted with the immensity of the aether and the insignificance of the ship; the domes blinking with lights in a blazing arc that felt far away until she looked at the distant stars.

And the gravity! At the halfway point, when they had jumped to the other side to return to their domes, they had weighed about half of their usual weight, and when they jumped down to the top of the container, they floated.

The rebreather in her suit's helmet ticked away, cleaning the air of her exhales. Her suit tightened a little around her as the aether pushed on it, and the cold struck her arms. She wished she had worn a heavier jacket. The full shipping container passed her going down, and the moment when she could have jumped on it to ride back to the surface also passed. Her feet rose off the counterweight as the centrifugal force normally holding her down had less and less effect; as she approached the center of the ship, she also approached near-weightlessness. She wrapped her legs around the chain link, though the bulk of her skirts through her suit got in the way, riding it as a man would a horse.

At the top of its arc, the counterweight came to a stop while the container on the surface was being unloaded. She didn't know how long that would take, so she only took a few breaths before launching herself toward central processing. She grabbed a strut and hung on, trying to orient herself. She could see tethered workers loading an enormous crate in the next open area. To either side of Darlington were Hardwicke and Castlereagh, and she was pretty sure the load they were preparing was going to Castlereagh, because past it she could see the brighter lights of London. Slowly, and terrified lest she lose her grip, she inched her way in the other direction. She could never have managed it in normal gravity, but she weighed so little here that the only challenge was to keep from losing contact with central processing and floating off into the aether to die slowly, unable to get back to the ship.

In the middle distance, a steam shuttle was dragging a captured asteroid. She paused to watch it, fascinated: she had heard of such things but from the inner surface of the ship, could never have seen it, as the shuttle would appear as only a series of faint moving lights from inside the domes. *Colonel Fitzwilliam could have captured that asteroid,* she thought. Perhaps someday she could tell him she had seen this. A cloud of steam and soot floated from the shuttle's vents and was diffused by the lack of gravity, each particle thrown in a slightly different direction. The cloud appeared to drift slowly backward over the giant rock, but actually stayed mostly still as the asteroid was towed through it toward her.

After a moment, she moved on and finally made it to the Hardwicke spoke. If she was wrong about London being the brightest nearby superstructure, and had therefore gone in the wrong direction, she would end up in Castlereagh instead and would have this all to do over.

A shipping container had been sent down a few minutes before and the workers had congregated at the far end of the loading area to load another container, so she snuck up onto the platform to steal an unused tether attached to the wall. The lamps over their working space made a round glow, and then a stark shadow, which she stayed within so that nobody might notice her. She was careful, and lucky, and successful. She attached the tether to her suit and worked her way over to just above where the counterweight would arrive, and clung to her strut there, on the underside of the workers' floor where she couldn't be seen. She watched the counterweight rise. It stopped at the top while the container was being unloaded on the surface. She watched it carefully, and began to pray steadily, and just as it started to sink again, she pushed herself lightly away from the underside of the loading bay toward the chain, slinging the tether like a whip around the chain. She collided with the chain and felt a shock along her whole body, and then she was clinging on. If she had weighed her normal amount, she would have slammed into it hard enough to bruise, she thought. She reattached the tether properly, and looked up, breathing hard, but nobody seemed to have noticed her little adventure; nobody was looking over the edge. They had no reason to pay any attention to the actions of the counterweights.

"Almost there," she whispered to herself.

She was clinging to a loop of the chain link that was welded to the counterweight. She slid to the bottom of the link, and held on to it with one arm while she slowly moved down to the next, and then reattached the tether to the bottom-most link. She lost her grip, and slid the rest of the way. Once she was standing on the top of the counterweight, she only needed to stay out of sight of the workers as the weight rushed toward their work space. She knelt, and then sat, and kept tight to the bottom of the chain. The whole way down, she became heavier and heavier, until she weighed her normal amount when the counterweight landed at the bottom of Hardwicke spoke.

She left the tether attached to the bottom link, and slid to the ground. The men down here were swarming the supplies they had just unloaded from the previous container, getting the space clear for the next one. Between their intense focus on their work, and her sticking to the unlit edges of the spoke, she was able to make it to the airlock unseen.

Outside the airlock, she removed her aether suit and packed it carefully in its bag. She looked all around, and recognized nothing, by which she hoped this was Hardwicke, and not Castlereagh. She hadn't made any particular point of looking at the spoke in Castlereagh when she had gone to visit Mary, but they had passed it there and back, and this looked wholly unfamiliar. She checked her watch; it had taken her only two hours to get from Lambton to here.

She waved down a passing hackney-coach and asked for St. Clement's dome, and when she was told with surprise that she was already there, for Fifty-six Edward Street, where she was taken immediately, though the driver made several rude comments about unaccompanied women and then an inappropriate offer that made her jump down from the coach while it was still moving, a block shy of her objective. She made sure the coach did not linger near the address she had given the driver before continuing on, but he was apparently satisfied with the bills she had left on the seat, and perhaps also with her having taken fright.

When Mrs. Younge opened the door, Elizabeth thought that she had a face that she would have liked if she had met her in any other way. The lady had a pleasantly lop-sided smile: a dimple only on the left side, the gap of a missing tooth on the bottom right. Her nose was freckled and her hair showed red highlights in the light from the lamps. She had dark circles under her eyes. She was a widow, and, from the cut of her clothing, poor; Elizabeth presumed the Darcys would not have given her a reference, ending her career as a governess, but there was no question of her starving to death, like there might have been on Earth. The ship needed babies and workers. Elizabeth frowned; Mrs. Younge hadn't needed to help Wickham prey on other women to survive; a few minutes later, when she saw how the lady looked at him with a kind of hopeless longing, she understood better.

Wickham was surprised to see her, and leered. "I would not have thought they would send *you*," he said.

"I have come anyway to fetch my sister," Elizabeth said.

"I do not think she will want you moralizing at her," he said. He made no motion to get Lydia.

Mrs. Younge, perhaps seeing a way to get rid of her rival, called up the stairs for her.

Lydia soon came down, still buttoning her skirt over her petticoats. "Oh, Lizzy!" she said. "What fun! Did you come to see me to church?"

"Are you getting married today, then?" Elizabeth asked with a great deal of relief, but Wickham was shaking his head no, and Lydia laughing.

"We shall marry soon, of course, but we must go shopping first." Lydia went to the little mirror by the door and began to finger-comb her disheveled hair. "George has promised me a nice dress and a new hat."

Elizabeth winced.

Wickham said nothing.

"And then when we go back to Brighton," Lydia continued, "you and Kitty may come with me and my charming husband and I shall find husbands for you both."

"I thank you for my share of the favour," said Elizabeth; "but I do not particularly like your way of getting husbands. I have come to help bring you home."

"I do not want your help," Lydia said, "and I will not leave George." She smiled at him.

He did not smile back, and that made her pout.

Elizabeth looked back and forth between them. "*Do* you intend to marry her, Wickham?"

"I cannot afford to be married," he said. "I have debts. Do you have one thousand pounds to pay them off, and the money for a marriage besides?"

"My father has authorized me to pay your debts," Elizabeth lied, "if you marry Lydia."

"We must have money to live on."

"You must work, then. What of your salary from Mr. Forster?"

"I find I do not like engineering," he said, and he smiled at her, by now perfectly at ease, sure that she would give him any amount of money to save her sister's reputation.

But Lydia said, "George, you *do* mean to marry me?" and when he did not answer quickly enough for her, she smacked him around his head and shoulders and pulled him up to what must have been their room. Their voices filtered through the floor, rising and falling and rising again. There was a smash of crockery, and more shouting.

Elizabeth quietly asked Mrs. Younge for paper and a pen, and wrote a note to her uncle that only said, "We are on our way to our house," unsigned and with no names, lest Mrs. Younge later decide to try her hand at blackmail. Her uncle would recognize her handwriting. She then sat silently, avoiding the satirical eye of her host, until finally Lydia came slamming down the stairs, carrying a valise, shouting back upstairs, "And I hope you choke on it!"

Elizabeth handed the note to Mrs. Younge. "For our uncle, in case he will not believe she has left." She grabbed the valise, checked that it contained Lydia's aether suit, and hustled her out the door and into a hackney-coach before she could change her mind. As the hackney-coach pulled away, she saw Wickham come bolting out of the door, and Mrs. Younge crying in the doorway behind him, holding her cheek, her bottom lip split open.

Explaining the mechanics of what she meant to do to get Lydia home again took the length of the ride, but it caught Lydia's imagination. "La! I cannot believe you would do something so unladylike, Lizzy."

"We must try very hard not to be seen."

"Just see if you can keep up with me." Lydia tossed her hair.

Once at the spoke, they donned their suits and crossed through the airlock. One of the workers unloading large boxes looked over at them, but they were anonymous in the bulky suits, and he must have assumed they belonged there, since he immediately turned back to his work. They walked into the darkness, where the harsh lights aimed at the loading area fell short, and waited for the men to finish unloading and send the container back, which would bring the counterweight to where they could unobtrusively climb on.

Lydia put her helmet against Elizabeth's. "Look," she said, "he must have followed us." She pointed, and Elizabeth saw Wickham by the airlock, wearing only his rebreather. Everybody knew you could not stay in the aether without a suit for long. He looked around, did not see them, and went back out.

They waited. Mrs. Younge's house was not so far away as to prevent him going back for his aether suit, and Elizabeth was anxious that they leave as soon as they could, before he could return, but the packet schedule worked against her. They waited for perhaps half or three-quarters of an hour, and finally the empty container began to rise.

The airlock cycled again, and a suited figure—surely Wickham—came in and began to walk slowly around the unlit perimeter of the spoke. The container was out of sight now in the darkness, and they knew the counterweight would come down any second. Elizabeth leaned her helmet against Lydia's. "Be ready," she said, "move fast when it touches the ground, but stay down."

"I've done this millions of times," Lydia said. "I have never been caught."

Elizabeth looked back to see where Wickham had gone, but couldn't find him in the darkness.

The counterweight touched down, and Elizabeth and Lydia scrambled up its sides. (Not for the first time, Elizabeth wished the skirts of ladies' aether suits allowed for a little more freedom of movement.) They each grabbed the first chain link, standing side by side and hugging the thick, heavy metal and each other. The jerk of the counterweight leaving the ground traveled through the link into their arms. Then Wickham was there, grabbing Elizabeth and prying her off the chain. She lost her balance and fell to one knee. He turned on her, and she could see his face within his helmet snarling. He kicked her hard in the ribs, overbalancing her so that she fell onto her back, and he looked down at her for a long moment before he turned to her sister.

If not for the suit, he would probably have broken her ribs; he might even have killed her. She tried to gasp, and couldn't. She couldn't breathe. Her lungs ached along with her ribs. Wickham, who some part of her had still hoped was misunderstood, who even now she thought might be redeemed somehow, had done this. The rebreather in her helmet ticked slowly, releasing precious fresh air that she couldn't convince her lungs to draw in. The lights of the ground fell further away. The struggling figures in front of her grew hazy and gray and anonymous. The counterweight was swaying—when she had traveled alone it had wobbled a little, but Lydia and Wickham's movements were making it rock back and forth, and Elizabeth's off-center presence was probably also destabilizing. She slid back and forth a few inches, first toward the center of the counterweight when it swayed one way, and then toward the side when it went the other way.

She was finally able to take a deep and shaky breath, and then, all at once, she realized three things: one, that she was, by increments, getting very close to the edge and could slide over at any time; two, that the tether she had left tied to the chain link when she had arrived was dangling very close to her hand; and three, that if she made a move to grab for it, she had better not miss, because anything she did now would make her slide off the counterweight and fall a very long way.

She grabbed for it.

Time was crawling by; her grab moved her hand through the air so slowly that she had plenty of time to think, *I am going to die, and he is going to throw Lydia after me, and nobody will understand what happened here.* It took her years to catch the end of the tether and wrap it several times around her glove as she slid halfway over the edge, awkwardly poised to fall.

Hand by hand, she pulled herself up by the tether. Wickham had grabbed Lydia, and pushed his head against her helmet; she had one arm around the bottom chain link, her valise in that hand held by her hip against the chain, and Wickham had his hands on her shoulders. They were getting high enough now that the aether replacing the air, even through her suit, was thick with cold, but he seemed unaware of it, his whole being focused only on Lydia. They were shouting: she could hear their voices getting higher and louder through the thinning air, but not what they were saying. Elizabeth passed the tether through her front and Lydia's back belt-loops and secured them both. The counterweight swayed slightly from side to side, too slowly; she kept countering the sway by leaning too far to the other side, her body accustomed to more gravity than this. The stars wheeled around them and the ship blazed in a high arc.

Then Wickham shook Lydia, as though to shake sense into her, and she slapped at him with her free arm. She stepped back from him, letting go of the chain link and stretching the tether to its maximum length, and he stepped back from her. For a moment he held up both his hands, as if to say, *calm down*. Each of them was only a step from the edge. They both had the casual stance of skilled packet-dodgers, their knees slightly bent, prepared to ride the sway of the weight without thought, but they were so focused on each other, they couldn't have much attention left over for physics.

And then the container passed them on its way down, and Elizabeth glanced at it, startled, just as the counterweight wobbled a little harder, perhaps from the slight wind of its passing, and when she looked back, Wickham was gone.

CHAPTER FOURTEEN

THEY REACHED LONGBOURN ON THE MORNING of the seventeenth. Lydia cried nearly the whole way from London to Meryton, and shivered all over.

"Shh, shh, hush now," Mrs. Gardiner said, rubbing the back of Lydia's neck. She had met them at the London spoke as promised, and they had found Mr. Bennet after a few hours of guesswork and driving around the City dome, so there were four of them in the carriage.

They passed several people walking on the road, and when they overtook William Goulding and his daughter, Ganymede, her father insisted that Lydia sit up and wave at the pastor, though her face was still white with shock.

Elizabeth had slept a little, dreaming of that moment when she turned and Wickham was gone, and waking, and impatiently telling herself to let it go, it was over and done and Lydia saved, and falling asleep again only to remember it again, and again jerk awake. She stared out at the passing town numbly, and her reflection in the window turned its eyes away from her.

Lydia slept a little on her aunt's shoulder, but only a little, and they were a very tired party when they finally arrived. Kitty and the young Gardiners came running out of the house, and the joyful surprise that lighted up their faces made Lydia smile for the first time since it had happened.

Elizabeth was the first out of the machine, and hugged her cousins hastily on her way to Jane, who was just coming to the door.

"We have Lydia," she said, taking Jane by the arms and steering her further inside. "She is safe. All will be well."

Then Lydia came in behind her, supported by her father, and Kitty went running for their mother, who was in one of her greenhouses, though Elizabeth could see she was pacing back and forth rather than doing any useful work.

The whole story was told while Mrs. Gardiner was engaged with her children. Elizabeth minimized, as much as possible, Darcy's role, and did not mention his sister or any particulars involving Bingley, to spare her sister pain. Nobody seemed to dwell overmuch on Darcy's role in the story; they were all very much shocked at the death of Wickham, as must be supposed.

Nobody could bear to task Lydia with the error of her ways, the closest being Mrs. Bennet's comment: "I have not had a wink of sleep since Mr. Bennet left, I have had such tremblings, such flutterings all over me, such spasms in my side, and pains in my head. But never mind," she added, seeing Lydia's face twist, "you are safe home and that is all that matters!"

Once the story was finished, and Lydia had given what confirmation of its particulars as she could bear to describe, she begged to be excused and went off to her chamber.

"Is there any possibility," Kitty asked quietly after she had gone, "that Lydia pushed him?"

"None whatsoever," Elizabeth said with a firmness she could not have called up in the immediate shock of the event. "He had stepped wholly away from her, so she would have had to step forward to do it, and I would have felt the tether pull, even if I had not seen it." She had only the previous day's experience of those tethers, and she thought what she said was true, but the actual physics of it didn't matter now. What mattered was that there be no question of Lydia's culpability.

"Let us hope," said Mrs. Bennet just as quietly, "that her innocence is never in question."

There was a silence as everybody declined to address the double meaning of this statement.

"Nobody knew Lydia was there but the people in this room, and the Gardiners, and the Forsters, and Lydia herself," Elizabeth said at last.

"And Mr. Darcy," Kitty reminded her with an arch of her eyebrow.

Elizabeth waved off the mention of him with one hand. "Unless—did anybody write to Mary? She would be sure to tell Mr. Collins, and he all the world."

"I did write her," said Mrs. Bennet, "but I have been so distracted, the letter is on my vanity upstairs still. I had some idea of holding the letter until you could join us here, Eliza, to add your own postscript, as I supposed you would come straight from Lambton at your sister's request, and nothing would be settled for days. I never imagined you would go haring off the way that you did. So it was never sent."

"And now never need be," Mr. Bennet said.

"Why, then, if Wickham's death is investigated at all," Elizabeth said, "I do not see how they would connect us to it, unless Mr. Forster were to betray us, or Mrs. Younge were to accuse us, but surely she would rather avoid the notice of the police."

"Well," said Mrs. Bennet, with her first smile of the day, "since the story is that I am ill, I must go back to my bed. Mr. Bennet, perhaps you can come and read to me. Children, we are not to be disturbed."

"I must write Mr. Forster," Jane said.

Elizabeth found Careful and hugged him to herself for a good ten minutes, until the dog began squirming too much and she could release him with a real laugh.

Later that day, Elizabeth went upstairs to change for dinner, and found Jane lying on her bed, reading old letters. Elizabeth recognized Miss Bingley's elegant handwriting before Jane slid them under her pillow. Elizabeth pretended she had not seen.

"Our mother seems much improved," she said instead. "Was she so very ill?"

"I have never seen her like it," Jane said. "She just closed the door to her bedroom and would not get out of bed. She kept saying that Father would have to fight Wickham to make him marry her, and Wickham would shoot him. And then she would stare up at the ceiling without moving for hours. She took no food, only weak tea."

"How did our father take it?"

"Much the same, but more quietly."

"Never have I been more grateful that we do not keep servants. We could never have kept it from them. Did anybody call during the last few days?"

"No, we put it about that our mother was ill, for she said she did not feel equal to seeing anybody."

"If Lady Lucas did not come offering condolences then you must have kept it all secret enough," Elizabeth said. "But I wish that we had been less secret before and made sure that Lydia, at least, knew Wickham's true character."

"We acted with the best intentions."

"If Mary were here," Elizabeth said, "she might remind us that the road to Hell is said to be paved with something very like."

"Do you really think we can simply bury the whole affair?" Jane asked.

Elizabeth frowned. "I have hope. Mr. Forster will not betray us, nor Darcy. He promised to keep our secret, and he may be many things, but he is a man of his word. The only other person who knows for certain that Lydia was with him is Mrs. Younge, and she only knows that he left to follow us. We do not even know if they will find a body. There was enough gravity he would have fallen toward the ship, but he could easily have missed the opening through which the shipments are transported. Without a—a body—" she stumbled over the word "—any searchers are apt to assume he is laying low someplace. I do not know, but I think we have a very good chance."

§

After a few days—having traveled in the traditional manner, he had been on the road nearly the entire time—Mr. Gardiner joined them, putting Elizabeth's note, given to him by Mrs. Younge, into the fire in front of her.

"What a pitiable creature," he said of Mrs. Younge. "I told her to come to me if she would like an honest job and is willing to relocate to London."

"That was very good of you," Elizabeth said.

"Perhaps we can give her some small measure of assistance, if she does not take Mr. Darcy's offer."

"Mr. Darcy's offer?"

"Yes, he came with me to show me where she stayed," Mr. Gardiner said, as if it were the most natural thing in the world. Her idea of who Darcy was did not include his voluntarily visiting the man who had attempted to seduce his sister, and yet. Her uncle was still talking: "It seems that she depended upon Wickham to some extent. News of his death was spreading through the dome when I left."

"News of his death! They have found his—him, then?"

"Yes, the body was found in the central spoke, rather mangled apparently." He saw her face, and put his arms around her. "I am sorry, my dear. I did not think. But how did it happen?"

Elizabeth told the story again, and begged him not to bother poor Lydia with any mention of it.

Elizabeth said, "Uncle, how did it come about that Mr. Darcy accompanied you to Hardwicke?"

Her uncle raised his eyebrows. "I assumed he was there more or less on your behalf."

Elizabeth coloured but kept her eyes steadily on her uncle's.

"He came with me to discover them. He said that it was his fault Wickham's character was not known."

Kitty then came in to have a muffin, and nothing more was said.

Soon after this conversation, the Gardiners left with their children for London, and Mr. Bennet called Elizabeth to the library.

"Lizzy, I bear you no ill-will for being justified in your advice to me last May, which, considering the event, shows some greatness of mind," he began. "But now that your aunt and uncle are gone, and the worst shock is over, I can confess that I am as shocked by your audacity as Lydia's wickedness. Everything has turned out well enough, but I could as easily have had to bury two daughters this week."

"Papa—"

"No," he said. "Do not apologize. I did not tell you not to do anything so foolish since it never once occurred to me that you would try, so I cannot rightly blame you."

"I had no intention of apologizing," Elizabeth said.

"I have shown a great poverty of imagination," he said. "I see now that you are the most ill-behaved of my children after all."

Elizabeth hugged him. "I will try not to worry you," she said.

She left the library thoughtful. She was struck by the justice of his complaint: she had never truly believed that she could come to harm, but of course, after Wickham, it was impossible to deny.

With the rumours of his death trickling in from Hardwicke—he had been pushed into the path of the falling counterweight, some stories had it, or had been packet-dodging and his fickle companions fled—Meryton was in a fever to produce the most salacious gossip that could be found about their former favourite. Wickham was found to have tried to seduce every innocent daughter in town, and to be in debt to every tradesman and gambler in the dome. Though she knew half of it must be exaggeration, Elizabeth heard enough that her relief at her sister's escape became still more profound.

Yet none of the rumours seemed to suspect anything other than misadventure, and no police came to their door, so that after the passage of a week, Elizabeth began to think they might be safe.

§

The peach pits had been forgotten in the immediate aftermath of Lydia's misadventure, and Mrs. Bennet found them again one day and set Elizabeth to the task of planting them. They had thoroughly dried out in the box they'd been sent in, and she was able to crack them open to extract their seeds, which she set to soak in some old crockery. After a few hours spent reading, she added some soil and took them to one of the cabinets that Mrs. Bennet had set against the back of their dome, where it was always quite chilly, so that the seeds would think it was winter. She would check them daily to see if they sprouted.

It was difficult, during the whole procedure, not to think about Darcy. His information about Mrs. Younge's whereabouts had been indispensable, but she wished that she had somehow been able to find out Mrs. Younge's address without acquainting him with her sister's elopement.

At Pemberley, and in Lambton, he had been so kind, and had sought out her company so determinedly, that she had been sure he still felt at least something for her, but any feelings he still cherished for her could not withstand this blow. Weeks passed with no word of him, and no way to get it: she certainly could not be so presumptuous as to write to Miss Darcy, though if the peach seeds sprouted, she might in a few months be able to send her the tiniest tree, as promised—that was something. But to wait so long!

Charlotte was in London now with Miss King, and Elizabeth wrote her there, but could not bring herself to put to paper everything that consumed her, so she wrote of her make-up work sessions: long night shifts of signal work with the taciturn Harriet Harrington, which allowed Elizabeth to read her mother's gardening books without her mother seeing her doing it and getting ideas about passing along her business; prepping loaves of bread with William Goulding's children, now old enough to join in the rota; countless carrots peeled and string beans trimmed. She was so busy she had no time to pine for Darcy, but somehow she managed it anyway, and Jane, she could tell, continued to think of Bingley, though his name never passed her lips.

Gradually, Lydia emerged from her chamber more and more often. At first she was entirely subdued, and then after a few weeks, her natural animal spirits began to assert themselves and she grew more interested again in comparing ribbons and clothes with Kitty. At the August Meryton assembly, Lydia danced only with a few of the boys whom she had known from childhood, and flirted, as far as Elizabeth observed, with nobody. She seemed a thoroughly reformed character.

At the assembly they also heard the news, which had apparently been going around the neighbourhood for at least a week, that Mr. Bingley was at last coming back to Netherfield.

§

Elizabeth walked down the rows of vegetables, picking away a few browning leaves and adding a little water to each of the cucumber plants. She hummed, and thought of very little. The arc lights also hummed (and, presumably, thought of very little), and the clockwork mister misted, and the smell of mulch and dirt and greenery filled her nostrils.

"Mamma sent me out to help," Jane said from the doorway, and Elizabeth looked up with a start.

"I think it is all finished," she said. "I was about to come in."

Jane came over to her, and put a hand on her shoulder, very seriously. "I saw how you looked at me at the assembly. I might have seemed a little distressed, but it was only because I felt that I *should* be looked at. I want you to know that I am entirely recovered from my tenderness toward Mr. Bingley. He may come and go as it pleases him and I will not be affected in the slightest."

"I understand," Elizabeth said. She understood perfectly that Jane would always value a calm façade over everything, including self-knowledge; it was the only fault she had, this one way in which her pride insisted she be insensible. She would not hurt her sister by pointing it out, however, since her façade would be her only comfort if Bingley really had no intention of renewing his attentions. From what she had seen in Lambton, she thought he would very much want to see Jane.

Bingley did not leave them to themselves. He visited the following Tuesday, the very first morning after he arrived.

Lydia saw him come through the airlock from her upstairs window, and yelled down the stairs so that the whole house knew: "Mr. Bingley and Mr. Darcy are just coming through the 'lock!" Jane kept trimming string beans in the kitchen, her head down, no expression at all on her face. Lydia skipped down the stairs into the kitchen, and Careful began barking at the door.

Mrs. Bennet raised her eyebrows at Elizabeth. "Miss Eliza, I had quite forgot, in all the talk of—" here she glanced at the kitchen, indicating she was thinking of Lydia, and changed whatever she had been about to say, "that is, in all the excitement of Lydia coming home, that a certain gentleman showed you so much attention in Lambton."

"No, mamma," Elizabeth said, with some confusion, but no wish to be teased. "I see what you are hinting, but I have no expectations there."

Mrs. Bennet only smiled. Elizabeth blushed. Then the men were at the door. Kitty ran to let them in, Careful on her heels. The beagle was still smelling the gentlemen's feet as they entered, and doing his best to trip them. Mr. Bingley smiled down at him, and called him a good dog, and Darcy knelt to pet him, and Careful barked and bowed. Kitty took him out and into the library, where his kennel was. Jane, very pale, took off her apron, and they all went to the parlour.

"How are your aunt and uncle?" Darcy asked once they were all seated.

"Very well," Elizabeth said.

"They stayed with us for a week in July," Mrs. Bennet said. "I heard that you met them in Lambton. I must thank you—"

"No—" Mr. Darcy said, and glanced at Bingley, who of course would not know about Lydia's misadventures.

Mrs. Bennet took the hint and only said, "They were very glad to meet you."

"And how is your sister?" Elizabeth said.

"She is very well."

He said nothing further, and Elizabeth did not know how to start the conversation again.

"You have been away for several months, Mr. Bingley," Mrs. Bennet said.

"Nearly ten months," he replied.

She asked after his sisters, who he said were well, and told him a little about Mary's wedding, and said how good the harvest had been. Lydia asked how long he meant to stay.

"A few weeks," he said.

He then asked Jane if she had been well, and then, with some confusion, if everybody else had been well. Finally Kitty demanded to know if he would dance with her at the September assembly, and Lydia—Lydia!—took Kitty from the room for a quiet conversation, from which Kitty returned chastened. Bingley ruined some of the effect by assuring her that he would be delighted to dance with her or with any of her sisters.

Darcy continued silent, and did not meet Elizabeth's eyes. He looked at Jane, and Bingley, and the floor. Elizabeth could not account for it. If he meant to renew his declarations, why did he not speak? And if he thought her beneath him, why had he brought Bingley?

After a few more minutes, the gentlemen rose to leave.

"You must both come to dinner some time this week," Mrs. Bennet said, and they agreed. When they were gone, Mrs. Bennet took Lydia and Kitty to be useful in the greenhouses, and Elizabeth was left with Jane.

"Well," Elizabeth said. "That was awkward."

"It was. . . tolerable," Jane said. "The first awkwardness is past us, and when he dines here on Thursday, we shall all be easy again."

On Thursday, Longbourn was at its best. Mrs. Bennet had Kitty arrange spherical bunches of white hydrangeas and soft pink dahlias in bowls, and slender porcelain vases of pink and white roses, in every room on the ground floor, and Mr. Bennet had hired a few people to help serve and invited several of his colleagues to fill the table and even out the numbers.

Darcy was seated by her mother, but Mrs. Bennet invited one of Mr. Bennet's colleagues to sit on her other side, and Mr. Bingley sat by Jane. Elizabeth, sandwiched between a middle-aged Mr. Brown and Lydia, was too far away to converse with Darcy, though she watched his animated conversation with her mother with pleasure.

She hoped that after dinner they might have some opportunity to speak. But when the gentlemen entered the drawing room, Mr. Brown came straight over to her to continue describing the proposed steam engine design that had formed the basis of their entire dinnertime conversation, and Darcy walked away.

Finally, she got away, on the excuse that she was needed to serve tea, but Darcy went to Jane for his cup.

But when he brought his cup back, he came to her, and having no other ideas for opening a conversation, she asked if his sister was still at Pemberley.

"Yes, she is there until All Saints' Day, at least. She sits her examination for admission to Babbage some time in November and we have hired a tutor for the intervening few months."

"I am so glad to hear that," Elizabeth said with a smile. "Are Miss Bingley and Mrs. Hurst still with her?"

"No, they left very soon after you did. Mrs. Annesley and the tutor, a Mr. Encke, are with her."

He stood silently next to her for several agonizing minutes, during which she considered and discarded a few other topics, each as insipid and stupid as the last, her cheeks heating, until he walked away. When finally they were done with tea and moved on to cards, Elizabeth looked for him, but the inconvenient Mr. Brown accosted him for whist, and they were soon seated at opposite ends of the room. Her eyes were often turned toward him, but he played with a steady concentration, and did not notice her.

The next morning, Elizabeth discovered that two of the Pemberley peach seeds had sprouted, and she potted them. When she stood from the task, she stretched to relieve her back from all the stooping she had been doing, and looked up at the glass ceiling of the greenhouse, and met her own gaze in her reflection with the acerbic look she would formerly have given Lydia at her worst. Did she really intend to send one of the little pots to Miss Darcy once she could be sure that it would live? Was such a stratagem to start up a correspondence beneath her? Yet, she thought of the healthiest of the plants as Miss Darcy's.

The next Saturday, Mr. Bingley came alone.

Mrs. Bennet was working in one of her greenhouses, and Jane and Kitty were in Meryton, so Elizabeth and Lydia sat with him for a short visit. After they had been talking for nearly ten minutes, and she could bear the suspense no longer, Elizabeth asked, with what she hoped was cool composure, after his friend; and Mr. Bingley said that Darcy was gone to back to Pemberley. Elizabeth bent all of her attention on her embroidery for some minutes, and left Lydia to carry the conversation, but then roused herself.

"You would be most welcome to dine with us tonight," she said, and Lydia's eyes flickered to hers.

"I am so sorry," Mr. Bingley said, "I am engaged to dine with Mr. Brown."

Elizabeth almost laughed. *The inconvenient Mr. Brown,* she thought.

"Perhaps tomorrow?" she said. "For tea?"

"I should be very happy," he said.

The next day, accordingly, he came for tea, and afterwards, when Mr. Bennet went to work in his library and Mrs. Bennet in greenhouse three, Elizabeth engaged Kitty and Lydia in Speculation, hoping the noisy card game would give Jane privacy to converse with Mr. Bingley, and she noticed that they chattered away just as they had done months before, and Bingley touched Jane's arm four times. The sisters did not speak of it, but Elizabeth was sure that there must be some kind of understanding between Jane and Mr. Bingley, or if not, there soon would be.

Mr. Bennet invited Bingley to see a mysterious new invention he was working on by correspondence with Faraday, which kept sputtering to a stop for no reason he could discern, and they spent several happy hours tinkering with it, and came in to dinner apparently well pleased with their repairs and each other.

They went on in this manner for half a week before Bingley proposed, at a moment when the only other person in the drawing room was Elizabeth, writing a letter to her aunt and paying little attention until she heard Jane say, "Oh yes!" in a tremulous voice. She glanced up: their heads were bent together, and Jane was smiling with tears standing in her eyes. Bingley immediately left the room to seek out their father.

§

Her mother had a dozen terrariums in greenhouse two, which she used to grow plants she would be moving to other people's houses, and wanted to protect from the aether or too much jostling on their route. They were about two feet square, and each had their own little world inside. Elizabeth traced her finger along the outside glass. They reminded her, a little, of Pemberley and Rosings, of the way their grounds came right up to the glass of their domes, instead of keeping their greenery, like most people did, in container gardens or greenhouses. That was easier, but was it good for people? On Earth, they would have had trees and plants around them all the time. She remembered wondering how it must change the way people like Lady Catherine thought about themselves, to have an entire park at their own private disposal. She remembered her conversation with Darcy about the expense of building a public park, but could not help imagining every superstructure having its own dome-sized terrarium, perhaps with walking paths like the forest at Pemberley.

Kitty came in then. "What are you grinning at? String beans, Eliza," she said, and Elizabeth came back to herself. They were hard at work harvesting them by the time their mother joined them.

"Do any of the superstructures have forests like Pemberley's, mamma?" Elizabeth asked. "But not owned by a single family."

"No," Mrs. Bennet said. "What would be the use of that?"

Elizabeth was opening her mouth to reply when she heard the airlock cycle. She straightened up to look out. Condensation had formed on the window, which she wiped away to see who it was that had come to visit. She would have guessed Bingley, but instead she saw Sir William just stepping through the 'lock, a few figures behind him distorted by the glass of the 'lock.

"Who is it, Lizzy?" her mother said.

The other figures stepped out from behind Sir William, and Elizabeth put a hand to her heart.

"Lizzy?"

Kitty answered, looking back and forth between her sister and the figures at the 'lock. "It's the pastor, Mr. Robinson, and Sir William, with a strange woman."

"You had better fetch Lydia," Elizabeth said quietly to Kitty. Then she turned to her mother. "Mamma, it's Mrs. Younge."

"Who, dear?"

"Mr. Wickham's. . . protectress."

"Oh! I see." Mrs. Bennet grasped her hands tightly and although Elizabeth could feel her mother's hands trembling, she nonetheless felt comforted when she looked deeply into Elizabeth's eyes and said, "All will be well, Lizzy."

The group was approaching the house. Mrs. Bennet swept out of the greenhouse and went to greet them. Elizabeth watched them numbly for a moment, and then sank down into the only seat in the place, an old velour armchair. A few empty pots poked her in the back. She put her head in her hands, and then found from the wetness on her fingers that she had tears in her eyes. She wiped them away, sniffed, and put on a smile. "All will be well," she told the string beans, and went to be arrested.

The tableau that greeted her in the drawing room looked very much like a play. The men stood clustered at one end of the room, as though to stop anybody from trying to flee. Elizabeth wondered for a moment if they knew about the second airlock. She could grab her aether suit and go—but go where? There was no point to it. Mr. Goulding and Sir William both looked very grave as they blocked the doorway. Mr. Robinson, a millwright and sometime handyman who Elizabeth only knew from the monthly assemblies, hung back uncertainly behind them. Mr. and Mrs. Bennet faced them, Mr. Bennet with his hands on his hips and Mrs. Bennet leaning forward, one hand stretched toward them as though in admonishment. Further in the room, Lydia and Mrs. Younge sat opposite one another, both of them sitting very straight, though Mrs. Younge looked faded and tired in her patchwork dress. Kitty sat next to Lydia, a little slouched, her face a shocked blank.

Elizabeth felt a moment of unreality, as if she were looking at paper cutouts of people, and then Mr. Goulding stepped forward to say, "Calm yourself, Mrs. Bennet," and she saw that he was wearing a red armband, and once she noticed it, she saw that Mr. Robinson was wearing one too. That meant, she supposed, that they were both acting as bailiffs. Meryton did not employ bailiffs, as a rule. She took a deep, sharp breath and felt the reality of the moment snap back into focus.

"There's the other one," Mrs. Younge said, pointing at Elizabeth standing at the back door.

"Yes," Sir William said grimly, "thank you, Mrs. Younge. We all know Miss Elizabeth."

"You won't let her get away with it just because you're all friends," Mrs. Younge replied with a sharp look.

Sir William bowed, though whether it was to Mrs. Younge or to the room in general was unclear. "I am here to arrest Miss Lydia Bennet and Miss Elizabeth Bennet on suspicion of murder."

CHAPTER FIFTEEN

ELIZABETH LISTENED TO THE AERATOR TICKING IN THE DARK. She'd been counting the ticks, in a half-hearted way, since she'd been put in the storage room, and had reached a thousand three times before giving it up. She thought she had heard somewhere that the aerators ticked once per second, and she tried to do the mental math to work out how long she had been detained. Her brain felt slow and foggy. She supposed she should be grateful not to be cuffed. And for the cot she was lying on. They could have left her to sleep on the floor.

The ship did not have an actual jail. Most of the crimes that occurred on board the ship were thefts and assaults, which were punished on an ad hoc basis. The only murder in Meryton that Elizabeth had ever heard about had happened when she was Lydia's age. Even London only had a few murders each year, dueling having been outlawed—typically crimes of passion and gamblers who couldn't pay their debts—and the punishments ranged from being made to do the hardest jobs in water reclamation without wages to being ejected from the ship.

Walking in the aether without a suit might well be her fate.

Mrs. Bennet had suggested allowing Elizabeth and Lydia to be on house arrest until they could be tried, but Mr. Goulding had persuaded Sir William that such leniency would be bad for morale. Consequently, they had been taken to the storage rooms behind the central kitchen, which were hardened against thieves and could, consequently, be locked. Lydia was put in with the vegetables and Elizabeth with the grains.

About sixteen and two-thirds minutes per thousand ticks, she finally worked out. So, she'd been there for at least three-quarters of an hour, plus however long it had taken her to do the math. That was hardly any time at all. The silence and darkness of her container already felt infinite and endless, and she had only been there an hour at most.

She heard a scraping sound, and she turned her head to listen to it, and then a sliver of light came through the door, and she realized somebody had unlocked the door and was now illuminating the tiny space: the threadbare cot, its thin pillow with its gunmetal gray pillowcase and its shabby gold woolen blanket, the bare metal of the floors and walls, and behind her, the large pile of faded sacks of wheat. She sat up on the cot and smoothed down her dress.

Mr. Robinson, still in his red armband, gave her a nod and an encouraging smile, showing off all of his crooked teeth. "Visitor for you," he said.

The man he let in was angular and tall, and extraordinarily gray in his clothes, skin, and hair. Elizabeth thought she had seen him before, perhaps at the monthly assemblies, but could not place him. "Miss Elizabeth Bennet," he said. "I am Oliver Eastaughffe. Your uncle works in my office and has perhaps mentioned me to you in the past."

He had not, but Elizabeth nodded anyway. "Has my father retained you?"

"Yes. I did his and your mother's wills, and helped your mother draw up a standard contract for her vendors. I must warn you, I have no experience with criminal defence, but then, very few do. The judge will probably not have any experience either."

"Have they chosen a judge?"

"Not yet. You are too well-known in Headfort for it to be anybody from here, and your mother works with the surrounding domes, so they will look for somebody from farther afield, perhaps from Saye and Sele or Arkwright since your mother has no business contacts there at all, and nobody could suggest any result was motivated more by interest than truth."

"Do you know how long I will be in here?" Elizabeth asked.

"Until Monday, I believe. We have to give witnesses time to get here. Now. I have already spoken with your sister. Tell me what happened, every detail, and I will begin to work on your defence."

She told him the whole story, omitting nothing, and before he left, asked him to see if he could bring her a lamp and a book to read.

After he left, she counted over five thousand ticks of the aerator before Mr. Robinson brought her some food, more for something to do than as a reliable way to tell the passage of time, and yet she found herself doing mental calculations of larger and larger numbers anyway. Mr. Robinson lingered in the doorway to watch her eat the boiled cabbage and greens, and she found herself grateful even for his company.

They had done nothing to restrain her. She could have easily gotten past him and run off into the night, but what would have been the point? Like sneaking out of Longbourn's back airlock, it didn't bear thinking about, because there was nowhere to go. She gave him back the plate and the fork when she was done, and when he said, "I'm sure they won't convict you, a pretty girl like you," she only smiled tiredly at him. When he closed the door, she lay on her cot, and did not bother to count the seconds. She listened, but the noises from outside of her room consisted only of mysterious scrapings and tappings. She heard no human voices nor godly ones. She spoke for a long time with Lady Catherine de Bourgh, who arrived on a flying chariot and declared herself the judge at her trial, and then with Bingley's horse, who had been made to stand as her lawyer and kept getting elements of the law wrong and angering her Ladyship. Careful kept coming into the courtroom and stealing important papers, and Lydia could not find a hair ribbon to hold closed the sacks of wheat. The wheat and the barley kept getting eaten by her lawyer, and her Ladyship was angrier about that than the murder. She declared that the whole family was to be made to walk from Longbourn to Pemberley without aether suits, and if they made it, they could live.

Elizabeth became aware that it was morning when Mrs. Clark stood in the doorway waiting to escort her to the privy.

"They just come in the communal kitchen and grab the first lady they see," Mrs. Clark said to her to explain her presence, "but I am happy to take you, Miss Elizabeth, and what I say is, if you did do it, then he must have deserved it."

"Lydia and I are innocent," Elizabeth said, "but I appreciate your confidence in me."

"The Bennets have always been good neighbours," Mrs. Clark said, and then, illustrating why there would be no jury, she said, "He was a bad sort anyway, with all of his lying and gambling. He tried to get my Franny to go off with him, too. A quick death was likely too good for him."

She said this as though no other opinion on the matter were possible.

Elizabeth said, "Hmm."

The rest of the day passed away very quietly and slowly, with only meals and regular walks to the privy to entertain her. Mid-morning, she was interrupted in her long reverie by Mrs. Clark's needing a sack of barley. Lunch came with a small valise with a few changes of clothes, for which she was grateful, but she would have happily traded them for reading material and light. Lying around in the dark for much of the day was much worse than she ever would have predicted, as a punishment: time passed with mysterious slowness and she found it difficult to hold her mind to a single subject.

"Quiet day," Mr. Robinson said that night, as he passed the keys over to Mr. Harrington, who was to guard her overnight.

"Will my parents visit me tomorrow?" Elizabeth asked them.

"Not allowed," Mr. Harrington said as he closed the door.

On the morning of the third day she awoke from a dream of being imprisoned for the rest of her life, and lay in the pitch blackness thinking about it: she would never marry, never have children, never run her own business. *I want to grow things*, she thought. *I want to put my hands in soil and squeeze.* Not to be locked up. Of course, nobody wanted to be locked up. But it was foolish to imagine that she would be imprisoned for years, for decades even. Nobody was imprisoned here. If a guilty verdict were brought in, she must hope for the unlikely leniency of a life of hard labour, though that mercy was generally for lesser crimes than murder. No, they would put her out into the aether with Lydia, or they would let the two of them go free. There would be no half-measures. The ship only supported idle people if they were very rich.

As if she had been summoned by this thought, Lady Catherine de Bourgh visited her a few hours later.

"I thought that I could not have visitors," Elizabeth said to Mr. Robinson, who had relieved Mr. Harrington at breakfast.

"No family," he said.

Lady Catherine looked around her, frowning. "We must have a light," she said, and Mr. Robinson brought one in.

"Do come in, your Ladyship," Elizabeth said uncertainly.

Her Ladyship made no reply, but entered the cell and looked at the sacks of grains and the cot, and remained standing. Mr. Robinson watched avidly, and after a moment she turned and raised one eyebrow at him, and he closed the door, though he did not lock her Ladyship in.

All was silence for a long moment, as Elizabeth waited for some explanation of the extraordinary visit, but Lady Catherine only prodded one of the sacks with her cane and frowned some more.

"Are my sister and her husband well?" Elizabeth asked at last.

Her Ladyship seemed to remember where she was, and said, "Oh! Yes, Miss Bennet. They are very well."

Elizabeth thought that her visitor might hand her a letter from Mary then, but she did not.

"I would offer you something to drink," Elizabeth said after another pause, "but I am afraid I have nothing."

Lady Catherine smiled a little in acknowledgement of the joke. "It is strange to be in a prison cell," she said. "I have never seen one."

"You still have not," Elizabeth said. "This is a storage room for wheat and oats. Now, how may I help you?"

"You must have guessed why I am here."

"Not at all," Elizabeth said. She wished that she did not smell so dustily of flour, and that whoever had packed her clothes had thought to include a comb.

"Mr. Collins has told me of your engagement," Lady Catherine said. "Naturally I have come to forbid it."

"*My* engagement?" Elizabeth raised her eyebrows. "Mr. Collins has made some mistake—"

"Mr. Collins is a clergyman," her Ladyship said sternly, as though clergymen were all faultless. She prodded another bag with her cane and made a small hole, out of which a slow trickle of barley poured.

"And why should you care who I marry?" Elizabeth demanded as she picked up the bag to put the hole at the top.

"My nephew's affairs are my own. I am intimately involved in every aspect of his life, and he turns to *me* for guidance, not to some upstart merchant's daughter. Pemberley deserves better than *you*."

"I see," Elizabeth said. She stood straighter and ignored the prickle of sweat running down her back, but inside she was screaming *Darcy! She means Darcy! How could this have happened?*

Perhaps Mr. Collins had tried to pass along the news of Jane's engagement and Lady Catherine had misheard and then refused to be corrected.

While she was thinking all of this, Lady Catherine was stalking back and forth across the only patch of floor the small cell provided, gesticulating with one hand and clutching her cane with the other. Her dull reflection in the metal walls of the storage room paced with her. She said, "You absolutely may not marry him. He is already engaged to *my daughter*."

"Is he? He and Miss de Bourgh certainly do not act like people in love."

Her Ladyship scoffed. "*In love*. How you talk. Before we even entered this ship, indeed, before Anne was even born, they were intended for each other. She was named after *his mother*. These are ties that are not broken on a whim."

"Mr. Darcy was, what, a year old when the ship took off? I do not think agreements entered into by his parents when he was an infant are binding upon him now."

Lady Catherine stopped pacing to face Elizabeth and point at her with the cane. The room was not quite big enough for this action, and Elizabeth had to sway backwards to avoid being smacked across the cheek. Her Ladyship's mouth compressed to a line and her eyes narrowed. "Would you make your sister's situation untenable? You know that I can make her very uncomfortable if I so choose."

For a confused moment, Elizabeth thought she meant Lydia, and then she realized that she was threatening Mary. "You have no power over Mr. Collins's living, once it has been granted," she said coldly, "and moreover, blackmail of this kind is beneath the dignity of a de Bourgh."

"Hmph," Lady Catherine said. "Do not think I appreciate your sarcasm."

"You would do better to ask your daughter what *she* actually wishes than to appeal to me. I cannot make him marry her, and if he does not wish to marry her—and I dare say that she does not wish to marry him either—then they are both free to look elsewhere."

Lady Catherine was quivering with rage, and Elizabeth found that she had to look away.

"You cannot mean to pollute his family line in this grotesque manner. Your father may be a gentleman, but has not a penny to his name. Your mother is a *merchant*. And who are her brothers?" Lady Catherine smiled with a cold triumph. "And if that is not bad enough, your sister is a wanton."

Elizabeth crossed her arms.

"Have you nothing to say to that?" Lady Catherine said.

Elizabeth walked to the door and knocked until Mr. Robinson opened it. "Lady Catherine is leaving," Elizabeth said to him in her calmest, most level voice.

"This is how you treat me! Obstinate, headstrong girl! Very well. I shall now know how to act." Her Ladyship stalked through the door and then, turning back, added, "I take no leave of you, Miss Bennet. You deserve no such attention. I am most seriously displeased."

Elizabeth did not answer, except by turning her face away.

When the door had been locked, and she was alone, she leaned against the door until her breathing and heartbeat had returned to normal, and then proceeded back to her cot. She laid down, and looked at the bare metal ceiling, and went over the conversation, wishing she had defended herself more fiercely or not at all, and wondering if Lady Catherine de Bourgh might bring pressure to bear on the judge, or only on Darcy. That depended, presumably, on the identity of the judge. The leaders of the ship all seemed to be related to each other in some way. Would she and Lydia be found guilty and left to smother and freeze in the aether because Elizabeth could not, just once, hold her tongue? After a few minutes, she leapt off the cot again and began to pace. What would happen when her Ladyship harassed Darcy on the topic, as she was bound to do? Her arguments would appear much more persuasive to him than they could to Elizabeth. She paused in her pacing, leaning against the door, and ran her fingertips lightly over the smooth wall. If he agreed with her Ladyship, he would decide on Miss de Bourgh, or Miss Bingley, or whomever, and she would see him no more. There was nothing she could do further to influence events. But that was not so different from before. When she had tired herself out with pacing, she realized that nobody had come to get the lamp, a flickering golden light that illuminated her tiny prison of metal and barley. As a consequence, Elizabeth found that she was more grateful for, than disturbed by, Lady Catherine's visit, but it was a close contest.

She counted the ticks of the aerator, and watched the tiny flame in the lamp sway first a little to the left and then a little to the right, like her father attempting a waltz, until she felt her eyelids growing heavy and put out the light, and finally fell asleep.

Her fourth day in the cell passed much like her second, with regular meals and trips to the privy and not much else, though she could at least now see the confines of her room. She examined every inch of her cell and studied the fine print on the sacks of grain as if they held the secret to her escape rather than details of where and when the grain had been packed. She shook out her sheets in an effort to keep them fresh. Mrs. Clark took away the pierced sack of barley, and brought her a hairbrush, and Elizabeth spent an hour getting four days' worth of tangles out of her hair. She was permitted to have a bath at a boarding house across from the communal kitchen, with Mrs. Clark overseeing. Nobody seemed overly concerned about her trying to escape. She again asked for a book, any book, and again was ignored. She asked for a bushel of potatoes to peel, or dishes to wash, or anything at all to do, and Mrs. Clark smiled and just shook her head. Mr. Robinson refilled her lamp when it guttered out, and otherwise left her alone.

The morning of her fifth day passed much the same, but when Mr. Robinson came to get her empty plate after the evening meal, he said, "You have another visitor, and you will never guess who. Shall I bring him back?"

"Is it my lawyer?"

"No," he said, smirking. "You will never guess it."

"Then I suppose you had better bring them back."

He brought back Mr. Darcy, dressed somewhat severely in all black, but for a simple white shirt and a bright blue necktie. He looked as handsome as ever, his dark hair as glossy as one of his well-bred horses, but that was unimportant now, secondary to his steady gaze and the way his eyes seemingly filled with light as he regarded her. Their twin delighted smiles while for a moment they were the only people in the universe. His thrilling, sudden movement toward her, as he took her hand and murmured, was she quite well, were they treating her quite well, was there anything he could have brought to her. Her quick relief at the certainty that his coming to visit her was an admission of his continued regard, that there could be no other reason for him to visit her here, risking his reputation and every other thing that he had once said mattered so much to him. That perhaps it did not matter so much anymore. He brought her hand to his lips, kissed her knuckles, and quickly released her and stepped back. She said that she was quite well, and had no complaints about her treatment, and meanwhile her eyes were shining and her mouth was curving into a helpless smile. Her shoulders lowered, her mouth softened, and her whole body relaxed out of a tension she had not even realized she was carrying.

Her jailer stood in the doorway, grinning at the two of them, until Elizabeth said, "I am on trial for murder, Mr. Robinson. I hardly think we need worry about a chaperone."

He looked at Darcy, and Darcy gave him what Elizabeth thought was a very sarcastic bow. Mr. Robinson closed the door to give them privacy.

At first, they were both silent; and then they both spoke.

"Thank you—"

"Are you quite—"

They laughed a little, and Darcy said, "Are you quite well?"

"Not really," Elizabeth said frankly. "I am constantly listening to the silence to try to get clues about what is happening outside this room, and I have nothing to do but think. What news is there? Are my family well? Has Mr. Bingley broken off his engagement? How does Lydia hold up? Who have they selected as the judge? Any intelligence you can give me would be very gratefully received."

He glanced at the cot, and, presumably considering it an improper place to sit, began to stack the sacks of barley so that they each had a seat. While he stacked, he spoke. "Your family is well, though distressed, of course. I mean that their health is well. The community has rallied around them. Lady Lucas is apparently not talking to Sir William, for his role in your arrest, for example."

"Oh goodness. It was his duty," Elizabeth said. "I do not blame him in the slightest."

"Very fair of you. To your next question, Mr. Bingley is standing by Miss Bennet. I had confessed to him, I should tell you, all of my interferences, and after some period of anger he has forgiven me. He is determined that he will not now fail Miss Bennet, and I have lent my support to him."

Elizabeth could not help smiling at his easy manner of directing his friend.

"And Lydia?"

"I have heard nothing about Lydia."

"That can only be good."

"Aside, of course, from the inevitable speculations regarding her guilt or innocence. I suppose that she is equally as bored as you are. There," he said, finishing with the makeshift seats. She took her place. When he folded himself into his, her dress just touched his knees.

"To your last question, the judge is Alexander Stewart, Viscount Castlereagh."

"Oh no," Elizabeth said. "Rosings is in Castlereagh dome."

"So it is, but it is his father, Robert Stewart, who lives there. Alexander lives in Arkwright, where he works overseeing water reclamation. He has been fetched from there as a person reputable enough to be eligible to act as judge and who has little or no connection to anybody involved."

"Is he very young?"

"I knew him at school. He was always a very measured, careful sort of person, and I believe he will give you a fair hearing."

They sat for a long moment, and Elizabeth watched her dress touch him and wished that she could do the same. Finally, she said, "I must thank you. This seems a million years ago, but I have not had a chance to speak to you of it. My uncle mentioned that you had gone with him to Hardwicke, and I can only imagine the scene that greeted you when you got there. I feel certain you meant to do far more for Lydia than she deserved."

"No," he said. "She did not deserve to be shackled to him. Nobody did. I am prepared to testify to that effect. I will keep Georgiana's name out of my testimony, naturally, but I have other anecdotes from his youth and can paint him as a villain very easily."

"Is that why you are here? As a witness?"

"Yes. I am to testify about the events of the morning you received Miss Bennet's letter about Miss Lydia Bennet's elopement."

Elizabeth coloured, and looked at her hands, and could not say anything. Her breath was stuck in the back of her throat; she almost thought she might cry.

He watched her a moment, and then said, "You are too generous to trifle with me. If your feelings are still what they were last April, tell me so at once. *My* affections and wishes are unchanged; but one word from you will silence me on this subject forever."

"Oh," Elizabeth said. She had tried so hard to expect nothing from him, to avoid disappointment; she had not quite considered how to act if he renewed his attentions. She wished now that she had practiced some gracious replies, such that a lady of fashion might say, but she had not, and here he was looking at her in suspense, a slow blush rising up his neck. She resorted to the plain truth. "My affections and wishes could not be more different than they were then. Since our conversation, and repeated readings of your letter, I have learned to think differently of almost everything you mentioned in it, my mother's profession excepted—"

"—and I hope you will forgive me for that criticism," Darcy said. "I have asked about the famine you mentioned, and your mother's actions now seem to me to be very admirable. Please destroy that letter. I wrote several unpardonable things in it."

"I would rip it to pieces right now, but of course I do not have it with me. It is still in Jane's suitcase, that I borrowed to go to Darlington," she said. "How long ago that seems."

"You can burn it when you get out of here, then," Darcy said with a smile. "We are agreed."

"I—I may not make it home," Elizabeth said. "If they find Lydia and me guilty, I think we would go straight from sentencing to—"

She found she could not say it.

He took her hands tentatively, looking at her expression to ensure that his touch was welcome, and she remembered how he had taken her hands when he had proposed, as though he already owned them. He was so changed, and yet she could see how she had misunderstood so many things. She curled her fingers around his, and squeezed them gently.

"That is one reason I came," he said. "On Monday, I pray that all of your troubles will be resolved. But if not, this may be my last chance to speak with you. I could not allow the opportunity to go by."

She looked down at his hands. They were so warm, and although she had not thought of him as an especially big man, his hands engulfed hers. His palm was very warm against hers. She entwined her fingers with his, fascinated with his warmth and strength.

"Was my aunt very terrible to you, the other day?" he said at last, his voice oddly breathy.

"Oh, yes," she said, almost laughing. "Yes, she was awful. Did she give you a full report of my insubordination?"

"She found you to be perversely stubborn and rude," he said with a grin. He moved his fingers so that he could stroke her palms. "It taught me to hope as I had scarcely ever allowed myself to hope before."

"I am glad that Lady Catherine's communications were so helpful. It ought to make her happy, for she loves to be of use."

Darcy smiled. "I will be sure to mention that aspect of the events of today when I relate them to her," he said dryly.

Elizabeth laughed. She disentangled their fingers so that she might move her hands around his, so that her palms rested against the backs of his hands. There was a lightness to everything, a luminosity as well as an airiness, and an enlightenment too, and she felt as though any second they would lift right off the ground and fly, as if in a dream, and when they landed it would be in a circle of the brightest illumination. Her tone, she thought, fairly bubbled with giddiness as she asked what he had felt when she had appeared at Pemberley.

"Surprise, of course." He mirrored her earlier movement so that his palms were against the backs of her hands now, completely engulfing them. It was beginning to be difficult to concentrate on their conversation. "Mostly I wanted to show you that I had listened to you, and held no resentment."

"Was Georgiana very disappointed that we did not attend her dinner?" She twisted her hands to hold his, slowly stroking the callouses on his fingers. How engrossing fingers could be.

"She was, a little; of course she liked you, as any reasonable person must, and she could see that I liked you, and was distressed at you going."

"Does she still want to be an engineer?"

"Yes. I might help you to be swift in your studies, whatever they might be, so that you can be an example to Georgiana."

"You are assuming I will be released."

"The Darcys still have some influence," he said with no trace of self-consciousness.

"So do the de Bourghs. I fear you and your aunt may cancel each other out. She was very decided about her plan when she left here."

His fingers tightened on hers. "I will do everything in my power."

"In any case, I do not want to be an engineer. I have another plan, which I will share with you, if I survive Monday's trial. Even Lady Catherine would not object to it."

"But that reminds me of one point I must ask about."

Elizabeth forced her hands to still, even though all she wanted to do was to keep touching him. "We did not kill him."

"I never doubted it," he said, raising her hands to kiss her knuckles. "I have only wondered how you managed to get to Lydia ahead of your uncle and me, and what happened afterwards."

Elizabeth described her journey briefly, with extensive preliminaries on the subject of packet-dodging, an activity he had been too well-brought-up to encounter. That the Bennet girls, and even Charlotte Lucas, had engaged in it had always been something of a scandal to those with more attentive parents.

He stared at her in frank astonishment. "Good Lord," he said. "You could have been killed."

"Indeed," Elizabeth said dryly.

He seemed to remember that somebody *had* been killed, and gripped her fingers more tightly. "So that is how it happened."

"What are they saying about his death? I have hardly dared to ask, and the reports that have reached me have been rather garbled."

"The story in London was that he was found crushed under the counterweight in the central spoke. He owed extensive gambling debts, and it was generally presumed that he was, er, made a useful example to others who might fail to pay up."

"Until Mrs. Younge came forward," Elizabeth said, remembering that lady's presence in her parents' drawing room. "If I am honest, it all seemed very theoretical. I did not actually see him fall, so it was as though he simply disappeared from our lives."

"How terrible for you," he said. He kissed her knuckles again, and she leaned forward until her forehead could touch his.

The gas lamp guttered out then. She heard his intake of breath. He ran his fingers slowly up her arm, giving her a lot of time to draw away, until he reached her chin and cupped it. Tenderly at first, and then hungrily, they kissed.

She thought, *I might only have a few days left to live. What does propriety matter now?*

She shifted from her seat to his lap, leaning against his solid warmth. He kissed her at the edges of her mouth, and then trailing along her chin to her neck, where he bit her very lightly. She could hear her breathing thickening. He kissed and bit along her neck until he reached her earlobe, and she sighed into the darkness. She moved her hands up to tangle her fingers in his hair. "Darcy," she whispered, and he groaned into her ear. He moved back to her mouth, slipping his tongue inside. His lips felt firm, and he tasted like smoke. She kissed him harder until her lips felt almost bruised. His hands moved down her back, and some instinct made her lift herself a little so his hands could cup her buttocks.

He put his face into her neck then. "We have to stop," he said softly.

"I could be dead in a few days," she countered.

"No," he whispered back, and then he stood her up, pulling her up with him, and simply held her. "I won't allow that to happen. You *will* be my wife."

After a moment, he stepped away and she heard a rasping sound in the dark. A tiny flame appeared in front of her, as of a candle, but as it brightened, she saw that it came from a small brass cylinder. "It's my invention," he said. "A handheld tinderbox." He lit the lamp and examined its reservoir. "We had better knock for Mr. Robinson. This light will go out again in a minute, and I hate to compromise your reputation."

"Ha," Elizabeth said, thinking that her reputation could hardly become more compromised than it already was, and he suddenly grinned at her.

"I hope you will teach me to be as free as you are from such concerns," he said quietly, and before she could reply, he was knocking on the door for Mr. Robinson to let him out.

When the lamp had been refilled and the door had closed again, she leaned her forehead against it, and stayed in that attitude for over a thousand ticks of the aerator.

He still loved her.

If she was found guilty, and made to step through her final 'lock, she knew that the certainty of his love would be her last thought and the loss of their future together would be her last regret.

An hour or so after Darcy left, Mr. Robinson handed her three novels to choose from. All, he said, were from the gentleman who had just left. Elizabeth promptly lost herself in the troubles of Dr. Frankenstein, grateful for a man who would send her books.

CHAPTER SIXTEEN

MR. ROBINSON LEFT TO GET SOME REST, having stayed up all night to make sure neither of them escaped. "Good luck," he said. On an impulse, Elizabeth hugged him goodbye.

After he was gone, Lydia crossed her eyes at Elizabeth, making her, very briefly, laugh. Lydia looked worn and somehow faded. Her hair was clean and simply held back from her face with an old ribbon. She had chosen to wear one of her most patched dresses, a shipmade linen with the seams visibly let out at the sides. Perhaps Mr. Eastaughffe had advised her to look poor to elicit sympathy from the judge, or perhaps it had been her own idea. Elizabeth had worn her best dress, the one her mother had bought on Earth as a young woman, and which was only patched and repaired around the hem. If she was to be marched out an airlock later that day, she wanted to at least look her best. Mrs. Clark had even kindly helped her put her hair up in intricate braids. She wondered now if she ought to have emphasized their relative poverty, but she didn't know enough about the judge's character to guess. Would he pity or feel contemptuous toward the poor?

She reached out to her sister and said, "Are you well?" but Mr. Brown said, "No talking, ladies." Lydia smiled at her reassuringly.

It was time. Elizabeth and Lydia were brought in together, separated by the bailiffs who held their arms. Had Elizabeth not known them, she might have been more cowed, but it was only

Walter Harrington and George Brown.

The courtroom was the assembly hall with tables and chairs brought in and arranged to make the place more useful. At the head of the room was the judge's bench, a beautifully polished desk of some dark wood that Elizabeth recognized from Sir William's study. A velvet-lined chair sat empty behind it, and the desk and chair were a little elevated over the room on top of some structure that had been built to raise them up a foot, and then covered over with rugs. In front of it were two long tables with chairs, and against one wall sat Mrs. Younge, Mr. Darcy, Mr. Forster, the Gardiners, and several people Elizabeth did not recognize. Behind all of this were rows of seats, and her family sat in the first row, Mr. Bingley by Jane, and Mr. and Mrs. Collins and Lady Catherine de Bourgh beside him, and spectators crowded all around them.

As they were led in, for a moment, the mirrored walls made the spectators look endless. Walter Harrington and Mr. Brown led them up the side of the room, past the spectators, who fell silent as they went by. The silence spread until her family, in the front, twisted around to look at them, and Mrs. Bennet gave them both a tremulous smile. Elizabeth's gaze settled briefly on her family, and then skipped to Mr. Darcy, whose face was his usual composed blank. As their eyes met, he winked, and then they were past him. They were led to the chairs behind one of the long tables, on either side of Mr. Eastaughffe, who whispered to them to remain standing.

Next, the prosecutor came in, the portly Richard Coffin. He sat at the other table. Lady Catherine went over to him and said something into his ear, and to Elizabeth's relief he only nodded at her and pointed at the gallery. She returned to her seat, frowning.

Viscount Castlereagh came in then, from the door at the other end of the hall, behind Sir William's desk. Walter Harrington, standing by that door, was proud to shout, "All rise!"

"All right, all right," said the Viscount, waving one hand and sitting at the desk. "Yes, yes, sit down, everybody. Court is in session."

They sat.

"Now," he said, looking at Elizabeth and Lydia in turn. "You know why we are here. Mr. George Wickham was found dead on the sixteenth of July and the evidence suggests that one or both of you killed him. Some other theories have also been floated, but a witness places you at the scene. We're here to get to the bottom of this. You will be sworn in, and so will the witnesses, and then everybody shall tell me what they know. If anybody gets out of hand—" here he gave a stern look at the spectators' gallery "—they will be thrown out. Your attorney may give you advice, but we will have none of these time-wasting legal objections we would have had back home."

Elizabeth had to think about this for a moment before she realized that he meant back on Earth.

He went on, "Our only purpose today is to find the truth."

Everybody was sworn in, putting their hands on the Bible and making their oath, and then the judge said, "Mr. Eastaughffe, how do the defendants plead?"

"Not guilty, my lord."

Somebody in the spectators' gallery scoffed, and the judge raised one eyebrow. The disturbance subsided.

"Mr. Coffin?" said the Viscount.

The prosecutor, a London attorney who was ordinarily an expert in business contracts, stood and spoke at length about the discovery of the body, the results of the investigation that had taken place in the Hardwicke dome, the alibis of the major money-lenders to whom Mr. Wickham was in debt, and finally the evidence of Mrs. Younge, whom Mr. Coffin referred to merely as Wickham's landlady.

She was called up to give her testimony. Like Elizabeth, she had worn her best clothes, though hers were still shipmade and had a few patches along the hem. The split lip that Wickham had given her the month before was healed, and the dark circles that Elizabeth remembered from under her eyes were gone. Her eyes were reddened, as though she had been crying, but otherwise she looked much better than she had when Elizabeth had last seen her.

"How did you know the deceased?" Mr. Coffin asked her.

"I run a lodging-house in Hardwicke, in St. Clement's dome," she said. Her dark red hair shone smoothly in the light from the gas lamps. She was the picture of respectability. "He was a lodger there, at the end along with the lady here on the right."

The spectators' gallery murmured and rustled. Lydia sat up very straight, her chin in the air.

Mrs. Younge testified to Elizabeth showing up at her house, Lydia's argument with Wickham, the girls leaving, and Wickham going after them. "He never returned," she said, and something of her grief broke through onto her face.

Lydia leaned over and whispered something to Mr. Eastaughffe. When his turn came to speak with the witness, he said, "You testified that your relationship with the deceased was landlady to lodger, but was he not also your ex-lover?"

Mrs. Younge flashed a hateful glance at Lydia and then turned to the judge. "I never, my lord."

"Had you known each other as youths?"

"Well," she said, "yes, we both grew up in Lambton."

"And were you not engaged to marry him?"

She raised her chin. "We spoke of getting married when we were young, but he had no money and I married Gerald Younge instead and have remained faithful to him even after he died."

"And you did not think it was relevant to disclose your long relationship with the deceased to this court?"

She did not answer, and the Viscount said, sounding a little bored, "You have made your point, Eastaughffe."

Next, Mr. Forster was called. He explained his wife's invitation to Lydia. "They are very good friends," he said. "I made guarantees to her father that I would carefully protect her, but I failed in that commission. One of the engineers on my project convinced her to run away with him. He seems to have had no intention of marrying her, but I can attest that she believed that he did. She wrote to my wife not to be worried at her absence, for she was on her way to London to become Mrs. Wickham."

"And when you discovered her gone, what did you do?"

Mr. Forster explained the steps he had taken and the communications he had made to her family. "But we could not find them," he finished. Eastaughffe declined to cross-examine. Several witnesses who had seen the pair along their route were called to confirm Mr. Forster's testimony, who Eastaughffe also did not cross-examine.

Finally, it was Mr. Darcy's turn to testify. He sat in the seat next to the judge, impeccable in a dark coat and bone-white shirt, his necktie a flash of red at his throat.

"What is your relationship to the defendants?" Mr. Coffin asked him.

"I have known the family for a few weeks shy of a year. And, as of two days ago, Miss Elizabeth Bennet is my fiancée," Mr. Darcy said.

Elizabeth turned to look at her family. Mrs. Bennet was staring over at her, her astonishment plain on her face. Mr. Bennet only smiled at her, and Elizabeth thought that Darcy must have visited him in the intervening day to ask for his blessing. Lady Catherine whispered furiously to Mr. Collins, who looked shocked and disapproving, but Mary was grinning at Elizabeth. Jane gave her her Madonna smile, and Mr. Bingley was smiling proudly at Darcy. The spectators whispered and gasped. The judge pounded the table. "I will have order in this court or I will turn you all out in the street." Gradually a hush fell.

Mr. Coffin's expression was sour, and he moved on quickly to his questions, which regarded Elizabeth receiving Jane's letter and her reaction to it, and the scene which had greeted Darcy when he had arrived in Hardwicke with her uncle.

"I knew Mrs. Younge would give Mr. Wickham shelter if he asked for it, and I suspected that he would go to her rather than to London. Not knowing yet that Miss Elizabeth Bennet had gone ahead of us, we reached the house to find Mrs. Younge crying in her kitchen. I do not wish to impugn Mrs. Younge's reliability as a witness, but she was most distressed over the loss of the young man whom she claims not to love, far beyond anything reasonable for the loss of a friend."

Mr. Coffin looked alarmed at this line of thought, and said hastily, "That will be all, Mr. Darcy. You may return to your seat."

Darcy turned to the judge. "I have known the deceased my whole life, and had hoped to testify about his character."

"I said that will be all," said Mr. Coffin, and Mr. Eastaughffe said, "My lord, before he is dismissed, I have a question for this witness."

The Viscount waved a hand negligently, and Mr. Coffin, his mouth compressed to a straight line, sat back down.

Mr. Eastaughffe turned to Darcy. "You became engaged while Miss Elizabeth Bennet was awaiting trial?"

"Yes," Mr. Darcy said. "That is how convinced I am of her innocence, and of the innocence of her sister. I stake my family's reputation on it."

Elizabeth caught her breath. The Viscount raised his eyebrows, and it was evident that Mr. Darcy's word would weigh highly with him.

Darcy stepped down from the witness stand, and Elizabeth followed him with her eyes all the way back to his chair, until Mr. Eastaughffe whispered to her to face forward again.

Mr. and Mrs. Gardiner next gave their testimony, and then it was Lydia's turn. She walked steadily to the stand, and sat with her chin raised. The gas lamps made her chestnut hair glossy. For the first time, Elizabeth was surprised to find that her sister was grown perhaps even handsomer than Jane, the reputed beauty of the family. She had never considered her sister as a stranger might have, but in her simple, patched dress and with her face drained of much of its usual colour she did not look like the young girl Elizabeth had known. Her ordeal had given her clear green eyes a depth and resolve rare in one so young. No wonder Wickham had wanted her.

Mr. Coffin ran through the events of July with her.

"He convinced me to run away with him," Lydia said. "He told me that he loved me, and that we would be married, and I was foolish enough to believe him. He convinced me that, since we planned to be married, it was permissible for us to live as though we were already."

The spectators' gallery murmured at this but subsided when the

Viscount pounded Sir William's desk with his fist.

"It was not until Lizzy—my sister, Elizabeth—came to bring me away that he said that we could never afford to be married, that my father did not have enough money to tempt him, and that he was growing tired of me already. We had an argument—Mrs. Younge has already described how noisy we were, and I do apologize to her most sincerely for my rude behaviour—"

The judge smiled at this, though Mrs. Younge did not, and Elizabeth was gratified to see his initial stern look softening towards her sister.

"—and during our argument, he struck me across my cheek, and I decided that I did not want him for a husband after all. I left with Elizabeth. She had used the shipping packets to get to Hardwicke from Darlington, and she knew that I often went packet-dodging with my friends, so her plan was that we would go home to the Headfort dome by the same method, and we would hope that we could pass off a lie that I had traveled directly from Brighton to see my mother, who we would say was ill. Then nobody need know that I had been so foolish as to run off."

A tear ran down her cheek, and the Viscount sat forward and said to her in a voice laden with concern, "If you need a moment to compose yourself, please let me know. It has already been a long day."

Lydia nodded and then, with some confusion, shook her head. Some colour rose in her cheeks as she said, "Thank you so much, my lord, but I would like to go ahead with my testimony."

He nodded, and she turned back to Mr. Coffin, who asked her to go on. "We climbed the counterweight and held on to the heavy chain. George—Mr. Wickham—had followed us there, and he pulled my sister away from the chain. We were in our aether suits, and they look much the same, you know, and we are a similar height, and similar colouring, and all, and I think he thought that she was me."

This interpretation of Wickham's actions had never occurred to Elizabeth, and she felt her hands begin to tremble. She clasped them tightly on the table.

"He kicked her hard, and I think, believing that she was me, he was trying to kill me. He had a fearsome temper when he was crossed, for all that he was so pleasant in company. When he kicked her, Elizabeth rolled onto her back, so he could see her face and realize his mistake. Then he turned to me and tried to drag me away from the chain, too. By this time we were pretty far off the ground, and a fall would have been very dangerous. Probably deadly. But I had seen what he had done to Lizzy, and I had had time to wrap my arms around the chain and lock my elbows, and I was able to resist him. If he had stuck to it, eventually he would have succeeded, I am sure, and dashed me to the ground, and he would be the one sitting here on trial. But Mr. Wickham was not the sort of person who sticks to one plan—" (behind her, Elizabeth heard Mr. Darcy quietly laugh)— "and instead he grabbed me by the shoulders and shouted at me. How dare I leave him, he wanted to know. Elizabeth had dragged herself back to the middle of the counterweight by this time, and she went behind me. I found out later that she was attaching us both to the chain with a tether that she had left there on her way to me. Wickham shook my shoulders, and I slapped at him, and—"

Her voice broke on a sob, and she raised shaking hands to her face. For a moment, the only sound in the courtroom was her crying, and then Elizabeth heard the low rumble of her father's voice, and Mr. Coffin said, "Miss Bennet, do you require a brief respite?"

"No. No," she whispered. "All that is left to tell, is that he stepped back when I slapped at him, and held up his hands." She mimicked the action. "We looked at each other for a moment, and then the packet passed us on its way down, and the counterweight wobbled, and—he slid off the edge."

The silence in the courtroom was complete.

Lydia stepped down, tears standing on her cheeks, and Elizabeth stepped up. She gave the testimony required of her: she had received Jane's letter, as Mr. Gardiner and Mr. Darcy had both testified already, and gone to fetch her sister, and everything had happened the way

Lydia had said. She explained about the tether, and how she would have felt it if Lydia had stretched it any further, since it was already at its full length. Her sister could not have pushed him.

As she stepped down from the witness stand, Elizabeth saw herself in the mirrors of the assembly hall, which were slightly cloudy with age, and made her appear, she thought, old and fatigued.

She looked over at her family sitting in the spectators' gallery, and saw her mother clutching her father's hand, and Jane leaning against Bingley's shoulder, and Kitty clasping her hands tightly in her lap. Lady Catherine de Bourgh gave her a look of such pure venom that Elizabeth faltered for a moment, and then her eyes swept past her Ladyship toward the one she most wished to look upon. Darcy was giving her a steady look, unsmiling, that she would have once regarded as judgement and now saw as simple support. His lips curled a little as she met his eyes, and hers curled a little in reply.

Once she was seated, the judge said, "I have heard enough, and I have settled upon my verdict. From the first I had determined that the punishment for murder is so terrible, especially to be carried out upon two women, that I would only convict if I were completely convinced of their guilt. The evidence against them is purely circumstantial, and their testimony, and the testimony of their friends, is so persuasive, that while I recognize the possibility of their guilt, I am nonetheless convinced of their innocence. I find both sisters not guilty of the murder of George Wickham, and they are free to go."

The spectators were all talking at once, and the roar of their voices shut out any sense they might have made. Lady Catherine stood, quivering, and swept out of the room. Lydia made a noise like a startled dog and slumped onto the table in front of her, her face in her hands and her shoulders shaking, and Elizabeth jumped up to comfort her. Then their whole family was around them, everybody talking at once and hugging her and Lydia and crying.

She noticed Mr. Darcy hovering on the edge of the circle of her family, standing next to Bingley. She went to him. "Thank you for what you said on the stand," she said. "'I stake my family's reputation on it.' Viscount Castlereagh's face could not have been plainer: if a Darcy believed us, then he would too."

"I doubt that very much," he said, taking her hands. "What won this for you was your own testimony. Nobody can hear you and fail to believe in you." His fingers tightened around hers.

She took a deep, shuddering breath, and all of the relief of the verdict and noise of the crowd smashed through her, and suddenly the future felt wonderfully vast and exciting. Laughter bubbled out of her. The two of them smiled foolishly at each other, and then Mrs. Bennet was there at Elizabeth's elbow, saying, "You certainly played your cards close to your chest, Eliza."

She turned to Mr. Darcy and said, "Come back to the house with us. We are not at all prepared, but I think we are going to have a celebration!"

§

Before they went back to Longbourn, Elizabeth insisted on finding Mrs. Clark to thank her for her kindness of the past few days. Then she and Darcy strolled slowly back to Longbourn, occasionally interrupted by the congratulations of well-wishers, exchanging whispers about the fears and hopes of the past few days, and the sudden promising brightness of their future together, and their amazement and delight in hearing the other speak of their love.

After they cycled through the Longbourn 'lock, they stopped just over the threshold to the dome. "Look there," Darcy said, very low, and Elizabeth followed his finger with her eyes: the lights of the greenhouse picked out the forms of Bingley and Jane, standing in a spot hidden from the house by the greenhouse walls, their heads leaning together, Bingley's bowed and Jane's lifted up, their hands clasped, and their lips just lightly touching. Darcy and Elizabeth crept forward a few paces until the couple was hidden again, leaving them to their privacy. They went in, and were almost instantly separated by the crush of people.

Elizabeth made her slow way to her father's library, suspecting him of having retreated there, and found the door closed. She knocked, and hearing his summons, went in.

Mr. Bennet was plugging figures into his difference engine. The columns spiraled as it processed his request, and, as she entered the room, he watched it instead of her, frowning.

"Lizzy," he said to the machine, "when Mr. Darcy visited me yesterday to ask for my blessing, of course I gave it to him. But I am hesitating to give it to you. Have not you always hated him? If this was a strategy to get out of a conviction, then I applaud your cleverness, and fear it, as well, but if that is all it is, you know you do not have to go through with the marriage."

Elizabeth laughed. "I wish I had not made such a point of my dislike. For many months now I have been changing my opinion—you know we were thrown together much at Rosings, and then—I was wrong about him. Father, I love him."

Her father looked at her at last. "He told me, amongst a long list of ways in which he plans to provide for you, that he will provide for your further education. Is this about going to Babbage? You do not need to make such an extreme choice, my dear. Once you have graduated, you will still need to live with the man."

"No," she said. "It is not that. It is. . . when I am with him, I feel as though I am more myself than at any other time. He makes me feel. . . capable. He is really very funny and kind, once you have gotten to know him."

"Extraordinary thing to say of such a man, and yet, I can see you really mean it. You must be in love. Nothing else could explain it."

She gave him a deep curtsey, which made him laugh, and then petted Careful before going back out into the rest of the house, which was packed with well-wishers. She found Darcy talking to Charlotte Lucas and Miss King. She said, "Papa has just given me his blessing."

Charlotte laughed and said, "As if anybody in this family could say no to you!" and hugged her long enough that Miss King began to look jealous.

"I am so glad you have come, and we must catch up later. I want to hear everything about London. But right now I am going to spirit away my fiancé before mamma notices that papa is done with me and puts me to work."

She took him out the back door and snuck him in to the smallest of the greenhouses. A flowering crabapple tree showered pink petals on the ground by the door. Further in, the peppery sweetness of nasturtiums drifted over them. High-end restaurants in London would pay higher for nasturtiums than more nutritional fare, since they were so pretty, and they grew so easily Mrs. Bennet found them a good supplement to her income.

"Thank you," Darcy said, smiling. "I was beginning to feel quite overwhelmed with the number of people and variety of conversations. I suppose a loud party is only to be expected when two members of the household have been cleared of murder charges."

"I assure you, it is nothing special," Elizabeth said. "The female Bennets are renowned for their high spirits." She supposed after a family that consisted only of Georgiana, with occasional visits from Colonel Fitzwilliam and Lady Catherine de Bourgh, her family must seem very boisterous indeed. "You will have plenty of time to become accustomed to us, and you can hide with papa in his library when we all get too loud for you."

While they had been talking, Elizabeth had been clearing off an overstuffed chair for them where her mother usually sat by the little stove, the cushion of which was a tumble of tools and stakes and water buckets and wooden quart boxes for berries. The greenhouse was always warmer than the house, despite the clockwork misting mechanism that Mrs. Bennet had had installed, and which she refilled every morning; the stove in the center of the greenhouse kept it what her mother insisted on calling 'summery'. Elizabeth felt pleasantly warm, whether from the temperature of the room or from the company, she could not have said.

He smiled. "That reminds me. Do you have any writing paper? I feel that I ought to send a note to my aunt."

"To rub salt in the wound?" Elizabeth said.

He smiled down at her. "To extend the hand of peace while I am still feeling so charitable. Just think, if she had said nothing to me, I might never have had the courage to come back to Meryton."

"Let her know that she will always be welcome at Pemberley when I am its mistress."

He laughed and put his arms around her, and for some time they did no talking. They returned to the house when the only alternative was to anticipate their wedding vows, and each privately vowed to marry as soon as possible.

Elizabeth hugged Lydia again and again, made endless quantities of tea and coffee, introduced Mr. Eastaughffe to Miss Grantley, took a bottle of wine away from Ganymede Goulding before her father could catch her with it, and even danced a song with Walter Harrington for old times' sake.

EPILOGUE

ELIZABETH DARCY STEPPED INTO AIR that smelled like the Pemberley forest. Some of the small birds that she had introduced into the park the previous week began chirping, warning each other that she was there. She loved walking in the park when the broad walk was still empty of workers and the decorative flowers looked smugly across at the tidily staked vegetable gardens.

Behind Elizabeth, the rest of her little party entered and the airlock cycled closed. A tiny form zipped past her, little legs pumping.

"Charlotte!" Elizabeth called. "Get back here!"

"I have her," Darcy said. He ran ahead, and came back a moment later, holding their toddler in a tight hug. She shoved her head into the crook of his neck and her thumb into her mouth.

"She will never stop running away if you keep running after to catch her, Fitzwilliam," Elizabeth said. "She thinks it is a game."

"I will always catch you, will I not?" Darcy said to his daughter.

Charlotte breathed an affirmative around her thumb.

"She is just like you were at that age," Mrs. Bennet said to Elizabeth.

Mr. Darcy replied, "All of our children should be so lucky," with a private smile to his wife; the two of them knew that Elizabeth was pregnant now with their second child, but at just four months, had opted to keep it between themselves until after the quickening.

Mrs. Bennet looked around at the small trees, protected by light fences, the cluster of mature oaks and Spanish chestnuts gifted from Pemberley, the broad walking trails made from the gravel waste from the mining of asteroids, and the banks of vibrant flowerbeds.

"Oh, Elizabeth," she said, "how wonderful!"

Mr. Bennet began walking ahead without a word to anybody. He, his wife, and his two youngest daughters as well as the Gardiners and Philipses had been staying at Pemberley for the previous week, and he had grown fatigued with socializing. Elizabeth saw him take a book from the pocket of his coat as he disappeared into the trees, and smiled after him.

Mary was meant to be arriving from Castlereagh any moment with Mr. Collins and their toddler son William in the hackney-coach Mr. Darcy had sent for them; whether or not Lady Catherine would deign to accompany them was still a mystery, as Elizabeth was still persuading her husband to forgive the abusive letter she had sent upon the occasion of their marriage, and the invitation he had written had been, if not rude, not actually particularly welcoming either.

Of the five sisters, that left only Jane, who had excused herself from attending the park opening. She was expecting her own second child any day and was closeted in comfort at Netherfield, where the Bingleys had chosen to stay permanently.

The park dome had been built a little over a year before, just after Elizabeth and Darcy had had Charlotte. Following months of community engagement on the design of the park, she had broken ground the year before. Like Pemberley, the lawn came right to the edge of the dome and sloped upwards to turn the whole park into a hill tall enough to make room for tree roots, but unlike Pemberley, nothing was planted in an orderly geometry. Elizabeth loved the lanes between the evenly-spaced trees of her home, but had wanted the park to look more like the paintings of wildernesses on Earth had looked: wild and asymmetrical and vivid with contrasting colours. That she had also wanted to provide vegetable gardens to give more people the opportunity to learn how to care for a garden had complicated that vision, and she had decided to put the vegetables into container gardens, since that was how most people would grow their own, and cluster them around the benches on the sides of the main footpath, while keeping the deeper paths decorative.

The flower beds were arranged with forget-me-not, hyacinths, and violas for spring. When summer came, they would have roses and ginger lilies, and for autumn, crepe myrtle and fuchsias. Then her team would impose an artificial frost and put shaved ice on the plants to mimic winter. Then they would wait for snowdrops to flower and start the cycle over again.

To add the final touch to the park, she directed a team of men to wheel a wagon with the final two trees to the central gazebo, where two holes were waiting for Pemberley's final gift to be planted: two of the four peach trees that had grown from the Pemberley seeds she had propagated before her marriage three years before.

(The third had been given to Miss Darcy two and half years before, for her birthday, as promised. It held pride of place in her little sitting room, where the clockwork chickadee often slept amongst its leaves. The fourth, and smallest, was in a container in the entrance hall at the Gardiners' house in London.)

People were filtering in, and Elizabeth braced herself for the public part of her work; happily, she only had to do this when the park was ready for the public, and after today she'd have a break for at least another year. She stopped to chat with some of the gardeners and their spouses, and with the workers who were wrestling the peach trees into place, with the members of the Lambton public, and with the leaders who had traveled from other domes to see how people reacted to a public park, and with Charlotte Lucas and Mary King, who had come to cheer her on and play with little Charlotte, their goddaughter.

Mrs. Bennet and her two youngest daughters were still loitering by the container gardens, Mrs. Bennet professionally interested, Kitty eyeing the young men coming in, and Lydia sitting on one of the benches, writing a letter, probably to Thomas Purvis. Tom was determinedly courting her, and the family all expected to hear of their engagement any day now, though Lydia was remarkably shy about any discussion of that matter. She insisted that they both had to finish their educations before they had any thought of marriage. (Tom was to become an aethernaut, and Mr. Darcy had arranged an interview with Colonel Fitzwilliam; Lydia had apprenticed with Elizabeth on her park project and planned next to work under one of the fancier florists in London, living with Mrs. Annesley, with an eye to expanding her mother's business in a few years.)

While talking to one of the workers, Elizabeth watched out of the corner of her eye as two women in fine dresses began to walk past, noticed the notorious Lydia Bennet, and turned around to walk the other way. Lydia glanced up at them and then went back to her letter, pursing her mouth a little. Some people would never accept her sister's innocence, Elizabeth knew, and even some of those who thought her innocent of murder still believed that her virtue was compromised, and some of *them* believed that to be the greater sin. Immediately after the trial, the people of Meryton had, with only a few exceptions, rallied around Lydia, and now that the people of Lambton were grown used to her, many of them seemed to have forgotten the earlier scandal and merely regarded her as one of the ladies of Pemberley. She was still barred from Mr. Collin's home, but Mary had not been prevented from coming to visit at Pemberley especially to see Lydia the previous Michaelmas, and they had made a very merry party.

Almost everybody was being their best selves, and it was just the sort of thing her mother excelled at, and that Elizabeth found so tiring. By the end of the day, she suspected she would be ready to join her father in hiding.

The mayor had arrived. The trees were next to their holes ready to go in, butterflies were waiting in their burlap bag to be released, and a long ribbon had been strung around the gazebo ready to be cut. The mayor cut the ribbon, and everybody cheered. The work crews placed the peach trees and the butterflies were shaken out of the bag, whereupon they failed to spiral beautifully overhead as Elizabeth had envisioned, instead settling sleepily over the trees, their wings flexing slowly, like clockwork running down. Elizabeth shoveled a ceremonial final bit of dirt over each tree and stamped it down, and everybody cheered some more. Finally, the mayor stepped onto the gazebo to address the crowd.

"Thank you so much, everybody, for coming," he said. "Thanks to the generosity of the Darcy family, and thanks to the hard work of Mrs. Darcy and all of her team, I am thrilled to open the first public park on our ship: the Lady Ann Darcy Memorial Park!"

He paused for applause, which was enthusiastic (those who remembered her, remembered her fondly) and then went on, "I would also be remiss if I did not mention the generous bequests from the Marchioness of Londonderry, Lady Eleanor Butler, and Sir Humphry Davy, none of whom were able to be here with us today. This is an historic occasion that you will be able to tell your children and grandchildren that you were here to witness! This ambitious park will help to feed us—you are each invited to take one of Pemberley's peaches home with you to eat and to propagate if you wish—and to nourish our souls."

Smiling, he turned to her. "Mrs. Darcy, anything you would like to add? No? In that case, everybody, enjoy a peach and some cake and a walk around our park!"

Elizabeth didn't like crowds, always having an obscure idea that at any moment they might coalesce into a new wild animal, with its own mood almost independent of any individual's within it, but this crowd was eager and happy, and could not be avoided. She worked her way through it, handing out peaches along with instructions on propagation.

The next dome was to be in London, and Elizabeth started the following week. She had been given a special dispensation to ride the first box of the morning to central processing, before the workers started their shifts, and to go down in the first load to London. She could go home in the evenings in the same way, in reverse. Enclosed within the conveyance, she didn't run the risks she had on her now-famous excursion to rescue Lydia. Word had gotten out, and there was talk of putting in some sort of elevator and making it available to everybody, which Mr. Darcy had pledged to help fund, but for now she would ride alone.

Mrs. Annesley had become Elizabeth's assistant soon after the Darcys had married, since she was no longer needed as a companion now that Georgiana was at Babbage. Pemberley had remained Mrs. Annesley's home, but she often remarked on how she longed to move back to London, and was looking forward to the park they would build there, with Lydia as an apprentice.

Elizabeth looked around the park, as finished as two years' growth could make it. She would miss the scale of the greenery here once she was working in London, where what awaited her was, at this stage, a simple pile of dirt; but she looked forward to shaping an entirely new dome. She looked out over the flowers and thought, I should have put in a lake, but perhaps for her first project it had been better to keep it simple. She could do a lake for her third park, location still unknown. London was to have a river, and they were going to call it the New Thames, of course, but it would only be about five feet across, with a clever contraption underneath to cycle the water that spilled out the end back to the beginning. Bingley was already fashioning the three arched bridges she wanted, and an artist friend of Charlotte's was hard at work on ten marble statues to be placed around the walkways. She could already picture the whole thing.

In a garden, she had said to Jane on one of her visits, everybody was equal: the soil and the seed did not care who you were but what you gave them, and the proof of your quality was not in your clothes or your manners but in the health of the harvest.

In their technologically-advanced society, gardening seemed to her to be a very traditional pastime, and yet Lady Catherine and Mr. Bennet and several of Darcy's business associates had expressed dismay that she, Mrs. Fitzwilliam Darcy of Pemberley, should be working, and worse, working at something which benefitted the public. She could have had the decency, they seemed to believe, to limit her activities to parks for the great and proud. Not arranging gardening lessons for blacksmiths and washerwomen. But, happily, most of her acquaintance were growing with the times. It was 1850: no time to be old-fashioned.

The pace of invention and innovation had been startling ever since Sir Humphrey Davy had worked out the properties of aether before Elizabeth had even been born. She expected to be surprised by numerous changes throughout her life, like the steam engine that could now take passengers from Kent to London, or the newest type of incandescent lamps, which made everything bright and sharp-edged. The hazy golden world of Elizabeth's childhood was slowly giving way to a clearer future.

Her husband joined her from the audience as the event wound to a close, holding a sleeping, floppy Charlotte. "It's wonderful," he said to her quietly. "I am so proud."

"Thanks, love," she said, and dipped her head to smell little Charlotte's hair and kiss her head. He put an arm around her, and she leaned into his warmth. "Let's go home." She put his hand on her belly, and added, "On second thought, let's find Charlotte and let her know she's about to be godmother to another Darcy." The baby kicked its little foot again and Darcy's mouth curved into a surprised smile.

The overhead leaves softened the light from the new lamps, and the green walkways seemed to radiate serenity. On her way to Charlotte, Elizabeth stopped to eat a peach.

ACKNOWLEDGEMENTS

My deep thanks to Peter and Sharon Merriam, who fed and housed me during the writing of this book, and to David Crews, who provided some of the ideas for the workings of the fictional aerator, counterweights, centrifugal force, and gravity.

Many thanks as well to Evelyn Elgie, Melissa Ren, and everybody at Inanna for their support and guidance, to Georgia Atkin for clarifying editorial advice, to Pei Yuan Li for the stunning cover art which brings Darcy's clockwork birds to life, and to my beta readers Charlotte Ashley, Mary Ellen Gilson, Claire Humphrey, Rebecca Kennedy, Jennifer Litowski, Deborah Merriam, Kristin Philips, Susan Stockell, Susan Swansburg, Royale Underhill, and Jessica von Handorf for their helpful comments.

Since the ship takes off in 1821, the novel's setting is more like 1821 than 1845 (aside from considerable scientific advancements and what I imagined would accompany them in social change). Accordingly, I am indebted to the following authors for their information about Austen and Georgian England: Roy & Lesley Adkins (*Jane Austen's England: Daily Life in the Georgian and Regency Periods*), James Edward Austen-Leigh (*A Memoir of Jane Austen, ed. Kathryn Sutherland*), Maria Grace (*Courtship & Marriage in Jane Austen's World; Jane Austen's Christmas: Regency Christmas Traditions; How Jane Austen Kept Her Cool: An A to Z History of Georgian Ice Cream*), David M. Shapard (both *The Annotated Emma*, for elements of Mr. Collins's first meal with the Bennet family, and *The Annotated Pride and Prejudice*), Patricia Meyer Spacks (*Pride and Prejudice: An Annotated Edition*) and Raymond Williams (*The Country and the City*).

The Kepler epigraph comes from "An Animated Guide to Humanity's First Interstellar Mission," *The Atlantic*, Sep 27, 2016. Mr. Bennet's difference engine is modeled after the Mountain View machine featured on Wikipedia. Careful and Neptune got their names from Richard Heaton's webpage on 1000 Georgian and Victorian Names for Dogs. For the trees and foliage at Rosings, Pemberley, and Lady Ann Darcy Memorial Park, I am grateful to the UK's Royal Horticultural Society and to the English Heritage website's description of Charles Darwin's gardens at Down House. The way to germinate peach seeds came from *Better Homes & Gardens*. Information about period-appropriate arrests and sentencing was informed by The Proceedings of the Old Bailey, though I made changes on the assumptions of what would be practical in a small shipboard society.

Of course, any errors and all liberties are mine.

ABOUT

Joanne Merriam is a writer and poet from Dartmouth, Nova Scotia. She is the author of the poetry collection *The Glaze from Breaking* and her poetry and fiction has appeared in dozens of magazines and journals, including *Astropoetica, The Baltimore Review, Escape Pod, Pank, Per Contra, Pictura,* and *Strange Horizons*. Find her at joannemerriam.com and @joannemerriam.bsky.social.